Waterdrops

Waterdrops

John Lucas

GREENWICH EXCHANGE
LONDON

Greenwich Exchange, London

Waterdrops
©John Lucas 2011

First published in Great Britain in 2011
All rights reserved

Printed and bound by **imprint**digital.net
Typesetting and layout by Jude Keen, London
Tel: 020 8355 4541
Cover design by Narrator
www.narrator.me.uk enquiries@narrator.me.uk

Greenwich Exchange Website: www.greenex.co.uk

Cataloguing in Publication Data is available from
the British Library.

ISBN: 978-1-906075-66-8

for Ben & Catherine & Emma & Chris.

But that the busy day
Wak'd by the lark, hath rous'd the ribald crow,
And dreaming night will hide our joys no longer,
I would not from thee.

Troilus and Cressida

In war, nothing is the truth but war.

There's No Home, Alexander Baron

The ribbon he winds loosely about his fingers no longer binds the pile of letters that lie face up on his desk. Repeated unrollings of the increasingly brittle paper have left some pages worn, though none so badly as to make illegible the lines of neat, schoolmasterly handwriting with which each sheet is covered. The words, especially those written in pencil, have in many places faded, but most are decipherable. Even the ribbon, which he will place on top of the letters when he once more returns them to his desk drawer, thinned to a near-translucent, rusty orange though it may be, retains hints, threads, of its original crimson.

Hunched in his chair in the cool of this early summer evening, he lifts his eyes to glance out at the garden and sees across the lawn spindly stalks of a lavender bush trembling in what could be a sudden stir of wind and is in fact the blurry weight of foraging bees. Two blackbirds bob springily about the fresh-dug earth, stabbing at invisible food — "look at nothing and then pick it up" he lets himself think — and, as he watches, a pigeon crashes clumsily into the top boughs of an old apple tree that leans against the brick wall at the garden's end. All things can distract him from the task in hand. Sighing, he forces his attention back to the letters.

What *is* he to do with them? He knows — at least, he thinks he knows — that he should make fair copies before they, and he, crumble to dust. But to what end? No publisher would want them. They aren't, as one told him, "of general interest," and the man's shrug and complacent, dismissive smile, confirmed his own doubts. A private printing, then? But the few people the letters most concern are now familiar with the story they have to tell. As for the story the letters *don't* tell, that, too, is known to those concerned. And who else could possibly care?

Once again he finds himself wishing that the letters would fly away as they once flew to England, would allow him to depart in peace, and at once some lines from a favourite poem come to mind, rebuking his wish. "And therefore, though it be a history/ Homely and rude, I will relate the same/For the delight of a few natural hearts." Homely and rude? Not really. Anyway, would those natural hearts, always supposing he can identify them, really want to know the story that the letters under his hand partly reveal? Perhaps, perhaps not. And what of "delight"? An altogether more difficult question, that.

The room begins to fill with dusk and at last he moves to switch on his desk-lamp. A pool of lemony light spills across the topmost letter.

Malta May 23rd.

Darling, I can't tell you how wonderful it was to get your last …

As always, the words catch at his heart. He looks away, then up, staring without really seeing them at the books lining the shelves above his desk. A door on the other side of the hall opens and now, suddenly, music surges into his study. Small group jazz. Instinctively, he picks up a pencil so that it nestles in the crook of his left thumb, first two fingers aligned along its shaft, thumb and tip of third finger holding the pencil steady, and as the Benny Goodman quartet swings effortlessly along on "Honeysuckle Rose" he begins to tap out an accompanying rhythm on the wooden arm of his chair.

PART ONE
1944

CHAPTER ONE

Sun dazzling the high west window became a searchlight through whose fixed beam they all had to pass, singing as they went.

Safely beyond the cone of glittering light, the youth carrying the cross at the head of the procession raised and waggled it as he began to head down the north aisle. *Piece of cake.* David turned to smile at the boy processing beside him and at once felt his ear gripped from behind.

"Eyes front," a voice hissed. Old Godwin.

A moment later the choir squeezed awkwardly, two by two, through the vestry door, the practice at last over. While men and boys struggled to unhook stiff, white collars and hang up surplice and cassock, the choirmaster ducked into the vestry from his place at the organ and began in his ashy voice to sprinkle them with praise and criticism. The hymns had gone well but the anthem was still ragged, did they agree? One or two nods. Well, no time for further work on it, unfortunately, but he would ask each of them to take mental note of the need to come in sharpish.

"Why, Gerald, was anyone flat?"

Godwin stared slowly round, his red-rimmed bulbous eyes behind thick spectacles inviting laughter, but apart from Mr. Collins nobody even smiled. Bert Mee, who made no attempt to hide his dislike of the postmaster, looked at the only other man there, known to the boys as "Knees-Up" on account of his odd, high-stepping walk, and raised an eyebrow. Knees-Up winked back at Bert, then passed a finger across his upper lip, ostensibly to smooth his bushy moustache, but really to indicate, as David had heard him mutter to Bert on a former occasion, that someone ought to bolt and padlock Godwin's trap.

"Where was your friend this evening?" Mr Monk asked.

"Robin Masters? Don't know sir." Then, discomforted by

Monk's steady gaze, David added, "perhaps he's not feeling very well."

"He was well enough to be at school today." Mr Collins, released now from church regalia, flicked a speck from the trousers of his habitual dark-blue suit, reached into his jacket pocket for his cigarettes and, after peering intently at the packet's contents, perhaps to count how many he had left, selected and raised a Woodbine to his lips. "He sat next to you, didn't he?" The teacher's words came as a gentle rebuke, as though he knew quite as well as David what Robin was up to.

"Well, when you next see him you tell him from me that I want him here on Sunday," Monk said. "We need every man Jack of you on parade, and that includes Robin. Understood?"

"Yes, sir."

"I take it there will be no objection if I wear my campaign medals."

Monk turned to look at Godwin. "Under or over your cassock?" he asked, his voice steady.

"I intend pinning them to my surplice," Godwin said, "unless anyone objects, that is." He stared at the two men opposite, who stared back. "Show these Americans that some of us at least have been through it all before."

"If it comes to that, Godbert, some Americans have been through it all before."

Godwin flushed. "They only came in when the war was as good as won," he said at last as he turned to Collins. "I was out there, in France, in the trenches, for over two years." A pause. "Years during which others were allowed to rest their backsides at home."

"Was you by any chance a volunteer, then, Mr Postmaster?" Bert Mee, straight-faced, gazed unblinkingly at Godwin. "Only I heard you was one of Derby's lads."

Godwin turned redder. "I'm not taking that from you, Bert Mee, or from anyone else."

"Now, now," Monk said, raising his hands in a gesture that reminded David of a goalie. "I'm sure Bert meant no offence, did you, Bert."

Bert Mee went on gazing at the choirmaster, but held his peace.

Monk's smile took in the entire vestry. "As soon as you've finished getting out of your clobber, Godbert, I suggest we all stroll over to the Cross-Keys and see if they've any beer worth drinking? Agreed?"

The other men agreed.

* * *

At the entrance to the twitchel David paused to look back, but nobody was following. Good. He sprinted along the narrow track until it ended at a stile beyond which Farmer Bailey's field, its lush, tussocky greenness studded with buttercups and dandelions' brassier yellow, slumbered in shadow. Clambering onto the stile, he watched a squadron of flies gleaming coppery green and gold in the evening sun as they hovered over a cowpat. The size of a dinner-plate, the pat was already crusting to tawny brown at its edges though the moist centre gleamed like liquorice. Flies descended and droned heavily across the sweet-smelling shit until they almost touched its quaggy surface. A daylight bombing raid.

Among the raggedy hawthorn hedges bordering the narrow field a few elms thrust up, and an old, storm-battered oak leant beside the stile opposite from where David sat. Under its shade maybe a dozen cows knelt, dozily chewing and drooling. But no Goebbels, thank goodness. Although Farmer Bailey's old bull was so slow these days that if he was up at the field's far end you had time to run from one stile to the other before the bad-tempered beast could muster either the energy or interest to lumber after you, any nearer and it was touch and go.

David launched himself from his perch and a moment later was standing on the stile beneath the oak, surveying an altogether larger field. "Long field," the locals called it and at this time of year it seethed with wheat that swept in a long, pale yellow curve down to a line of osiers. The Fox gang had been here, he could see that from paths they'd trampled through the corn, all of the paths leading to a flattened circle in the field's centre. That was where they set up den in defiance of Farmer Record's various threats to put the police on them, or to give them a hiding to last a lifetime if he ever got hold of one of them. They laughed at such threats. "Gotta catch us first," they'd yell, running back up to the village.

But they weren't here now. Nor, he realised, when he reached the safety of the plank bridge at the field's bottom and peered over its wooden railings, first down and then up the stream, was Robin. What at first he hoped might be his friend, that shape loitering among the osiers on the bank a little upstream, he realised at a second glance was a tree trunk, its apparent motion a trick of light, ripples of water reflected on its smooth bark.

David couldn't blame him. Two hours earlier, when the pair of them were trudging up the sunlit fields and Robin had suddenly declared as they reached the bridge that he wasn't going any further — "Can't be bothered with practice, tell them I'm ill or something" — they'd agreed to meet by the bridge once David was released from practice. But then Monk made them process right round the church in their robes rather than going straight to the choir stalls, and as if that wasn't bad enough old Godwin, loving the sound of his own bass voice, had insisted on several run-throughs of the anthem, in which of course he had a major part, after which they'd sung *all* the verses of *all* the hymns, sometimes having to repeat a fluffed entry, and finally, and instead of being allowed to nip back to the vestry to change the quickest way, they'd been made to line up for the full, slow recession. He should have known that Robin wouldn't wait all that time.

Stilling his disappointment, he began to jog home along bottom meadow, although it wasn't any longer a meadow and the footpath no longer cut across it because the meadow had been ploughed up. All part of the war effort, so people were told.

"Nothing to do with making a tidy profit," Bert Mee had been overheard muttering. "He's a proper patriot, old Record is."

So the farmer had given over what was once pasture to raising beets, and such villagers as still bothered to come this way had to keep to the merest strip of grass between hedgerow and the beginning of ploughed land. Few bothered. Only those who lived in the straggle of small, semi-detached houses that lined the road beyond bottom meadow, the fences at the end of their back gardens marking the meadow's furthest extent, took the field path. Most went by road. In the summer months David was allowed to squeeze through a gap in the palings of his garden fence, but in winter or bad weather he had to follow the hedge-path out onto the road by way of the wide gate through which the farmer steered his gunmetal grey tractor. "I don't want you treading wet clay about the house," his mother said, although he was sure he collected as much soil going through the rutted, puddled gateway as by following the path that curved round beside the tall, shaggy hedgerow.

But this June evening the path was dry. Whistling now in time to his movements, he thumped down hard on every third stride. *Wish me* **luck** *as you* **wave** *me good***bye.**

He passed the gap where the hedgerow was broken to allow passage to a further field, a stretch of waste known as the sand-pit because nothing apart from docks and thistles grew on its humpy surface, passed the wide-branched elm at the far end of the gap, then, ratcheting up the volume, thudded along beside further hedgerow that would stop only when it met at right angles the back-garden fencing of the last house in the row among which his stood.

He was some way beyond the gap when behind him a voice suddenly said, "My, my, that's some whistle, young fella."

Shocked into silence, he stood still before spinning round. An American soldier — he knew from the man's uniform that he had to be an American — stood leaning against the elm, smiling at him. "Bob White'd be proud to claim that for his own."

"I — I'm sorry," David said. "I didn't see you."

The soldier opened his mouth to laugh, and David thought he'd never seen such white teeth. "Well," the soldier said, jerking his head backwards but without turning away from David, "I guess that's because we were the other side of this greenstuff."

And now David saw that a woman was standing behind the tree against which the American leant. Head bowed, she had her back to David. But he knew her well enough, recognised that dark, ringletted hair, the black leather shoulder-bag, the fawn, square-shouldered jacket.

"Anyways," the soldier said, "There's no call to apologise. You whistle pretty good."

"Thank you," David said. He took in the man's height, taller than Collins, taller than Monk even, registered his easy, wide-eyed smile, cropped fair hair, the trim uniform, tan shoes. So this was a Yank, as everyone in the village called them. The man looked steadily back at him and David, realising he was staring, felt himself redden. "I'm late for supper." The words seemed to speak themselves.

"Gotcha," the soldier said, pointing a finger at David and then waggling it slowly up and down. "Most folk sing for their supper, but you whistle for yours. Is that so?"

"Yes". David laughed with delight. "When mum hears me whistling she knows it's time to lay out my food."

The man returned his laugh. "Better get to it then, while it's good and hot."

"It won't be hot," David said, "but I'd better go." He wondered whether to say anything more — in his last sermon the vicar had talked about the need for the village to extend the hand of friendship to those he called "our American cousins" — but the woman, who was edging further out of sight behind the tree, evidently didn't want to speak, so he waved farewell to the man who said, "s'long, young fella."

"Goodbye," David said.

Then he turned and ran for home.

CHAPTER TWO

Darling,

I can't tell you how wonderful it was to get your last and to read all you have to say about yourself and the nippers. I'm writing this mid-morning, having just had a late breakfast of soggy toast and stewed tea, courtesy of the canteen wallahs. Last night I was fingered for watch, along with one of the newer boys. Jimmy Miles, by name. He'd been shaken out from a rag-bag assortment recently delivered here from North Africa. Surplus to requirements on the Italian front, so he told me, as we marched off under a full moon to the gun emplacement we'd been allocated, though further enquires revealed that the batch of which he was a part had all been wounded in pursuit of Rommel — not sufficiently to entitle them to be shipped home but badly enough to put them out of the reckoning for front-line duties. So now you know: Malta is officially off the critical list. We've been downgraded to a kind of field hospital, where the half-fit are sent. "A cushy number," according to him. I told him he should have been here two years ago, when the raids came thick and fast and we spent more time in caves and shelters than above ground and lived in what we thought was the certainty of imminent invasion. His reply was that if I thought Malta had it so bad I should have tried Egypt. I explained that I had. So we agreed to shake hands and settle for an honourable draw.

After that, of course, he wanted to know why I was still here. He'd heard, you see, about the order that those who've been on the island for two years can now get a home posting. I had to explain that the order only applied to the R.A.F, not the poor bloody infantry. All this while he was rigging up his machine gun, swearing about what he claimed were the gun's various inadequacies — don't ask me what they are, I haven't a clue — and I stared at the Med. No inadequacy about standard issue field glasses. They'd spot a sprat a mile off. But all quiet. That is, until a damned big splash near to shore made us both jump. But no, it wasn't a U-boat, merely a dolphin enjoying a midnight frolic. We watched it make several leaps while Jimmy lined it up in his sights. Then it went under for good and silence resumed its lonely reign. I can't begin to tell you how absolutely quiet that hillside was. No trees, as I think I've mentioned before, and precious few bushes for the wind to get into, always supposing there'd been a wind, which there wasn't. Not even a breeze. No wonder we were both soon sweating. I'd taken the precaution to bring along a canteen of water so we were able to keep our throats moist. But as Jimmy said, the moon not only made the place as bright as day, the temperature seemed better suited to noon than midnight. (Although he put it rather more vividly.) The sea was like a sheet of vitreous enamel, and where we lay, about a hundred feet above the shore line, we could see for miles across the Med. I told Jimmy about a fisherman who was shot up a couple of weeks ago — he'd ignored the curfew and taken his boat out for some night fishing. The night had apparently been a cloudy one. That, anyway, was what the gunner who winged him claimed. I was back at barracks deep in sleep, so I can't vouch for his story, but there are rumours that once the fisherman — inevitably dubbed "Pedro" at base — is out of hospital, he and some of his mates are going to come looking for whoever sent his boat to the bottom and nearly did for him. The view from our side is that he was lucky to get away with a few flesh wounds, and that he should be grateful for the fact that, once they'd realised he wasn't a Fritz, the lads fished him out of the sea. But it's created some tension between us and the locals, adding several degrees of chill to the less-than warm atmosphere that seems to be developing now that Musso is gone and Hitler's finest almost certainly won't be troubling us.

It's funny, or rather it isn't, it's not funny at all, that while the invasion scare was at its most intense and during all those terrible air-raids, there was a really good feeling between us Brits and the Maltese, whereas now that the threat has lifted all the signs of friendliness I'd thought were part of a genuine regard are disappearing, and fast. I don't know that anyone actually admits to sensing the difference, but I'm sure we all feel it. Shopkeepers who used to nod and smile when I bought things from them now look surly and take my money without so much as a "thank you". People I pass in the street with whom I used to stop for a chat, scuttle past or cross to the other side to avoid having to talk to me. I go into the bar in the town square and the locals stop speaking and either try to stare me out or duck their heads away if I so much as look towards them. I don't mean everyone behaves like this. Maria and Marcus are still good friends — at least, I think they are. But others, no.

The truth is, the Maltese want us gone. They probably hold us to account for all the houses and churches that the Luftwaffe flattened or left in ruins, and they may well think it's our fault that the seas around the island are virtually clogged with shipping blown up by stukas and U boats. I imagine that now the worst is over they want to be left alone, as the film actress has it, and in all honesty I can't say I entirely blame them. Sooner or later you want to have your own place to yourself. (Is that a cry of "Yanks Go Home" I hear echoing from various corners of dear old Blighty?)

Anyway, once Jimmy and I had lain and watched the empty sea and sky for over an hour, I was free to take him on a short recce., drawing his attention to all the desirable features of our estate. I didn't need to point out Filfla, sticking like a petrified tree stump out of the water, but explained that the infantry used it for target practice and that the artillery had been known to lob bombs at it in the interest of range finding, which, since it's only a hundred yards offshore, isn't difficult to get right. "About as much of a problem as hitting the side of a barn," he said. "Try whapping a tank when it's coming at you full tilt. That's what sorts the men from the boys." I said that no doubt it did, then marched him up to the statue of Congreve, "Sir Walter Norris," d. 1927 and buried at sea "Between this spot and Filfla Island" as the inscription has it. "Don't suppose he gets much rest with that artillery racket going on," Jimmy said. 'Bombs to the left of him ...'" "Cannon, actually," I said, and the look he gave me made me wish I hadn't. After that I showed him the other gun emplacements scattered across the hillside, explaining that in the past year local farmers had taken some of them over to use as hen coops and sheep pens, so not to be surprised if he heard animal noises coming from them. Strictly not allowed, but if you had any sense you turned a blind eye to such goings on, though their possible use as love nests for soldiers and local girls was absolutely forbidden. So not **those** animal noises. Anyway, I said, there's always the town shelter, now more or less surplus to requirement against Goering's finest. That's where lovers end up most evenings, although according to one of my informants it's often as crowded as Piccadilly on a Saturday night. Jimmy said he thought he'd give it a miss.

Finally and for good measure I pointed to the two sets of standing stones above us, one to the right, the other to the left and farther off but still distinct in its massive, settled rockiness. "Know what they are?" He surprised me by saying that **of course** he knew. "Megalithic tombs, right?" He'd been shown pictures of such tombs in Egypt, he said, as part of a lecture at base camp in Cairo which they'd all had to attend. The lecture, which had been given by some "geezer" with a bow-tie and posh accent, was about "Treasures of the Mediterranean and Middle-East," and was meant to explain what the allies were fighting to preserve from Teuton barbarism. "You been up there to have a look?" he asked me, nodding towards the tomb above us on the right, and when I told him all the tombs were off limits, he said "Yes, but have you ever been up to have a shufti?" I said nothing but from the way he grinned I think he knew what the answer would have been. "Old, old tombs," he said, his head moving back and forth as he studied now one, now the other of them where they stood, "loomed," I suppose I should say, against the bare moonlit hillside. Suddenly he dropped his voice and whispered "you reckon the Maltese could still be pagans?" But when I turned to him I could see that he was grinning. I told him that the Maltese were Catholics and took their religion seriously. "But they don't want anyone mucking about near the tombs," he said. "Why not? Do they reckon they're sacred places, or what?"

No more than the English do Stonehenge, I told him. "That's different," he said, "we're not sodding Druids, are we. Don't go in for blood sacrifice or nothing."

Don't we, I thought. Don't we just. But I kept my mouth shut.

I'm enclosing a letter for David. How I wish, **wish** I could be home with the three of you. But soon, surely, the day will come. And

Sunday," he added, "because we'll be performing in front of dignitories. What are dignitories?"

"Oh," she said, "the mayor and corporation together with Lord and Lady Muck I shouldn't wonder."

"*Who*?"

She laughed again. "It's a saying. Lord and Lady Muck. People with money. Poshos. People with their noses in the air. Like this." And tilting her head back and closing her eyes, she lisped "Don't know ya, 'pon my word, don't know ya."

This time they laughed together, and then, suddenly anxious, he asked, "But you will come, won't you?"

"Yes, of course we will," she said, reassuringly, serious now, though her smile still held traces of the laughter that came from so deep within her that it was a guarantee against all his fears. "Sarah and I will sit at the back, among the great unwashed."

Happy, he said, "unwashed is mucky."

Again, she laughed. "I can see you've been to Sheffield," she said. Then, glancing at the mantle-piece clock, "Now, young man, if you've finished your supper you'd better hop it. Up to bed with you. And don't wake your sister. She's sound asleep, or was when I last took a peek at her."

She stood up, carefully moving her chair so as to avoid scraping it against the table's thick steel leg, and, having kissed the top of his head, stepped across to her fireside chair, picked up the knitting that was draped across its seat, sat, reaching as she did so for the switch on the wireless that stood on the small table beside her.

He lingered by the door. "Is there any news?"

"That's what I'm about to find out," she said, her hand hovering over the knob. Then, "oh, it'll be the same, I imagine. Allied armies advancing on all fronts. As far as I can make out we're about here." And half rising she indicated on the map stuck to the wall beside her a small red flag pinned halfway up the leg shape he knew was Italy, its foot poised to aim a kick at the misshapen lump just by its big toe.

"That's good isn't it?"

Her gaze was intended to reassure him. "It must be," she said, then turned back to study the map.

Still he lingered. "What about dad?"

Flopping back into her chair, she reached for her cigarettes, lit one, and, sighing as she exhaled smoke, said, "He's bound to be safe now. I think he'll be on Malta for the duration." She paused and then, not looking at David, said more softly, "unless orders change and they want him further forward."

"You mean in Italy?"

She nodded without speaking and he knew that she was more worried than she would say. Then, turning the wireless knob and watching the needle waver into position, she said over her shoulder, "now, off you go. I'll come up and check on you in a few minutes."

He went then, though careful to leave the door ajar, so that as he climbed the stairs he could hear the well-known voice announce that this was the BBC and that here was the nine o'clock news.

* * *

Not ready yet for sleep, he lay, staring into the dark, hearing the regular, metallic ripple, the shuffled clinking that came from far across the fields on the other side of the road and were, he knew, coal wagons being backed into position at Hinckley's marshalling yard. "Coffling," his mother called those sounds. They were dying away now but they would be back as other wagons followed the line to and from the nearby mines. He didn't mind, he even liked them, they weren't frightening, unlike the heavy drone of aeroplanes pulsing low overhead as they made for Leicester, Coventry, Birmingham, for towns that were to him only names but which everyone spoke of with sighs and a shaking of heads as they studied newspaper photographs of mounds of brick, twisted girders, and half-ruined houses whose broken, jagged walls looked like bits of the petrified forest that illustrated one of Sarah's story books. Though the people clambering through the rubble or walking the broken streets, men in belted coats and trilby hats, most of them, and headscarved women, some pushing prams, others holding onto the hands of small children, were unlike the creatures of the forest. They looked far more like those he was used to seeing in the village. The only difference, the big difference, was that although one night a bomb fell into bottom meadow — a German plane "shedding its load before it scuttled for safety" so the vicar told his congregation — the village hadn't been attacked from the air and now it wouldn't be.

At all events, his mother had told Sarah and him that the Luftwaffe would be unlikely to trouble them again. That meant no more tumbling out of bed as the siren sounded its alarm and then making their way downstairs to crouch under the table that was supposed to save them from all but direct hits. Recently, people in the village had begun to talk of there being "an end in sight," of Hitler being "on the run," of peace around the corner. Meanwhile, his father was far away, on the island of Malta, a dot on the map so tiny that when their mother had shown them it, Sarah said "but he can't be *there*, there isn't room," a response with which David, though he had told her not to be silly, secretly agreed. But the letters that came regularly from their father were postmarked from Malta, so it had to be a real place.

He thought then of the most recent letter. It had arrived yesterday and the part meant for him was now lying on his bedside table. He had read it when he got home from school, then later, propped up in bed, read it twice more, until he knew its contents by heart.

*Dearest David and Sarah, I wonder if the weather in Leicestershire is as hot as Malta's. Somehow, I doubt it! Today, I have been swimming with a few other soldiers. One of them, who swam a good way out from the beach, tried to frighten us by saying that he saw a submarine underneath the water, while another tried to scare us even more by saying it must have been a shark. I suspect if anything **was** out there it would have been a porpoise or dolphin. We see plenty of them, leaping from the sea during the daytime and, sometimes, at night. David, if you'd like to read about dolphins, look in the bottom of the bookcase in the front room. Mum will help you find the book I mean.*

Anyway, we were perfectly safe from attack by sea! And the skies above Malta have nothing in them now but clouds — and not many of those. "The clouds roll by," as my friend Corporal Morris says, adding that he's sure we'll all be home soon, safe and sound. I hope he's right. Until then, give Mum a good big kiss from me, and remember how much I love you all."

Together, he and his mother had hunted for the book and read the account of how the "agility and grace of dolphins" as they played about the bows of ships, entranced watchers. There was more, too much to take in, although he paused over the sentence which told them that dolphins in the Mediterranean "usually measure 6 to 8ft. in length." "But that's as long as my bedroom," he said, amazed.

Now, peering into the dark, he didn't know whether to be scared or excited by the thought of so huge an animal moving through sea water. Turning on his side in order to face the photograph propped on his bedside table, he imagined the smile which in the dark he couldn't see, the beret angled above the light, curly hair, and he tried to hear his father's voice. But he couldn't make it come.

Instead, as sleep dragged at his eyelids, he heard another, more recent voice. "My, that's some whistle, young fella," it said. And then, "Bob White would be proud to claim that for his own." Bob White. Who was Bob White?

∾ CHAPTER FOUR ∾

Darling, this is being written early in the morning, 6 am, and already the heat is rising. If I look from the window of my hut I can see some twenty yards off the monster fig tree under which I sometimes lie in the heat of the day. For now it's still netted in mist, although once that's lifted and the cicadas have pressed their starter buttons, we're promised what Dave Morris prophesies will be "enough heat to drive Satan out of hell." Anyway, that's what he said last evening when I set out to walk down into town. At first I'd thought of going in the other direction. I've still not explored the Inquisitor's Summer Palace, though I've walked past it once or twice. Seventeenth-century, I'd say, and according to the locals used by the Pope's representative for drunken orgies. I've no idea whether I'd be able to get into the grounds let alone the house itself, which I've peered at through the closed iron gates — very handsome, it is, too, three-storey, and no doubt in a state of dilapidation.

But at seven o'clock last evening the heat was still so intense that I decided I'd be better off strolling down to Siggiewi rather than clambering up to the Palace, especially as that would take me in the opposite direction from town and further off from any watering hole. Besides, I needed a haircut. Dave didn't want to come. He'd had a hard day tinkering with the moving parts of some trucks needed for duty elsewhere. According to him he's working on equipment that should really be pushed over the nearest cliff — well, his actual words are a bit too ripe to commit to paper though I'm sure you can guess what they were. So I went on my own.

Even the walk downhill was pretty demanding. I took the donkey-track through olive groves the locals keep marked off from each other by stone walls, but the trees don't give much shade and the dust gets into your eyes and throat. By the time I came out on the road above town I was in such a sweat that I might as well not have taken the shower I'd splashed about in half an hour previously. But the heat hadn't put a stop to the building trade! The repair work on houses the Luftwaffe damaged but didn't manage to flatten is going on pretty well. I stopped to inspect a few of them, which I'd not done before, largely because I didn't want to give the impression of snooping. (He snoops to plunder.) From the look of it, the incendiaries jerry dropped here hadn't done as much harm as in northern Europe, probably because the houses are built of stone so can't be so readily set ablaze. Yes, you see the occasional smoke-blackened wall and there are burnt-through rafters, but overall Siggiwiggi got off comparatively lightly. There are still piles of rubble scattered about the place, but they don't begin to compare with the chaos in Valetta. Hardly a building there that hasn't been damaged, the city's streets still look like frozen cataracts of stone, and though I don't want to repeat what I've said in previous letters, I can't help being amazed that anyone could survive in a place that took such a pounding, let alone marvelling that they stayed sane through all those days and nights. But they did, and in Valetta, too, as all over the island, men are clearing the rubble and beginning to re-build. The George Cross is the least the island deserves. Of course it helps that the local stone is plentiful and easy to cut. They have saws that can slice through the limestone the way you'd slice through a piece of cheddar. It makes for a hellish amount of dust, so that any place where building work is going on is surrounded by a thick, yellow mist — there's just such a mist now on the road into Siggiewi — but it does speed up the work. Much quicker to arrange square blocks of stone on top of each other than to lay bricks. (No wonder the pyramids got built in a day. Ha.)

You'll want to know that I paid my usual respects to Professor Zammit. Because I rather like stealing up on him, I took a left road into town itself, and there he was, his back as always to me. So round to his front I go, and bid him good evening. Naturally he doesn't answer but nor is he surprised to see me. And while he remains in his accustomed pose, I'm free to observe him, his bow tie and frock-coat. Very dignified, right hand resting lightly on his hip as he looks over my head, though I think of his gaze as turned inward, considering the wisdom stored in the books that are piled within reach of his left hand — a few more lie at his feet. Is he contemplating Malta's future, I wonder, or that of the entire world? I also wonder whether I'll ever be able to introduce you to him? Who knows, after the war is over I might bring you here so you can see for yourself why I like him so much, why looking at him soothes me. He has the face of a man who's survived a full look at the worst.

But this isn't what I especially want to tell you. Having said farewell to Professor Zammit, I went to get a trim and shave. At that hour the shop was, as I'd guessed it would be, empty of customers. Only Marcus and brother George present, and Marcus his usual welcoming self. "Good evening, Mr Stephen, nice to see you, sir, you are here for a haircut, then let us start immediately."

An odd mixture of the deferential and the genuinely friendly, our Marcus. Having returned his welcome and agreed that I did indeed require his professional attention, I added that I was also there for the pleasure of his company — which is true, although you wouldn't have thought so from the look George gave me. George doesn't like me one little bit. I've met him before in Marcus's shop and he's never been overflowing with human kindness, but on this occasion he excelled himself. When I arrived he was sprawled in the leather armchair reserved for customers and he showed no sign of moving until Marcus gestured to him and he made great play of prising himself out of it. Then, and only then, he spoke to me.

"Why you say 'evening?'" he wanted to know. "It is not evening yet." The truculence in his voice took me aback. It was as though he was spoiling for a fight.

"In England evenings begin after six o'clock," I said.

"But you not in England now."

"True."

"But perhaps you wish you were."

Marcus did his best to lower the temperature by reminding George that I was a regular customer and a friend. But it did little good, I'm afraid. George simply changed tack, reminding me that I'd been on Malta for two years which I no doubt thought was too long, although "you wasn't here during the worst."

"No, I wasn't," I admitted, but added that North Africa had been no picnic, either. So then he wanted to know what a picnic was and I said picnics happened wherever the Germans weren't, and Marcus laughed, but George went on staring at me.

"You think this war soon be over?" he asked, as though to imply he couldn't wait to see the back of us, and when I said, yes, he wanted to know why I was so confident. I muttered something about how convoys were at last getting through pretty easily. Almost like civvy street, I said, trying to make a joke of it, regular supplies of all we needed. Food, tobacco, oil …

"Women?" he asked, nastily, as though we must be bringing in shiploads of ladies of the night, and Marcus said "George, you swallow your tongue. You go now." So off George went, without a backward glance as they say, and I could breathe more easily.

"Mr Stephen, I am sorry about that," Marcus said as he got to work with his scissors. I said I could understand that now the raids were a thing of the past and the blockade lifted, the islanders would want Malta to themselves, but Marcus explained that it wasn't so much that as his brother's being the father of a girl, "Anna, and Anna is seventeen, an age, you know, when fathers begin to worry. Me, I have boys, so I don't have the same worries. But George, he fears for his daughter's honour. Because if Anna is dishonoured, he is dishonoured, the family is dishonoured."

I was beginning to twig. "Is your brother worried because of the presence of British soldiers?" Had she perhaps formed a "romantic attachment" with one? A silly form of words, I know, but I didn't know how else to put the question. And I'm certainly aware of tensions, even the occasional fist fight, between some of the locals and troops over girls of the island who've abandoned their Maltese boyfriends for the "glamour" of service uniform.

That was the problem exactly, Marcus agreed. And then he added that George had told him of one soldier who was "many times" coming to their house, asking to see Anna. "Perhaps you know this soldier?"

"It's not very likely," I told him. "There are hundreds of us still here, and plenty of airmen and sailors, if it comes to that."

But Marcus was insistent that the young man in question was in the army. He had been seen in soldier's uniform at the wheel of an army truck and he'd even left the vehicle standing outside the house where George and his family lived when, on one occasion, he had knocked on the door in order to enquire about the young woman.

"He did that?"

"Yes," Marcus said. Then, having once again apologised for George's behaviour, he explained that at the moment I arrived his brother had been telling Marcus that he, George, thought I might know the soldier in question, "because you are a mechanic who is friendly with all the drivers." You'll have spotted the exaggeration in Marcus's narrative. **Many** times coming to the house turned out to be **one occasion**. Besides, friendly with "all" the drivers. I think not.

Still, I let that pass, as I did George's habitual surliness, for which this once there might, I had to concede, be some excuse. I didn't want to offend Marcus. I did, however, point out that not only was I one of several mechanics at our base but that there are other bases on the island. The man could come from any of them.

But Marcus knocked that down. "Not if he drive through our village every day. He must come from your camp, Mr Stephen."

How to reply? "I wish your brother had talked to me about his worries," in the circumstances seemed reasonable, and I said as much while Marcus whipped away the sheet in which I'd been wrapped and then stood in front of me, doing his best to brush stray hairs off the shoulders of these god-awful shirts we have to wear. Short-sleeved they may be, but you can't get rid of their wire-wool feel, and in this heat, well — Nessus could have taken lessons from whoever came up with the design and material of the damned things. Anyway, having done his best to save me a night of intolerable itchiness, Marcus once more apologised for his brother's bad temper, then said, "I agree, Mr Stephen, he should have asked you himself but he find it not easy to talk to … to outsiders." Which is most certainly true.

Then Marcus dealt me the Hanged Man. "Mr Stephen, the soldier left his name at the house. George says he is called Mr Derek Southern. You know him?"

"No," I said, which was the truth. "I don't." But as Marcus went on looking at me, I realised that I would have to promise to make enquiries.

"Mr Stephen," Marcus said, "I tell you this as a friend. Fathers here take great care of their daughters. If a daughter don't do as her father wants or if she bring dishonour on her family then … " and *he pointed two fingers at my heart. "Pouff," he said. "If you find out who this Mr Derek Southern is you explain to him what I tell you. Tell him he must be very careful to be a good man. You understand?" One glance at Marcus and I could see he wasn't joking.*

Darling, I'm going to break off now. There's more to tell, but I'm going to swallow some breakfast before the day becomes too hot to think of food, then I've a morning's worth of maintenance before we go over to Valetta to pick up whatever the latest supply ships have brought in. I'll resume this in the cool of the evening, once I've washed off the day's muck sweat.

* * *

OK. It's now ten o'clock pip emma and I'm back at base after a tedious day driving in convoy round half of the island dropping off goods at various camps. Dirty, tiring work, though I shouldn't complain, I know. We're well away from the enemy. In fact, if it weren't for the bomb damage Malta would seem a little world entirely remote from war. (As long as you turn a blind eye to the military camps and the forces personnel and the heavy-duty trucks and lorries and motor bikes and, in the harbour, the battleships and cruisers and…)

*Anyway, you'll be pleased to learn that I found our mystery man, Derek Southern. No great sleuthing required, either. Here's how Sherlock Willoughby did it. After I'd shaken the hairs of Marcus's shop from my heels, I took myself to his sister, Maria. If **he's** reliable, you could set your watch by **her** movements. As always, she was sitting on the old wooden chair she takes on to the cobbles outside her shop, knitting, and, as always, surrounded by tommies dunking bits of bread in the tea she supplies. Lining their stomachs, no doubt, for their later visits to the bar on the other side of the square. She does a good deal of washing and darning for them, so in buying a crust and a cuppa they are, as it were, paying their respects and helping to fill her purse.*

As soon as she saw me, she complimented me on my hair cut and asked how Marcus was. Marcus was fine, I told her. So Maria crossed herself and said "Thanks God." This from someone who sees her brother probably half-a-dozen times a day and whose bakery is all of fifty yards from his shop. Perhaps it comes from living halfway down the square which is dominated by a whacking great church. And, as I think I may have told you before, at the square's lower end is a hefty statue of the local saint Nicola (a man) on a pedestal, right hand dispensing bread and with a basket of rolls by his feet.

Bear with me. Divagation by way of illumination! The church here does feel like a controlling and containing presence. Most days we drive to Valetta via a town called Mosta where a German bomb lodged in the roof of the church but didn't fall on the congregation then packed in for service. I know I'm not repeating myself telling you **this**, because I only heard the story today The man who told me added that it was God's intervention. Choosing to save his faithful worshippers from death that can fall from the sky or hit you unexpectedly at any time. E.M. Forster, I seem to remember, says that one difference between the north of Europe and south is that in the south death comes suddenly. "A man can be well in the morning and dead by evening." Something like that. Perhaps this explains why Maria gives thanks to God for sparing the life of a brother she sees every day. In the midst of life and all that. Besides, belief in God's mysterious ways is as much a part of her life as the air she breathes. She wears her widow's black as a matter of course. It's simply what she **does.** Choice doesn't come into it. She's older than Marcus but not, I guess, by as many years as her appearance suggests. Her two lads who work the fields where a bomb killed her husband are still only teenagers. But you look at her old dress and her grey hair and you think she must be sixty at least. Our lot no doubt like it that way. She's the mum, even the gran, they're missing.

And now the illumination. For **of course** she knew who Derek Southern was. I had only to ask and Maria pointed him out, one of a group sprawling on the doorstep of her shop. She called him over.

No threat here, I found myself thinking, as he sauntered across. A large, tow-haired youth, with blue eyes and a face reddened by sun. Nothing out of the ordinary but certainly no suggestion of Lothario about him, nothing to make men lock up their daughters. Naturally, his mates watched us with some interest, and when I suggested that we step into the bakery because what I had to say could perhaps best be communicated in private, there were the inevitable cries of "Oo er, wot you bin up to, Derek," "Naughty boy," that kind of thing. He didn't seem bothered, shrugged, said nothing, and to be honest it was me who felt embarrassed.

After all, what **was** I to say? But once we were inside that hot little space he made it easy for me. "So, then, sarge?" I liked his grin, not cocky, genuinely enquiring, and his voice, south London at a guess, and reassuringly without edge. I explained as well as I could the gist of what I'd learnt from Marcus: about brother George having reason to believe that his daughter had been pestered by a soldier … . At which point he stopped me by laughing outright. "Pestered? If you're talking about who I think you are then I can tell you I've not said a dickie bird to her. I don't even know her name."

"Her name's Anna," I said, and then wished I hadn't.

"Anna, is it. Then you know more than I do." I thought he was going to clam up at that point, but after a moment or two of silence he said, "if it helps, I don't mind telling you this much — which is all there is to tell. See, I'm a driver, well, you probably know that. Deliveries to all parts. OK. So a few days ago I'm driving down through the town and I see this girl sweeping the path outside some house or other, one of the those that's being repaired, and she's … well, she's lovely. Next day, she's there again, and the day after that. So I decide that I'll try to find some way to talk to her. Sure enough, the next day as I drive up, there she is. But when I stop the truck she scarpers round the back of the house and as I'm walking up the path some man opens the front door and stands there, arms folded, glaring at me like I'm the Means Test Man. Her dad, I guess. I don't know what to say, that's the truth. It was spur of the moment, that stopping, and there I am clueless, not a word in my head. I think I asked him if I could speak to the young lady I've just seen going round the back, something pretty sophisticated anyway, but he's not too impressed. In fact he looks at me like he don't understand English, which for all I know he don't. So, and I know it must sound a bit stupid, I ask him to hang on a minute, get out a bit of paper, write down a message, ask the bloke to give it to the young lady, then hop it back to the truck."

Naturally, I asked him what had been in the message.

He mumbled a bit over his reply. Did I really want to know? I did, I said, and I could sense his embarrassment even in the dark of that little bakery. "I said I'd like to see her and wrote down my name. And that was all." He stopped, sighed, then said, "Pretty silly, I know, but I wouldn't call it pestering, would you."

To be fair, the only answer I could have given was that I agreed. But I didn't say that. Instead, I told him that Marcus had asked me to warn him — not off, exactly, but to be careful. Family honour was at stake and Marcus's brother, Anna's father, wouldn't stand for any 'hanky-panky.' I tried to give the phrase an ironic twist but I doubt Southern noticed. He simply repeated, insisted, that nothing had happened between him and the girl. So I said that I'd report back to Marcus what I'd been told and tell him that in my opinion the soldier in question could be trusted.

"Oh, I can be trusted," Southern said, laughing. "No wife waiting for me in blighty, no nasty diseases. Anyway, even if I manage to get as far as persuading her to take a walk, father willing, she'll have to bring a friend, won't she? A chaperone. To make sure she comes to no harm."

He knew that much of local customs. "And there are three brothers," I told him, not adding that two of the three were still juniors and the oldest was in America. There are some things better not said.

"Plus the dad with a shotgun waiting to blast me to kingdom come if I as much as lay a finger on her. Is that it?"

"You got the picture," I said in my best Cagney accent.

He laughed, then shook his head and said ruefully, "I don't know why I bother."

I couldn't resist it. "Then why do you?"

"Ah," he said, suddenly serious, "If you'd seen her you wouldn't ask that question."

Will they prove to be star-crossed lovers? I doubt it. More likely a young man's far from home sudden stirring of fancy under a hot sun that will wither and die from lack of encouragement. Meanwhile this not-so-young man apologises for his rambling letter and closes by saying that he yearns to see you all again and sends you his dearest love.

∼ CHAPTER FIVE ∼

Letting himself into the house by the back door, he called out a greeting, but as he'd hoped his mother and Sarah weren't yet back from the dentist. Good! Upstairs, he stared at his face in the bathroom mirror. The lump above his right eye showed blue but the scratch down his nose was no longer bleeding. He dabbed at it with cold water then, careful not to wipe his face on a towel, rubbed his nose on his shirt-sleeve and looked again. Better. As for the sleeve itself, he could say that the grass and mud stains came from having tripped while running, and that would also explain how he'd bashed his face.

Downstairs, he poured himself a cup of water, drank it, re-filled the cup and took it into the living room. There, he settled at the table with pencil and paper and began to write.

Dear Dad, it is Friday and I have no more lessons until Monday.

Then he stopped. What to say next? What he wanted to say was that the fight he and Robin had been in wasn't a fair one.

Images of the fight kept breaking in on him, followed by memories of the gang's jeers as he and Robin finally ran off, their cries of *"Custards, custards. Eyeties. Canaries."* Jamming his hands over his ears did no good, nor did whistling to try to drown out the sound of Neville Fox's contemptuous laugh, his squawk of delight when he, David, tripped and fell as he stumbled after his friend.

He looked about him, trying to focus on something, *anything,* in the room that would blank out the memory… Suddenly, he found himself staring at the note pad that lay on the carpet beside his mother's easy chair. Her fountain pen, uncapped, lay across the pad, as though she had stopped in the middle of what she was writing, perhaps realising she might be late for Sarah's appointment.

He swung off his chair and tip-toed across to where the pad lay.

*Darling, your most recent letter arrived this a.m. Though I'm sorry to hear you've been drawn into the romantic "imbroglio" — if that's the word for it — you tell me about, it's wonderful to know that you're otherwise well and free of harm. You say there's a change of atmosphere in Malta. There's a change in England, too, though here it's a cheerier one. I can even hear it in the voices of the BBC news readers. They **were** cautious, guarding against hope, so I always felt, but now there's a new spring in their step — well, announcements. And of course we all follow the news of where the allied armies have got to and it seems that as far as France is concerned the Germans are being pushed back fast. I can't tell about Italy, the news from there is rather more vague. And the far east doesn't sound quite as promising. But the Red Army has reached Poland. Isn't that amazing when it seems only yesterday that we were worrying Hitler would overrun Russia? I know there's a long way to go yet, and we're always being urged to "exercise caution," but we're going to win, aren't we! When I think that David and Sarah might have had to become little Nazis (or worse) 1feel such **relief** that I want to run up and down the road shouting for joy.*

*Meanwhile, the village has been invaded by Americans! One of the regiments sent to Normandy has a sort of reserve camp — I don't know what the correct term is — which is based up at the old Children's Home. Two Sundays ago they were at church, presenting their flag. Brass band, lots of parade ground shouting and saluting, the vicar in his element, and David singing his heart out in the choir. Sarah and I huddled behind a pillar among the usual crowd including, of course, that extraordinary man who makes a point of reading **The News of the World** all the way through the sermon. Nobody knows who he is, he appears to materialise out of thin air for Sundays only at St Mary's. "The devil incarnate," Godwin calls him, and so he may be for all anyone knows to the contrary.*

He paused in his reading. Hastily dropping the pad, he crept out into the hall and waited. But no, there was no outline shadow against the frosted glass. He tiptoed back into the living room and, as he bent to retrieve her pad, found he was still clutching his mother's pen.

David, would you believe, has actually met one of the Americans.

Our boy first ran into him first when he was coming back from evening choir practice nearly three weeks ago. Apparently the soldier complimented David on his whistling. I rather think from what David says he must have disturbed a bit of hedge-side canoodling (ahem) the American was going in for with a woman David swears was Beth Morton. Oh, lord! Of course, I told him he must have been mistaken and hope he was. I know there have been one or two rumours and I remember you saying that you thought Beth was a bit too "lively" for Dick, as well as being too young for him, but when Dick isn't at work they can be seen together in the village looking the image of married contentment.

*Anyway, on the Saturday after the big church parade, David met the American again, at one of Hetty Raynor's tea dances. (Now that the Americans are here she's turned them into weekly events.) According to David, he's called Jay Krassner and in "real life" is — wait for it — a drummer in what I suppose is a professional dance or swing band. Needless to say, as soon as he discovered this, our son was in raptures. The upshot of this was that without breathing a word to me he took it upon himself to invite the man to our house to give him some lessons. When Sarah and I got back from the village some days ago I found the two of them pounding away at what David calls his drum-kit — biscuit-tin and that old snare drum a misguided neighbour gave him — happy as Larry. Naturally, I was civil, offered Uncle Sam's Drummer Boy a cup of tea before sending him on his way. David wanted to make an arrangement to see him again but I wasn't having that. I know we're encouraged to welcome our "American cousins," but there are limits. So, "it may not be easy to find a suitable time," I said, and waved Mr Krassner off the premises. Since then David's been in something of a sulk, but he'll come round. I hope you think I did the right thing. It wouldn't be right, would it, to have a young American visiting the house while you're not here. No matter how innocent the explanation, it's how it **looks.** But of course it's terribly difficult to explain this to David, poor boy. I tried telling him that it was fine for him to be friendly with Mr Krassner but that inviting him home wasn't such a good idea, but he wanted to know why it wasn't, and what could I say? The best I could come up with was to suggest that Krassner's time* *wasn't his own and that his hours of freedom might not coincide with ours, and I don't need to be told how feeble that sounded.*

Oh, darling, I do miss you so terribly. As do the children. It nearly broke my heart the other day when Sarah asked me, "What does daddy look like?" I think she can't believe the photographs are of the real you. I have to remind myself that she was only two when you went away. Hurry home, dearest. We need you and …

At that point the letter broke off. David replaced the pad, laid his mother's pen across it in what he hoped was the right position, and went back to trying to write his own letter. After a few moments' thought, his hand now steady, he once more picked up his pencil. He knew now what he wanted to write. *I have met an American soldier,* he began. *"He is a very nice man who is a drummer and he has given me a pair of drum sticks. They are long but he says I will get used to them. I would like him to come to our house to show me how to play properly.* He read the sentences over again before adding *I looked up about dolphins. I think they must be as long as my bedroom. If you see any more I would like to know. With love, David.*

"Have you been in a fight?" his mother asked, as the three of them sat over tea. She reached out a hand to stroke his face but he flinched from it, shaking his head as he did so.

"I fell over," he mumbled, "running too fast."

"It's bad to run fast," Sarah said, as though repeating a well-known rule.

"No, it's not."

"It is. It makes you fall over and dirty your clothes. And spoil your face."

"You'd run fast if Goebbels was after you."

"You mean that you had to run from the bull?" Sarah stared across at him, enthralled.

"Sort of," he said.

Before she could ask for further explanation, their mother broke in to tell him that they'd seen Mrs Rayner up in the village, "and she asked to me to remind you about tomorrow's dance. She'll be expecting you to help as usual. Not that I imagine you need any reminder." She paused, looked smilingly at him, and then, as though holding out the promise of an indefinable reward, added, "No doubt your Mr Krassner will be there."

* * *

But the tea-dance began without him. For a while David lingered outside the hall, beside the blackboard on which one of Mrs Rayner's assistants, Doreen, had scrawled

DANCE STARTS 3 PM.
TEA 4. 30 pm.
FREE ADMISSION IF IN UNIFORM
EVERYONE ELSE 1/6d

ALL WELCOME. HELP THE WAR EFFORT!!!

But the American didn't come.

And an hour later, by which time he was busy with his responsibilities at the gramophone — "time for a waltz, David, settle our tummies a bit," or, "let's have a gee-up, pet, something to get them twirling" — the soldier still hadn't appeared. Why not? He thought he knew the answer. Krassner must have been put off by the way he'd been given the cold shoulder — wasn't that what people called it — when he'd offered to repeat his visit to David's house. All he'd done was offer to show David a few "tricks of the trade," as he called them. What was wrong with that? Krassner after all *knew* about drumming. Just as he knew who Bob White was. A bandleader, so he answered David's question, of what was apparently "a pretty ordinary outfit," and White himself "did a whole lot of whistling." And in reply to another question, Krassner had said, "My favourite drummer? Well, I'd have to say Dave Tough." And then he added, laughing, "perhaps we should call you Tough guy." After which he began to show David how to hold his drumsticks the Dave Tough way.

And at that moment David's mother and Sarah had come in and everything was spoilt.

He was shaken out of his reveries by Mrs Rayner putting a hand on his shoulder as she said urgently, "David, change the record will you love. Get that one off, put on something more lively." "That one" happened to be Ray Fox's orchestra playing "Love is the Sweetest Thing" to which, he now saw, several couples were dancing, although the word hardly applied to one or two pairs who did little more than clutch each other as they swayed in time to the music. Among them was a young village woman who, with her older husband, ran the newspaper shop. She was in the arms of a GI, head resting on his shoulder, while her husband glowered from the sidelines.

David lifted the gramophone arm. Dancers stopped and looked in his direction, there were whistles of complaint. As he dropped the record into its sleeve and began to lift one from a different pile, Mrs Rayner said loudly, "Tea time, everyone." She laid a restraining hand on David's until the floor was cleared.

Cries of "otch up" as people began to arrange themselves along the wooden benches. Mrs Rayner watched the newsagent reclaim his wife, then said to David, "alright, Pet, let the music play," and left him as she went to supervise the tea arrangements.

He guided the needle into position. Softly at first, the music picked its way through the accentuated beat, fat chords of brass beginning to answer the saxophones' cushiony sound.

From behind him a voice he recognised, said, "*Cherokee*, eh? Not a bad outfit, Barnett's, though it sure can't beat Goodman's."

Jay Krassner. He'd come after all.

∼ CHAPTER SIX ∼

Stephen sat with Dave Morris in the doorway of Maria's bakehouse, half in and half out of shadow, drowsy from the day's work. Even at eight o'clock the July heat lay like a stupefying power over the town's empty square. Muffled laughter and the sounds of raised voices came through the open door of Tony's Bar on the square's far side, but the two men had the bakehouse to themselves as they munched on hunks of bread. On the cobbled pavement outside, chair tilted back under the house eaves in order to avoid the worst of the heat, Maria darned socks while directing occasional remarks to the pair of them, though without bothering to turn her head in their direction.

"How is your family, Corporal Morris?"

"What bleedin' family? I've told you, Maria, there's only me and me old mum." But the words came gently, more regret than rebuke.

"And how is your mother?"

"Not a clue. Not 'ad a letter in months."

"Do you write to her?"

"Oh, yes," Dave said, winking at Stephen. "Regular as clockwork."

Dave was not, as he himself said, "much of a scholar," and his mother was completely illiterate. The few letters sent in his name were therefore addressed to the old lady's next-door neighbour who could read, though she wasn't to be trusted with confidences. "Leaks like a length of perished hose," Dave once told Stephen. "Mention anything intended for ma's ears only and in two shakes the whole street knows." As a result, communications with home were kept to a minimum, in both frequency and content. *Dear Mother, the weather here is hot, as per. I am well and hope you are in the pink also. I am looking forward to seeing you again. Your loving son.* "That's enough to keep her happy," Dave said, the first

46

time he dictated a letter to Stephen. "Don't mind doin' this, do you? I mean, you're writing's a sight neater'n mine, what with you being a teacher an' all."

"And you," Mr Stephen," Maria asked. "How is your family?"

"All well," Stephen told her. Jean's latest, which had arrived that morning, lay unopened in his bedside cupboard, a present to himself to be opened and read last thing at night.

A pigeon landed on cobbles in front of the bakery, peered dowager-like about as it waddled in search of crumbs, then, after stabbing moodily at a crumpled, empty packet of *Lightweights*, decided there was nothing here to detain it and blundered back into the air.

Perhaps prompted by the sight of a bird which a year earlier would almost certainly have brought some hungry islander running with a gun, Maria said "I think the war, it goes well for us now, is that not so? And then, when it is finished, you will all want very much to be with your families."

Was this a non-too subtle hint that the armed forces had outstayed their welcome? Stephen thought not. For Maria, the family — her family, any family — was the centre of existence. Family was what gave you entry to full membership of the human race. It followed that men now far apart from wives, children, parents, cousins, even, must want above all to be with them once again.

"Not me," Dave said. "Got a cushy number here, what with all this sun and no Teds to worry us, not any longer. Once they've raised the white flag I reckon I might try to find a nice little Malta Miss, make a life for myself here. Gotta be something I can do. Open a garage, maybe. Not much I can't make go. Bring me your dead and I'll fire 'em up."

He grinned at Stephen, and Stephen smiled back, as he did so inclining his head in honour of the hours they had spent that day exposed to the full glare of a pitiless sun while they crawled beneath a clapped-out truck or took it in turns to lean over its innards, until finally, in the late afternoon, and after Dave's prolonged, expert ministrations, the engine coughed, rumbled, and shook itself into life. "Like an old dog coming out of water, just to prove it ain't dead," Dave had said, laughing.

"And you, Mr Stephen? Do you wish for your home?"

"Yes," Stephen said, "I want to go home." He paused, cleared his throat, momentarily overcome by the surge of emotion that thickened his words. "Nothing personal, Maria, but I want to be back in England."

And as Maria turned to him, nodding her approval, he said, "I joined the army to fight fascism, but since leaving Egypt I've done precious little of that. I'm beginning to feel that we're not doing much good where we are. We're no bloody use, are we, no bloody use to anyone. The war has left us behind." Like flotsam, he stopped himself from adding.

"They also serve who only stand and wait," Dave said sententiously. "You can't argue with Shakespeare."

"Milton."

"Oh, Pardon my mistake. I must 'ave been off school the day we done 'im." Then, lowering his voice, he said to Stephen, "anyway, you are useful. Keepin' the course of true love on track. Speaking of which … "

"Evening," Derek Southern said, looming in the doorway. "Alright to come in, or are you two in private conflab?"

They shifted their chairs to let him pass. He was followed in by Maria, several balled pairs of newly-darned socks cradled in her arms.

"Here you are, you Englishmen," she said, doling out pairs of the socks. "I wash for you, I mend for you, I cook for you. And where is my reward." She smiled broadly at them, her teeth showing surprisingly white in the semi-dark.

"You'll get your reward up above," Dave said, answering her smile. He blew her a kiss. "Lusso in cielo, as the Eyeties say. Sommat like that, anyway. Right, I'll be off. See you, lads."

They watched as he strode across the square, tall, wide-shouldered, and disappeared through the door of Tony's Bar. "Built like a brick shithouse," someone had once said of Dave Morris. Not bad.

"So," Stephen said, registering the scent of Southern's pomaded hair, his fresh-pressed army shirt, "I assume you're hoping to see Anna."

"Right you are, Sarge." Southern offered a mock salute. Dropping into the seat Dave had just vacated, he watched Maria's movements as she pushed aside the curtain that divided the room where they sat from the bakehouse and passed through to begin the preparations for next day's bread. They listened to the low screech of an oven door opening, heard the scrape of Maria's wooden shovel among cinders, and then, turning back to Stephen, and bringing his head close as though to whisper the words, Southern said, "she's bringing a pal with her, so there's no need for you to hang around."

"For god's sake," Stephen said, "it's not as if I *want* to be dancing attendance on your meetings." But noting Southern's startled expression and realising the other hadn't intended to be offensive, he said more reasonably "well, at any rate I'm glad that so far at least the —" he was going to say "affair" but changed it to — "romance seems to be going well."

That didn't sound right, either. He tried again, this time allowing for a mocking disclaimer. "Your true love has your heart and you have hers." Worse still. I, on the other hand, haven't seen my wife for the best part of three years and for all I know it may be another three years before I see her again. Ah no, he couldn't say that. Instead, and ruefully, he said, shrugging, "who knows when this bloody war will end." There, would Southern understand.

But before he could answer, Maria's voice said "Mr. Stephen, I pray that before long you will be re-united with your family." She had ducked back through the curtain and now stood, crossing herself and smiling reassuringly at him. She at least understood.

"Thanks, Maria," he said. Then, to Southern, "Let's believe in the power of prayer. After all, we don't want to be wrinkled, white-haired ancients before Hitler's in his grave, do we. How old are you, by the way?"

"Twenty one," Southern said. Adding, "In November."

"Older than I was when I met my wife-to-be."

"When was that, sarge?" The question was polite, dutiful, and Stephen didn't bother to answer it. Instead, he levered himself up from the chair on which he'd been sitting for the past hour, becoming aware as he did so of the clamminess of the shirt sticking to his back. In this climate nothing stayed clean or dry for long. He waved goodbye to Maria, stuffed the pair of socks she'd mended into a pocket of his shorts, and left the bakery. Then he turned to face Southern who had accompanied him out of the shop and now stood, hand shading his eyes against the glare of the lowering sun, peering down the square in the direction from which Anna and her companion for the evening would come.

"Enjoy yourself," Stephen said to him. "And no stepping out of line, OK?"

"That's what I love about the army," Southern said, continuing to look down the square rather than at Stephen. "I'm old enough to get killed fighting for freedom, but not old enough to enjoy any freedom of my own."

"It's not that, as you perfectly well know," Stephen said, turning away. Over his shoulder, he added, "You're alright, Derek, but when in Rome, remember … "

Propped against the doorway, Southern looked briefly at him. "I'll remember," he said.

* * *

Marcus's door was, as usual, half open. Inside, in the cool gloom, the hairdresser sat smoking in the leather chair which he had pulled over to the deep-embrasured window in order to look out onto the dusty fields below.

"Good evening, Mr Stephen," he said in reply to Stephen's greeting, and without looking round. "You are well?"

"Very well," Stephen said, dragging a wooden chair across to join Marcus. "And you?"

Together they watched three men bent among the growing corn in the field below. "They are very pleased," Marcus said, nodding in the direction of the men, "the crop, it promises well. I, too, am well, thank you. My soul is at peace."

"That's good to know." There was a pause while Stephen dug inside his shirt pocket for his *Lightweights*, and, having chosen and lit a cigarette, carefully pushed the spent match back into its box.

"And Mr. George, he is well?"

He watched Marcus's brother in the field gradually ease himself upright, push his straw hat to the back of his head and arch his spine as he pressed his hands to the back of his ribs. He must have spoken to the other two men, because, having turned their heads to look at him, they slowly, slowly, began to straighten themselves. "Strong Labour got up with his pipe in his mouth," Stephen murmured, "and stoutly strode over the vale." But there was no hint of a stride about these men's fatigued movements. The three of them stooped again, this time to gather up tools, a wooden rake, hoes, forks. When they passed beneath the window and then out of sight, it was not even a weary plod, more like a round-shouldered shuffle.

Only then did Marcus turn to face Stephen. "George is pleased," he said, smiling candidly, opening his arms wide as he did so. "He tells me that Anna is happy with her Englishman. He is a good man, he treats her with respect. My brother thinks they will marry."

"*Really*?" He hoped he hadn't revealed the unease he felt.

"Why are you so surprised?"

"Well… " How best to put it? "I suppose I was caught off balance a bit. They've only known each other for a short time — three weeks, isn't it?"

"But the young man, Mr — " He paused, looked enquiringly at Stephen, who said "Southern, Derek Southern" — "But Mr Derek, he agrees to go to church with Anna. He meets Father Marco, one, two, three times."

"You mean Southern is taking Instruction?" This time he couldn't keep the incredulity out of his voice.

"Why is that a bad thing? Anna cannot marry if she does not marry in church, and the church is a good church. The True Church." He gave the three words an especial emphasis. "You should think perhaps of going yourself, Mr Stephen."

"Oh, I'm already married," Stephen said lightly.

But Marcus did not join in his smile. "You should not joke about this matter," he said.

"No, you're right, sorry." Stephen drew heavily on his cigarette, licked thumb and index finger and pinched the end of his *Lightweight* before returning the half-unsmoked cigarette to its packet.

"How is your wife?" Marcus said more gently, acknowledging Stephen's apology with a nod.

"She's fine."

"No, I mean *how* is she? Is she tall? What is the colour of her hair? Does she bring you children? You never tell me anything about yourself. If we are to be friends I think you must tell me about how you live when you are in England. But you say nothing."

"English reticence," Stephen said. Marcus must have heard from Maria about David and Sarah. Perhaps he needed to receive such information from his customer in order to confer friendship. "We're a tight-lipped lot, I'm afraid. Used to Keeping Mum as the saying goes." And then, as Marcus opened his mouth to ask the obvious question, "'Mum'. From Mumming. Acting without speaking. That's the English for you."

"You are a teacher, I think, Mr Stephen?"

"That is indeed my profession," Stephen said, making a mock bow.

"And you will be a teacher again when this war is over."

"Yes," Stephen said, "I will. It's an honourable profession," he added, sensing the blood coming to his cheeks.

Marcus burst into delighted laughter. "Now you speak from the heart. Now we can be true friends."

He got up, crossed the room to an old dresser, from which he retrieved a bottle. Uncorking it, he sniffed the contents appreciatively. "This," he said, carefully tilting the bottle and filling two small glasses to the brim, "is very special." He handed Stephen a glass.

"What is it?" Stephen said, trying not to recoil from the dark, aromatic scent.

"Island brandy. Very rare. We will drink to friendship."

"I don't usually drink brandy," Stephen said, then immediately, "but I will certainly drink to friendship."

"And to the profession of teacher."

"In that case," Stephen said, "I propose a toast to Dr Zammit."

Marcus widened his eyes in pleasure. "You know about Dr. Zammit?"

"Not really, I'm afraid," Stephen said. "Only what I can deduce from the statue."

"He was a good man," Marcus said solemnly, raising himself on tiptoe as though meaning by such a gesture to demonstrate the full intensity of his regard. Then, sinking back onto to his heels, he stared up at Stephen, his eyes gleaming. "He gave to the children of our town his love for learning. So, yes, let us drink to Dr Zammit."

They clinked glasses and drank to Dr. Zammit.

"I'd also like to propose a toast," Stephen said, "to our friendship. You and me."

"That is good," Marcus said. Again they clinked glasses and drank.

"And now we are friends" Marcus said, taking and refilling their empty glasses, "we may say what we like to each other. It is what friendship is for." In the half-gloom he watched for Stephen to nod his agreement. Dropping into the leather chair and motioning Stephen to the wooden chair he'd drawn up, he said, "So. Please to tell me about your wife. Is she also a teacher?"

"No," Stephen said, as he sat and sipped the brandy. "Before our marriage she worked in a music shop, selling sheet music, records, even gramophones. Her boss gave us a gramophone for a wedding-present, a portable, one you can take with you on picnics."

"But why the gramophone? Why not take a guitar?"

"Because not so many people in England play the guitar, or any musical instrument that can be carried any distance. But you can carry a gramophone and then you can dance. Or simply listen to the music."

"And you did that? You took the gramophone with you?"

"Not often," Stephen admitted. "It's too heavy to lug for any great distance. We didn't take it if we went by bus. But it went with us whenever I could borrow a car.

"And whose car did you borrow?"

"My father's," Stephen said, watching Marcus half-stand and reach across to splash more brandy into his glass. "He ran his own business, supplying tableware to hotels and restaurants. The car was needed, you see, to ferry his goods about. But at weekends he'd sometimes let us take it, drive right out of London, which was where I taught. Not far away from my parents, although that I found a post near there was pure coincidence."

"You mean you didn't want to be near to your parents? Why not? Did you not like them?" Marcus's question suggested the inconceivability to his mind of separation between parents and children.

"No, it wasn't that," Stephen told him. "I came from the city but Jean — my wife — was a country girl at heart. She used to say that she preferred a sheep-pen to Shepherd's Bush." And as he said the words he could almost hear her voice, the light syllables, the hint of laughter that seemed to inhabit everything she said.

The room had suddenly grown dark, the window with its deep embrasure behind Marcus's head leading out to the warm night air and distant sintering of stars. Marcus got up, crossed to the small table pushed up against a far wall and, without bothering to pull the shutters, lit the oil lamp that stood on it. Few on this side of the island bothered any longer to obey the black-out.

Lulled by the brandy's glow, Stephen watched shadows spill across the floor and come lapping at his feet as night insects droned and flittered about the room.

A soft rap at the half-open door startled them both.

"Mine's God." Marcus stood suddenly up from the chair he had re-assumed, open palm slapping his forehead. "The time, I forget the time. I have to go to shave a sick friend."

He bustled across to the shelf where he kept the instruments of his profession, scooped some into a small leather bag, and as another rap, harder this time, came, he turned to Stephen and said, shrugging, "that is his wife, sent to fetch me. She will not come in. Please, you stay here. I will be only a few minutes away." He motioned Stephen to sit where he was.

"I come," he called out in English. Then he was gone.

Stephen drained his glass and stood up. He should go. But then he thought, why? Why not believe that Marcus meant what he said, that the invitation to stay wasn't merely a form of words but was that of a friend, that his words were genuine, "con amore," as Italians said, that Marcus might be hurt to find the room empty on his return.

Re-filling his glass, he reached for his half-smoked cigarette, went back to his chair and sat down. Now that he had begun to talk about Jean there was so much he wanted to tell Marcus. Previously he'd tried to keep her to himself. Beyond the merest mention of his marriage and of David and Sarah he'd said nothing to anyone about his family, as though words casually spilled would dilute the intensity of their presences, presences he could summon whenever he wanted and who always came before him, to look, to move and to speak with a bright, unshadowed clarity. Jean, in particular, wasn't to be offered to anyone else. But now, with Marcus at all events, he felt he could trust himself to speak. What should he tell his friend about her? Where, as storytellers said, to start?

Slumped at ease in the warm, lamplit room, listening to the low buzz and occasional whine of creatures blundering around the lamp's glass dome, some sizzling to death, he sipped his brandy and, sucking in what strength he could from his cigarette, remembered a summer day by the Thames when the two of them had driven out of London in his father's Morris, heading west, all windows down in the heat.

The road they took eventually brought them to Reading and from there they followed the written instructions of a teacher acquaintance of Stephen's who came from Berkshire and often spoke of the countryside around the town, and especially of Mapledurham, which was, so he assured Stephen, the kind of place for which the word idyllic had been invented. The instructions led them through the town and across the Thames at Caversham Bridge, thronged with sightseers who all seemed to be watching boaters splashing about on the river beneath, though in answer to Jean's shouted question one of them turned long enough to motion with his hand to a road beyond the bridge.

There was no road sign to what Stephen's informant had explained was a village, hamlet really, with a grand house which had originally belonged to the Blounts, friends of Alexander Pope. The house had long since stood empty, was a property where "the mole now labours, and spiders knit."

"Pope?" Jean asked.

"Hardy."

"Pedant."

Once over the bridge, they swung left as directed and found themselves on a steep, upward curving road that cut through a wooded landscape, occasional clearances offering a glimpse of thatched cottages and larger buildings, probably farmhouses.

"Over my shoulder goes one ca-re," Jean began to sing, her voice accentuating the upper-class syllables, and Stephen joined in, warbling in daft falsetto.

After a mile or so the road levelled out. They stopped beside a signpost which announced CHEZEY HEATH.

"We're lost," Stephen said.

"Never more to be found." Jean buried her head in her hands and sobbed theatrically as he swung the car left down a steep, rutted track that had, he announced, to lead to cottages whose thatched roofs they could make out among a group of elms below them.

"Old ragged elms, old thorns innumerable," he intoned.

"There aren't any thorn trees," Jean said.

"Pedant."

The car jolted on down through a thick screen of trees and then, "I think I can see a water-wheel, cap'n," she said, "down there," pointing to where the trees thinned.

"And where there's a wheel there's a way."

"Which we're on."

"I mean W=E=I=G=H. Weighbridge. As in weighing sacks."

The track had become a flat, gravelled expanse around which at the bottom in a kind of hollow were a few cottages, windows open to welcome the thin stirrings of the breeze. Beyond these, the water-mill loomed.

"We've arrived," Stephen said. "Thanks entirely to the driver's skills. Move over Nouvelari."

"For which you get the millstone award." She squeezed and he yelped.

The mill was abandoned. They stepped across the rickety

wooden bridge. Gapped planks creaked above the dark, weed-thronged waters of the mill-race — "home to the fabled Berkshire pike," Stephen said, "it roams the land by night, bringing terror to the locals and savaging feral sheep and wild boar" — and followed a deep cut of water out onto a strip of grassland beside the alder-fringed Thames. In the afternoon's deep heat everything, even the bumming drone of flies, seemed drugged, torpid.

"No sign of the house," Stephen said, after they'd walked some way along the riverbank.

"Perhaps this isn't Mapledurham," Jean said. "There's no sign that anyone's been along here for donkey's years." They turned to look back along the path they'd made for themselves in the tall grasses, reedbeds fringing the water to one side, on the other overgrown hedgerows starred with dog-roses. Then, once over a shallow ditch, they peered through a small gap in the thick greenwood and saw beyond the hedgerow rough meadowland leading up to a screen of trees and, away to the right, the cottages, although the mill itself was cut off from their line of vision by a slight curve in the river.

"Do you think there could be a house somewhere beyond those trees?" Jean asked. "If we could find a way through this hedge we might be able to work our way toward it."

Following the line of the thickset, sprawling bramble and hawthorn, they searched for a possible gap.

"Here we are. Just what the doctor ordered." She jumped down into the dry ditch, began to part grasses that screened the bottom of the hedgerow. Insects took to the air like a sift of sundust.

"We'll not get through *that*."

"Oh, yes, we will," Jean said, "or never call me Carruthers."

The gap she was pointing at, less than two feet wide, looked as if it had been made by an animal — fox? badger? — repeatedly forcing its way through the tangle of brushwood where green had died back to rusty brown.

"But what about your skirt? Catch that on a spike of hawthorn and it'll be ripped to shreds."

"Then I'll take it off." She gave a quick look to right and left but nobody was about. A moment later she had stepped out of her white, pleated skirt and was now undoing the buttons of her dark-blue blouse. "Hand them through to me when I've made it," she said, rolling the clothes into a bundle and giving him a kiss. "I go where man has rarely been." In knickers and bra, she knelt to peer into the gap, then, like a swimmer easing into water, crouched forward and in one swift movement disappeared.

He waited for a cry, a scream of protest as thorns ripped at her flesh. Nothing.

"Jean, are you alright?" he called out.

Still nothing, nothing apart from the drone of nearby bees and the just-audible soughing of leaves in the alders behind him. Then, "easy." Her voice muffled by what lay between them, was triumphant. "Come on, it's your turn. The water's lovely. And don't forget my clothes."

He pushed the bundle inside his shirt, knelt and, beyond the tunnel, could make out Jean's naked legs, one of them faintly streaked with blood.

"You scratched yourself," he shouted.

"Well, hurry up, then. I need a doctor to save me."

"Then here I come." He dived in. "Bloody hell."

"Hold still," Jean said, a few moments later. She was cradling his head on her bare knees as he lay full-length whimpering for the nurse, cushioned in soft grass and allowing her to stroke the scratch across his forehead. She lifted a finger to show him. "Barely a drop of blood," she said. "In a few years you'll be completely cured."

Stephen shaded his eyes as he looked up at her. "I'll never be cured of you," he said.

"I should hope not." She bent, put her lips to his.

Reaching a hand, he undid the red ribbon she always tied round her hair and watched the freed gloss cascade over her bare shoulders.

A while later, minutes, an hour, her voice husky, she said, "Darling, do you think what we're doing constitutes an offence against public decency."

"I do hope so," Stephen said.

And later still, fully clothed and languorous from the afternoon's heat and their love-making, they strolled hand in hand along the unkempt meadow until they almost stumbled into a wide, deep ditch, brick-walled on the steeper, far side.

"Aha," Jean said, "A ha-ha. The house must be somewhere near."

The sunken curve brought them to a narrow bridge. Once over that, the outline of a gravelled path curved left, away from the river. For a few minutes more they pushed through tall stands of grass, of willowherb, meadowsweet, dock, skirting low whinbushes and bramble, and a large, red-brick, three-storied house came into view. Like the mill, it was in an advanced state of decay, sky showing between the mansard roof's rafters and purlins where slates had cracked and fallen. Swallows flickered in and out of the glassless windows, darted among the clusters of tall chimney stacks.

Stephen bent and broke off the stem of a cornflower that showed blue among the haze of grasses. He threaded it through the ribbon now once again securing Jean's hair. "Yourself a fairer flower," he said, and kissed her lingeringly before turning to look at what lay in front of them.

It was the ghost of a formal garden. A flight of stone steps, mossy and weed-choked, led to a balustrade and, beyond, what once must have been a large square lawn, running the length of the house whose back they were facing. Now all was feathery grasses and straggles of bush about which, as hand-in-hand they climbed the steps, insects, rising to protest against this intrusion, made the air thrum. Almost lost among the grasses, four life-size statues, weather-stained but otherwise intact, stood on plinths to confront the landscape that fell away down to the river.

"Who are they?"

"I'm not sure."

Stephen pushed his way among the statues, parting the grasses to look at them more closely. "This one will almost certainly be the God of the River, Tamesis." He rested his hand on the buttock of a frothy-bearded, muscular, naked figure which poised a shell-encrusted urn on its shoulder. "Always propitiate the local deities. And this has to be Diana. Look, she has a quiver-full of arrows by her side, though someone's gone off with her bow. And there are these." He tapped her shins. "Greaves," he said. "So the animals she hunts can't bring her down if they turn and bite."

"What could she have hunted round Mapledurham?"

"Feral sheep and fanged boar. To say nothing of night-creeping pike. Now, this one with a circle of bay leaves round his head is almost certainly Apollo, and this lovely lady will be Flora, fruitful Flora."

"Or Ceres? Surely that's a stook of wheat under her arm, and, look, there's a sickle in her belt."

Stephen considered. "Yes," he said, "you're right. It is Ceres." He paused, turned to Jean who was staring at the goddess. "You know more than you let on."

Standing behind her, he put his arms round her shoulders. "I wanted it to be Flora," he said, resting his chin on her head and speaking so softly he wasn't at first sure that his words would reach her.

But she looked at him expectantly, and he went on, "so then I could tell you that you were more beautiful than any Goddess of Flowers."

She half-turned away then, the flower vivid blue in her hair, and it was as though she herself was sculpted into stillness, her outline clear against the screen of elms that deepened into grey-blue as the sun dropped behind the tree line. When she turned back, her eyes fixed on him, unwavering. Then, slowly, she raised an arm and brushed his lips with her outstretched fingers.

"I do love you, Stephen," she said.

* * *

He became aware of Marcus standing in front of him. "You were asleep, I think, my friend."

Stephen pushed himself upright. The glass, clutched in his hand, was, he saw, empty. "I shouldn't have accepted that last drink," he said, yawning. "It was a bit too much for me."

Marcus sank into the leather chair, laughed, then sighed.

"How is your friend," Stephen asked him. "Well shaved, I hope."

"I shave him for the visit of the priest. He wants to look good for when the Father comes."

"Oh, I'm sorry, I'd no idea … "

"No, no". Marcus laughed, waved a hand dismissively. "It isn't the end for him. But he wants to be … " He paused, said, "I think he likes to believe he is still young. Not due yet for this," and he drew a finger across his throat, then crossed himself. "Years ago he had many women in love with him. He was a handsome man."

"And now he's old."

"Yes," Marcus said. "Now he is old." And again he laughed, though it wasn't an unkind laugh.

Stephen stood, stretched, and handed Marcus his glass. "Well," he said, "the love of one woman is enough for me."

"And that love you have."

"Yes."

Marcus looked swiftly up at him and Stephen realised he had spoken with unusual emphasis, as though rebutting a scepticism entirely absent from Marcus's question.

"Anyway," he said, "I'd better be getting back to barracks. Time for bed. But thanks for the drink, Marcus, and for the chat. They were much appreciated."

In the room's warm shadows, Marcus stood to shake hands. The two men faced each other unsmiling, in silence, held by the solemnity of the moment.

"It is as it should be between friends," Marcus finally said.

Stephen took the outstretched hand, gripped but did not shake it. Then, releasing it, "agreed," he said.

A few minutes later he was walking up the road out of town, glimmers of light from partially-shuttered windows throwing shadows across his path. Farther away, down the island, lamplight from distant houses lights flickered and shimmered across a wide stretch of fields. *Some candle clear burns somewhere I come by.* Did *anyone* bother with black-out now? Even the canteen tales of the breaking of curfew, of people being caught in the streets or out at sea long after hours, tales which once formed part of the breakfast routine, had withered away. For the islanders at least, many of war's immediate effects were no longer a concern. For those in uniform it was, of course, different. Bullshit orders had still to be obeyed.

As he climbed away from the little town, the road became a dusty, unmetalled lane curving left toward the army camp, the path lined and partially screened by dry-stone walls, limestone glimmering dull white under hanging clusters of stars.

Marcus's brandy lay warm in his stomach. Marcus was a good man. He owed it to him, and to George and Maria, to see that young Anna came to no harm with Southern. Whatever is done out of love takes place beyond good and evil. Who had said that? Anyway, he didn't believe it. Too much evil had been done out of what its perpetrators called love. *Deutschland uber alles.* All nationalism was like that. "I vow to thee my country the service of my love." The old lie, Wilfred Owen called it. It was, too.

Swinging his arms in a parody of marching as he turned off the lane onto the donkey track, Stephen thought of the aged man in Elizabeth Gaskell's novel who said to a friend "I'm a man and you're another, but nation's nowhere." Unfortunately he was wrong, as the sanctioned deeds of a pressgang soon showed him. But he was also right. At all events, it felt a damned sight more worthwhile thinking you were fighting for "the brotherhood of man," as the phrase went, than for any national flag. Jean and he were in agreement about that. It was why she had accepted his decision to volunteer. As he stumbled along the uneven track, he thought of the wireless broadcast they had listened to not long before war was declared, a talk in which Jean's favourite novelist E.M. Forster had spoken of Love, the Beloved Republic as alone deserving three cheers. Stephen was inclined to mock the wispy voice and, as he suggested, equally wispy sentiments. "Cockaigne," he murmured, smiling at her as they sat across from each other in the back room of their newly rented house, the tiny children safely asleep upstairs. "Where the beggars raffle the bank-notes and the giant is enchanting to Jack." Her face had been averted, chin resting in the palm of her hand as she propped her elbow on the side of her armchair, listening hard. But when she turned toward him he saw at once that her eyes were full of tears.

"A world free of hate," she said, fiercely. "That's what he means." She paused. "Wouldn't you want that for our children? For all children?"

"Yes," he said, abashed by her fervour, "yes, of course I would."

Her words came back to him as he stopped, listened to the sounds of small night creatures scratching among the tinder-dry undergrowth. They, too, had a life to live. The night was so warm that any slight stirring of air felt like a lover's breath against his cheek. He looked up at the stars. "She is all States, and all Princes, I, Nothing else is." Tears pricked his own eyes and he shook his head, fiercely, to clear his vision. He loved those exuberant, extravagant words. But in the end perhaps it was fantasy, as much a fantasy as that dream of Love, the Beloved Republic, or the claim that you could make one little room an everywhere. Who, lying in bed with the loved one, had not wished that. And for as long as the moment lasted you could believe it to be possible, just as it was possible to eclipse the sun with no more than a wink. But then you opened your eyes and the sun was still there, the day and the world came back to you. God or whatever meant the good couldn't stop time. Guns roared their readiness to avenge. The guns of avenging nations, of avenging fathers. Let Southern take care, at least until he'd married Anna or got her safely to England. And that wouldn't be until this bloody war was finally over. And when it was, when at last they could all go home, then he and Jean and David and Sarah would once more be a family.

Meanwhile, her letter awaited him.

More briskly now he began to stride along the track and then, with lengthening strides, broke into a run.

As David knelt on the carpet to wind the gramophone, there was a knock on the front door.

Neat in his linen uniform, cap tucked under his shoulder tab, blond hair with ripple lines as though he had just combed it, Jay Krassner looked, David thought, surprised and, for a second, perhaps not altogether pleased to see him. But in a trice the look disappeared.

"Hi," he said, his face relaxing into its customary grin. "I guess I didn't expect to find you in today." And then, as David, peering round the half-open door said nothing, he added, "I was out for a walk, strolling along with the breeze, and what d'you know, my feet pointed me in this direction."

More silence.

"Mind if I come in?"

David shrugged, uncertain what to say.

"Is that a yes or a no?" Jay looked puzzled, unused to this show of reluctance on David's part.

"Mum's not here." The American was, he now noticed, swinging a leather grip in his right hand.

"But you are," Jay said, reasonably enough.

He was trapped. The initial rush of pleasure he'd felt at seeing Jay fell back and he looked away. It was as though he'd been caught out in a lie. But how was he supposed to tell the American that he shouldn't visit them, wasn't welcome.

On an impulse, he stood aside and let Jay squeeze past him into the narrow hall. "In here," he said, leading the way into the front room and watching as Jay took in the bookcase, the shabby lovat-green settee, the improvised drum kit and, beside it on the blue-pile carpet, the open gramophone, a record ready on its turntable.

"Can I ask a question?"

Here it comes, David thought, tensing. He stood beside his drums, trying meet Jay's eye.

"By my reckoning it's Wednesday and as for the time" — Jay eased a wrist watch from under his buttoned shirt sleeve, its silver band gleaming in the early afternoon light — "just gone 2 o'clock. So how come you're not in school?"

David almost laughed in his relief. "We've been given the afternoon off," he said.

"You have? Why?"

"Because the teachers are all going to a funeral. In Leicester." And as Jay raised an enquiring eyebrow, he said "For someone important, important to education, anyway that's what the head teacher told us."

"Must have been a top man, to get you the afternoon off," Jay said, laughing. "Funny, I thought a moment or so ago you looked a bit like I'd caught you playing hookey." And, when David stared at him in bewilderment, he added, "hookey. Getting out of school without teachers' permission. Like deserting from the army. Running off. Lighting out for the territory, doing what Huck Finn does. You heard of Huck Finn?"

"No," David said, "is he a musician?"

Jay laughed. "No," he said, "though he could have been. Leastways, he gets friendly with a nigra feller, Nigger Jim, gets along with him real well, like, say, Goodman and Wilson. Anyway," he said, gesturing to the drums, "as you're practising you could probably use this."

He squatted beside the gramophone and drew from the leather grip a record in what looked to be a brand-new card cover. Lifting the record David had placed on the turntable, he said as he read the label, "Fats, eh? *Ain't Misbehavin'*. Mr Zutty giving out on the traps. Good stuff. But this one'll singe your eyeballs. Want to give it a try?"

"Yes, please."

But as though he needed no answer, Jay had already wound the gramophone, guided the needle into position, and now sat back on his haunches motioning David to do the same.

"Well?" he asked, minutes later.

But David had no words for the elation that had poured through him as the music powered to its climax. When he could finally trust himself to speak, he asked, "Can we hear it again?"

"Attaboy," Jay said, and rewound the gramophone. Again the music began.

"What is it?" David asked, when for the second time the record span to a close. His whole body seemed to throb with sound.

"Goodman. 'King Porter Stomp'. And that's Gene Krupa doing the honours on drums." Jay carefully lifted the record off the turntable and slipped it into its case before, half-turning to David, he said, "have you *ever* heard drumming like that." But it wasn't a question and he seemed not to be talking to David, but to himself, his voice full of awed wonder.

"I thought Dave Tough was your favourite."

Jay stood up, holding his hands aloft in a gesture of surrender. "So he is. But this is something else, don't you think? I mean, this … This … "

But whatever words he was trying to find remained hidden because the door they had closed now opened and a woman's voice said, "I thought I heard voices."

David's mother stepped into the room. She was wearing her dark-blue summer coat, open to reveal a white blouse with ruffles, and a grey, pleated skirt. Briefly aware of how smart she looked, David was more alert to the frown behind her eyes.

So, obviously enough, was Jay. "Hope I'm not intruding," he said, transferring the record to his left hand and holding out his right.

For some moments David thought she was going to ignore it. Then slowly, reluctantly, she extended her arm and briefly shook hands. "David knows that I don't like him inviting strangers to the house when I'm not here," she said. "I'm sure you can understand that. Mr… Mr Krassner."

"Jay Krassner," he said hopefully. He looked swiftly at David. So that was what you were trying to tell me, the look said. "Yes, sure, *of course* I understand," he said. "But he didn't invite me. I invited myself. See, I'd got hold of this record" — he held it up in explanation —"and I guess I thought he'd like to hear it and I was coming round this way so — well, the fact is I didn't even reckon on him being here. I was going to leave it on the doormat with a note." His apologetic smile asked forgiveness. "No offence intended, ma'am."

There was a short silence. "And none taken," she said at last, inclining her head slightly. Another short silence. "As you're here, perhaps you'd like to stay for a cup of tea."

The offer, briskly made, was no more than formal, but to David's joy, Jay accepted.

"David, show Mr Krassner into the back room," his mother said, unsmiling, "I must run upstairs to change."

"Mum's been at a meeting," David said by way of explanation as the two of them stood at the French windows at the back of the house, looking out over the small garden with its collapsed greenhouse and, beyond, the fence through whose gaps he had access to bottom meadow. "It's called W.I. Women's Institute."

"Uh, hu." But Jay clearly wasn't interested in asking about that. Instead, he said, "Guess your ma has heard tales of Uncle Sam's soldiers." He smiled wryly, then, staring across at the wall map, he said as he moved towards it, "Hey, tell me about this. This is Europe, right? What are the flags all about?"

"To show where the different armies are," David said, as he came to stand beside Jay. "Do you know where your friends are?"

"My friends?" Jay glanced down at him, perplexed. "Oh, you mean the guys in France. Well, I sort of know. Normandy for sure, and the last I heard some of them had got as far as a place called Carentan." He peered more closely at the map. "Don't see it marked up but I guess it'll be hereabouts." With an index finger he traced a line inland from the Normandy coast.

"My dad's down here," David said, "Malta. He can write to us now but for a long time, when he was in Africa, we didn't know where exactly he was."

"Malta? Not a good place to be, I guess. From all I hear they had it real rough."

Jay repeated the remark as the three of them sat round the table, drinking tea out of what David recognised were his mother's best white china cups.

"Unfortunately, they had no choice in the matter," she said. The tone was one she adopted when she wanted to show she'd have "no truck" with views of which she disapproved. He'd heard her speak like that to old Godwin when, confronting her in the post office where she and the two children had gone to post a parcel, he'd offered to explain the wrongs of someone who seemed to be called Beveridge and who, according to the postmaster, was "an enemy of the nation." "My enemy's enemy is my friend," she replied, and David watched the man's face turn peony red as her meaning dawned on him.

But Jay was unruffled. "I guess in wartime none of us does. We all have to come to the aid of the party."

"Though some come later than others."

At that he did colour, slightly. "Well," he said, putting down his cup and staring into it, "I have to tell you, ma'am, that from Gary, Indiana, Europe looks an awful long way off."

"And might have continued to do so but for Pearl Harbour."

He looked up at her but said nothing.

"Is that where you live?" David broke in. "Gary?"

Jay turned gratefully to him. "It's where I was born and had my start," he said. "But I went to school in Chicago. I guess you'd call it university."

"What did you study?" It was civilly put. Perhaps an apology for her former tartness.

"I majored in engineering," he said. "But I'd have to say that the day work was a whole lot less interesting than night life."

She looked at him expectantly, but said nothing.

Leaning back in his chair, suddenly relaxed, he said, "that was when I began to hang around listening to jazz and where, after I was out of school, I got to play a bit. I mean I'd been with some outfits in Gary, but they weren't like the ones in the Windy City." He paused, shook his head as though in rapt memory of the music, and, straightening his shoulders, said, "but then Uncle Sam came calling. 'You're in the army now, Mr Krassner.' So here I am. Though not for long, I guess. The rumour is that we'll soon be getting our marching orders." He spread his hands and, as though searching for another subject, bunched one hand into a fist and rapped it on the table. "Say, is this made of metal?"

"Steel," David said as his mother sat silently sipping her tea.

"A steel table. How come?"

"It's a shelter as well as a table. If there's an air raid we have to crawl under it. There are wire-mesh sides we have to put into position once we're inside. I can show you if you'd like."

But Jay ignored David's offer. Instead, looking from son to mother, he said, "And you've been under there?"

"We have. Oh, yes, we have." She set her cup down, her eyes crinkling now with laughter at his wonderment. "Of course, the luckier ones among us have Anderson shelters, built at the bottoms of their gardens. The couple next door, for example. But getting there when a raid has started can be a risky business. Tell Mr Krassner what the Fishers do, David, when they run to their shelter."

"They put saucepans on their heads," David said, "like tin hats."

"You're kidding me."

"No, I'm not," David said, "we've seen them running across the grass holding onto the saucepans, haven't we, mum." He was laughing now, partly at the memory, partly at the look on Jay's face, and partly because the mood, formerly so difficult, had subtly altered.

"So tell me, what use is a saucepan against a falling bomb?"

Jay looked at his mother as he asked the question and, "not much, I suppose," she said. "But as the air-raids have now stopped I suppose we'll never find out."

"You English," Jay said, shaking his head in mock wonderment, and they both laughed.

It was as though the afternoon sunlight, which had begun to filter into the room, falling in stripes across the red-and-white check tablecloth, had warmed her into friendliness, and now talk came easily to them. While David chewed on a piece of bread with marrow jam, she told Krassner of her husband's readiness to volunteer for active service as soon as war was declared, even though several friends of theirs tried to argue him out of it. "They were in the Party, you see, and took the approved line that this was a war between decadent capitalist states."

"Party? What party?"

"The Communist party," she said, "most of the people we knew were in it, still are, for that matter. Stephen joined when he was at university."

Jay looked uncomfortable, as though he wanted to get off the subject. "What does your husband do?" he asked. "I mean what did he do before he joined up?"

"He's a teacher," she said, "of English. Although the army saw fit to turn him into a motor mechanic and part-time driving instructor. In Egypt he serviced tanks, even drove one or two, but on Malta I think he spends most of his time crawling about under lorries and jeeps." She glanced at her wristwatch. "Oh, lord, I'll have to dash. I left Sarah at a friend's house and it's high time I went to fetch her." She laughed. "No doubt her clothes will be drenched. She was promised the chance to make ice-lollies."

"I'd better get along, too," Jay said, standing.

"Is Sarah at Mrs. Morton's, then?" David asked. And, ignoring his mother's warning look, he said to Jay, "she's got a fridge, you see. Do you know what a fridge is?"

Jay considered the question. "A fridge," he said, nodding gravely. "I guess I do, though back home we call it an ice-box."

"David, *every* American household has a fridge — ice-box."

"Well, let's say most do. This Mrs. Morton, would her name be Beth?"

He asked the question lightly enough, and lightly enough she answered. "One and the same. Do you know her?"

Jay nodded, smiled. "She's a real friendly lady. I was with her when I first met David here. She took pity on this poor, wandering boy she met up in the village. Gave me a guided tour of the place. Well, say hello to her from Jay Krassner, if you'd be so kind."

"I will indeed."

"And thanks for the tea," he said, once again reaching out his hand, "it was much appreciated."

"That's nice to know," she said, and then, to David's amazed delight added, "You must call on us again while you're here. I know that David loves to watch a real drummer at work. Or should that be play?" "

The two adults shook hands and Jay said "that's good of you, ma'am. Next time I'll try to give you some advance warning."

"That might be advisable." But the remark was accompanied by a smile.

And as he stood at the front door to wave the American off the premises, Jay, looking down at him and with a hand resting lightly on his shoulder, said, smiling, "See you then, Tough guy." And off down the front path he strolled.

CHAPTER EIGHT

Darling: I read your lovely letter when I got back to barracks late last night and it's probably as well that I did, because this morning I woke with a thick head. Writing comes rather more easily than reading would! I'd spent the evening with Marcus, you see, who in between protestations of eternal friendship plied me with rather more brandy than I'm used to or than is good for me. Not that I had more than three glassfuls, but his brandy punches well above its weight. My own fault for not saying no, but I've grown fond of him and I think he means it when he calls me a friend. It's more than can be said for some of the other islanders. They get surlier by the day. Dave Morris was telling me at breakfast that last evening he narrowly avoided getting involved in a bar brawl on the other side of town. It's not a bar I've ever been into and it isn't one of his regular ports of call, either, and in the light of what he tells me I certainly won't be setting foot in the place. According to Dave, a Private Jenkins, who works with him, insisted on his — Dave — being part of Jenkins' birthday celebrations. If Dave is to be believed the celebrations nearly turned into an almighty dust up. The details aren't clear but a local took exception to a remark he claimed to overhear one of our men make about island women. Dave reckons that the man, who was drunk, was spoiling for a fight with a Brit. The soldier he targeted — not Jenkins — was, in Dave's words, knee-high to a grasshopper and wouldn't have stood a chance, so Dave 'interposed his body' between the two of them. You'd have to be either very stupid or built like Joe Louis and Tommy Farr rolled into one to take Dave on, but even so I gather the man's friends had to drag him away before blows could be traded. Dave was, he says, worried in case they might be waiting outside, perhaps with reinforcements, but when he and the others emerged some time later all was quiet and they got back to barracks unscathed. Still, he tells me that the atmosphere in the bar itself was far from friendly and the would-be celebrations proved anything but.

I don't really know why I bother to report all this, except that it adds to my growing conviction that the sooner we're away from Malta the better for all concerned. When will that be? Your guess is as good as mine, but as you say, the day can't come soon enough. Your talk of summer in England, of the ripening wheat you can see from the window where you sit to write, of the trees and hedgerows, reminds me of all I'm missing. Well, not all, of course, although here the weather — but you can't really speak of 'weather' on Malta. It's simply an unvarying diet of hot days which after a while become, can you believe it, boring. I'd love to be able to lift my head and see clouds filling the sky above me. (Though lifting my head in my present condition isn't easy to do!) Nimbus, cumulus, cirro-stratus: simply writing the names down makes me homesick. That soft grey, crumbling light. Even rain would be welcome. Here, everything is hard-edged, glaring, **obvious.** I'm trying to recall Wordsworth's description of the hedgerows he sees at Tintern Abbey. 'Lines of sportive wood run wild' and something about pastoral farms green to the door. Could you look them up for me and write them into your next letter? I've so few books here I feel bereft. I remember how the poem starts, though.

Five years have passed, five summers, with the length
Of five long winters! And again I hear
These waters rolling from their mountain springs
With a sweet inland murmur.

I used to think he was overdoing the repetition of the number five, but now I understand that he's simply emphasising the sense of absence from what he loves, its duration.

And now it comes to me that 'dure' as a verb can mean to survive. Love has to survive, doesn't it. That sweet inland murmur could be you whispering in my ear! Oh, my dearest, let it not be five years before I see and hear you again.

All my love to the three of you and I apologise for the shortness of this, but Dave's off to Valetta any moment now and he's promised to post the letter from there. I'll write at length next time, and I won't repeat the dosings of Marcus's brandy!

The back door was half open. For a moment he stood, listening in the kitchen. Then, bursting through the into the room where the two adults sat facing each other across the table, he said, grinning, triumphant, "I *thought* it was your voice."

Neat as ever in his uniform, elbow propped on the green-velvet cover, fingers lightly supporting his chin, Jay smiled at him. David went and stood beside his mother who put an arm round his waist and drew him to her. But it was Jay he greeted.

"Hi, Tough guy," Jay said. "Met your mom and sister coming down the lane and they were kind enough to ask me in, so," he paused, spread his arms and said, "so here I am."

"Tough guy?" His mother looked into David's face, her voice tinged with the faintest hint of disapproval. "I'm not sure I want David to be one of those."

"It's a joke between us," David said. "Dave Tough is a drummer. Jay says he's the best."

"One of the best. Remember Krupa."

It was more than two weeks since Krassner had played that record and in the intervening period he had seen nothing of the American. Jay hadn't even gone to the tea-dances. "Been away," he said now in answer to David's query. "Army business." Then, in ripe imitation of a posh English accent, he added, "fraightfully hush hush. Not a peep out of me shall you get, old man, what. Walls hev ears. But I'll be back on parade at the village hall tomorrow, what, what. A promise is a promise, or so I'll hev you know." He turned to her. "Reckon I'd pass for an Englishman?"

"Not a chance," she said, laughing. Then, to David, "run upstairs and change out of your school clothes. You won't need those again until Monday."

As he released himself from her arm, David asked Jay, "will

there still be time for some practice?"

"Drumming, you mean? It's why I'm here," Jay said.

David wanted to whoop for joy. "I'll go and get my drums," he shouted, already running up the stairs as she called after him, "twenty minutes, no more. Then it'll be tea. Tell your sister, will you, I think you'll find her in her bedroom."

Sarah was sitting on her bed, cradling her favourite doll to whom she was crooning a wordless lullaby. "Don't make a noise," she whispered. "I don't want her to wake up."

"What's the matter with her?"

"She's poorly. She's got dried ear."

"She's got *what?*"

"It means she has to keep going to the lav."

"Well, mum says you've got to get ready for tea."

"Is *he* still here?"

"Who, Jay? Mr Krassner. Of course he is. He's come to help me learn how to play the drums."

"If you can call that noise playing the drums," Sarah said, lifting her eyebrows heavenwards in passable imitation of their mother. "Anyway, if you ask me he's here because he's ill. He needs feeding." She looked at him briefly, then once again bent over her doll.

"Don't be silly," David said, irritated but, despite himself, impressed by Sarah's confident diagnosis. "Of course, he doesn't need feeding."

"He wouldn't understand, would he?" Sarah whispered to her doll. Sighing, she got to her feet, still holding the doll to her breast. "You'll have to come with me, my poor love. I can't leave you here to be ill on your own."

As he set up his drum kit in the front room, David looked across at Jay, who was bending over the gramophone. *Was* he thinner than he should be. "What are you made to eat in the army?" he asked as he watched the soldier take a record from its sleeve.

Jay looked up in surprise. "*Made* to eat? I guess we're not made to eat anything. The food we get's pretty good, to tell you the truth. Makes me kinda embarrassed to talk about it, seeing how you folks … . " He stopped, shook his head, and by way of changing the subject, said brightly, "Hey now, you know what a rim shot is?"

"A rim shot?" David said. "I've never heard of it."

"So let me show you." Jay guided the gramophone arm into position and the lesson began.

* * *

That afternoon set a pattern for the following weeks. Each Friday David would come back from school to find Jay and his mother sitting at the table in companionable talk, the tea things spread between them, Jay with drumsticks at his elbow. Sometimes Sarah was with them, sometimes they'd be on their own, but always the atmosphere was one of casual contentment, a kind of settled ease. As for their talk, it might be of war, of the hastening, inglorious retreat of Hitler's forces from Eastern Europe, of allied advances through France and Italy, of those "damned Nips" causing so many American casualties in the Pacific; or Krassner might be telling her of a film that had been shown in camp — one, *Cabin in the Sky*, he'd sat through three times, he said, because of the singing of someone called Ethel Waters. "The way she sings 'Stormy Weather', I'm telling you it would bring tears to the eyes of … " He broke off, seeking for an appropriate name.

"Al Capone?" she asked.

He laughed. "Well, maybe not him."

"Who is Al Capone?" David asked, as he stood by his mother, listening.

A crook," Jay said, "from Chicago, the Windy City. Where all the best hoods come from." And, in response to her warning shake of the head, a gesture David sensed rather than saw, Krassner began to tell them of the railway lines that crossed the streets of Chicago's south side, where freight trains bearing the carcasses of thousands upon thousands of hogs rumbled in and out of the city all day and night. "Hog butcher to the world, that's us," he said, holding his nose, "no wonder the stink carries for miles."

In exchange for the American's stories about life in America,

David made her tell Jay of the flat East Anglian village where she had grown up.

"I don't think Mr Krassner will want to hear about that," she said, smiling dismissively.

"Try me," he said.

"There's precious little to tell. It was small and there were fields on all sides. And when you've said that … "

"What about the telephone box?"

She shrugged off David's prompting. "Oh *that*." Then, after a pause, "the annals of the parish, part one." And, seeing the enquiring look on Krassner's face, she began to explain. "What happened was that the villagers got together to ask for a telephone box to be installed on the green. Not many families could afford to own their own telephones, you see. Anyway, the GPO eventually agreed to our request and this was thought to be of such importance that when it arrived the vicar was asked to bless it."

"The vicar blessed a *telephone box?*"

"Certainly he did." She laughed at his incredulity. "Dressed up in all his robes for the occasion. Full fig. Not only that. A newspaper from Peterborough sent along a reporter and cameraman, so our vicar posed for photographs, standing beside the box, hand raised, villagers all around him, then he was photographed emerging from the box, as though he'd just made use of the phone, with the crowd applauding."

"Tell him how you got to be included in the photograph," David ordered her.

She blushed faintly, shook her head.

Jay looked enquiring from mother to son.

"Dad spotted her," David said, "and asked her to stand beside the box so he could take a special photograph of her alone."

"Your dad was the photographer?"

"He wasn't our dad, then, and she wasn't our mum. But that's how they met, isn't it?"

"Yes," she said simply, "that's how we met. Not that Stephen was a professional photographer. He was simply helping out." And as Jay raised a questioning eyebrow, she explained that while

Stephen was waiting to go to university he had gone to stay with a friend of his father's who, as luck would have it, happened to be the editor of the newspaper planning to send a reporter to the village. "And as their only photographer was on another assignment Stephen went along with his camera."

"And the rest is history."

"History is rather a grand way of putting it. But a moment of good luck, I'd certainly be prepared to call it that. "

"Because the young man — Stephen — sees a pretty young woman and asks her to look the birdie in the eye and gets to capture not merely the picture but the lady." And he snapped his fingers. "Sounds good to me." He sipped some tea, then, putting his cup down, asked, genuinely interested, "Was your husband considering becoming a journalist? I mean, was that why he was staying at this place in Peterborough?"

"Yes," she said, "for a very brief period Stephen did wonder about newspaper work. But then he changed his mind, and I'm glad he did. He's a school teacher. When he's at home, that is."

"And this is home."

She paused before answering. "No," she said, eventually. "No, I like it here, but it's not where I want to spend the rest of my life, not where I want David and Sarah to grow up. That we're here at all is, like so much nowadays, a matter of accident."

"Accident? Why accident?"

"Because Stephen taught in London, and his school was evacuated to the midlands at the beginning of the war. We found this place to rent, and then, almost at once, he was off to join the army."

"So here you are."

"Yes," she said, "here we are. It's nice enough, but I think I had more than enough of village life when I was a child." She paused to sip her tea, as though considering her remark. Then, putting down her cup and smiling as though in apology for some tactlessness or other, she said, "I mustn't give the impression I was unhappy there. I had a perfectly normal, contented childhood. The countryside couldn't be called spectacular, not by a long stretch of the imagination, but then you don't notice that when you're small, do you? There were fields and streams all about, and my parents let me them roam them with friends. What more can a girl want?"

"Brothers and sisters?"

She shook her head. "Like Stephen I'm an only child. That may be why my parents found it a wrench when I wanted to get away. But I *had* to go," she added, as though justifying herself. "There was nothing doing in the village. Nothing, that is, to keep me once I'd finished my schooling, and even for that I had to go to a nearby town. Well, once I was out of junior school." She laughed. "My first taste of real freedom. Taking the bus as an eleven-year old schoolgirl. Journeying to foreign parts." She pulled a face, pretended to shudder.

He nodded. "I guess I understand that," he said. "Getting to Chicago was a big break for me, too. I don't think my folk minded too much, though. In fact, they told just about everyone I was off to make my fortune. Reckon they felt it was about time someone in our family did."

"Were they poor?" David asked before he could stop himself. He blushed as his mother frowned but Jay said, "Well, it wasn't skid row, but we didn't have much to throw around."

"Nobody did, did they?" she said quickly, as though to cover up for David's directness. "My father was head teacher of the village school, as indeed he still is, but we got by on precious little. His salary was a pittance and at one point the national government even lowered it. *And* he was expected always to wear a suit and be smartly turned out. He and my mother often found themselves providing free meals for some of the poorest kids in the village, ones who came to school without socks and shoes." Her voice now was edged with an anger David had heard before in her words whenever she told him and Sarah about their grandparents' lives. A pause for more tea-drinking and when she next spoke her voice had lost its momentary fierceness. "Having the school house helped, of course," she told Jay, "but it came without running water or electricity. Now, in these enlightened times, water has arrived." Again, the flicker of anger.

"And they've got a telephone," David said. He felt the need to defend his grandparents' house. It was a house he always loved going to and its oil lamps, lit each evening, were for him part of its attraction.

"True, as David says, they have a telephone. They had it installed as soon as I left for the big city, which was as soon as I decently could after I'd waved goodbye to my school years. Life begins at sixteen, well, seventeen in my case. I had to phone them once a week to let them know how I was surviving among the fleshpots and the palaces of sin." She was smiling, back in control.

"London?"

She nodded. "A friend had found work in a music shop, and a vacancy came up at a place nearby, so she recommended me, I went for interview, and, as they say, Bob's your uncle."

Jay looked mystified.

"It means knowing someone who can help. Friends in high places. Not that I'd call *Hawley & Co* a high place. It was a biscuit manufacturer. *Hawley's Home-Baked Harvest Crunch*. Now don't disappoint me by admitting me you haven't heard of it."

"*Hawley's Home-Baked Harvest Crunch*." Jay pretended to consider, sighed deeply and said, "It shows what a one-horse town I come from. Sorry to say, ma'am, that I don't recollect the name."

"Shame on you," she said lightly. "America cut off from the world."

"Not any longer," he said, studying her, suddenly serious.

As though his words disturbed her, she looked away.

For some moments nobody spoke, then Jay, asked casually, "So you met Stephen even before you got to London?"

David answered for her. "Mum was home for the weekend. She was working in the music shop by then, weren't you, mum? But granny and granddad wanted her to be at home when the telephone box was put in. There was a dance afterwards, at the village hall. To celebrate."

"There was." She looked gratefully at David, reached over and stroked his cheek with her fingers. "With Willie the one-eyed fiddler to play."

"Didn't the guy have a surname?" Jay asked her, but she went on looking at David as she answered. "Willie the one-eyed fiddler was what everyone called him. He lived in a shack at the bottom of the village and he played for all the dances for miles around." Then at last she turned to the American. "He reckoned he could play any tune he was asked for and the parts he couldn't play he whistled." And, shaking her head, she laughed quietly at the recollection. The good mood was restored. "That's when Stephen and I met," she said, "he stayed on for the dance."

"And by the time it finished it was too late to get back to Peterborough," David said, who had heard the story several times, "so dad slept in a barn opposite the schoolhouse."

"Yes," she said, smiling round at them, "sad to say, all the village's three-star hotels were fully booked that night."

"That's a good story," Jay said to David, "Hollywood'd love it." Then, to her, and as though changing the subject, he said quite briskly, "So after the war you aim on getting back to London?"

"If we can. From all I hear and see the bombing has been terrible. Stephen's school was flattened. Imagine the deaths of so many children if it had still been open." She shuddered, looked away from them both., and when she looked back David could see that her eyes were full of tears. He knew what she was thinking. It could have been us. "Oh, how I hate this war," she said, "*hate* it."

Again the mood had darkened.

Jay was the first to speak. "Yeh," he said, sighing, "it's not good. Can't say I'm much enjoying being so far from home." Then, colouring, "no offence, ma'am, I'm truly grateful for what you and all the villagers are doing to make us welcome, but, still, you know ... ."

She looked up and perhaps prompted by the sudden sadness in his voice said, "Have you left a girlfriend behind? A wife, even?"

"Oh, no," he said, staring into his cup, shaking his head. Hunched still over his cup, he raised his eyes, met her gaze. "No, nothing like that." And then, again, he said "But, still, you know, there are things I miss."

"Like your music," David said.

Jay nodded, smiled appreciatively at him. "Like my music," he said.

"What I miss most," she said, looking away, "is the chance to talk to Stephen. People complain about the rationing, the lack of this, of that, of having to put up with living off scraps, of dried egg, rotten cheese — when you can get it — of coupon clothes that don't fit and fall to pieces almost as soon as you put them on. Well, I can bear all that. But it's the *silences* I can't stand. At first his going was so strange that I couldn't believe it was real. I spent most of the time reassuring the children that he'd soon be back. But after the stupid army, instead of putting him in the educational corps, turned him into a motor mechanic and he was posted overseas, I began to realise that it would be ages before we'd see him again."

"I guess there were too many teachers in uniform to get the jobs they wanted," Jay said, placatory. "Plenty of the guys I'm with came out of classrooms."

"You told us that Dad wanted to be a *proper* soldier," David said, wanting to defend his father's honour.

"And so he did." Again she reached over, touched his cheek in propitiation. "Sorry, I sometimes say things I shouldn't. Yes, of course, Stephen — your father — was determined to fight against the Nazis. He wants a better world for you and Sarah to grow up in." She looked at her daughter's anxious face.

Until that moment Sarah had said nothing, merely concentrated on helping her doll to food. Now she said, "and what about *her*," as she did so drawing the doll into her lap. "Will *she* be safe?"

"Don't worry, love, we'll all be safe once Hitler's in his grave. And in the meantime … In the meantime we just have to grin and bear it. Whistle a happy tune." Then, as David began to whistle in an attempt to cheer his sister, she said, putting on an exaggeratedly mournful expression, "but after you and your brother are tucked up in your beds, I don't have anyone to talk to."

David ceased his whistling. "What do — did — you and dad talk about?" he asked, genuinely curious.

"Everything," she said emphatically. "Books, music, the pictures, you two, friends, family, the world." She threw up her hands. "Anything and everything."

"There are three movie houses in Hinckley," Jay said as though this was a surprising piece of information he thought he might share with them. He looked around the table. "Perhaps while I'm still stationed here we could all make a trip to one of them some afternoon."

"Yes," David almost shouted, "can we, mum?"

But, looking at Krassner, she shook her head. "Not when you're at school," she said, and then, almost as the thought came to her aid, she added. "besides, on Saturdays you have to assist Mrs Rayner, remember."

"A real nice lady," Krassner said.

"Not everyone thinks so."

"Really? Why?"

The surprise, even disbelief in Krassner's voice, echoed David's silent thought. Why should anyone not like Mrs. Rayner?

But he pushed that away. The American's offer of a visit to the cinema was uppermost. "I don't have to help her *every* Saturday, do I?" he said, trying to work out what her answering look meant. Was she cross? No, he didn't think so. She was looking now at Krassner. He knew that look. It was a look of appeal, like the one she gave when she was asking her children to join her in some tedious but necessary task about the house. Yes, that was it. She wanted the American's assistance. But for what?

As though in answer, she stood up, began to clear the table. "It's out of the question," she said.

~ Chapter Ten ~

Darling, as usual your letter comes to save me from myself.

> *No nightingale did ever chaunt*
> *So sweetly to reposing bands*
> *Of travellers in some shady haunt*
> *Among Arabian sands.*

*Not that Wordsworth was ever in Arabia, so how, you might say, does he know? And not that Malta is a desert, although the German bombing certainly aimed to make it a lone and level place. Now that re-building is in full swing all over the island, the sounds of hammering and sawing, as well as the dust — which gets **everywhere** — would drown out whole squadron of stukas, let alone nightingales. Every time I go across to Valetta I can see that more streets have been cleared of rubble and houses and public buildings are beginning to emerge from hills of masonry that two years ago would have made anyone despair. And as this goes on, Dave Morris and I have been recruited with others to do our own re-building of machines we thought were fit only for the scrap heap. "Deeds of great pith and enterprise … " Well, I can say no more.*

I can however report that young Southern still seems to be behaving himself and that his romance with Anna flourishes. Marcus proclaims himself happy and brother George looks forward to Derek S becoming his son-in-law. So, at least, Maria says, though I can't say George's face cracks into a smile whenever I bump into him. I suppose we can regard as progress the fact that he no longer scowls at me.

My talent as scribe has been put to the test recently. Not by Dave, who never wants me to address more than a few lines to his mother, but by one of the artillerymen who a week ago received a "Dear

John" letter and didn't know how to reply. The trouble was not so much his wife telling him that she'd found true love in the arms of another man and would "appreciate it" if he agreed to a divorce but that the only mention she made of the kids, of whom there are apparently three, was a sentence in which she "assured" him that they'd be looked after. "What's that supposed to mean" he asked me? "Is she taking them with her or having them put into care?" He then broke down, said he didn't care about her so much, but he was damned (he used a stronger word) if she was going to steal the children from him. (The oldest is ten, the youngest four.) "They're mine as much as they're hers," he said. " It's their future I'm supposed to be f-ing fighting for." Sad, sad. Not the first time of course I've come across this kind of thing, but his misery upset me a good deal. I've spoken to the CO on his behalf and we're hoping to get him compassionate leave and send him back to England asap. But while we're waiting for permission to come through — always assuming that it's granted — I've been writing letters on his behalf, both to the wife and to his parents, asking them to let me have the name of a solicitor we can retain. Just in case the wife plans to disappear with the children before he can get back to Blighty.

On a lighter note, I loved the story about your dad's misadventure with the pheasant on his evening walk. Fancy "winging" it with a stick. But they are lumbering creatures aren't they? Still, he really should have had the courage to carry it home himself, rather than expect your mother to come running over the fields to collect it. No wonder it had gone by the time they returned. The likeliest explanation of course is that he hadn't killed it, merely stunned the bird, and that while he was absent it came to what few senses it had and made itself scarce. And if it **was** dead no doubt a local Reynard had gathered it for the pot. Here, the hungry natives have by now winged so many pigeons that the army no longer tries to use them as messenger birds. Pope has a line about how the shot pheasant "Flutters in blood and panting beats the ground." Remember Mapledurham, and how we, too, panting beat the ground that far-off afternoon? Wouldn't it be lovely to take David and Sarah there some time to show them the house and the garden. I wonder if the statues are still there? And what of the house itself? By now I can *imagine it's not much more than a mound of rubble.*

Looking at the calendar, I realise that you'll soon be packing your bags for the summer holidays. A home from home, I know. (I mean exchanging one village for another.) But David and Sarah get on so well with your parents they'll love it, and it will be good for you to be able to savour your mother's home cooking. I've no doubt that your dad's position in the village means that while they may not be able to live off the fat of the land some goodies find their way into the larder — even if pheasant is off the menu. "The blushing apricot and woolly peach Hang on thy walls, that every child may reach." I don't recall that the orchard at the far end of the schoolyard runs to either fruit, but there are apples and plums enough to give our kids the collywobbles unless their eating habits are monitored.

*Oh, sorry, I shouldn't be fussing about this, you're obviously a wonderful mother to them. Blame it on the distance between us. I can't help worrying about the three of you in both big and small matters. I sometimes wake up in the middle of the night gripped by panic at the thought a bomb might fall on you, might have **fallen**, then remember that the skies over England are now free of enemy planes (at least, so we're assured). But then I worry about whether you've enough money to live on, if there's food to go around, if you've clothes for your backs, or dreading the thought that one of you may fall ill or simply be unhappy and I won't know about it and that anyway there's nothing I can do to help. Being apart is **hell**, isn't it. This far apart, apart for this long. Hell, hell, and hell again. But I mustn't go on. Snap out of it, as Dave Morris would say.*

As for our son, whose writing has come on in leaps and bounds, he tells me that Mr Krassner is with you most Friday afternoons, giving him drum lessons, which must be a thrill for him, if not for you. How on earth do you cope with the noise?

All my love

As July progressed, the days settled to warm skies of high-banked clouds moving slowly over the ripening corn. David walked up to school when dew was still beading the stiles and the wheat rustled in the day's first breezes. Coming down from the village after school was over, the fields smelling now of dusty warmth, he and Robin stripped off sandals and socks before paddling along the stream beneath the wooden bridge, on the lookout for the arrowy shadows that meant minnows, and the blue, needle flash of dragonflies.

But one Friday afternoon they were forced into a lengthy detour. As he stood on the top stile to scan Farmer Bailey's field for Goebbel's whereabouts, Robin suddenly stiffened, jumped back down, and whispered to David, "they're in the next field."

Crouching behind the hedge, they listened. Bodies were crashing about in the wheatfield below the pasturage. Then, as they looked at each other, they heard Neville Fox's voice, raised high in song. "Roll out the barrel, we'll have a barrel of fun. Jump on the choirboys, kick them all up the bum." This was followed by a cheer and other voices joined in.

"Do you think they've spotted us?" David whispered.

"Dunno, but we'll have to go round by the road."

"That'll take *ages.*"

But Robin was already leading the way back up the twitchel.

As they trudged down the main road out of the village, Robin said, "anyway it's only another two weeks, then term's over."

David knew what he meant. After that there'd be no risk of running into the Fox gang. They could get to the stream from bottom meadow.

"You going away?"

"Yes".

"Same place?"

David nodded.

"Must be boring always going to the same place," Robin said, as they turned into the road where their houses stood. He himself never went anywhere. There was a grandmother, "old gran," who lived in his house, who looked after him whenever their mother disappeared "to visit to her sister," said to live near a place called Newcastle. These visits occasionally lasted for weeks and during her absence Robin had what he called a holiday at home. "A real holiday," he said, grinning. "No rules. Sit up late and eat when I want." And it was true, with his mother away Robin seemed free to do more or less as he liked. In her rusty black dress and with her short-sighted scowl, his gran might look fierce, but whenever at a time of her stewardship David went to call for his friend, he'd find her more often than not at the kitchen table, overflowing ashtray at her elbow and in front of her a glass of pinky liquid, with Robin sitting placidly opposite her. "Hello, pet," she'd say to David, "come to see your friend. Mind 'ow you go, then, the pair on yer."

"What's that your gran drinks," David had asked after once seeing her drain her glass and immediately pour a refill. "It looks like cough medicine."

"Cough medicine." Robin's laugh was dismissive. "That's a good one. I'll tell her that. Still, she calls it her medicine. Don't half make her sing." And he laughed.

David was intrigued. "What does she sing?"

"Anything. Hymns, funny songs, something about a porter who dropped her off at Crewe, and one about her old man telling her to follow the van. Not that she's got an old man. Mum says he went off years ago. Before I was born, so I've never seen him."

"You mean he died?"

"No. Like I said, went off. With what mum says was a Fancy Woman. And he's not been heard of since. Where does your gran live?"

"I've got two grans. The one we're going to lives in Huntingdonshire."

"Any good."

"It's alright." David guessed, correctly, that Robin meant the place rather than his grandmother. Where she and his grandfather lived was better than alright, far better, but he didn't think it fair to say as much, not when there was no holiday home for Robin to go to. And that reminded him of a more immediate pleasure in wait.

"I'd better run," he said. "Don't want to be late for my practice."

"With that Yankee? He's at your place a lot, isn't he."

"He comes on Fridays." David was breaking into a jog.

"Mum says she saw him in the road two days ago. Wednesday."

Something about the way Robin spoke the words made him stop and turn to his friend. "Probably going to see Mrs. Morton," he said.

But Robin shook his head, definite. "No, she said it was your house he was coming out of. Fancy a game of cricket tomorrow?" he called as David began to run.

He didn't stop running until he reached home.

But the house was empty. He called up the stairs, called again as he peered in the front room, noticing the open gramophone, called once more as he pushed open the back-room door, but nobody answered. The table was laid for him alone and as he sat down, still gulping for air after his run, he read the note propped beside the jar of marrow jam. *Sarah and I are out collecting. Tea is on the table. Help yourself. Love, Mum. PS Jay's sorry but he can't come today.*

He pushed the note away. So that was that. Jay wouldn't be here.

* * *

He was on his second piece of bread when the back door opened and, even before she burst in on him, Sarah was shouting, "Guess what? Mrs Pugh gave us tea. And I had a butterfly cake, with strawberry jam."

As his sister stood at his elbow listing all she'd had to eat and drink, their mother came into the room. She was wearing her grey, pleated skirt and a green-and-white striped blouse that brought out the dark tints in her hair. "Hello, darling," she said, "enjoying your tea, I hope." She smiled brightly, as though feeling the need to apologise for something. "No cake, I'm afraid, but I'll bake a sponge tomorrow."

He finished eating before he spoke. "Why couldn't Jay come?"

"David, I'm sorry." She came and knelt by his chair, put an arm round his shoulder and pressed her cheek against his forehead. "Don't look so sad. He can't always be here, you know. He's a soldier. He has to obey orders."

"What orders?"

She straightened, began to clear away his plate and mug. "I'm to blame, I quite forgot to tell you. Jay left a message on Wednesday to say he was being called away for special manoeuvres — oh, I don't know." She turned, again gave her bright smile. "But he promises he'll be here for next Friday. I'm so sorry, I should have passed on the message but by the time you got back from choir practise it had slipped my mind."

In the doorway, she turned back, the smile now even brighter. "Anyway, the good news is that he left you a record. It's all ready, waiting on the gramophone. I set it up before Sarah and I went out. Do go and see it for yourself."

He slid off his chair and went into the front room. Kneeling, he lifted the record off the turntable. *You Made me Love You*, the title was, which meant nothing to him, although the singer's name did. Judy Garland. She was the girl in that film, *The Wizard of Oz*, which he and Sarah had been taken to see in Hinckley and which they'd had to leave half-way through when Sarah began to scream at the Wicked Witch. He was still holding the record in his hands when his mother came in. "Why not play it?" she asked, "I've wound the machine and put a new needle in for you."

He knelt to his task and, as the music began, stayed crouching, listening to Judy Garland's voice, that full-throated plaint: *You made me cry for I didn't want to tell you, I didn't want to tell you. You made me feel so blue...*

The song came to its close.

"Like it?"

He turned to look up at her but her gaze was averted.

"It isn't much use for practice, is it?"

"I expect Jay would know what to do," she said, as though speaking to herself, then, turning to him, and now her voice was stronger, "let's play it again."

More to please her than himself, he once more set the turntable spinning.

Again, the voice, ardent, yearning, soared, swooped in plaintive submission to its fate. *You know you made me love you.*

"Robin said his mum saw Jay leave our house on Wednesday."

She did turn to him then. "I told you, darling, he dropped in with this record and to apologise for not being able to come today."

Then she turned back to attend to the gramophone. Over her shoulder, she said, "he was especially sorry because he knows how much you look forward to his visits."

"You do, too, don't you?"

She didn't at first answer. Then, getting to her feet, she looked at him, opened her mouth to say something but no words came. What had he said to displease her. The laugh when it came sounded false, her voice sharper than usual as she said, "I'm pleased to see him, naturally, because I know how his coming here bucks you up."

"Like Andrews Liver Salts."

She reached out an arm to ruffle his hair and now her laugh came more easily. It was an old joke of theirs. Anything that lifted their spirits — ITMA, JUST WILLIAM on the radio, the old record of the Laughing Policeman, now badly scratched through repeated playing, Farmer Record's wife who used the Catholic church at which she was a regular attendant as excuse for occasions when she forgot their daily milk supply , "I had to pray for the holy souls in purgatory" (they converted this to Coventry) — all were awarded an imaginary tin of Andrews Liver Salts. Runners up such as Charlie Chester had to make do with Epsom Salts and third, who was usually Eric Barker, received a packet of Carter's Little Liver Pills.

Later, all three sat in the back room to listen to the six o'clock news. The announcer spoke of further allied advances in Europe, adding some details of battles or "engagements," and including the names of places that meant nothing to David. Malta wasn't mentioned. Was that a good thing? From the table, where he and Sarah sipped their milk, he looked across to where their mother sat in her armchair, hand under her chin, staring unseeingly at the rug beneath her feet.

"I think Dad must be safe now," he said to his sister, almost in a whisper.

"David says Dad is safe," Sarah said loudly. "Mum, David says Dad is safe. Does that mean he can come home?"

They looked her, waiting for her to speak, but she gave no sign of having heard them. Sarah got down from the table, went over and put her arm round her mother's neck. "Are you tired, mum?"

She looked up, startled. "Tired, no. Whatever makes you say that?"

"Because you didn't hear what we said. I thought you might be asleep."

"Not much chance of that with you two muffins around." She hooked an arm round Sarah's waist, drew her close, then, as Sarah burrowed in, kissed her daughter's head, its mass of brown curls.

Sarah straightened up, looked candidly at the face smiling at her and said, "Don't be sad, mummy."

There was a pause. Then, "I'm not tired and I'm not sad," she said firmly, and, withdrawing her arm from Sarah's waist, clapped her hands loudly once, twice. "There, that's got rid of the blues." And as Sarah opened her mouth to ask perhaps what that meant, she said, "now, finish your milk and it's up to bed with you."

As the older, David was allowed to sit up for a further twenty minutes, which he filled by standing at the French windows and looking out at the patchy garden with its parade of blue and pink lupins, the blaze of nasturtiums in front of the greenhouse, and then, beyond the broken picket fence, the row of elms at the far side of bottom meadow about which rooks swung lazily, like hinged commas black against the sky's deepening blue. The sound of the village church bells came faintly through a half-open window. Friday night was practice night for the bell-ringers and he pictured the four men, coats off, shirt sleeves rolled up, hauling bent-kneed on the ropes as he'd occasionally seen them do when the choir had been called in for extra practice, gripping, bending and then letting go of the bell-pulls before straightening up.

The only one of the ringers he knew was Mrs Morton's husband, Dick, a tall, grey-haired man whose limp had been caused, so everyone said, when the jack holding up the car he was repairing suddenly collapsed and the car fell onto his foot, crushing it. Each morning Dick Morton walked up to the village, joining the main field path where the stream ran under the wooden bridge, his limp not preventing him going at a lively pace, although from time to time children following behind would imitate his lop-sided gait, suppressing their giggles in case he turned round and caught them at it. He always wore the same brown trilby with the same brown-and-white check sports coat and flannels, on wet days adding a raincoat which he seldom buttoned, exchanging these clothes for his grease-stained overalls once he was at his lock-up garage. There he worked until early evening, sometimes much later. A good worker, so people, even old Godwin, said, and kept busy by all the farmers about, who brought him their machinery to repair and maintain in working order.

David and Robin would often stop outside his garage opposite the school, peering in at the cluttered cave-like space where he worked, a visor pulled over his face, in his hand a thin metal pipe that sparked flame as he applied it to a tractor frame or chassis. "I wouldn't mind being one of those when I grow up," Robin said as they watched Dick Morton bent over an upended two-wheel trailer, hammering at one of its iron bars. And when David said, "What, a trailer?" Robin grinned and said "No, you ruddy nit, a garage owner. My mum reckons he makes haystacks of money. That's how come they've got a fridge."

"They've got a fridge." Or, as Jay called it, an ice-box. Jay, whom he'd first seen with Mrs Morton. Where was the American now? On special manoeuvres. What were they?

"Penny for them." His mother, whom he hadn't heard enter the room, came and stood beside him, putting an arm round his shoulders as she did so.

"I was thinking of ... " he'd been going to say he'd been thinking of Jay, but some impulse made him say instead, "I've been thinking of Dad. I was wondering when his next letter would come."

"Wonder no longer," she said. "A letter arrived this morning."

He looked at her. "You didn't tell me."

"I haven't had time," she said, apologetically. "Sorry." She pulled a face. "There now, that's the second time today I've had to say sorry."

He moved away slightly in order to look at her as he asked, "well, what was in dad's letter?"

"Oh, the usual. I don't suppose he can tell us all or much that he'd like to. Not allowed to risk passing on information that might fall into enemy hands. Anyway, he's still safe on Malta. Or he was at the time of writing."

"I wish he was here," David said. And, after waiting a moment, "Don't you?"

"Of *course* I do," she said, looking down at him, then, turning her face to the window and sighing, she said, "and I also wish I'd got something better to cut the grass with than that old mower Robin's mother lent us."

He studied the faint reflection of her face in the glass and as their eyes met her expression changed to a smile and she said, "now, my love, bedtime. You can have a few minutes to read and then I'll be up to say goodnight."

"Did he add a letter for Sarah and me?"

She had turned away, was moving to her armchair, and without looking round she said, "No. No, I don't think so."

He wanted to say "but surely you know," then thought better of it and left the room.

* * *

He'd not been in bed long when she tiptoed in to see he'd come to no harm, as she always termed her goodnight kiss. Bending over the bed, where he was propped up, bedside lamp angled onto his open book, she said, "let's hope this weather is here to stay. Sun for your holiday. Just what the doctor ordered."

"We could ask gran and granddad to order good weather," he said. "When will we be going?"

"Oh," she said, kissing him and straightening up, "in two weeks' time, I expect, just as soon as you've finished school. Huntingdonshire, here we come."

She went over to the window, drew his curtains across. But after the war —" spinning round, she threw her arms wide, said in a loud whisper so as not to wake Sarah, "we'll be able to go anywhere. The world will be our oyster." She was filled with sudden gaiety, as though determined to make up for her earlier, uncertain mood. "Now, where, if you wished upon a star, would you like to go?"

He thought about it. "I'd like to go to Indiana," he said, then, seeing her expression, the sudden look in her eyes, almost of pain, he said loyally, "no, perhaps Malta."

"But east is east and west is west," she said slowly, "and never the twain shall meet."

Once more she bent to kiss him, then, telling him he must read for no more than five minutes, was gone, pulling the door softly shut behind her.

Soon enough he snapped off his light, then lay awake, hearing the ripple and clank of coal trucks from beyond the fields and woods on the far side of the lane and, now distant, now nearer, now fading again, an owl's watery whoooo. *Whooo*, he thought, *blooo*. What had she said? "That's got rid of the blues." What did she mean? What exactly *were* the blues? As though in answer to his question, Judy Garland's voice came back to him. *You make me feel so blue.*

He was drowsily puzzling over the word, hearing in his head the singer's deep, bruised tones as he turned over on his side and pressed his ear to the pillow.

He sat up. The voice *wasn't* in his head, what he could hear was the record itself, faint but unmistakeable. He listened as the song came to an end. A pause and then once more it started out of silence. But she never played records of an evening, not wanting to wake the children, whose bedrooms were directly above. He lay back down and as he did so his nostrils caught a trace of the aroma she had left on the pillow as she bent to kiss him. Not soap, not powder, but something sharper and at the same time sweeter. Something unfamiliar, something new.

~ CHAPTER TWELVE ~

Darling, Thanks as always for news from the home front. It's good to know that David is now, so you say, as 'happy as a dog with nine tails', but I worry that this Krassner is requiring rather a lot of you. Fine for him to be passing on to our son something of his skills, but from what you say — or rather, don't say — I get the impression that he must be imposing on your hospitality by turning up quite so regularly. If I were you I'd hint that not every Friday afternoon can be set aside for him. I certainly don't see why you should, as you say, hurry back from your activities in the village in order to offer him his cuppa. What would Professor Zammit advise, you ask? Well, aside from keeping a marble or a bronze repose (marble in his case), I think he might suggest that good fences make good neighbours. But I'll consult him about the matter next time I'm down that end of the town. I don't suppose Mr Priestley's homilies offered much on the responsibilities of neighbourliness, did they? Anyway, I gather Jolly Jack has ceased his BBC chores.

You say the children want to know how I'm coping. I'm trying to recall what it is Elizabeth Bennet says about looking forward to the moment when marriage means that she can remove herself from society "so little pleasing" to her — isn't it? Substitute "after the war" for "marriage" and I imagine you have a statement that will hold true for countless thousands of us. Not that I can complain of all who make up the society I live among. Dave Morris is a good, reliable friend, and I'll continue to sing the praises of Maria and Marcus. The islanders' grumbles get louder by the day, but I don't blame them. The food we try to foist on them is — I choose my words carefully — not all it might be. Most of the rabbits and pigeons vanished into stew pots long ago, and farming here is only now beginning to get back on its feet. Few greens and I suspect that not even Squeers would find much to say in praise of the bread on offer.

Maria's apart, that is, but then she gets first choice of George's flour. On the other hand, convoys, including food ships, now get through with next to no trouble. Unfortunately, the quality of the food they offload falls some way short of A1. (Or perhaps all that disappears into the black market.) At least fags and beer are plentiful and keep the service personnel relatively happy. But as conditions improve so the former cheeriness of the we-can-take-it Maltese has changed to something less agreeable: a kind of dourness. Understandable, but not all that reassuring. However, "mustn't complain". The weather at its best is glorious: hot, dry, with plenty of chance for swimming, or as Dave says, "frolicking in the briny." (Which the Med. isn't of course.— Briny, I mean, not to anyone who's swum off an English beach.) Most days we're simply too hot to do anything beyond regulation maintenance work. That goes on as per. Yesterday was a stinker, but fortunately from early morning to late at night Dave and I were testing machines up on that headland above Ziggiewi we call "Clapham Junction," and where there's at least the semblance of a breeze.

I'm not sure I've described the junction to you before, have I, so here goes. It really is very strange. A stretch of land with long, straight fissures in the rock and soil nobody seems able to account for, though it must be some geological freak, perhaps alternate strata of limestone and harder rock laid down over millennia and then tilted up by earthquake activity. The limestone presumably wore away, the harder stuff remained. The overall effect is of an abandoned railway junction, as though hundreds of lines laid down long ago have since been lifted up and carted off. As I say, very strange, but perfect for testing the steering and suspension of army vehicles. Trucks, gun carriers, motor bikes, you name 'em, we've tested them. And the breeze allowed us to escape the grilling that affected everyone who stayed down here.

But apart from professional grousers, we're contented with our lot. We've no choice! Stiff-upper lips prevail. Nobody curses the heat, nobody mutters mutinously and, to speak personally, I breathe a sigh of relief each time I observe or hear that Southern is continuing to play Ferdinand to Anna's Miranda. I'm not quite sure why I feel so involved with the pair of them. I suppose partly because young love *does rather catch at the heart and then — I confess —there's that hope, a frail one I know, you'd probably tell me it's a fantasy, that the relationship of an English youth and a Maltese Miss may signify a future of amity rather than enmity for us all. Anyway it's a relief that George isn't required to be the heavy-handed Prospero. I think he'd have a hard time trying to take the part of his nobler reason 'gainst the fury he's capable of. For now, though, he's so content that he almost smiles when he sees me coming.*

*Truth to tell, I'm probably better off for companionship than you are. And when I want to withdraw I can lie on my bed in vacant or in pensive mood, reading your letters (**many, many** thanks for writing out "Tintern Abbey" for me) or imagining our future. I try not to let fears of the immediate present darken my mind, though it's sometimes difficult to blot them out, whether it's the dread of some terrible illness affecting either of the kids or yourself, or some other unimaginable disaster. I know I've said this in previous letters but such fears do, inevitably, prey on my mind. "My whole life I have lived in pleasant thought." Good for Wordsworth. But for us who are separated by getting on for three years and countless miles, pleasant thought doesn't come so easily. One that **does** is the memory of that Sunday morning, the first of our honeymoon, when we lay in our hotel bed after the previous evening's showing of the Bob Hope film, and the maid came in with our breakfast while we singing that song. "No tears for us, hooray for us." And she **joined in!** Remembering that always gives me a lift. I'm not sure why. Oh, I suppose because we were so happy. God send us more such days as that. But God damn this bloody war that's keeping us apart. When will it end? When waterdrops have worn the stones of Troy ...*

He stopped what he was writing, put down his pen. He should cross those words out. He didn't want to think about *that* ...

He became aware of a tap on the shoulder. Dave Morris hovered above him. "Time to go," Dave said. "The gang's all here."

Stephen stood up, drained the last of his mug of breakfast tea — cold by now — and followed his friend out into the dazzle of morning sun.

Gathered in a semi-circle in front of the hut some fifteen or so young men and women were sitting astride the Nortons which for the past week he and Dave had been working on and which the riders were now revving up as they studied their two instructors. Stephen let Dave explain what they'd be doing that day. He spoke slowly, clearly, while the group listened attentive, silent, their olive-complexioned faces for the most part screened by long, dark hair, their eyes fixed on the speaker. They were a handsome lot, insouciant, determined, and in all likelihood they would soon be dead.

"This morning we're off up to 'Clapham Junction'," Dave told them, and they laughed and nodded, their English good enough for them to understand the reference. "It's a useful place to practice given that you'll be avoiding roads once you get to where you're going. You'll be travelling by cart tracks and riding over rough ground and scree. Leastways, that's what we've been told." He paused, looked enquiringly at them, and they nodded in agreement. Reassured, he went on, "Good. Now as you've probably noticed, Siggiwiggi's got sod all by way of mountains, but we're hot on cart tracks and what we're supposed to call uneven terrain. I can see you're all mad buggers" — he paused to allow for further laughter —"but me and the sergeant here have spent a lot of time and effort making sure that your machines in are good working order so we'd be grateful if you didn't wreck them before you get to where you have to use them for real. And to that end we're going to spend some time teaching you how to strip an engine down in the hope you'll learn to repair whatever can be repaired. If it's past saving we'll teach you how to booby-trap the bike just in case a passing Fritz takes a fancy to it, OK."

Nods, laughter, applause. Stephen studied one young woman in particular, her expression intent as she listened to Dave, her oval face framed by dark, wavy hair that was held in place by a ribbon. Perhaps aware of the intensity of his own stare she looked briefly at him and at once he looked away, smiling awkwardly as he did so. Anyway, it was a blue ribbon.

"Right, then." Dave slapped the saddle of his own bike before straddling it, "wagons roll." He kick-started the bike, the others did the same, and amid a coughing roar of engines and blue-grey clouds of exhaust smoke, they began to move in slow, wavering single-file up the lane towards the headland, Stephen at the back, watching their progress and wondering how on earth this group of partisans, which he and Dave had been working with for the past month, would manage once they were back home, taking on not merely a ruthless enemy but the inhospitable weather and mountainous conditions over which they would be fighting. Was it for this the clay grew tall. Their gaiety astounded him, the laughter with which they dismissed the chances of death, laughter which, as he lay in bed at night brooding over each day's training sessions, brought him to the verge of tears. He thought of the moment when, after one such session, someone had produced a box Brownie and they'd all lined up for a group photograph. "Something to remember us by," one of them had said in broken English, and Dave had muttered, "smile while you can." None of this could be told to Jean, of course. Another reason to hate the bloody war. It forced its way between those who ought to be closest to each other.

* * *

That evening, hot, sweaty, tired, Dave, he, and the young Yugoslavians, sat in the canteen drinking beer, all of them too fatigued for more than the most desultory of conversations. Tomorrow morning the group would be transferring to Valetta, where they were to expect a ship that would take them across to their disembarkation point. Where that was, however, they either didn't yet know or weren't allowed to say. All they did know, or anyway told their instructors, was that they were intending to link up with one of Tito's outfits. And after that?

"Then we rid our house of the rats."

The woman who spoke was the one who wore the blue ribbon. She sat diagonally across from Stephen and as she spoke she stretched out her arm in order to clink her bottle against the one he held in front of him. Startled, he looked into her eyes, saw the flicker of excitement in them, but almost at once realised that it wasn't sexual. She was aroused by the thought of the fighting ahead. Suddenly, he wanted to tell her not to go, that where she was heading would lead to certain death, she was too young, beautiful …

But before he could even suppress the words he knew would be entirely pointless, Dave said, "Well, I'm for shut eye. Coming, Sarge?" and Stephen, tilting his bottle to swallow the final drops, said "With you, Dave," and stood to join the corporal in shaking hands with the entire group, wishing them good luck, safe voyage and a happy landing. All the usual meaningless but heartfelt clichés.

"What do you reckon their chances?" he asked Dave as the two strolled across the darkening patch of open ground towards their huts. Cicadas were ratcheting down now, the warm air soothing the men's bare arms and legs. A half-moon stood directly above them, so that their shadows moved below them like watery refractions. Dave looked down as though to check his own shadow before he replied, "Dunno, but rather them than me."

He stopped, looked up at the moon. "Poor buggers," he said, cleared his throat and spat.

They walked on a few yards in silence, then Dave spoke again. "How about you, are you alright?"

"Me?" Stephen said, turning from opening the door of his hut to look at Dave. "I'm fine. Why?"

"Oh, nothing," Dave said. "Only I thought you looked a bit … well, a bit peaky, my old mum would have said. You know, this morning, when I came to fetch you."

"I was writing a letter," Stephen said. "To Jean."

Dave said "Everything all right at home?"

"Yes," Stephen said firmly. "Everything's fine."

"Glad to hear it. In that case, I'll be off. See you in the morning."

Stephen watched Dave amble away into the dark. Then he went into his own hut.

Inside, irritably aware of the clammy heat, he pulled the curtains across, a ridiculous precaution now but one the army still pretended to insist on, then dragged a chair into position under the hut's one electric bulb, notepaper on his knees, and read again the words he had been writing that morning when Dave's arrival interrupted him. *When waterdrops have worn the stones of Troy ...* What was it about her letter that had nagged at him, had throughout the long, exhausting day, come buzzing about his mind like an irritating presence he wanted to swat away? He went over to his bed, reached under the pillow, and drew out the several hand-written sheets of paper he had put there for safe keeping. Turning them slowly over, he scanned the pages until he found what he was looking for. Yes, there it was, very near the end. *Soon David's summer term will be over,* she had written, *and then of course they'll be off as usual to Mum and Dad. Fingers crossed that the good weather continues for the holidays.* Was that a slip, the kind of mistake you made when you were rushing to conclude a letter so as to get to the post in time, as she said, for that's day's collection?

He read the words over again. "They'll be off". They, not we. But if it wasn't a slip, what could she possibly mean? That she wasn't going with them? But why? No, it had to be a mistake. She could hardly let them make the long train journey on their own. Besides, they always went to her parents for the summer, all of them, without fail.

He put the letter back under his pillow and returned to his seat. *When waterdrops have worn the stones of Troy.* He took up his pen and sat looking at the words, uncertain what came next.

CHAPTER THIRTEEN

"It's not fair," Sarah said. "*Why* can't she come with us?"

She was perched on the end of David's bed, her dressing gown heaped untidily about her, eyes, which she scrubbed with the heel of one hand, still bleary from sleep. The other hand was being used to clutch to her side a teddy bear on which dangerous spots had just been found. "I don't know *what* to do for the best," she said dramatically, bending over the bear. "I really ought to stay here with Archie if he's going to be ill."

"You can't stay here," David said, "you know that. Bring it with you, perhaps it needs a change of scene."

"It's *HIM* not *IT*," Sara said crossly. "And of *course* I'm not going to leave him behind." Sliding off the bed, she went to look out of the window. "Do you like being in this room?" she asked.

"Yes," David said, meaning it. And in answer to Sarah's inevitable "why?" he told her that he preferred the view from the window. He didn't tell her that he also liked the room's smallness, the sense it gave him of being in a secret cave, a place which felt special to him. But underneath the show of protest he'd put on when he was asked to move out of his front bedroom, the prospect of changing to the back thrilled him, even though it would be for two nights only. And when they returned from their grandparents they'd find their own rooms would be good as new, their mother promised.

So he and she manoeuvred his bed and then chest of drawers along the landing and into what she called the box room where he would sleep before he and Sarah set off on holiday. Sarah's room being bigger, her things had been pulled into the middle of the floor, leaving walls and skirting-boards free to be "got at." On an expedition up to the village earlier in the week, Sarah had helped choose the new colours for her room. White walls and, for the woodwork, dark green. David said he didn't care what colours his room was painted and accepted with a shrug the choice of blue for the woodwork, but now that he was in the box room with its faded yellow wallpaper on which was imposed patterns of spindly grasses, he realised how much he wanted to stay there.

From downstairs came the clatter of breakfast things, then their mother's voice calling them to hurry. As Sarah trailed disconsolately away, David levered himself up and out of bed. Standing at his window, he looked out to where, beyond bottom meadow, layers of early-morning mist, thin as tissue paper, spread over the ripening corn and clung in soft tatters to the lower branches of osiers that marked the stream's narrow course.

A sudden movement made him shift his attention to the man who stood in the nearer wheatfield. Farmer Record. He was in his usual blue overalls, head bent over hands that were pressed together as if in prayer. But he wasn't praying. David knew what that posture meant. Farmer Record was rubbing ears of corn between his palms to see how readily husks came away from the kernels they surrounded. As though satisfied with the result, the farmer spread his hands wide, then slapped them together, rubbed them, perhaps to free them of wheat chaff, perhaps to signify delight, and then, very slowly, raised his arms towards the cloudless sky. And at that moment the sun, lifting clear of the brambled hedgerow that bordered the still misty wheatfield, dyed his hands and wrists vermilion.

From downstairs came the call, "David. Sarah. Breakfast. Quick now."

Reluctantly, he turned away and nearly tripped over the small suitcase they had packed the night before and which held his freshly-ironed clothes and the few books he'd chosen to take with him. He wanted to include his drumsticks, but had been persuaded him to leave them behind.

"They'll be safer here."

"Oh, well, Jay can use them if he likes." He'd meant it as a joke, and was startled by the sudden look she gave him. "Sorry," he'd said, involuntarily, unsure what there was to apologise for.

Now, putting on the clean shirt and shorts she'd left out for him overnight, he wondered when he would next see the American. Though Jay still came to their house most Friday afternoons, he hadn't been at last Saturday's tea-dance, which meant that David couldn't ask him about what one of Mrs Rayner's helpers called "a clear out of the Yanks," and another said, with a meaning look, some would regret more than others. Three weeks away. Would Jay still be here when he and Sarah returned?

Suppose the American had gone? In that case he might never see him again. The thought, like a blow, sudden, sharp, almost winded him.

"I think I've got an ache," Sarah told David across the breakfast table. "I must have caught it from Archie."

"Nonsense." Their mother, coming in with a tray on which were boiled eggs and toast, said briskly, "you can finish your cereal after you've had your eggs. A special holiday treat. They were laid last night, so Mrs Record assures me."

"I don't want an egg," Sarah said tearfully. "I don't feel like one."

Crouching down beside her, their mother ran her fingers through Sarah's chestnut curls. "Darling, you have to eat, you're going on a train journey, remember. And this egg is extra special fresh."

"Ugh," Sarah said, "I don't want to eat what came out of a hen's bottom."

"Oh, Sarah, *please.*" Her tone was placatory, almost wheedling.

"Why don't you eat it, Mum?" David asked, "you say you're going to be busy day and night while we're away. You need to keep *your* strength up." He did his best to imitate her manner of speech, smiling to show he meant no harm.

Sarah turned from scowling at her egg to studying her mother. "Are you going to paint in those clothes?" she asked critically, looking at the green silk frock that rarely came out of the wardrobe, and the black, open-toed shoes.

"Of course not." She straightened up. "I've put on my glad rags because I'm taking you to the station. I want to see you off in style. But as soon as I'm back here I'll dress to look like a tramp's wife.

Whistling Billy's, perhaps." She was trying to make them laugh.

"Whistling Billy sleeps in a tin bath." David tried to join in the attempt at jollity. "You're not going to do that, are you, mum?"

"Certainly not." The smile came and as quickly went.

"How do you know he sleeps in a tin bath?" Sarah was wide-eyed, her question balanced between wonder and accusation.

"Because we've seen him, Robin and me, when we were out nutting. It's in the ditch at Lane End spinney on the way to the woods. He was snoring."

Sarah clapped a hand to her mouth as thought to stifle giggles, then, releasing it, began to chant, "It's raining, it's pouring, the old man's a snoring."

"Sleeping off a skinful I shouldn't be surprised," their mother said. And, registering their puzzled looks, "I expect he'd been in the pub." Now, Sarah, why not do as your brother's done and finish off the egg before it gets cold."

She bent to help Sarah and as she did so Sarah hooked her arm round her mother's neck. "I don't want to go to gran and granddad's without you," she whispered.

"Oh, Sarah, you know you'll have a wonderful time there." But though her voice was pleading, the words themselves came matter-of-fact. "It's only for three weeks, you'll have a lovely time being spoilt, and think of the rooms you'll be coming back to, all ship-shape, Bristol fashion."

Plates piled on the tray, she paused at the doorway, said, "Besides, we'll talk to each other regularly."

"How?" Sarah was suddenly interested.

"Because I've saved up a fistful of pennies so I can telephone you and then you can tell me all your news."

"I'd like that," David said, looking at his sister, who said nothing. "But what if it's raining?" Bad weather was always her excuse for not running up to the box at the top of the road.

Going towards the kitchen, their mother called over her shoulder, "I'll take my umbrella. Now, you two run upstairs and make yourselves presentable. Hurry now, the taxi will be here soon."

She sat between them on the back seat of the ancient car that doubled as local taxi, an arm round each, trying to get them to join in a song they'd so often sung while huddled together at night under the steel table. "Bang, Bang, Bang, BANG, goes the Farmer's gun." David, gripping his suitcase to his stomach, dutifully helped out, but Sarah, lips set in a straight line, stared silently ahead. And as they boarded the train at Leicester, where they were handed over to their grandmother, she turned away from her mother's kiss so that all the way to Peterborough the side of her forehead remained gashed with lipstick, like a wound.

* * *

The four of them were just finishing tea in the room that gran called her parlour when they heard the telephone's shrill sound echoing through the stone-flagged hall.

"You take it, Harold."

But he was already lifting himself out of the wooden chair with its padded arm rests, using an index finger to brush his moustache clear of non-existent crumbs as he made for the door.

The ringing stopped and their grandfather's voice came to them, but not his words. Sarah looked expectantly at the closed door, David tried to concentrate on the honeycomb that sat meltingly in a blue, shallow bowl beside a saucer of butter, but was first out of his chair when they were called: "David, Sarah, hurry, your mother is running out of coins."

Sarah was handed the receiver first. Grabbing it with both hands and pressing it to her ear she shouted "Hello, mummy, we've had our tea and I had an egg and the train was late and Granny said it's the fault of the war ... ." She turned to her grandfather, who leant against the parlour door, listening and smiling. "Mummy wants to know why our being late is the war's fault?"

"Not enough coal to go round, tell her."

"Not enough coal to go round," Sarah shouted into the phone, while their grandfather winked complicitly at David.

Then it was his turn. "Hello." The word was little more than a whisper. He cleared his throat, tried again. "Hello, Mum." He felt awkward speaking to someone he couldn't see, and when she replied, his mother's voice, distorted by distance, sounded unfamiliar, as though it wasn't his mother at all. It was only after he'd managed to push this thought away that he realised she had been telling him something about how she had already started painting his bedroom walls and that she was counting the days until they'd all be together again. He nodded.

"Your mum can't hear a nod, young man."

David turned to his grandfather. "Sorry," he said.

"Sorry? What for painting your bedroom?"

"No, sorry, mum, I was saying sorry to Granddad."

"Oh. Well, I hope you've done nothing to be sorry for. No, I'm sure you haven't." And it was the sound of her laugh alright that came unmistakeably through the earpiece. "Remember to look after Sarah, won't you."

"Yes."

"And give gran and granddad my love." A pause, and then her voice, again now unmistakeable, but lowered, deeper, almost a whisper, as though what she was saying was for him alone: "and all my love to you both."

"Mum?"

"Yes?"

"Has dad written?"

A brief pause. "Why? I mean is a letter due then? I can't remember."

"We wrote to him two weeks ago."

"So we did. Well, perhaps one will come tomorrow. As your gran says, it's the war's fault."

Another voice came on the line. "You have ten seconds left," the operator said.

"David, I simply must go. But I'll phone as soon as I've heard from your dad and ... ."

There was a click, followed by a low, continuous burring sound. David returned the receiver to its cradle.

"And how's your mother, has she heard from Malta?" A long, white pinafore now covering her habitual, blue-and-white polka-dot dress, their grandmother turned from her task of clearing the table as the three of them trooped back into the parlour.

David shook his head. "No, no letter today. She says she's been busy painting my bedroom."

"As no doubt she has," his grandfather said, "she sounded to me as though she'd had a bellyful of it," while his wife, glancing towards him said, "Ah well, they say that no news is good news." She went on arranging plates on a large, wooden tray. "Now, would either of you like to finish off this last piece of apple tart. No, not you, Harold," slapping her husband's wrist as he pretended to reach out for it. "You behave yourself, my lad. This is for the young ones. Share?"

They shared.

* * *

In the mostly sun-filled days that followed, they were free to roam the open country lying all about. The fields opposite the schoolhouse were given over to grazing cattle that stood or knelt under clumps of elm or the line of alders that fringed a muddy stream into which the cows, as they dipped their heads to drink, lifted their tails and let fall liquorice-dark platelets of shit.

One morning, soon after their arrival, David and Sarah watched squadrons of flies hover above the stream where two cows stood.

"Bombs away," David shouted. One cow briefly lifted its head to look at him, then once again lowered it to the water.

"They're drinking their own poo," Sarah said, with appalled fascination.

"And the flies eat the rest."

"Ugh, that's really horrible." Flapping at a few of the black-gold insects that had broken off their business over the stream to target her head, she began to run further off down the field away from her tormenters.

David followed her. At the field's lowest corner was a pond, its black, oozy margins heavily trodden by the hooves of cattle. It was fringed by wild grasses and reeds from which coots and moorhens scuttered out onto the water, a kite-tail of chicks behind. When the mother birds reached the middle of the pond they turned for home, their movements creating an unbroken echelon of vees like an arrow tracking its target. The water at the pond's edge was furred with green scum, but further out the surface cleared and here it was patterned by white and grey cloud-drift and, toppling deep down, the old oak that had years earlier been struck by lightning and which, gnarled and bare-branched, stood in the hedgerow at the field's end, its hollow trunk a nesting-place, so their grandfather told them, for a little owl. This was an uncommon enough bird for him to have published a letter in the local newspaper about its arrival, and the letter, properly framed, now hung on the parlour wall.

As David knelt beside her, Sarah pointed silently, aghast, at a steel-blue dragon-fly that quivered above the water near her sandal, its blunt head and thin straight body like a darning needle, until it suddenly lifted and veered at her, at which point she screamed and hid her head in her hands.

"Silly," David said.

"It's not silly."

"Yes it is. Baby-silly."

"It's NOT." Her shout subsided into a sob and tears splashed on her cheeks.

Then there was silence.

After a few moments, during which, her sobs subsiding, Sarah continued sitting on her heels as she wiped her eyes with the back of her hand and frowned across the pond, she opened her mouth and, without looking at him, spoke.

At first, he wasn't sure that he'd heard her correctly. When he realised he had, he was shocked into numbness. But almost at once feeling returned, his whole body trembled, blood pounded at his ears.

Rage, though, kept his throat constricted, left him unable to speak. Slowly, slowly, then more swiftly, the pounding in his ears lessened, until he could clear his throat and, as he stared, not at her but at a moorhen that had just bustled out from the reeds, he at last found his voice. "I don't believe you," he said. Then, shouting,

"I don't *believe you.*"

Startled, the moorhen turned tail and disappeared back into the safety of its grassy habitat.

David scrambled to his feet. Still refusing to look at his sister, "I don't believe you," he said once more, his voice this time a fierce whisper.

Sarah reached up to take his hand, but he snatched it away, turned and ran to the far side of the field where he stood looking at but not really seeing the thick tangle of hedgerow. Beyond, a dusty lane curved between wide stretches of grass. Think of something, *anything.* Gipsies. They sometimes camped here and the lane was also used by one of the villagers who tethered their goats along it for daily browsing. No man's gardens. That was what his grandparents called these stretches of green. What were the names of the three goats owned by the woman, Jedson she was called, who brought them titupping down the lane each morning and returned for them later in the day. Dora, George … ?

From behind him, Sarah's voice, small, scared, said, "I'm sorry, David." And again, and this time it was no more than a whisper, "sorry."

He turned then, slowly, saw her anxious, tear-stained face.

"Alright," he said at length, "but you mustn't say that again. Ever."

"I won't," Sarah said. She sighed with relief, smiled apologetically. "I didn't mean it, anyway."

"Good." Then, looking over her shoulder, he said, "I didn't believe you, anyway."

Dumbly, she nodded.

And although there were occasions in the following days when, caught off his guard, her words swarmed back, stinging his mind, he managed to beat them off, for a while at least.

* * *

As the days passed, David found he needed his sister as a companion. At home, he had Robin. Sarah lived a separate existence, with a gaggle of small girls, chief among them Mary

Record. The girls used each others' yards for hopscotch or skipping games with complicated rules and rhymes, except when, frocks tucked into their knickers, they would practise handstands, heels pressed against wall or fence, white arms and legs making them look like the row of animal carcasses he'd once seen in an old picture book. They rarely if ever went into the fields. But here, brother and sister, alone together, had the freedom not only of the fields but of their grandparents' orchard, separated by a crumbling, moss-damp brick wall from the bottom of the school playground, its tangled grass mined by fallen apples and pears among which wasps cruised. On an earlier holiday both had been stung — Sarah on her neck, David on his lip, which, despite repeated applications of the blue-bag, refused to return to normal size for several days — and now they tended to avoid the orchard unless either grandparent went with them.

They preferred the open fields. By day the two of them roamed at will, and each evening, with their grandparents, they struck out along a path that took them towards a farm to which most of the land around belonged, although they never met the farmer. The boy who came to collect the cows for milking was a former pupil of their grandparents, a shy lad called Charlie, who always greeted the strollers by lifting his cap but saying nothing, and who stumped along behind the cows in boots and corduroy trousers far too big for him.

"He's learning all he needs to know for when his dad retires," their grandfather said, poking at tufts of grass with his walking stick or kicking at them. He was trying to start rabbits and one evening succeeded in dislodging a young one from its hiding place. They watched as the frightened animal took off in a swerving run that ended with a leap into a field-side hedge.

Their grandmother, following the rabbit's movements as it raced for cover, said, "Did your mum ever tell you of the time your granddad found a pheasant and I was summonsed to bring it home?" And although they did know the story, they asked to hear it again. When she finished, she said, "I can't imagine your dad expecting your mum to drop everything for a little thing like that."

"That would be difficult, given that she's in England and he's on Malta," their grandfather said, laughing. Then, to David, "have you any plans to follow your dad in his line of business?" nodding to the boy plodding along the track some way ahead of them.

"Harold! David's a young lad. He doesn't want to bother with questions like that. Time enough, when he's older." Then, to her grandson she said, smiling, "although teaching is a good profession, as we know," adding, "If you're a man, that is. Imagine, I had to give up my career as soon as I was married."

"Then that's one reason to thank Mr Hitler." And, seeing David's startled look, he said, "with male teachers in the services it's all hands to the pump. Imagine it! We're forced to ask married women to help us out in the classroom," and he skipped nimbly away from his wife's pretend clout to his head.

As they turned for home, their grandfather more seriously said, "Anyway, I've no doubt your dad will be glad to get back to the classroom. Teaching's a profession that runs in families. Like doctoring."

"But Stephen isn't our son. And his father isn't a teacher." His wife, leading the way with Sarah holding her hand, paused, looked back. "If what you're saying is true, then it's Jean who should be in the profession."

"Well, maybe it runs in families in a zig-zag pattern, like that rabbit we watched."

David found the courage to say, "I'd like to play the drums when I'm old enough. I mean *really* play. In a band."

They stopped, stared at him. "What's brought this on," his grandfather asked, genuinely surprised. "Your mother's told us that you bang about a bit at home … "

"It's *not* banging about," David said, hotly. Then, seeing his grandmother's expression, lowered his voice. "I'm learning what Jay — Jay Krassner, the American who comes to see us — calls 'tricks of the trade.'"

"An American?" They exchanged glances.

Sarah said to her grandfather, "he's a soldier. He comes to our house and he teaches David how to b… " she changed the word to "play."

114

"He comes from Gary, Indiana," David said, "but he learnt to play properly when he was in Chicago."

"Chicago, eh?"

"Yes," David said, "Jay — Mr Krassner — says it's called the Windy City." So then he had to tell his grandparents about how he'd first met Jay.

He was still telling them all he knew about Krassner as he and Sarah sat in their bedclothes at the parlour table sipping glasses of milk. For good measure, he began to explain about the tea-dances and how Mrs Rayner let him choose the records to which people danced, and then, as his grandmother said, tongue flapping like a sail loose in the wind, he added that the GIs who came to the dances brought records with them and that they danced with village girls in a way that upset the village men, especially when they did the 'jitterbug' — at the mention of which his grandfather said "you mean throwing the girls over their heads and all that mullarkey? I don't wonder they don't like it. Imagine me trying to throw your grandmother in the air like that."

"I wouldn't mind if I thought you'd catch me."

"Precious little chance of that," he said and they all laughed.

* * *

Some mornings, if they were out of bed early enough, they were allowed to clamber up onto the baker's horse and cart when the roundsman, Eric, stopped outside the schoolhouse to deliver that day's bread. David seated beside him, Sarah behind under the cart's tarpaulin cover, they swayed and creaked slowly up the village street, David dropping off to take to each house the bread that Sarah, under Eric's instructions, handed him. Warm and sweet-smelling from the oven, the bread was kept under white starched cloths on wooden trays. "Mrs Gunnis, number 6, one tin, six cobs," Eric would announce without turning his head, shaking the reins of the old piebald horse so that it ambled to a stop. "Ma Youngman" — a name which, considering that it belonged to an old woman bent almost double with age always made them giggle — "one baton, one cottage, though I dunno how she copes with 'em, she ain't 'ad no teeth since Methuselah were a lad."

At the end of their round, they were given a cob apiece. Sarah saved hers to share with Archie, but David at once jabbed through the baked, brittle outer crust so that he could lift the cob to his nose, inhaling its moist warmth. Then, waving goodbye to Eric as the brown-and-yellow painted cart — POTTS FINE BREAD AND CAKES — turned in the lane to make its way back to the bakery, he would take the roll he'd earned indoors, break it open and spoon over its white flesh honey from the honeycomb his grandmother kept under a glass dome on the parlour table.

As the days went by they grew accustomed to the six o'clock jangling of the telephone that summoned them from supper. "Jean, come most timely upon her hour," their grandfather would say, glancing at the mantelpiece clock as he put down his napkin and padded out to the hall. After a minute or so he would call out, "Children, your mother," and out they would go, Sarah always first, eager to speak, David less prompt, never able to shake off the strange awkwardness of talking to the mother he couldn't see. His answers to her questions were invariably monosyllabic, not because he didn't yearn to say more but because, watching his grandparents study him from the parlour room door, he felt instinctively that he needed to guard his tongue, though against what he didn't know.

Sarah had no such inhibitions. She reported all she had done that day and made sure to include progress reports on Archie's condition — much improved, thank goodness, spots nearly gone — as well as accounts of what they had eaten. Finally, prompted by her grandfather, she gave reluctant way to her brother. He heard the voice at the far end of the telephone, imagined the box on its little patch of green, those stale smells trapped in its confined space. How had his day been, his mother would ask? Alright. Was he eating well? Yes. Was he looking after his sister? Yes. "Well," she said one evening after a string of his single-word answers, "you're as close as an oyster," adding, as she laughed, "you'd make a dumb man sound like a chatterbox."

"Sorry," he said, then "have you finished painting the rooms yet?"

"Very nearly done," she said. "Two shakes of a dog's tail and they'll be ready for you both."

"That's good," he said. "And dad? Have you heard from him."

Yes, she'd heard and all was well. He knew that David and Sarah were at their grandparents and had written a note for David which would be waiting for him when they returned from holiday.

Then, silence. She was waiting for him to ask for more information, perhaps. He too waited, then, after an aching moment of indecision, said his goodbyes, handed the phone to his grandmother, and went back to the parlour.

* * *

She was to phone the evening before their return in order to "confirm arrangements" for meeting them at the station. That day the weather broke. From early morning a wind slammed across the fields, bending the trees and scattering rooks about the grey skies. Fistfuls of rain battered against the schoolhouse windows and there was a whistling in the chimneys as clouds of smoke poured out into the parlour where David and Sarah sat huddled over the fire which had been lit to dry their freshly-washed clothes.

"Drat the weather," their grandmother said, as she draped shirts and dresses over the clothes horse. "You'll be glad to get home if this keeps up."

Late that afternoon, after their clothes had been folded and packed, the tin bath was taken down from its hook on the scullery wall and saucepans of water heated on the kitchen range. Sarah sang loudly as she soaped herself and even David had to prevent himself from whistling. Tomorrow evening they would be at home.

Warm in pyjamas and dressing gowns, they sat fidgety with suppressed glee at the parlour table waiting for their supper. "Going home," Sarah whispered loudly, then covered her mouth with both hands, her eyes wide with the shock of delight at what her words signified.

"If it gets any darker I'll have to light a lamp," their grandmother said, setting the supper tray down and turning to look out of the window pearled with rain water. A figure in yellow oilskin trod heavily past the front gate.

"Jedson going to fetch his wife's goats in for milking," their grandfather said, as he came into the room and stood to watch. "Rather him than me. A day like today, he'll have more water than milk in his pail, I shouldn't wonder."

"If you light the lamp will you have to draw the curtains?" Sarah asked, bouncing on her seat.

"We might risk leaving them," her grandmother said, smiling at the little girl's new-found surge of energy. "Nobody much bothers any longer with the blackout rules, not in the village. Anyway, Miss Shufflebottom, we'll manage without the lamp as long as we can see to put our hands in front of our mouths." Then, turning to her husband. "What time is it?"

He drew the gold watch from his trousers pocket, flipped up the lid, and held it in his hands as though weighing it. "Near enough six o'clock," he said, "she'll be phoning any moment now," and David heard his sister's sharp intake of breath, the excitement that nearly burst out into a cry of joy.

Obeying his grandmother's request, David took a piece of plum tart and reached for the milk jug. It was covered with a square of muslin fringed with blue beads from under which, as he lifted the muslin, a large, sloe-black bluebottle blundered out into the air. It flew at Sarah's face. She screamed and hit out. The blue-bottle droned down to crawl across the table's green-and-white oilcloth. Their grandfather studied it briefly, then his fist came down and there was the sound as of a boot grinding wet gravel.

The fist lifted off. Sarah stared at the berry-red splodge on the oilcloth and shuddered dramatically. David pushed his plate to one side.

"I'll get a rag and wipe that off." Their grandmother left the parlour saying, as she went, "now be sure to listen out for the phone."

"Aye, aye, cap'n." Facetiously, their grandfather cupped a hand to his ear and winked.

They sat there silent, expectant. Their grandmother returned with a rag, wiped the remains of the bluebottle away and began to stack up the supper things. Again she left the room, again she returned, this time without the flowered apron that had covered her polka-dot dress. She sat in her accustomed place, glanced round the table, said "we'll do the washing up after the phone call," and lapsed into silence.

After what seemed an age, during which David kept imagining he heard the phone begin to stir in its cradle, their grandfather said as he looked from one to the other of them, "I hope you give your mother a good report of your gran and me. We can give a gold-star report on you two, can't we?"

"We certainly can."

"Thank you for having us," Sarah said. Her words were enunciated with rehearsed care. "And Archie is a lot better now."

"Well, we're pleased to hear that."

"I didn't like the look of him when we left home," Sarah explained to her grandfather. "He was covered in spots."

"Was he, indeed. What colour spots?"

Sarah rolled her eyes at such an imbecilic question. "Red of course." Then, as a concession, she added, "although I had to look carefully to see them all."

"Hard to spot the spots." He smiled briefly at David who more from politeness than any pleasure smiled back.

Once more silence took hold. A sudden gust of wind banged into the windows, made them all jump.

David began to whistle and at once stopped. "Whistling in the dark," his grandfather said, and David said, "Jay says I whistle like Bob White."

"Bob White?" the adults said together, plainly mystified.

"An American bandleader. But he plays old-fashioned music."

"I expect it would be right up our street."

And speaking over her husband, their grandmother said "And you say your Jay — Mr Krassner — prefers jazz?"

Nodding, David began to list the bands to whose music Jay had introduced him. "And his favourite drummer is called Dave Tough," he said by way of finishing the catalogue of names.

"He calls David tough guy," Sarah said, and giggled. "Tough guy, tough guy, poke your eye and make you cry."

"Don't be silly," David said, feeling himself redden.

And then, at last, the phone rang.

"It's mum, it's mum," Sarah shouted, beginning to clamber down from her chair. But her grandmother put out a restraining hand. "Let granddad answer it first. We don't know for sure that it's your mother." He was already in the hall.

But Sarah wasn't to be held back. One foot on the ground, she swivelled awkwardly to face her grandmother, hands behind her as she gripped the chair back. "I shall tell her she's late," she said, "we might have been in bed when she phoned. And then we couldn't have talked to her."

"If it *is* mum."

Red-faced she turned on David. "Of course it's her. Don't be so stupid." She let go of her chair, tried to push it away and it tilted and fell back on the parlour floor. "Now look what you've made me do." She was close to tears.

David got off his own chair and went round to the other side of the table, intending to pick Sarah's up, but as he did so their grandfather came in shutting to door behind him. They watched as he sat down, looked first at his wife then the other two and said, "your mother couldn't stay on the phone, I'm afraid."

Sarah's mouth opened wide in disbelief. Then her lips came together, began to pucker. "But she *said* we could speak to her. She *promised*." Her voice became a wail of protest, of dismay.

"Never mind, pet, you'll see her tomorrow." And her grandmother reached out to draw the little girl to her, smoothing her hair as Sarah hid her face in the polka-dot dress.

"I'm afraid there's been a change of plan."

David looking at his grandfather, saw at the edge of his vision Sarah's body become rigid, her grandmother's hand cease its movement.

"What on earth do you mean?"

"I mean that Jean can't after all be at the station tomorrow," he said to his wife. "But of course," and now he looked at David, "your mum's taken good care that there'll be someone to meet you. Mrs Rayner. And you'll be staying with her — but only for tomorrow night." He spoke the last words quickly, with what he no doubt hoped was a reassuring smile, for now Sarah had spun round in her grandmother's arms and was staring at him, eyes wide, appalled.

"Staying with Mrs Rayner?" she shouted. "But I don't *want* to stay with her. I want to be at home. I *hate* not being at home."

"That's rude," David said, though privately he felt the same as Sarah.

"What's happened?" his grandmother asked, ignoring Sarah's outburst. "Why on earth can't Jean meet them?" Suddenly, her expression changed from bewilderment to consternation. She looked at her husband in panic, put a hand to her mouth. "Oh, no," she said, "no". And hearing her indrawn breath, seeing the look in her eyes, David felt a chill run through his body.

But his grandfather shook his head. "No, it's not Stephen," he said. Then, to the children, "it's not your dad who's … who's in trouble."

Their grandmother let out her breath. "Thank God for that," she said softly, then, "but in that case who … ?"

"A friend of Jean's, apparently, who needs her — needs your mother to be at her side for a couple of nights. I guess it's a lost husband or son. Who knows?" He spoke half to his wife, half to David, for Sarah, head buried in her grandmother's lap, was now sobbing uncontrollably.

"Shshsh, pet." She bent her head over her granddaughter's while David watched, forlorn.

"Just be thankful it's not your dad who's come to harm," his grandmother said. She lifted her gaze enquiringly to her husband, who was staring at her in silent dismay. Then, placing a hand under Sarah's chin she gently raised her granddaughter's head until she could look into her eyes. "Come now, pet, dry your tears and we'll get you upstairs to bed. Whatever happens, you've an early start tomorrow." She rapped softly on the table with the knuckles of her free hand. "Touch wood you'll never know the sorrow that your mum's going to be coping with." And, with an attempt at humour, "we'll have to stick your name tags on your noses, in case Mrs Rayner doesn't recognise you." But the only response to this was a further wail from Sarah.

"It's all *his* fault," she said.

* * *

He woke in what at first seemed pitch blackness. Raising his head from the pillow, he saw the strip of light under their bedroom door. Sarah, worn out by her crying fit, was asleep in her bed under the curtained window, its outline shaped by the merest glimmer of moonlight. He eased himself out of bed and, lino cold to his bare feet, tiptoed across to the door, slowly, slowly, turned the handle and slowly, slowly, teeth clenched, edged it open. A pause, but Sarah did not stir.

Sitting on the top stair, hugging himself against the landing's draughts, he stared down to where the parlour door, ajar for night sounds, leaked soft yellow light across the hall floor. The light outlined the small table on which stood the telephone and, further along, two suitcases, ready packed, over which his and Sarah's coats were draped.

His grandparents' voices were mere mutterings, part of a medley of sounds, the creak of chair-springs, leaves chafing against windows in the night wind and, far across the fields, the strange, scratchy cry of a bird, hunting or being hunted.

But then, as his ears grew accustomed to the night, he found he could hear his grandmother's voice, could distinguish her words.

"It isn't like her, it isn't right. First she doesn't come with them and now ... . " But at that point the voice, which been had been raised in fretful perplexity, tailed away into silence.

His grandfather's reply was low, a mere murmur, no word audible. If it was intended to reassure it failed to do so.

"And what did Sarah mean, 'It's all *his* fault.' *Whose* fault?"

Again, his grandfather's reply was too low for him to make out the words.

It was followed by silence, as though the two of them had retreated into their own thoughts. Suddenly there was the sound of a chair being pushed back. A second later David was under the bedclothes and watching breathlessly through half-closed eyelids the shape of his grandfather's head looming round the bedroom door.

"David, Sarah, either of you awake?" But the words were spoken so softly that he knew he hadn't been detected. It was a routine check. A pause, then the head withdrew and the door silently closed.

In the fretful dark, unable or unwilling to sleep, he lay thinking about his grandmother's question. It's all *his* fault. What had Sarah meant by those words? She couldn't know. Well, *he* knew, at least he thought he did. Those words his sister had flung at him on that occasion when he'd taunted her for being scared of the dragonfly came crawling out of hiding once more, and it was as though his skin burnt at their touch. "Anyway, you needn't think Jay is *your* friend," she'd said. "It's mum he comes to see, not you."

CHAPTER FOURTEEN

Lying beneath the fig tree's shade, Stephen raised his head to stare briefly around him. The hutments' tarry, acrid, blistery smell, like burnt toffee, together with the shimmer of corrugated roofs, suggested that at any moment they might burst into flame. Between them and where he sprawled, the sandy parade ground was empty except for a single soldier who, in singlet and shorts, was choosing to do press ups, his rhythmic grunts carrying across the stalky grass bleached white as raffia, the few clumps of dried-out bushes. Squinting against the sun's glare, Stephen at last recognised the man. "Fists" Francolis, a boxer who a few years previously, so rumour went, had won several "eliminators" for the British middle-weight championship, and who now took pains to keep himself fit for when he could return to London and once again take up his career.

"Fists" was one of the soldiers on the island who before the war had been professional sportsmen. "You could make up a bloody good first-division team from some of the lads we've got here," Stephen was told on more than one occasion, but as he didn't follow football the reeled-off names meant nothing to him. Some he thought he recognised from cigarette cards, though he couldn't be sure. One or two, he was assured, had been at the top, others on their way there. The same was apparently true of Francolis. But "he'll be too old after this is over," some sceptic commented, and when reminded that a good old 'un could always beat a novice, replied that it depended how old that was and how long the bloody war would go on.

"Fists" was in his late twenties. If Hitler could be seen off inside the next two years, "Fists" would still be in his prime. That, anyway, was what was opined by some of those who claimed an understanding of the fight game or what they called the noble art of self-defence. And to the suggestion that there were plenty of ex-boxers among the Bevin Boys who were waiting their chance to throw away their miners' lamps and hammer the likes of "Fists," they replied that working down a pit might add brawn but it didn't do anything for your brain except fill it with coal dust. Besides, their man not merely knew how to look after himself physically but he was artful as a wagonload of monkeys when it came to using the tricks you needed to keep you out of trouble— thumb in an opponent's eye, arm round his back to draw him onto an uppercut, a crafty jab in the goolies; though how this squared with boxing being a noble art wasn't explained.

Francolis, having completed his press-up routine, was now running on the spot, arms stretched taut above his head, then down, followed by windmilling, backwards, forwards, first one, then the other, then both arms together. Merely to watch him made Stephen feel dizzy. Labouring into an upright position, each slow movement enough to start a trickle of perspiration that gummed his body to the shirt he'd put on fresh that morning, he propped his spine against the fig tree and reached into his shirt pocket for Jean's half-read letter.

Earlier, over breakfast, he'd been forced to abandon his reading when Dave Morris arrived with orders, so he said, from "up top." They were to drive over to Valetta to pick up replacement parts for a couple of trucks that might soon be needed as part of the Italian campaign.

"Now?"

"Or sooner," Dave said, mock-posh. "Convoy came in last night, unloading's well under way, can't lose a minute, got to get this war jolly well won … These two trucks may make all the difference, Morris." He grinned affably at Stephen, who swallowed the remains of his tea and, as he stood, pushed the hastily-folded letter into his pocket.

"Everything hunky dory on the home front, sarge?," Dave asked.

"Of course."

Now, balancing the sheets of paper between fingertips to avoid blurring the ink with his sweat, he found the place where he'd had to break off.

They'll be happy as Larry without me being there to boss them about. I took them as far as Leicester where they had to change trains and, as arranged, mum was already waiting to collect them and take them on from there. (The plan is to reverse roles for the return journey. Mum will bring them as far as Leicester where I'll meet them.) Sarah was a bit mopey at the start but as soon as she saw her gran waving to her on the platform tears turned to smiles. When the Peterborough train came in she could hardly wait to get on board. I phone them nearly every evening from the box up the road and can tell that they're having a whale of a time. Our daughter in particular will love getting her grandparents to do her bidding and they're of course delighted to have the kids to themselves for a few weeks. The truth is that the break will be good for us all. I sometimes worry that the three of us have become too dependent on each other — no, I don't mean that, but as I'm the only adult here the children inevitably rely on me more than is good for them. They'll enjoy having other grown ups to talk to, to give them a different slant on things.

Not that I plan to twiddle my thumbs while they're away. In fact, I'll be hard at work re-decorating their rooms which, believe me, are in need of brightening! I've decided that new paint means a new world, new beginnings, the fresh start we all want. [That sentence had been scratched through] *So I managed to buy some cans of Co-op paint with tokens I've hoarded over the past three years. Sarah came with me and we chose green for the woodwork in her room, while David is to have blue. Beth Morton's promised to lend me their step-ladder and Next-Door — Robin's mother that is — has come up trumps with some spare brushes because, oh dear, ours when I rescued them from where they'd been hiding under the stairs were stiff as boards and beyond use.*

Poor Robin! He's been rather hanging around since our pair went. I've found him loitering in our garden on several occasions, almost as though he expected to summon the ghost of David to keep him company. I've taken pity on him, given him a few odd jobs, running up to the shops, tidying the back garden, and he's done them all and come back for more. His mother says he misses his dad, who's in aeroplane reconnaissance somewhere, as of course ours miss theirs, but I suppose because Robin is an only child that makes matters worse. And then there's the fact that his mother is away quite a lot — supposedly visiting a "sister" — which means that Robin has to rely for company on his gran. From time to time I see the pair of them up in the village, Robin carrying the old lady's leather bag which clinks as though she'd got a mobile off-licence stored in it! Not much fun for the poor boy. No doubt he's aching for David's return.

He tilted his head up to study the underside of the leaves above him, black against the ferocious sun. Mine eyes, they dazzle. Breathing in the fig tree's dark, sweet odour, his hands steady, he turned the page and found himself at once confronted by her closing words. She sent him all her love. *Jean.*

After a pause, during which he studied the words as though trying to decipher a secret message they withheld, he allowed the letter to fall to the bare earth beside him. Only when he had reached for and lit a cigarette could he bring himself to take up and look again at the brief last page. *All my love. Jean.*

All my love, Jean. Smoke trickled through his nostrils and he watched as it thinned and vanished in the heat. The cigarette tasted grittily stale. His mouth was dry.

All her love. Wasn't that enough? Well, no, it wasn't. Something was lacking from those closing words. The endearment felt somehow routine, formal rather than genuine. Why not the ending he was used to, words that told him how much he was missed, how greatly she wanted him at home.

He drew in more smoke, shaded his eyes against the sky's glare, tried to wriggle his shoulders into a more comfortable position. But the ground was resistant, inhospitable, unyielding.

Then it came to him. Use your grey cells. Jean's letter was a mixture of hope and fear. Hope for the future. A fresh start. She meant what she said. But at the same time she must fear that even this simple act of painting the kids' rooms could be tempting providence. How much longer might the Germans hold out? And what of the Japanese? Few signs that the Nips thought they might be on the losing side. Splash paint over old walls, by all means, announce a coming gaiety, but keep the lid screwed down on extravagant dreams. No talk of a new world, of new beginnings, not until this bloody war was over and they could be together again.

Cigarette clamped between his teeth, he became more than ever aware of the army shirt pasted to his arms and body, the sweat pooling at collarbone and armpit, and as he did so Sarah's question as reported by Jean came back to him. "What does daddy look like?" What indeed. A red-faced, perspiring soldier in a far off place, ill-at-ease in his uniform, loathing army life and longing for an England that would in all probability have changed beyond recognition when he once more saw it.

If he once more saw it. No, think no more of that. Think instead of what his daughter would look like when he next saw her. But, try as he might, he couldn't. All he knew was that the girl he hoped to see would be very different from the tot, not long out of infancy, he had left behind. And David? He too, would have changed.

Would they be strangers to one another? Well, yes, they would, at first, anyway. No doubt about it. He loved receiving the brief letters his son enclosed with Jean's, but their dutiful plainness gave no clue to the writer's personality, which was in a way what made them so heartbreaking. *I like playing at cricket and going on walks with Robin. We found an old hut in the woods but could not see inside. School is alright. I am learning to play the drums properly now and Mum says that when you are home I must give you a concert.* Underneath that most recent note, Jean had written "*He really **is** improving, though goodness only knows how we can get hold of a proper set of drums for him (or "kit" as Krassner calls it). I took your advice and managed to find a copy of **Robinson Crusoe** for his birthday, a rather well-illustrated one. Not the whole gubbins, but plenty for a nine-year old to get his teeth into. I doubt, though, that it will replace **Treasure Island** as his favourite book. Goodness knows how many times he's read that.*

And then Jean. The woman he loved. Would she, too, have changed? Time hath, my lord a wallet on his back, In which he puts alms for oblivion.

Perhaps. But he at least would never forget that afternoon when in the ruined garden at Mapledurham she had unloosed the scarlet ribbon that bound her hair and stepped across to him, so purely beautiful that now, as then, it took his breath away. Could such a moment die? To one mind, never.

Involuntarily, his body stiffened. Suppose any of them should die before he was able to see them again. "It's not possible." He looked around to see whether anyone had heard his involuntary utterance. But the place was empty. Francolis had disappeared from his exercise spot on the parade ground, and in the battering Maltese heat not even the cicadas could manage more than a low buzz, like a dentist's drill winding dully down.

It's not possible, he told himself again. The bombing raids had ceased, and while, as Jean complained, this meant that there was less reason to draw the curtains so that in the double summer-time now in operation it was difficult to get the children to believe their bedtime had arrived — "But mum," Sarah had apparently protested one evening when being chivvied upstairs, "the sun hasn't even had it's *tea* yet" — they were safe from the Luftwaffe as, for the last two years, they had been safe from fears of invasion.

How different from when he'd been posted to Africa. Then, he and all the men who went with him knew they were leaving behind people jittery with dread that storm troopers might at any moment be stepping up onto English soil. It was a dread those bound for Egypt took with them, one neatly summed up by the man who, as they docked at Alexandria, said to Stephen, "if I have to fight fucking Fritz I'd rather do it on a fucking English beach than fucking foreign sand."

At least those fears had gone. There were even rumours that coastal defences were being relaxed and beaches cleared of land mines and the endless rolls of barbed wire intended to delay if not prevent stormtroopers from goose-stepping along every high street.

Except that death wasn't merely doled out by an enemy falling from the sky or clambering across beaches, an advancing tide of field-grey uniform. There were accidents, there were illnesses.

Even in Siggiewi's depleted camp, men would from time to time report the deaths of those "safe" in England. One had lost a nephew to asthma, another mourned a brother, a Bevin Boy, crushed by a fallen pit-prop, cancer had taken someone's father. They also die who only sit and wait. All over Europe now people were waiting for an end to the war, and it occurred to him that as they waited so they would be holding their breath, newly cautious, terrified of being betrayed by an upsurge of optimism they simply daren't acknowledge, even to themselves. They had come so far, it would be cruel to be denied at the last, like a spent swimmer who thinks he's reached landfall and then finds that the rock onto which he's hauled himself is crumbling beneath him. No wonder Jean was frightened of putting into words hopes that might, as people said, tempt providence. He had been too unguarded in his recent letters, too full of his plans or at least hopes for their future. In his next letter he would take care to speak only of the present.

* * *

He woke to find Derek Southern looming over him. Blinking as he tried to shield his eyes from sun that was now lancing through the tree's canopy, he said, or tried to say, "I could do with a beer," but managed no more than a croak. He pulled himself awkwardly into a sitting position, still groggy with sleep, peered at his watch. Four o'clock. He'd been spark out, as Dave would say, for the best part of two hours. Working some saliva into his mouth, he managed to ask whether there was anything he could do for the young man looking down with concern at where he lay.

"You could try staying out of the sun, sarge, for a start." The words blended rebuke with concern. "Get roasted in this oven, it could give you heat stroke, melt your brains."

Stephen grunted assent. Then slowly from a crouch he hauled himself upright and stepped out, staggered rather, from what remained of the fig tree's shadow. Black dots spawned in front of his eyes. "A beer," he said again, "that's what I need."

"We should be able to manage one," Southern said, making to

take Stephen's arm. "You alright, sarge, you look a bit done in."

"I'm fine," Stephen said, straightening up and, as he did so, throwing off the last of the dream he only now realised had so disturbed him, a dream of arriving home to find his house a smoking ruin, rubble and splintered woodwork naked under a grey sky, nobody there, all gone, the road where the house had stood itself empty of movement. Blinking away the sweat that stung his eyes, he looked about him. The usual. Huts, parade ground, wire perimeter fence interrupted by the guard post where nobody stirred, the flag pole from which the union jack drooped in abject listlessness. This was the reality of his waking life, this dun aridity was where, for the moment at least, he belonged, under a sky whose metal sheen seemed to seal in the intolerable afternoon heat.

From the back of the encampment, where the workshops had been erected, came the dull, flat clatter of hammer on steel as someone adjusted a cam shaft or straightened an axle. A tiny lizard quivered at his foot before its needle-shadow vanished into the tree's shade.

"Let's get out of this," he said. His voice, he noticed, had returned to normal. He led the way towards the mess canteen. "Even if we can't get a drink we'll at least be out of the sun."

They pushed through the mosquito-netted doorway and stood for a moment, letting their eyes grow accustomed to the gloom. Stephen tugged at the arms and then back of his short-sleeved shirt, working to free his flesh from its clammy hold. A swim was what he most needed, but the nearest beach was a couple of miles off and he wasn't going to walk there, not in this heat. Maybe later, after dinner, he'd get away, wash the sweat and dust from his body. After which he ought to drop in on Maria, who would have ready for him some fresh-laundered shirts and underwear. Then a visit to Marcus, perhaps.

Which reminded him. Southern. He'd not really answered the question. *Did* he want anything of Stephen? And if so, what?

As though in reply to Stephen's unvoiced words, the younger man said, "I've got a bit of a problem, sarge. Let me get some beers and I'll tell you about it."

He sauntered away, disappeared through an open door into the kitchens, leaving Stephen to choose a table far from the kitchen smells where the two of them could sit over their drinks. He sat watching Southern as the youth — he really wasn't more than that — returned, thumbs over the open tops of the beer bottles clasped in each hand. He moved with the kind of casual energy which suggested that he was ready, in the words of some novelist whose name Stephen couldn't for the moment recall, to meet life more than half way.

"You know," he said, as Southern sat down facing him and pushed a bottle of ice-cold beer into his hand, "if you described this place to someone who hadn't seen it, you could make it sound like paradise. We may be in the army, we may be in a war, but what have we actually got? Sea, sun, a little tinkering with clapped-out motor vehicles and bikes, and for the rest nothing to do but drink beer." He raised his bottle and drank from it.

Southern did the same, swallowed, then set the bottle down and looked long and steadily at Stephen. "I'd say that's near enough Paradise, yeh."

"No it isn't," Stephen said, "it's bloody boring."

"Try telling that to the troops up north."

From the kitchens came the sounds of saucepan lids being thrown onto metal surfaces and someone beat out a tattoo on what was probably a standard-issue can of beans.

Southern sniffed the air. "Now what tells me that tonight we'll be offered sausages, accompanied I shouldn't wonder by boiled potatoes, carrots, beans and all drowned in gravy you could use to build a mud hut. It beats me. Don't they *know* how to cook anything else?"

"It's what gets sent, I suppose."

"You mean some brass-hat bastard in London looks up Malta and says 'ho, yus, what those chaps in the Med need is a good hot meal.' Reckon the lads on Arctic convoys get to tuck into salads and ice-cream?"

"Oddly enough, food isn't what I want to think about at the present moment, Derek. It's finishing this beer, then having another. Oh, and I'm waiting for you to tell me about your problem."

Southern nodded, took a further swig, then, brushing his forearm along his mouth, said, "Ok, sarge, I'll come to the point. Have you heard anything about possible movements? I mean, have you heard anything of plans to shift us from this little number?"

"No." And, because Southern was looking at him with a half-disbelieving smile, Stephen added, "as far as I know, we're here for the duration. Why? What have you heard?"

"There's rumours flying about of a new posting for us all." And seeing Stephen's look of disbelief, he said, "Well, it makes sense. I mean, we're sod all use here. Besides, we're being run down, aren't we. Every day more of the lads are being sent to the mainland. Soon enough there won't be anyone left."

He finished his beer, pushed back his chair and stood. "I'll get two more of these."

While he was gone, Stephen shook out the last drops of his beer onto the back of his hand then licked them up, relishing the slightly sour, brackish taste, and thought about what Southern had said. Rumours abounded here as no doubt everywhere in the army. But he couldn't believe that Malta would be left undefended. Valetta, where ships and subs on duty in the Med came to coal up, to get refitted and repaired, and through which armour and much else besides passed on its way to the Italian campaign, *had* to be safeguarded. Besides, as he'd recently discovered, the island was being used as a base for training Balkan resistance groups. So no, the rumours had to be wrong.

"I reckon you've got Malta fever," he said, lightly enough, as he and Southern clinked the new bottles slippery with moisture from the canteen fridge. "Otherwise known as Anna. Am I Right?"

Southern took a minute to lower his bottle and when he did he studied it carefully rather than meet Stephen's gaze.

"I'm taking Instruction, see," he eventually said. "We're planning on getting married, but now all these rumours about how our lot's going to be off up Italy ... Well."

"So what's the problem? Oh, no, you haven't ... "

"No," Southern said, jerking his head up to look straight at Stephen. "I haven't. Anna's OK. I told you. It's a problem, not a crisis." He paused, took a deep breath and then drank some more beer. "Only the point is that if we're shunted out of here before I've finished my Instruction I can't get hooked. I've got to be proper RC or her old man won't let me marry her. It's that simple."

"It sounds pretty complicated to me," Stephen said. "This love will undo us all."

"Come again?"

"Sorry," Stephen said, "it's from Shakespeare. *Troilus and Cressida*. Love in a time of war." Then, waving away his momentary melancholy, he added, "and there are consequences, you know, of joining the Roman church."

"Like no johnies."

"That's certainly one."

"Not a problem for me," Southern said, grinning. "I like children."

"So do I," Stephen said, "I've got two of my own."

"And missing them, no doubt."

"More than I can say."

"And your wife."

For a moment, suddenly unable to speak, he merely nodded. But when the rush of emotion that seized and shook him had quietened, he said, to change the subject, "these rumours usually have as much substance as a fistful of fog. Where did this one come from?"

"It's all over camp," Southern said. He finished his beer, put the bottle carefully down on the table and watched a fly as it struggled to find a way out of a ring of condensation where the bottle had previously sat. "According to what I've heard, plans are pretty far advanced. A big convoy's expected any day now and it'll be loading us plus lorries etcetera on board for Naples, that's what the blokes reckon. Some of 'em say they can't wait to get shot of this place." He laughed briefly. "Me, I can wait for ever."

Stephen looked at the fly. Was it dead? No, it twitched suddenly, resumed the scramble to escape its fate. He doubted the rumour, but still … "I wouldn't mind a bit more by way of action," he found himself saying.

"I thought you'd had enough of that in Africa."

"Africa seems a long time ago."

He looked at Southern, saw his eyes, even in the gloom of the canteen, large, watchful, alert with what seemed a mixture of concern and foreboding. "I joined up to help defeat fascism. We're not doing much of it, are we, twiddling our thumbs in this place. You know, Derek, the other week when we waved those partisans off for Yugoslavia I half wished I was going with them. And I don't suppose I was the only one."

Southern, elbows on table, chin cupped in his hands, stared at the table, muttered something inaudible.

"What?"

"I said the poor sods are probably all dead by now."

Then, deciding to meet Stephen's eye, he said, more reasonably, "I know those bastard Nazis have got to be done for, but to be straight with you, sarge, when this bloody war is finally over I want to be still alive."

His voice took on a new note, half aggressive, half pleading. "I've got something to live for, see."

Stephen drank the last of his beer. "Haven't we all," he said.

CHAPTER FIFTEEN

The train wheezed and shuddered to a stop and along the platform Mrs Rayner's fleshy bulk emerged from shrouds of steam. She was wrapped in a heavy, dark-woollen coat, although the storms of yesterday had, as their grandfather said when he kissed them goodbye, blown themselves out, and today was warm with the scent of harvested wheat that drifted through the open carriage windows as the train shuffled its stopping course from Peterborough to Leicester.

Sarah, gripping her grandmother's hand, held back, but David, running despite the suitcase banging beside him, managed to dodge between slower moving passengers, until he reached Mrs Rayner's substantial side.

"Hello, pet." She put an arm round him, and then, smiling toward the other two who were making their way forward, "so this is your gran. We'll have to hurry, I'm afraid," she said as they shook hands, "the Hinckley train's due in any moment." And so, after a redistribution of luggage, the four of them climbed the railway bridge, the two women exchanging small talk, Sarah, with Archie wedged firmly under her arm, dragging on the far side of her grandmother, unwilling to let go of her hand.

But a few minutes later, after hurried farewells, they all three found seats on the train now leaving the red-brick houses of Leicester behind.

And a little later, time enough for David to unpin from his pullover the label his grandmother had insisted he wore and to tell Mrs Rayner that, yes, they'd had a good time at their grandparents and yes, the weather had mostly been good, they were yet again pulling into a station, theirs, Sarah prepared to let Mrs Rayner lift her down from the carriage but, a sullen "thank you" apart, which was anyway addressed more to her bear, not yet ready to speak.

It was only as they made their way out through the booking-hall that she said, "are we going home by taxi?"

"We're not going home," David began to explain, but Mrs Rayner cut across his words. "I thought we'd go to a nice place I know for some tea and then take the bus back. An end of holiday treat. How would you like that?"

Sarah's face began to redden and her lip quivered. "I'm not hungry," she said, and, after a pause, "nor is Archie."

She was still buttoned into her coat which, despite her grandmother's repeated suggestions, she had refused to take off. Now, hot, disconsolate, she was on the verge of tears.

"We had sandwiches on the train," David said as they stood uncertainly in the empty station forecourt. "And home-made tarts that gran brought with us. Lemon curd."

"So your stomachs are full?" Mrs Rayner was at last removing her coat, beneath which she now revealed a grass-green silk dress with dark stains under the armpits. Tucking behind her ears strands of the thick black hair which she wore in a bun, her wide, white-powdered face with dark eyes surveying both children in turn, she said, "Sarah, pet, won't you feel better if you take your coat off, like me?"

By way of an answer Sarah said, "Can Archie have a teacake?"

"If we can find him one, pet, he can have it for sure."

And in the café, Sarah behaved impeccably, feeding toasted teacake to Archie, even consulting David about which slice of sponge he'd prefer before choosing the one she wanted. On a previous occasion, when they'd been to this same café with their mother, Sarah had complained bitterly to her that "David has left me the cake I didn't have my eye on," but this time there was no such complaint. And later, on the bus back to the village, Sarah seemed entirely content, bouncing Archie on her knee and getting him to wave at people and a fieldful of sheep they passed as they turned into their own road.

But once inside the Rayner's house her mood swung round. They followed Mrs Rayner into the front living room, the light here dim from velvet-brown window drapes, and while David sat obediently on the edge of one of the easy chairs, its stiff grey material, like the texture of the carriage seats in the trains they had been on, rasping against the backs of his legs, Sarah stood on the blue-and-grey patterned carpet in the middle of the room, rocking Archie in her arms. "Archie wants to go home," she said. Then, avoiding Mrs Rayner's eye, "*I* want to go home." Her voice was muffled; she was once more close to tears.

Breaking off from her announced intention of going to turn down their beds, Mrs Rayner paused. "Sarah, pet, it's just for tonight. You'll see your mum tomorrow." She looked across to David, seeking his help.

"It's an emergency," he said to his sister. "Gran and granddad explained that to us."

Mrs Rayner was now kneeling in front of Sarah, an arm round the little girl's shoulders, looking steadily at her, smile clamped to her lips, the material of her dress, David noticed, strained round her thick thighs and large-bottomed curves.

"Your mum's promised she'll be here as early as she possibly can be. And just think, you've bedrooms as good as new to go back to." She spoke with a determined jollity.

"What emergency?"

Yes, David thought to himself, what emergency? And he, no less than Sarah, looked expectantly at Mrs Rayner.

Mrs Rayner went on smiling. "I'll leave your mum to explain it to you."

"Don't you know?" And then, when the woman got groaningly to her feet without speaking, Sarah said, enunciating the word slowly, experimentally: "ee-mer-gen-cee. I don't know what an ee-mer-gen-cee is. Is it bad?"

"No, I'm sure it's not *that*."

"Then why couldn't she meet us?"

Mrs Rayner opened her mouth but, without a word, closed it again, and for the first time it occurred to David that she didn't know what to say. He thought of the look on the faces of boys asked to explain why they'd scribbled nonsense in their exercise books. That was how Mrs Rayner looked.

Was that made him blurt out a question of his own? "Are the

Saturday tea dances still going on?"

The abruptness of her counter-question startled him.

"Why?" Then, perhaps seeing the alarm in his eyes, she softened her tone. "I mean, why do you ask? Why shouldn't they go on?"

"I just wondered." And, as she looked at him as though searching for a hidden meaning to his words, he said, trying to explain, "I wondered whether you'd want me to help you again now that I'm back. I'd like to." It seemed to him that he had no choice but to go on speaking, that he had to find a way through the entanglements of doubt, of uncertainty, that grew out of her gaze and in which, the more he said, the more he was becoming trapped. "I've missed listening to the music. It wasn't ever on the wireless at granddad's but that's because they only ever listen to the Home Service, so gran says, and she says that granddad doesn't like the other programme, it's not serious."

He was gabbling now. "Brass band stuff or choirs, that's what granddad prefers. Not what Jay ... " He stopped. Why did she seem to think he meant harm by his words?

"Well, there won't be much more of *that*," she said, pausing on the way out of the room, her hand on the door frame.

"Why not?"

Sarah, startled out of her self-communing by the urgency of her brother's voice, looked at him in surprise.

Mrs Rayner had her back to them. "Because the American soldiers have been ordered overseas and I expect their music will be going with them." She turned to face them, fleetingly. "Those that haven't gone already will be out of here by the end of the week. So from now on it'll be as you were. All the records for the Saturday dances will have to come from home stock."

"But what about Jay?"

"Mr Krassner will be off with the rest of them."

"You mean I won't see him again?"

Sighing, she shook her head. "No point in taking on, pet," she said, turning away. "This is war." And she left, pulling the door shut behind her.

"You see," Sarah said, her face buried in Archie's fur and

speaking to her bear so quietly that David could barely hear her words, "it's all *his* fault."

* * *

The next morning, as they were finishing breakfast, they heard a knocking on the front door, at first faint, then louder. Then the doorbell. It was followed by further knocking. "Well," Mrs Rayner said, getting heavily to her feet, "it can't be Michael. Hubbie never forgets his key." She pushed across the newly-opened packet of Force Flakes to David. "Here," she said, trying for jollity, "have another spoonful to help you leap over houses." *High oe'r the fence leaps Sunny Jim. Force is the food that raises him.* He knew the motto but wasn't interested in further cereal.

Sarah too was listening hard as the front door opened. They heard Mrs Rayner's words, "Ah, so you remembered. Come on in, then." They looked enquiringly at each other.

A moment later Robin put his head round the dining-room door, grinning shyly. "Oh, it's *you*," Sarah said, her voice wavering between disappointment and outright dismay. "I was expecting mummy."

"I met Robin yesterday when I was up in the village," Mrs Rayner said, following him into the room, "and he helped me carry my shopping home, didn't you? So I suggested he might like to come here this morning, to welcome his friend back to the village." She sat down behind the teapot as she smiled round at them all. "Though I didn't expect you *quite* so early." She glanced at the clock on the mantelpiece. It was not yet nine o'clock. "Have you had your breakfast?"

Robin nodded without speaking.

"Sure? There's bread and jam."

But Robin wasn't to be tempted.

"In that case," she said as she poured herself a cup of tea, "I've got something you lads can do for me." Swivelling round, she reached for the notepaper on the dresser behind her chair. "Here's a list I made last night." David saw Robin stare wonderingly at the ring-encrusted finger with which she tapped the paper. "Rings belong to Hetty Rayner as pegs belong to a gypsy," she'd once told him. "The only difference is, I'm not selling."

"You can get everything on this list from the Co-op," she now explained, "give yourselves a couple of hours to play, no longer, and by then your mum will be here, David. My Co-op number's written at the bottom of the page." She winked at him. "By the time I get round to claiming my divi. I'll be worth a fortune."

"Really? When will that be?" Sarah was genuinely interested.

"About the same time as Tessie O'Shea gets to be queen of England." Mrs Rayner swallowed her tea in one gulp and got to her feet. "And while you're gone, Sarah and I will do some baking, won't we, pet."

* * *

As Robin led the way along the narrow baulk age between hedge and Farmer Record's beets, he called over his shoulder, "You heard about Neville Fox?"

"No."

"It's all round the village. His dad got killed. Him and his mum have gone to stay at their gran's."

"Where's that?"

"Dunno. Miles away. Anyway, he won't be back for the rest of the summer." He turned to face David. "The gang's disappeared, too." His smile turned to a grin. "Got the fields to ourselves."

"Where was his dad killed?"

"Italy, I think. Hey, want to see some sticklebacks?" Robin began to run, the shopping bag Mrs Rayner had given him trailing behind. David followed.

Soon, out of breath but triumphant in their new-found sense of freedom, they leant side by side on the wooden bridge, Robin pointing down into the tea-brown water where, he claimed, the fish could be seen.

But each flash that David thought might be a stickleback was a sliver of sunlight.

"They're quick," Robin said, chin resting on his hands as he stared into the water. "Too quick to catch, but I've seen them alright."

Then, after a moment's silence in which they both leant over the bridge's rail, Robin whispered "Look. There." And now David could see flashes among strands of water weed.

"How do you know they're sticklebacks?"

"Because when they flip over you can see they've got red bellies. And I'll tell you another thing. They build nests."

"What, like birds? Have you seen one?"

"No," reluctantly. "But old Godwin told me about them when we was at choir practice last week. Turns out he knows heaps about fish." Robin turned away, began to walk up the long field. "Come on, let's get to the village."

But David, walking beside his friend through the freshly-cut wheat field, wasn't ready to let the subject go. "*Godwin?* Talking to *you*? He's never spoken to me except to tell me off."

"I know, but he was alright last Thursday. Must be a change in the weather. He even laughed at one of Bert Mee's jokes."

"I wonder what put him in a good mood all of a sudden?" A possible explanation came to him. "I bet he'd heard that the Americans are going."

"Yeh," Robin said casually, "that's probably it. He hates the Yanks, he does." The pair of them walked on for a few moments in silence, their sandaled feet scuffing up a thick carpet of strawy dust.

"They turned up at church again last Sunday," Robin said. "All of 'em. A proper parade, we had, band, flags. The vicar said a special prayer for their safety. Bert Mee says he reckons they'll need it where they're going."

David looked about him. Three weeks ago this field had been shoulder-high in wheat, now sheaves stood in groups like miniature straw hutments. Sparrows, starlings, pigeons, all pecked about the stubble-wrack in brief fraternity, unfussed by the boys' passing. Everywhere was the warm, sweet smell of harvest. But the field looked bare, wounded.

"Was Jay — Mr Krassner — at church?" David eventually asked.

"That bloke who's been coming to your house?" Robin pretended to consider. "No, I don't think so. I didn't see him if he was."

They arrived at Farmer Bailey's field, hoisted themselves onto the stile and peered about to see if the bull was anywhere within sight.

And mum, had she been at church? But no, he couldn't bring himself to ask that.

* * *

He heard her voice as soon as he stepped through the Rayner's back door. It came from the front room. In reply to some deep-toned question from Hetty Rayner, his mother said, "Oh, no, you've done quite enough. We'll manage."

Manage what?

"If you're sure." Mrs Rayner again. "But Michael can usually get hold of extra sugar."

Then Sarah's voice cut in. "Mummy, mummy, I want to tell you about the wasps at granny's."

"In a minute, darling."

"Not in a minute. Now."

"As soon as we get home you can tell me all about your holiday."

He stood in the kitchen doorway, listening hard. What held him back? Why this sudden reluctance to join them? Did her voice sound different? Would she look the same?

While he hesitated, the back door opened and behind him a voice said, "Hello, young man."

Michael Rayner was in his factory overalls. As David made to speak, the man dropped his brown trilby onto the small kitchen table and raked fingers through his mass of thick, grey curls.

"I've been shopping for Mrs Rayner," David said, feeling the need to explain his presence, then, realising he was whispering, added more loudly, "I've only just got back."

"And been beaten to it by your mother." Smiling, Mr Rayner jerked his head in the direction of the front room as they heard her voice raised in mock protest at something Sarah must have said. "Well, it's up to us men to break up the parliament of women if I'm going to have any lunch today." Like his wife, Mr Rayner pronounced *have* as *haff.*

Hetty Rayner was already on her feet when the two of them entered the front room. Beyond and almost behind her, his mother sat on the sofa, her dark-blue jacket contrasting oddly with the salmon-pink cushions on either side of her upright body, Sarah on her lap, an arm round her mother's neck, cheek pressed against hers.

Nerving himself to meet her gaze, he found her eyes fixed steadily on his. Slowly her face relaxed into a smile and he saw that her lipstick was slightly smudged. "Hello, my love," she said. "I hear that you and Robin have been making yourselves useful."

Still not trusting himself to speak, he nodded, then, at last finding his voice, began to tell Mrs Rayner that he had left her shopping in the kitchen. She acknowledged this with a brief smile before, explaining to his mother that her husband was on early shift, she flapped her hands in his face, saying as she did so "Now, then, Michael, shoo, shoo. Out of here and I'll see to your food." As the couple left, Mrs Rayner pulled the door shut behind her.

Only then did he allow himself to see his mother's outstretched arm. He let her pull him in and kiss him on the cheek. Gazing into her eyes, he saw the violet shadows under them.

"You look tired," he said, more abruptly than he meant.

An expression he didn't understand flickered across her face and was gone, but before she could speak, Sarah said, "Our bedrooms have been painted and we can go and look at them, can't we?" She jumped off her mother's lap and began to pull at her free arm. "Come on, I want to go home. Now."

"When you've both thanked Mrs Rayner for looking after you."

They trooped into the kitchen. Michael Rayner was standing at the table, picking at a plate of cold meat, lettuce and tomatoes, while Mrs Rayner busied herself at the gas stove.

She turned as they made their entrance, wiped her hands on the flowered apron she'd wrapped round herself, stooped to embrace the children and then, altogether more tenderly, drew their mother into her arms. "You're sure you'll be alright?" she said, her voice little more than a whisper.

"Yes, yes, I'll be fine now I've got these two scamps to worry about." But it was the briefest of smiles.

Hetty Rayner came with them to the front door. "Be sure to let me know if you need me," she said, wrenching it open, then followed them down the path to the front gate, which she clicked shut behind them. He turned to wave goodbye and saw the expression of concern as she watched them go.

As he and his mother, carrying their luggage between them, turned in at their own open gate — Sarah, running ahead, was already within the porch, jumping up and down while calling out "Hurry, Hurry" — David asked his mother, "is your friend better?"

She looked down at him, bewildered. Then, her expression clearing, she said, "Oh, yes, right as rain. A great relief." Though her strained smile didn't suggest she herself shared in it.

"Where does — where do they live?"

Her mother turned to close the gate behind her. Turning back to where he faced her, her eyes locking on his, she said, "Coventry. Her name is Eve Roberts and she lives in Coventry."

And as though to forestall further questions she pushed ahead of him and silently unlocked the front door, leaving him to consider whether she had ever before mentioned that name. Eve Roberts. He was sure she hadn't.

But inside, with the smell of new paint in their nostrils, Sarah ran ahead of him up the stairs, squealing in delight as she pushed open her bedroom door. "David, David, come and look."

He peered over his sister's shoulder at the newly white walls, the glossy, cabbage-green skirting-board and window frame. "That's really nice," he said, meaning it.

"Nice!" Sarah said scornfully. "it's not *nice*. It's *grogeous*."

"I'm sorry that I haven't had time yet to re-hang your pictures."

Their mother had followed them upstairs, was now standing in the doorway of Sarah's bedroom, smiling at her daughter's glee.

"Doesn't matter," Sarah said, throwing herself onto her bed, where she wriggled onto her back, then rolled over until she fell off the bed, straightened up and ran to hug her mother. "It's *grogeous*," she said again. "Thank you, thank you, mummy," and as her mother bent towards her, she threw her arms round her neck and kissed her extravagantly. "I love you," she said, as she at released her grip. "Now I want to see David's room."

"Ah, now that's a surprise."

And it was. Because she led them to the box room at the back of the house and he saw that in his absence it had become his bedroom. "How did you guess?" he asked, at once amazed and overjoyed as he stepped through the door and, in a few strides, was looking out of the window over the back garden and toward ploughed-up bottom meadow and the hedgerow beyond. Only when he turned back to face the room did he notice that the wallpaper, with its thin, feathery grasses, hadn't been taken down or painted over, and that the woodwork was glossed not in dark but pale blue, so that the room, small though it was, seemed full of light. A cave of light.

"Are you pleased?" his mother asked, anxiously, it seemed.

For a moment, he could only nod. Then, "how did you guess I'd rather be in this room?" he asked, once again looking out of the window.

Standing just inside the door, Sarah in front of her looking silently around, his mother said, "intuition perhaps." He turned to her to speak his gratitude, noticed that she coloured faintly as she said this and made to turn away, and his words were silenced.

Sarah, clinging to her hand said, "poor mummy, doing all this work while were on holiday."

"Luckily I didn't have to do it all. I had some help."

"Who?" they asked together, made curious by the unexpected remark.

She stepped out of the room and from the landing , so that they couldn't see her face, said "Oh, your friend Mr Krassner, David, dropped in once or twice to lend a helping hand. Setting up the back room for you was his idea. He said he was sure you'd want it as your bedroom. You'd prefer the view. Apparently, he had a similar room at home when he was a small boy."

She was going down the stairs now, hand clutching the banister as though she was frightened of losing her foothold, and because her back was turned to him he had to strain hard to hear her words. "He's very fond of you, David."

146

He watched her as she went slowly down. "Is it true what Mrs Rayner says?"

Almost at the bottom of the stairs, she stopped but did not turn. "What does Mrs Rayner say?"

"That the American soldiers are leaving."

In the indistinct light that filtered through the frosted glass above the front door he thought he saw her nod.

"So I won't have any more drum lessons?"

Without shifting her stance she said, the words so faint that he could hardly hear them, "No, I'm afraid not."

"Good," Sarah said from behind him. "I didn't like him coming here."

There was a silence. Then their mother walked briskly through the hall into the kitchen and slammed the door behind her. A moment later they heard the back door open. David leading the way, they tiptoed back into his room and, looking from his window down onto to the patch of grass beyond the greenhouse, saw her standing with her back to them, head tilted upwards, as though she was looking at the sky past bottom meadow. She stayed like that for several minutes, quite still, fists gripped either side of her, body rigid.

It was Sarah who finally spoke. "Mummy's crying," she said.

* * *

In the following few days, days in which his mother seemed to resent all noise about the house and even, he sometimes felt, her children's presence, David stayed outdoors as often and as long as he could, trawling the streams with Robin, venturing up to the village recreation ground for games of cricket, returning home only for meals and at bedtime. Sarah spent long hours alone in her room, dressing up and making stories for herself and her animals to act out, though once at least when he came in for tea he heard their mother singing with her daughter. "Over the Rainbow" it was, and for a while, despite the tune or words or way they sang causing in him an almost unbearable sadness, Sarah's chatter brightened the table, and when she praised Archie's new-found reading skills — "I think he needs a book a day so I'm trying him on the Bible" — they could all laugh, and that night he went to bed happy.

The following day, Saturday, he ran up to the village to help Mrs Rayner with the tea-dance, but without the Americans it wasn't the same. Few locals were in attendance, the dancers, elderly couples mostly, requested waltzes rather than the music he loved, and when the time came to empty the hall and clear away the tea-things, he overheard Mrs Rayner tell one of her helpers that the game was no longer worth the candle.

"Gonna jack it in, then Hetty?"

"That's about the size of it," Mrs Rayner said. "I don't imagine there'll be much wailing or gnashing of teeth in the village about it, will there. I'm not expecting a vote of thanks." He wondered at the short laugh that accompanied these words, its bitterness almost, and at the embarrassed look of the woman to whom she'd spoken.

A few days later he came in to find his mother, chin cupped in hand, staring at the pages of a letter or letters spread on the table in front of her. He stood hesitant in the doorway until, suddenly alert to his presence, she straightened her back, smiled at him, the smile though uncertain, brief, and said, as she handed him one of the sheets of paper, "For you, my love."

He recognised at once his father's careful uncials. "Is Dad alright?"

"Yes, of course he is. Why?"

He couldn't say, because you've been crying. Instead, he pointed to the wall map beyond where she sat. "You haven't moved the flags since we've been back," he said. "I wondered if perhaps the Germans are starting to win again."

She shook her head, made to laugh, though it was more an involuntary expulsion of breath, and said, "no, no, David. We're winning the war. Although this new bombing of London is a worry." And this time she did sigh.

He went over to stand beside her, still not daring to look into her face.

"Flying bombs, Doodlebugs, they're called," she said, in answer to his silent question. "Horrible." And she shuddered. "Too much for your other grandparents. They've decided to leave the city and sit out the rest of the war in — where is it?," and she picked up a sheet of blue writing paper, smaller than the ones his father used. "Woodbridge, a town in Suffolk. The blitz didn't manage to shift them but they say that these new attacks are more than they can bear. They suggest that once they're installed in the cottage they've rented we might go to visit them."

From remarks she'd let drop and the intonation of her voice when she spoke of his other grandparents he guessed she didn't much like them. Trying to keep any enthusiasm out of his voice therefore, he asked, "and will we?"

"I don't know, but I don't think so. You and Sarah have had one holiday already. And school starts again in under two weeks' time. Besides ... " Her voice tailed away as she stared blankly at the table in front of her. He wanted to put an arm round her, ached for her to put an arm round him, but before he could move she stood, abruptly pushed back her chair and said, "run upstairs, will you, and tell Sarah that tea will be on the table in a jiffy."

The smile she turned on him had something of her old gaiety in it. "The cup that cheers but not inebriates," she said, and when he stared uncomprehendingly at her, added, "a line from some poem or other. You dad was forever quoting it."

"But what does that word mean? Inebriates?"

"Well, now, why not look it up in the dictionary. After you've had your tea, of course." But then the smile faded and as he left the room she was busying herself in gathering up the letters.

On the landing he paused. Sarah was talking to her bear. "Did Mrs Willoughby speak to you to-day?" A pause. "No, she didn't speak to me, either."

"Tea's ready," he called out and went into his own room, his eyes momentarily scanning the letter his father had sent him. The weather in Malta was still hot and some soldiers had managed to swim far enough out from shore to find themselves among dolphins. Then came a passage that held his attention. The people of Siggiewi were thinking of closing the town's air-raid shelter because it was no longer needed. They were worried that it would become rat-infested and so breed "pestilence and plague. Unlike the table under which the three people who mean everything to me had to sit while enemy aircraft passed over the village." He thought he knew what plague meant, but pestilence? Another word to look up.

He laid the letter on his bedside table. He would read it more carefully when he went to bed.

As he turned away, he glanced out of the window. A boy was outlined against the hedgerow on the far aside of bottom meadow. Robin. His friend stood stock still, shading his eyes as though trying to see whether he could make out any movement in the bedroom where he, David, stood, now waving. But there was no response. He guessed Robin couldn't see that anybody was at the window.

"Tea," his mother called from the foot of the stairs, and as he called out an answer of "coming" a memory came to him, one so powerfully sudden that it seemed to jerk his head back and it was as though he stood on the spot that Robin occupied, looking towards the house as Robin now did.

It had been earlier that summer, before he had met the American soldier. He'd been running home from school when, as he turned into bottom meadow, the brown-and-white of a bird's wings arrowed across his path and into the thickset to his left. He knelt to peer among the hedgerow's tangle of leaves and twigs and after a few seconds made out a darker clot of twigs that had to be a next. And at that moment he heard his mother calling to him.

"Tea, David."

She was leaning from the window of what was now his bedroom, waving a yellow duster, and even at that distance he could see her smile. Or perhaps he realised that she must be smiling because she now shouted, the gaiety of her voice carrying across their garden and the intervening field, "There's a letter from your father waiting for you to read."

He'd abandoned his study of the bird's nest then. "Coming," he shouted back.

* * *

Tea, his favourite meal. And yet now, looking at the plate of sliced bread, jam in its blue pot, the as-yet uncut sponge cake, the white cloth his mother had laid so as to cover the steel table, he felt no great desire to eat.

The meal itself didn't count. The chance for the three of them to be together did. Tea-times were the best of times, especially in the winter months when the fire was lit and he and Sarah were allowed to make toast, skewering each thick-cut piece of bread before holding it to the flames. As soon as it was browned on both sides, their mother would spread on it the dripping she lifted on a knife from a brown pudding basin, sprinkle salt over the gelatinous, white-flecked mixture, then arrange the toast on a large blue-patterned plate decorated with ladies who walked under parasols among what looked like monkey-puzzle trees. The trees stood among small hills where streams flowed beneath crook-back bridges, while in the plate's middle was a summer-house called, their mother said, a pagoda. As the toast was eaten so the three of them invented stories to explain the picture details that came increasingly into view. The ladies were on holiday and waiting for their husbands to join them, not knowing that this could never happen because an earthquake had buried the men. That, anyway, was David's version. In Sarah's, the men had been swallowed by a dragon. As for their mother, she suggested that the ladies were part of a troupe of actors rehearsing their latest play, which they intended to perform for the king, called the Mikado. Unfortunately, the Mikado had been captured by the Pirates of Penzance. Uttering the last word she would prolong the sounds — *Penzzzzzaance* — and roll her eyes in monstrous fashion until Sarah clamped her hands over her ears and, squealing in mock-terror, slid under the table.

But that, and similar tea-times, belonged to the past. Since returning from their grandparents, tea was eaten in near-silence, the children facing each other while their mother sat smoking in her chair beside the wall chart, gazing unseeing ahead of her. On this occasion, when he remarked that he had eaten all he wanted and intended to go into the front room to look up the meaning of the word "inebriates" as well as "pestilence," she stared at him in an abstracted manner, before repeating, "*pestilence*? I don't know what you mean. Who said anything about pestilence?"

"Dad," he said, as he moved towards the door, then stopped and turned to her. "He says there's an air-raid shelter at the town in Malta where he is and it's going to be closed down because of pestilence."

Her expression cleared. "Oh, I understand. Yes, it's some underground burrow at the bottom of the square, I think. He did once write to me about it. I imagine it's not needed now that the air-raids have ceased, any more than we need black-out curtains, let alone gas masks. 'Pestilence'. Ugh." She shuddered. "Rats scampering about there, I shouldn't wonder."

"Do you think we might ever see it?"

"What, Ziggiewi's air-raid shelter? Why on earth would you want to see that?"

"Malta," he said, "I'd like to see Malta. Perhaps we could all go one day."

She looked at him, then away. "Goodness only knows what we'll be doing 'one day'," she said, her voice heavy, dull.

* * *

There were still occasions when she joined them at the tea-table, shared in their chatter, asked them question, listened to their replies. But she rarely attended for long to what they were telling her. "That's good," she said once in response to Sarah's account of Archie's latest illness.

"It's not *good*, mummy, it's *bad*," his sister protested, and had to be coaxed out of her sulk. And if either of them suggested a game of the kind they'd formerly played at the tea-table — "I Spy" or "Man and his Object" — she would either forget when it was her turn or put them off by saying she had a headache. "Let's leave it until tomorrow." But it was she who had taught them that tomorrow never comes, "because when it's tomorrow it's today," and sure enough the following day she would more often than not find some excuse for not playing or, if she did join in, would soon become so inattentive that it seemed scarcely worthwhile to ask her.

He once tried to ask how Eve Roberts was, thinking that it might be the other woman's problems that were behind his mother's new, uncertain temper, her bewildering shifts of mood, from forced gaiety to gloom, but when he mentioned the name she looked at him as though she had no idea what he was talking about before recognition came in the form of a short, dismissive laugh. "Oh, *she's* alright," she said. "Nothing wrong with *her*." And that was the end of the matter.

* * *

But still she read to Sarah each evening out of books she'd help her daughter choose from the village library, although listening to the murmur of her voice along the landing as he sat on his bed or stared from his window across bottom meadow to the fields beyond, he thought for sure that the readings didn't last as long as they once had. After she had finished with Sarah she'd come into kiss him goodnight. Once, when she did so, he was arranging his father's letters in a neat pile on the bed. What was he doing, she asked. "Putting them in order so I can read them like chapters in a story." He turned from concentrating on his task to see her gazing at him, her lips twisted in what seemed a spasm of pain before she smiled and bent her head to kiss the top of his. "Good idea," she said, spinning away and leaving the room.

* * *

On the Saturday before school re-opened they planned a concert to cheer her up. David was to perform some conjuring tricks he had been assiduously practising — mostly learnt from Robin who had been taught them by his gran — and Sarah would act out the story of Red Riding Hood with Archie as wolf and a rag doll as grandmother. Sarah herself was to take the part of Red Riding Hood. The concert, to be held as a prelude to tea, would close with an invitation to the entire audience, consisting of their mother, Robin, and Mrs Rayner, now free of her responsibilities as organiser of the tea-dances, to join in the singing of "Two Lovely

Black Eyes." After that, there would be Refreshments.

They spent much of Friday rehearsing and in the evening, when he went upstairs to bed, David wrote out the programme. It included "Tea which does not Inebriate and Sandwiches with no Pestilence".

But the concert never happened. On Saturday morning, as Sarah and he were at breakfast talking over their plans for the day, their mother, still in her dressing-gown, came from the kitchen to tell them she felt so unwell that she would have to go back to bed. And certainly, David realised, she did look ill. Her hair hung lank about her face, her tired eyes were red veined, and when he went to stand beside her as she sat slumped at the table, head propped on her cupped hands, his nostrils were troubled by the stale must of cigarette smoke that clung to her.

"Perhaps you'll feel better this afternoon," he said hopefully, trying to hide his own dismay and looking across to where Sarah sat watching them, her mouth open in unabashed distress.

She sighed, tilted her head to catch his eye, trying to smile as she did so, then reached out a hand to stroke Sarah's hair. "Perhaps," she said. And he knew at once that she wouldn't.

* * *

But the following afternoon, the day before the new school year began, she made them an especially lavish tea. David, who had stayed behind after Matins to hear from Monk about the choir's role in the forthcoming Harvest Festival service, came home to find his mother and sister in the kitchen, singing together as they greased baking trays and stirred the contents of a large mixing bowl.

"Divine Harmony," his mother said with a mock bow. "Singing for the troops." "No, *that's* not our name," Sarah told her. "You said we could call ourselves the Willoughby Sisters."

"That too."

"Can I call myself that at school?" Sarah was due to start at Infants the next morning and the tea was a way of marking her entry into a new phase of her life, a celebration of her becoming,

154

as their mother said, "a proper schoolgirl." Archie would be going with her and she worried, she said, that he might not like the food. Besides, he had never before drunk milk. David had explained to her that everyone was given a half-pint milk bottle at morning break, which you could drink straight from the bottle or through a straw. Sarah decided that Archie would be safer with a straw.

David agreed. "That way you don't need to remove the lid," he told her. The bottle lids, which were made of cardboard, came with small u-shaped areas marked out by dotted lines, and you simply pushed your straw through at that point. Although, he added, when the weather was cold the milk in its crates often arrived at school frozen and the bottles had therefore to be stood against radiators to thaw out. And even then you might find shards of iced milk in your bottle, sharp as glass, although in response to Sarah's protest that Archie couldn't possibly drink frozen milk, her mother assured her that it wouldn't be essential.

Tea was almost like old times. The three of them talked over, across and to each other. David and his mother agreed to laugh at Archie's joke about a blue-fly that turned green with envy of a blackfly, and then their mother made them choke with laughter as she imitated Godwin snorting down his nose at customers in the post office who dared to appear in public without carrying their gas masks, "In spite of the clear instructions of HIS MAJESTY'S GOVERNMENT".

Then, as though to add to this suddenly festive atmosphere, Mrs Rayner, in her habitual heavy coat, "popped in" to wish Sarah good luck — "now that you're off to the new world of school" — and was persuaded to stay for a cup of tea. They were all glad to see her, Sarah keen to show off the scarf Archie would be wearing next day, David to tell her that, now he was moving into the top class, his teacher would be Mr Collins — "That's nice, everyone says he's a good teacher, and we know he's a nifty dancer" she said, smiling broadly at him and winking — and their mother, because Mrs Rayner was after all a friend.

"How are you keeping, Jean?" the older woman asked, shaking her head at the offer of a cigarette as she lifted the cup to her lips. Sarah had by now taken Archie upstairs because he needed an early night, and David, about to leave the room with a tray on which tea things were piled, paused when his mother, lowering her voice, said hesitantly, "better, I think." Then, even more quietly though he was able to overhear, "But there have been rocky moments." He sensed her look swiftly in his direction, a look that was warning the other woman from speaking while he was within earshot, and when he re-entered a few moments later the two of them sat, silently drinking tea, each staring into her own cup.

"David? What do you want? The table's cleared."

The sharpness in her voice disconcerted him. "I ... I ... was looking for a book."

"All your books are in your room. I tidied them up earlier, while you were at church. So you'll have to look upstairs." Her voice eased back to somewhere near its normal pitch. "Now, off you go, love." A smile and nod towards the window. "The weather's still fine, why don't you and Robin enjoy one last half hour of freedom before I call you in for your bath?"

"Robin has to stay in to look after his gran."

"Well, then, you'll have to go to your room and find the book your were looking for." Her laugh, gentle as it was, dismissed him.

As he walked through the hall he heard her get up and shut the door behind him.

Half an hour or so later, when he was on hands and knees in the front room idly flicking through the dictionary, he heard the dining-room door open again and the two women's voices as they emerged into the hall. He had been careful to close the door to the room he was now in, so they could not see him as they walked towards the front door. A moment later the door creaked on its hinges and Mrs Rayner said "Well, love, be sure to look after yourself and those two kiddies."

Whatever his mother said in reply was so indistinct that, though he paused in the act of replacing the dictionary, listening hard, he could make nothing of her words.

He turned away from the crammed bookcase and as he did so noticed that the gramophone in its customary position behind the sofa was, unusually, open. On hands and knees he went over to inspect it, noticing, as he came near, that a record, broken into several bits, lay on the turn-table. He picked up one of the larger shards, inspected its black label with the white lettering. *Judy Garland … You Made Me …*

The door opened. He turned to see his mother staring at him.

"I came in to look up a word," he said, feeling himself blush.

Her nod was barely perceptible and she did not speak.

"*Quaint,*" he said desperately. "It's a word I heard granddad use."

Still she studied at him, then switched her gaze to the piece of shellac in his fingers. "An accident," she said. Her voice was a harsh whisper, as though something gripped her throat. She hesitated, then swiftly crossed to where he crouched, knelt beside him and gathered up the other pieces of record which she dropped into his open hands.

As swiftly as she had knelt, she stood again, gesturing at him to do likewise.

"Drop that mess in the dustbin, will you," she said. "It's no use to anyone now, is it."

Nodding numbly, holding the fragments of record in his hands like a broken offertory plate, he left the room.

PART TWO
1994

∼ CHAPTER ONE ∼

Maggie brought the car smoothly to a stop. "Let me know what time you plan to return," she said as he unclipped his seat belt. "You can phone when you get there — from the house, if the phone's still connected."

"And where will you be?"

"In the studio. And if I have to pop out I'll take my mobile with me. I'll expect you back early evening. Good luck."

"Thanks." He kissed the cool cheek she tilted toward him, squeezed her denim-clad thigh, then levered himself out of the passenger seat. From their station's forecourt he watched as she expertly reversed their small Fiat and fluttered her fingertips at him before she joined the traffic of nine o'clock delivery vans, slow-moving buses, and mothers in family cars returning from the school run.

An hour later, his half-empty mainline service left St Pancras. Once beyond the station's arced gloom, the train eased its way under surprisingly bright, wintry sunshine, past a clutter of hoardings, then what looked like brand new supermarkets, each constructed out of material he thought of as hospital white and giving the impression of planned anonymity — our aim is not to offend — until, realising the view did not entertain, he opened his leather bag, took out the copy of *Anna of the Five Towns* which Susie had given him for his birthday, found his place and began to read.

He had never before looked into any of Bennett's novels, taking for casual granted the assurance of academic colleagues that they were what one of them, a specialist in modernist writing, called "exercises in drab realism," and so was unprepared for the subtlety with which Bennett opened up the hidden, thwarted lives of his provincial characters. He had reached that part of the novel where Anna Tellwright, the much put-upon daughter of a domestic tyrant, is invited by wealthy friends to holiday with them on the Isle of Man, and, despite her father's opposition, joins them on the boat, rejoicing in what for her is an entirely new experience of freedom.

"Anythink from the trolley-service, sir?"

Reluctantly, he looked up from his book. The man was early middle-aged, grey trousers, grey waistcoat, the train company's green shirt, frayed and buttoned to his thin wrists, a pale, anxious-to-please smile.

"A cup of coffee would be nice."

"Afraid there's no coffee, sir."

"Tea, then."

"Afraid there's no tea, sir. There was a public announcement, sir, as the train commenced its outward journey, regretting that due to staff shortages the on-board bar facilities would not be available and that the trolley-service was not equipped to provide hot liquid refreshment."

"There's not much point to it, then, is there?"

"We have a wide range of soft drinks, beers and spirits, sir. Plus we have a selection of freshly-made sandwiches. And crisps."

"No thanks." David went back to his book. The holidaying party arrived at its destination, accompanied by Henry Mynors, a family friend known to the ingenuous Anna. Easy to foresee what would happen. And, yes, it did. It *would*. On the last night of the short holiday, Mynors proposed to Anna. Reading was now a form of anguish. Don't do it, he wanted to beg her, walk away. But of course she said yes. Bennett, that astute psychologist, knew why, given the hour, the holiday atmosphere, the sheer joy of being temporarily released from the prison of home, Anna would accept Mynors's offer of marriage. The next day, when the party returned to the Five Towns, was, Bennett commented, the high point of Anna's life, "a bright expanse unstained … marking the apogee of her existence. In the years that followed she could always return to it and say to herself: 'That day I was happy, foolishly, ignorantly, but utterly. And all that I have since learnt cannot alter it — I was happy.'"

Putting the book down, he gazed out of the window at green fields stretching away to a low, tree-fringed horizon etched by wintry sun. He thought of his adored daughter and of how, until her recent and pray god successful marriage, she had gone through a number of painful love affairs each of which, when it broke up, left her for a while emotionally shattered. And could the memory of past happiness then help Susie with her ache of disappointment, of defeat, betrayal? Bennett seemed to think that it could.

Nor was Bennett alone. Since his undergraduate days he had carried in his head Hemingway's remark about how, if people brought such courage as they could to the world, the world broke them but afterwards many were strong at the broken places. True, you could, if you wanted to, imagine that Hemingway was thinking of courage under fire, but everyone knew that *A Farewell to Arms*, where the remark occurs, ends with the death of the hero's loved woman and that this was Hemingway's way of attempting to come to terms with a doomed love affair of his own. Anna's remembrance of past happiness might seem a less powerful antidote, yet after all she *chose* to remember, chose *not* to sink into self-pitying defeatism when, as Bennett would surely go on to reveal — why otherwise would he anticipate her thought — her later life failed to sustain the joy of that brief holiday and what it led to.

"Men have died from time to time, and worms have eaten them, but not for love." Not true, not true, as the Shakespeare who had already written *Romeo and Juliet* perfectly well understood. But then Rosalind's caustic flippancy not only scorched Orlando's papery mooniness, it was meant to cauterise her own pain, her not knowing whether he loved her and whether, if he did, his love was worth having — for she was altogether too sharp not to realise that while Orlando might be an excellent strong wrestler he was an emotional weakling. Yet, knowing all this, she knew, too, that she'd survive —until the worms got her, and after all even a king must go a turn in the guts of a worm. Rosalind would live because she chose to, that was what made her a true heroine. Susie, too, had chosen to rise above her disappointments and was now rewarded with a happy marriage. Good for her. And good for Anna, choosing to find life bearable, able to call on the remembered happiness of that night when a man told her he loved her. He took up the book once more.

But the words that slid beneath his eye now formed lines of senseless type. He closed the novel, pushed it into his bag, and settled back to look out at the English midlands though which his train ran, the canal that meandered and curved beside the track, fields divided from each other by shaved bristlings of hedge, houses and farms where it was easy to think that life must be uneventful, unheroic. Shakespeare and Bennett had, after all, invented Rosalind and Anna. In the lives of actual men and women, suffering took away heroism, or perhaps disguised it so effectively that it turned into something else — the dogged failures that seemed no more than daily happenstance, mundane accidents. Such failures were too ordinary to be remarkable, too familiar to be notable. Familiar, a ghost, familiar, of the family. No. No. He pushed that thought away.

At Leicester, where he had a short wait before the local service arrived, he walked up and down the platform, peered into waiting rooms, the café, a bookstall, but of course everything had changed. He recognised nothing, no sign or sound tugged at his memory. He might have been anywhere.

A two-carriage train trundled in. "Is this for Hinckley?" he asked the turbaned driver who, leaning out of his window, stared dully along the platform, and for answer received an unsmiling nod. He climbed into a carriage which had one other occupant, a young man, fast asleep, body sagging across the aisle, head wagging up and down as the train began to judder out of the station, though the motion did not wake him. Nor did the youth stir when, as Hinckley was announced over the crackling intercom, the grubby cross-country train began to slow, then squealed to a gradual halt.

He stood, shouldered his bag, walked quickly to the end of the carriage and, when he reached for the handle, found that his hands were sweating and that he was trembling so violently that, for a panicky moment, he couldn't open the door.

Yet once on the anonymous, featureless platform, the brimming of his nervous anticipation quite drained away. He looked around him. No, nothing. As with Leicester, he might have been anywhere. Well, what had he expected? He crossed the footbridge, walked through the small, grubby space of what could hardly be called a booking hall and out onto the yard.

"Hello, David," Sarah said, "you're looking well."

She leant towards him to be kissed on the cheek. Hair glossily chestnut, skin smooth to the touch of his kiss, lightly scented, he saw as he stepped back a little that her body, though a shade bulkier than he remembered, was shapely in the professional pin-stripe suit she wore with grace. Doubtless she regularly worked out, as she'd call it, in some expensive health club. "It's lovely to see you," he said, "I've not kept you waiting, have I?"

She shook her head, looking him over as she did so, took in the brown sports coat showing under his open mac, blue shirt with red tie he so seldom bothered to wear, black cords.

"Maggie sends love," he said, as she led the way to a low-slung, sleekly black coupé. "Yours?"

Without bothering to reply, she opened the passenger door and he bent to lower himself into the seat. He slid a hand over the leather upholstery. "What is this, by the way?"

"The car? Top of the range Honda. Given me by a grateful client. Nothing flashy. The car, that is." She manoeuvred out of the station yard, foot tapping impatiently on the accelerator as she waited for lights at the junction to turn green. When they did, she swung the car expertly right onto the road out of town.

"You don't mean it."

The car began to move at speed, overtook a bus, and immediately afterwards, a police car. Sarah glanced in the rear mirror, smiled faintly. She had no fears of the boys in blue.

"Don't mean what?" her brief laugh was more of a snort. "I can see you've no idea *what* grateful business men will be prepared to offer their accountants. Holidays in Vegas. Diamonds as big as the pyramids." She dropped her mocking tone. "But no, I bought this with a bonus that recently came my way."

"So business is good?"

"Never better. And you? How's retirement?"

"Oh, fine. I was glad to get out."

"But?"

"But nothing." He waited until, accelerating powerfully, she overtook a slow-moving lorry that was blocking a good half of the narrow road, then, blowing out breath, said, laughing, "I suspect that unlike you, life in the slow lane suits me to a T. No more of aims and objectives, no more committee meetings, no more listening to men in grey suits talk of the need for mission statements."

"Have a care. Some of my best friends wear grey suits."

"And do they *talk* like men in grey suits?"

"How do men in grey suits talk?"

"The ones I've met — the ones who've begun to infest universities, all of them with their degrees in Business Studies — talk about biting bullets, grasping nettles, taking painful managerial decisions."

Sarah laughed and shook her head. "You're out of date, brother. We're now into user-friendly mode. Her voice took on a wheedling, babyish tone. "'My name is Tracey. How may I help you. Have a nice day.' Hadn't you noticed?"

"That's girl talk."

"The men are worse. Now her voice dropped to a purr. 'How are you today?' Deep, personal, caring. As if they did."

David laughed in genuine pleasure at his sister's imitative skills. "Thank goodness I'm spared all that."

"And Maggie? How is she?"

"She's fine. Her dealer's got a new show fixed up for her. Some of her smaller pieces, woodcarvings mostly, so she's busy preparing for that. Good god, we're *here.*"

"Not quite yet." They had turned onto a road he remembered only too well, the road he'd walked along so regularly fifty years earlier, a road which now looked altogether narrower and shabbier than he remembered it, but nevertheless and unmistakably the same road, even to the telephone box on its patch of green beside someone's front hedge. "I should warn you," Sarah said, and now, despite the cod-officialdom of her words, her voice had shed any of its bantering tone, "that what you're about to see may come as a not very pleasant surprise."

The car slowed as she eased it across the road and brought it to a stop by a low front hedge over which they could see, set back a little, past rockery and front lawn, a small, semi-detached house. Brother and sister stared at it, silent. The house's stained pebble-dash looked leprous with rot, blotches of grey wood showed through long-ago black painted window frames, the windows themselves curtained by what appeared to be old, grey drapes carelessly pulled across, the blistered and peeled front door in its keyhole porch, brickwork flaky, porous. There was an air of abandonment, neglect, defeat about the place.

Brother and sister sat in silence for some minutes before David could trust himself to speak. "Poor woman," he said at last. Then, "poor mother." He let out his breath. "I'd no idea things were so bad." Awkwardly, he raised a hand and let it rest lightly on Sarah's shoulder. Without turning her fixed gaze, she reached across and touched his fingertips with her own. "Yes," she said, her voice a mere whisper. "Poor woman."

"You've been inside?"

"Had to. I came as soon as the police contacted me. Drove down, stayed the night — not in the house of course," shuddering, "but I went through the rigmarole of signing the Death Certificate. And then of course I had to be here for the undertakers."

"It *would* have happened while we were snatching a few days' holiday."

"Not your fault," Sarah said, turning to him.

"Even so I feel guilty." He looked at her, then away. "Suppose at the last she'd wanted to see us?"

"I doubt it. Anyway, she did see us. Sometimes."

He stared through the windscreen, trying to remember the location of Farmer Record's farmhouse across the way, but now there were new houses strung along the road where, before, fields had led down to the woods. "Yes, she did," he said after a pause. "But only when we suggested it. It was never the other way round, was it?" He stared again at the house, winced. "And we never came here. Anyway, I didn't. Once, when the kids were young, I wanted to bring them, show them the place where I spent some of my childhood, but she wouldn't allow it. And I could never persuade her to stay with us, not even for a night, not even come to see where we lived."

"It was the same with me, you know." She spoke emphatically, as though expecting him to deny it. Then, half-apologetically, she shook her head, as if to clear it of troubled memories. "Well, are you up to seeing inside?"

But as she began to undo her seat belt he knew he couldn't face it, not yet. "Do you mind if we get the funeral over first," he said. "I thought that afterwards we might have a spot to eat and then come back here." His voice tailed off, picked up. "I've been travelling since early morning."

His sister looked across at him, a faint smile on her lips. "You're in need of Dutch courage?"

"Anything you say."

Without another word, she re-fastened her seat belt, turned the ignition key, and eased the car away from the kerb.

* * *

"It really *was* death from natural causes?"

"No doubt about it." Sarah looked around at the few customers in the pub's saloon bar talking quietly among themselves or scanning the newspapers they had propped against their beer-glasses. Lowering her voice, she said, "I'd half wondered whether there might have to be an autopsy, but her doctor signed the death certificate without any fuss. The official explanation was heart failure. But he did let drop that she'd not been looking after herself. She was apparently underweight. I don't suppose she ate properly, and as she'd never had central heating — remember she always turned down our offer to pay for its installation — the house was running with damp. As cold as charity, she might have said." She shivered, made a slight *moué*. "I had the distinct impression that as far as the doctor was concerned I was the heartless daughter." She shrugged. "Well, let him think what he wants. I certainly wasn't going to try to explain how matters stood, let alone justify myself to a stranger. Or anyone else, if it comes to that."

Her voice held a certain steeliness, and David thought that anyone who didn't know her well might well consider her, if not uncaring, then arrogantly sure of herself. And certainly, she had a self-confidence, an assurance, he knew to be lacking in himself.

He picked up his glass and, without drinking from it, put it down again. Staring into the beer, he said tentatively, "You do wonder though, don't you. I mean, what had she got to live for? To judge from that apology for a funeral, she had no friends in the village, she'd as good as cut herself off from her family and then ... then, that house." Involuntarily, he shuddered a little, thinking of the dilapidated frontage he had been forced to stare at not two hours past.

"A house without love," Sarah said, as though anticipating his words.

He did look at her then. She was staring steadily back at him and he realised that she was willing herself not to cry. Abashed, wondering whether what he felt was after all guilt, he turned his head away and found himself studying a couple of framed black-and-white photographs on the wall beside the bar. One showed a football team framed within goalposts under a sagging crossbar, the other was of cricketers, variously sitting or standing on the steps of what he at once recognised as the pavilion of the village recreation ground.

Sarah followed his gaze. "Do you think you might recognise anyone in either of those?"

"I doubt it." But he got up, crossed the room to stand in front of them. "I suppose that could be Collins," he said, as Sarah joined him. He pointed to one of the cricketers, a thin, dark-haired man sitting on the bottom step, his head tilted upward to the camera, smiling faintly.

"And who might Collins be?"

"A master at the junior school. He was due to teach me in my final year. He sang in the church choir."

"Well, I wasn't at the school," Sarah said, "and why should I remember anything about that damned choir."

"Sorry," he said, hearing the edge in her voice. "I'd forgotten it was male voice only. Did it bother you that much?" When she refused to answer, he went on staring at the photographs. Neither carried any identification, of dates or names, but at a guess they belonged to the same period. The footballers' shorts were baggy, hair, cleanly parted, was almost certainly slathered in brylcreem, the panelled ball under the boot of the man who stood with folded arms at the centre of his striped-shirted team showed its lacing, there were trim moustaches aplenty, and the round, wire-framed spectacles worn by several of the cricketers suggested standard issue from the early days of the national health service. After a while, he said, shrugging, "No, I'm not sure that is Collins and I can't honestly say I recognise any other faces there. It was all so long ago."

"Those happy, bygone days." He looked swiftly at her, saw the twist to her lips, and guessed something of the feelings that must be gnawing at her.

Abandoning the photographs, they went back to their seats. A few minutes later, subdued, unsmiling, mute, they watched a middle-aged woman come out from behind the bar carrying plates of sandwiches.

"Ours, I hope." David took the chance to break what was becoming a difficult silence.

"One cheese, one ham."

"That's us." While David smiled his thanks, Sarah asked the woman "Are you local, by any chance."

In the act of turning away, she paused, looked at his sister as though she was under accusation. "Lived here all my life."

"Would you happen to know any of the men in those photographs?"

The barmaid followed the direction of Sarah's finger. "One or two," she said, relaxing, "but most of 'em 'll be dead by now." She walked across to where the photographs hung. "Bert Mee. He went last winter. He's in the back row." She jabbed at a stocky-looking man with wide, fixed grin in the cricket team. "See. That's him." She came back to their table. "A lot of 'em was in here after the funeral. Had a bit of a knees-up. He was club president. There was a piece about him in the local paper."

"Bert Mee," David said. "I didn't know he played cricket. 'Knees-Up' now." He laughed, then, aware of her surprised expression, decided to explain. "It's an odd coincidence you using that expression. Bert Mee had a friend known among the choirboys as Knees Up because of the way he walked. They both sang in the church choir," he told her.

"That would be Jack Parker," she said, "he died some years back. Bert was never the same afterwards. Thick as thieves those two were. Often in here of an evening, laughing and joking."

"And both of them and a man called Godwin, who was village post-master, and Collins, a schoolteacher, and Monk, the organist, they all used to troop over to this pub after choir practice."

"Monk!" she said. "I heard about him. Seems he got caught with his fingers in the till, or anyway lifting plate money. He did time for that. Dunno what happened when they let him out, but he never showed his face round here again." She hovered, as though about to offer or receive further reminiscences but, when they said no more, left them to their food.

"Well, well." Sarah bit into a ham sandwich. "A rotten apple in the church barrel, eh? Though I can't believe that Monks or whatever he was called could be any worse than Godwin. He terrified me once when I called him Mr Postman. 'You will call your elders and betters by their full name. *Mister Godwin. And I am not a postman.*' "

"His Christian name was Godbert."

His sister looked at him in joyous disbelief. "Godbert? Godbert Godwin? Oh, why didn't I know that."

He laughed, remembering. "Godbert. That was how he was addressed at choir-practice when anyone was trying to soothe him, which was most of the time. And it was written on the side of the box he kept his gas-mask in."

"And which he always had with him. Do you remember how he used to stop people in the street to ask why they weren't carrying theirs, even after the need for them had gone." She paused. "A nasty, officious little man."

"Little? He was certainly a bully. Gave us choirboys a bad time of it. But little, well, I don't know. I didn't think of him as small. He always seemed big to me."

"But you were little yourself."

"True."

There was a silence during which Sarah looked searchingly at David. "Actually," she said, and the laughter in her voice had now gone, "I was using *her* words. It was *she* who once called Godwin a nasty, officious little man." She paused, waiting for him to speak.

"Are you going to tell me why?"

She finished her sandwich, wiped her fingers on the serviette, then, nodding, looking at him gravely, said "I think I ought to."

"*Ought?*"

"Yes," she said, having considered, "ought." She paused again. "I need to tell you." Once more she stopped, as though wondering whether to go on, then said, "Believe it or not, I'd forgotten all about the words until just now. It was hearing his — Godwin's — name that brought them back. Phew!" She steered bread crumbs about her plate, head lowered, and eventually said, her voice low, solemn almost, "at the time she swore me to silence, you see. And later, when I could have told you, I think I must have buried the memory as something belonging to a time I'd rather forget. Well, you understand."

Studying her bent head, the carefully-styled hair, her discreet make-up, the air of impeccable grooming, he thought how out of place she looked in this village pub, and yet how at ease she seemed, how in command of herself. But when she looked up, her gaze was troubled. She said, "it was sometime that summer, I don't remember when exactly, but I think it must have been not long before you and I were due to go off to our grandparents. Anyway, she and I were alone in the house early one evening — perhaps you were at choir practice, or out in the fields with your friend — she had the wireless on, and I was drawing at the table, I remember that alright, and suddenly there was a bang, bang, bang, on the front door. One of those knocks that immediately seems, you know, official. But it was still full daylight and as she switched the wireless off she said, 'well, whoever's trying to wake the dead, it can't be the ARP.'" Then she went quite pale, and put her hand to her mouth, and although it didn't occur to me at the time I realised later that she must have feared that whoever was at the door might well be the bringer of terrible news, our father's death, perhaps. 'You stay here' she said, and she almost ran out of the room, and I heard her yank the front door open — you remember how it used to stick — and then a man's voice."

Sarah raised her glass of soda water, sipped, put it back on the table and revolved it, wholly given over to her thoughts. Then, "I couldn't hear what was said, but I could hear her beginning to shout and finally she yelled 'Think what you damned well like' and the door slammed shut, so loudly even the table seemed to tremble. And after that, for a few moments, nothing. I was beginning to wonder whether she might have left me in the house alone when the dining-room door opened and she came in. She was very red in the face and I could see that she was shaking."

Sarah sipped some more of her water. She was looking past David now, seeing the events of fifty years ago. "She stood with her back to me as though she was studying that wall-map we used to have, remember, the one that showed troop movements across Europe. I'd never seen her so upset and for some time I couldn't speak, couldn't think what to say. But at last I must have asked her who'd come to the door because she said, 'Godwin, that's who.' And then she grabbed the cushion from her chair and hurled it across the room. 'Damn him', she shouted, and again, 'damn him.' I'd never seen her like that before, so, so *wild*, she always seemed entirely calm, didn't she. It's frightening when you first realise that grown ups can lose their temper, worse, can lose control of themselves. Of course, she soon calmed down. She turned and apologised to me for becoming upset, she said, over that 'nasty, officious little man.' Officious. I hadn't a clue what the word meant but she made it sound as though he had some sort of power over her. And no doubt because I was so frightened I asked her a stupid question. 'Does he want to send you to prison?' Guess what she said."

David finished his beer. "No idea."

"'He would if he could.' Then she laughed and said I wasn't to worry, and that men like Godwin always thought they had the right to interfere in other people's lives. And then she swore me to silence. I wasn't to tell you. It was as though she was suggesting that only if I let on about Godwin's visit would anything bad happen to her, or to us."

She looked at her brother across the small table that divided them.

David looked back. "So he knew."

"Oh, yes," Sarah said, "he knew."

"And you never told me."

"David," she said, with a shrug and a shake of her head. "I've just explained that she swore me to silence and remember, *please*, that at the time I was a small girl. I may have been frightened of her, I was certainly frightened *for* her. Godwin was like a wicked magician, he might have carried her away and what then would have happened to us."

She paused, smiled apologetically. "Alright, I think I probably enjoyed the thought of having a secret that she and I would share, the two of us. I often felt that you two shared secrets from which I was excluded." And when he opened his mouth to speak, she waved him to silence. "I know, I know. It comes of being the younger child. Besides, she explained that if you knew about Godwin's visit and how it had upset her you might mention it to your father in one of your letters and she didn't want him to be worried, not when he was far away from his family, helping to win the war."

"That was thoughtful of her."

Sarah reached across, put a hand on her brother's knee. "Don't be harsh on her," she said, "especially not today."

David covered his sister's beautifully manicured, ringless hand with his own. "No," he said, "you're right." He gathered up his mac from the chair beside him. "Well, if you're ready, I suggest we make a move. Time to see the house and decide what to do about it."

She was up at once. "I'm ready," she said.

* * *

174

Twenty minutes later her car again drew up outside the house they had once lived in. David followed his sister the few yards along the weed-tufted, broken-flagged path before they came to a halt at the step up to the porch. While Sarah dug in her bag for the house key, David turned to survey the front garden, the patch of rank grass ending at a dishevelled rockery and, beyond that, the hedge which divided garden from road. "I used to think this garden was as big as a prairie," he said. Behind him, he heard the door grunt open and followed Sarah inside.

The place smelt of rot, of decay. Strips of wallpaper flapped loose in the draught their entry caused, the lino on the hall floor, darkened from age and neglect, was worn through, and the woodwork, once white, was scabbed with burst blisters of paint, grimed, wretched. David opened the first of two doors leading off to the right and stepped inside. In the dim light caused by the drawn curtains he could make out an old, sagging sofa in badly-faded lovat green, pushed up against the inner wall. Two easy chairs, in the same material, stood under the bay window. Moving across to the sofa, he rested a hand on its nearer arm. It was cold and gritty to the touch, and when he raised his hand he saw that his finger nails were rimed with dust.

"I don't think she can have used this room at all," Sarah said from the doorway. "The back room's not so bad."

"She kept the table all this time," David said, shaking his head in wonder and — what was it he felt — dismay? — as they stood side by side in the room where, as children, they had eaten their meals, watched their mother adjusting flags on the wall map, listened together to the wireless, been for a while happy. Map and wireless were both gone, but her chair remained, old and decrepit like everything else but recognisable, as was the mirror above the fire-place, badly tarnished now and smeared by fly tracks.

The small kitchen held an antiquated gas-stove and badly warped wooden cupboards ranged either side of the wide stone sink in which stood an upturned metal tea-pot and a single blue-and-white ringed mug. Opening the door to the larder that backed under the stairs, he peered in at shelves holding only a few tins of soup and empty kilner jars, though one, he saw as he squeezed into the larder's narrow space, contained white flour, and another was a quarter-full with what had to be split peas. He prised off the top and shook some into his open palm. They lay there, as hard and dry as beetle cases.

"We used to creep in there to hide," Sarah said, as he backed out. "Remember?"

He nodded, smiling. "And to search for the biscuits she made. I loved the ginger ones especially. So did you, didn't you."

"So much that I fought you over who got to cut the pastry they were made from. 'Cut the pastry, get a tasty.'"

He stood leaning against the sink. "I've never really given the matter much thought," he said, "but I suppose she was a pretty good cook."

"Given the materials she had to work with, she was excellent." Sarah was opening the cupboards, peering in at saucepans, neat piles of crockery that looked as though they hadn't been touched in years. He studied her as she tilted her head to inspect the shelves, trying to see in this successful business woman the small girl she had once been, the one, memory told him, who insistently carried a bear around with her at all times of the day and sometimes wore her hair in a pigtail, or was it bunches?

Her present voice broke in on his reverie. "I imagine we had an easier time of it than those living in cities. We could count on eggs and cream." She banged the last cupboard door shut and turned to face him. "I don't recall cheese, though. Do you?"

"Only that bloody awful stuff she made from sour milk. She'd hang it in a muslin bag she attached to the window catch and drain it into a jug. Ugh!" He grimaced. "I think I'd rather have eaten boiled turnip."

"You hated vegetables."

"No, I hated turnips. And swedes. Woolton pie. I know they kept us healthy but give me Hetty Rayner's strudel any day."

"Gosh, Mrs Rayner." Sarah's hand went to her mouth. "I'd completely forgotten. Do you think I should have tried to contact her?"

"How could you? We don't even know where they went after the war. Presumably back to London to take up the rag trade again. But there are a lot of Rayners in London. Anyway, they're probably dead by now."

"Like most of the people she knew." She shook her head, sighed. "I found an address book in her bedroom. I don't think she'd added to it in years, although she'd recorded our various moves — more mine than yours, of course — and noted her grandchildren's birthdays. But I'm not sure even all that was up-to-date." She looked enquiringly at him.

"I told you at Susie's wedding that we'd invited her, but of course she wouldn't come, though she did send a cheque. And a card," he added.

She put out her hand, touched his arm. "Sorry," she said, "but that funeral was pretty dreadful, wasn't it. I'd arranged for notices to be put in the local papers and I saw the one you'd sent to the *Guardian*. I kept hoping somebody would show up, but we had her all to ourselves."

"Apart from the vicar and the sexton and the undertaker's men, yes." He smiled wryly. "Not much of a way to go, is it. These last years she must have lived like a recluse." He ran a finger over the gas-stove, inspected it for grease and found none.

They stood facing each other. "What else could we have done?" he said at last. "She wouldn't come to either of us, she wouldn't let us come to her. She never had a telephone. If I wrote, months might go by before I got a reply and then it was never more than a note. How on earth could we keep in regular in touch with her?" He heard his voice, its mixture of bewilderment and truculence, saw that she understood.

"I know" she said, and again, "I know." Then, "let's go upstairs. You need to see the bedrooms."

As they stood on the landing, he asked, as lightly as he could, "Do you ever hear of Jeremy?"

She paused and had she been a man he'd have thought her gesture one of squaring her shoulders. "No," she said, her head in profile, a faint smile vanishing as quickly as it came. "I heard that he'd gone to America but someone reported him as now back in London. He still has dealings with our firm, though naturally I'm not asked to act for him. No hard feelings though." She turned fully to him now. "I don't think either of us was cut out for marriage." There was a brief pause, and her smile returned. "Unlike you."

David bowed his head in mock assent. "Uxoriousness is my middle name," he said.

"Well, that's one in the eye for child psychologists," Sarah said, laughing. She led the way towards the back of the house and he followed her into the box room which for precious months some half-century earlier had been his bedroom. There, he stood, looked around. The wallpaper was now so faded he could barely make out the grass designs that trailed and spread across it, and the woodwork that had once been glossily blue had become a blurry slate colour. But his wardrobe was still in place, as was the chest-of-drawers beside the single bed.

"Come over here," Sarah said, leaning to peer out of the window from which she'd twitched back the curtain, "though whether you'll want to see this I'm not sure."

He joined her and she moved aside a little to give him the better view. Below, the back garden was an unkempt wilderness in which the ruins of the greenhouse lay collapsed in a heap of wooden struts and mouldering brick. He fixed his eyes on that for a moment, not wanting to acknowledge what had already registered on his sight. But eventually he forced himself to look beyond the garden, past the brick wall which stood where once had been the fence with its gaps through which he and his friend, Robin, had so often squeezed on their way into or out of the fields.

But there were no fields. No bottom meadow, no line of osiers, no wheatfield leading to Farmer Bailey's top pasturage and his old bull. Instead, stretching up to what he knew would be as far as the churchyard, were houses, row upon row of them. An estate of houses, complete with roads and closes, covered the green, open spaces which he and Robin had once roamed. And it wasn't merely the fields which had gone. Everything had disappeared: trees, hedgerows and no doubt the stream, all flattened, grubbed up, lost under cement, brick, tarmacadamed driveways and streets.

"Lower Binfield comes to the midlands," he said, when he could speak, but Sarah had left the room.

Nostalgia is a sickness of the soul, a now-dead friend, a poet, had once said to him; but was what he felt nostalgia? He thought of Cowper, a poet he especially loved, and of those lines lamenting the loss of some poplars. "Twelve years have elapsed since I last took a view/Of my favourite field." But at least Cowper still had a field to look at. A memory flashed into his mind, a memory of his boyhood in this house when he'd liked to take out one of the books housed in the front-room bookcase, not because the words it contained interested him, but because he was fascinated by its illustrations, line-drawings they must have been, including one of a man sitting on a felled tree trunk, hat in hand as he gazed at a row of downed trees which, David now realised, were surely poplars. He must have been holding in his hands a copy of Cowper's poems, one of his father's many collections of poetry. "'Tis a sight to engage me, if anything can,/To muse on the perishing pleasures of man." But, as he muttered the words, he began to mock himself, exaggerating the throb in his voice. Sentimentalist, don't be such a bloody fool. People need to live somewhere and when did you last care about this place.

He stood there, brooding. Time passed, then Sarah came back into the room. "Well?"

"I suppose it was inevitable," he said, turning to her. "But, yes, it came as a bit of a shock." He paused. "It must have been a shock to her, too. No more field path up to the village. I wonder why she never mentioned it. Or did she tell you?"

"Of course not. Why on earth should she." It was not put as a question and silently, bowing his head, he acknowledged the propriety of her swatting away his momentary show of petulance. Then, looking up again, he saw that she was holding a bundle of papers tied in faded red ribbon.

"What are they?"

"Letters," Sarah said, her asperity forgotten, her voice softening as she spoke. "I found them in the back of her wardrobe. I must have missed them when I was going through the house last week." She looked appraisingly at him. "Would you like to see them?"

"You already have, I take it."

"I've only had time to glance at a few. They seem to be love letters."

"Really? Who from?"

She raised an eyebrow, shook her head reassuringly in response to the urgency of his question. "Her husband. Our father. They're from Malta." She handed the tied bundle to him and, without looking at them, he pushed the letters into the pocket of his mac. "Go into the other rooms, if you want," she said, turning away, "but I've had enough. I'll wait for you downstairs."

"No, I don't want to see any more."

He followed her down the old, frayed stair treads back into the front room.

Once there, Sarah, drawing the curtains aside so they could see the better, said, "By the way, since we spoke on the phone I've managed to visit her solicitor. I found his name in her address book. Local, of course. I called on him yesterday afternoon. Rather to my surprise, she'd made a will, leaving everything to be divided between us".

"I can't imagine there's much, is there?"

"Hardly anything. The rent was paid up to date, and all bills were dealt with by standing order, which I'm assured leaves a tiny amount in the bank. According to Ryan and Bagot she had no money in shares or other accounts, not that I thought she would have. So we're free to divide the 'effects' between us." Quizzically she gazed about her, took in the room's dilapidated furnishings. "I don't want anything, but if you do, then say the word. The rest is to go to the Sally Army. I've arranged for them to come in tomorrow and clear the place."

She was all business woman now, cool, efficient, brisk.

He wandered over to the bookcase, squatting to stare along its shelves, empty save for a row of dog-eared paperbacks and old, stained, faded, hardbacked editions of novels that looked as though at various times they'd been rescued from remote corners of junk shops. Speaking over his shoulder, he asked. "What happened to all the books?"

She came to stand beside him. "Goodness knows. Thrown out, I suppose, along with so much else. Have you noticed how bare the place is?"

David looked around. the room, then at his sister. "Bare?"

"No mementoes. No pictures. No photographs. Of the family, of us, of him — her husband. Nothing to show that she'd once been a wife and a mother."

He drew in his breath, let it slowly out. "I see what you mean. She must have got rid of it all. Didn't want anything to remind her of the past." He thought for a moment. "I assume the army returned whatever of his they could. Books, clothes … ."

"Almost certainly. But if so she threw all that out, too. Although she couldn't apparently bring herself to part with his Shakespeare. That was here."

He quickly scanned the shelves. "It isn't now."

"No," she said, "I took it. I thought you wouldn't mind."

He stood, shook his head. "No," he said, "I don't mind, though it feels sad, doesn't it." He gestured to the empty rows. "His books — they must have meant a good deal to him."

She looked at him expectantly, but he found himself incapable of putting into words his sense of loss, of lost loves, lost lives. The waste of it all.

"And you don't think that Paul or Susie would like anything?"

He thought of his children, both now married, both settled into their lives. "They didn't know their grandparents." He could hardly say, but there's nothing to take.

"Just trying to be the attentive aunt," she said.

As he turned from the bookcase, he looked down, let out a small cry. "Hey."

She stared at the square black box he dragged out from where it had been wedged into a space between sofa and wall. "So she kept the gramophone."

Kneeling beside it, he snapped the rusted locks, pushed up the lid and raised the tarnished steel arm, peering at its sunflower head. "It's still got a needle in it. Do you think it might work after all these years?"

Not waiting on her answer, he found the crank handle, fitted it in, wound it once or twice and smiled almost in wonder as the turntable began to revolve.

"Don't you need a record to complete the pleasure?"

"Yes," he said, in his enthusiasm ignoring the satiric edge to her remark, "and I know where to find them, that is if she kept them." He ducked down, peered beneath the sofa. "Ahah."

Still on hands and knees, he drew out a pile of brown-paper encased ten-inch records, tipped one cover up and watched the record slide into view, balanced in the palm of his hand. "This needs a wipe," he said, passing his sleeve over the shellac, before blowing on it and gazing at it critically. "There, good as new."

"What is it?"

He studied the plum-coloured label. "His Master's Voice. Fats Waller. *Viper's Drag.*" He turned to look up at her. "A classic."

With almost reverent care, he placed the record on the turntable, watched as it gained speed, then, crouching so that he was on eye-level with the spinning, gyrating disc, gently guided the needle into position. There was a sound as of cold water hitting hot fat, and then, faintly, as though far off and tentative, notes from a piano began to emerge from the seethe of crackles and hisses. Watching, absorbed, he raised an arm and gave the thumbs up.

"It's slowing down."

He grabbed the handle and turned vigorously. From within the box came sounds of tearing, splintering wood, followed by a metallic clang that eddied slowly into silence.

Sarah rested a hand on her brother's shoulder. "I rather think that concludes the afternoon's entertainment," she said.

∾ CHAPTER TWO ∾

He must have been shouting in his sleep because Maggie was shaking him awake. "Sorry," he whispered into the dark.

"No need," she said sleepily. "But why are you whispering?"

"I didn't want to wake you." It was an old joke of theirs.

He lay there until he sensed her relax back into sleep, then eased himself from bed and made his way downstairs. In the kitchen, he flicked open the stove's vitreous glass door, laid some kindling across the red-hot ashes, waited until the first flames sputtered up, then added a couple of apple-wood logs and swung the door shut, watching the yellow flames subside to an orange glow. Odd, how even the most trivial of domestic routines brought satisfaction. Or perhaps it wasn't odd. The idea of order, well, practice of orderliness, was what provided a momentary stay against confusion. And yet how weak and little was the light. Standing at the sink, he turned on the cold tap, let it run for a moment before filling the kettle, dropped tea-bags into the brown pot, and a few minutes later was heading for his study, carrying on a small round tray the now heavy tea-pot together with his favourite mug.

His desk-lamp threw a circle of lemon light around familiar objects: the small silver-plated tankard from which thrust an assortment of pens and ready-sharpened pencils, the arranged stack of notebooks and, propped beside his computer, the framed photograph of Maggie with Paul and Susie on a sandy, sunlit beach, ten-year old Paul smiling self-consciously at the camera, skinny-thin in his striped swimming trunks and looking fraily vulnerable beside his younger sister's stocky, candid little body. Like her mother, Susie wore a black, one-piece costume, although her plump shape was in marked contrast to Maggie's elegant slimness. And now Paul was almost as old as his father had been when he took that holiday snap of his family in Norfolk, and had a wife and children of his own whom his parents saw whenever they could, which was less often than they wished, and as for Susie, although she still lived in London and therefore nearer to her parents than did her brother, her recent marriage almost certainly meant that she'd see less of them. And quite right, too, he said to himself, failing to stifle the envy in his thought.

He poured himself a mug of tea and began to look through the small pile of letters from the previous day's post which Maggie had left on his desk. Two were cards of condolence from distant relatives of his father's, both expressing formal sorrow at the news of his mother's death, neither offering any information about themselves. Presumably Sarah had written to them, either that or they had seen the *Guardian* death notice, although from the little he could recall of either relative they were unlikely to read such a newspaper. No, they must have been alerted by Sarah. So why hadn't they replied to her as well, for he was certain she'd mentioned no such letters? Oh, of course, because he was "head of the family" and therefore the one to whom all communications should be addressed.

He put the cards to one side. He'd send them on to Sarah and let her decide whether to reply, though he rather hoped she wouldn't. The next letter contained a flyer inviting subscriptions for a new journal "Combining the best of current Theory and Praxis." It went straight into the wastepaper basket. A brief note from a former colleague told him that a mutual acquaintance was suffering from terminal cancer and was unlikely to last more than a few more weeks. Perhaps they should try to see him while there was still time.

The last letter was from his publisher. Fitzroy Frobisher felt it necessary to remind him that his typescript was already three months overdue and that "as the market for academic books is now extremely sluggish it is imperative that our authors keep to their contractual obligations." Bullshit. What contract? What obligations? Alright, eighteen months ago he had signed up to produce a "general study" of eighteenth-century poetry aimed at "students and interested parties" — whatever they were — but absolutely no money changed hands and the deadline was put in purely for form's sake. Irrespective of when his book finally appeared, it would have precisely the same number of buyers who, institutional purchasers apart, would almost certainly be fewer than the number of its reviewers, and who would read it with a good deal less attention; because why pore over a book whose inadequacies you weren't invited to identify and comment on in some academic journal or other. What possible good could come from not being able to harm someone else's reputation?

Sipping his tea, he stared out of his study window into the blackness beyond, considering whether he should write to Fitzroy Frobisher. Where *did* they get that name, by the way, had they bid for it at auction, as Maggie suggested. But what could he tell them? That the book was taking longer to finish than he'd anticipated because he found himself entering into radically new terrain and fully expected the hermeneutics of his methodology, or should that be the methodology of his hermeneutics, to impact the interface of his valorised subject areas with a profound supplementarity of implication. Or should he simply ignore their letter? He decided to ignore it.

He let his mind rove back over all that had happened the day before. The journey to Leicester and beyond, the meeting with Sarah, their lunch together and, most of all, their re-visiting for the first time since childhood that desolate, desolating house. What had Sarah called it? A house without love. The bleak truth. Yet love *had* been a familiar presence there. It was their home, the place where, when they went there they had to be taken in, though "had" was wrong, because for all the deprivations of wartime England, that small, jerry-built, semi-detached place had once exuded warmth, laughter, safety. Until, that is, those things were suddenly withdrawn, became known only by their absence, grieved for by children who had no way of recovering them and who themselves were soon evacuated from a site damaged not by enemy bombs but by hidden, inexplicable forces they could not understand.

He poured himself more tea, drank it, and then, at last, from the top drawer of his desk, he drew the rolled-up sheaf of letters

Sarah had handed over. For some moments he let his fingers play above the faded red ribbon in which they were bound, then slowly, reluctantly, pulled free its bow knot. Held for so long in the ribbon's grip, the pages slowly, partially opened, like a flower gradually unclenching itself in the sudden warmth of spring sun. He bent to sniff the paper, sensed its frail, dry mustiness. More minutes passed. Then, teeth pressed against his lower lip, aware of the slight trembling of his hands, he lifted clear the top letter, smoothed it down on the flat surface of his desk and prepared to greet his father.

Malta, May 23rd, '44

*Darling, I can't tell you how wonderful it was to get your last letter. Now that our post seems to be getting through so much more promptly, we can, with luck, be back in regular touch. (Though I know too much about army ways to hang myself in the expectation of plenty.) Still, I'm going to risk writing you a long letter in the hope of giving you a more accurate impression of life over the past two years than I could have done earlier. You make it seem as though the three of you are positively **enjoying** the difficulties rationing brings. I suppose it isn't as bad for David and Sarah, who won't have known much "real" food, but I can't believe an endless diet of root veg and grey bread is much fun for you. Until recently, it was even less fun for the Maltese, as you can no doubt imagine, and as they keep reminding us. For a while, there was virtually no food at all on the island. Once the supplies they had were exhausted they had no means of getting any more. Our Company arrived after the worst was over, but for those with eyes to see there's still abundant evidence of malnourishment.*

But the Maltese are hardy people — they have to be to put up with the battering they took — and they even managed to draw some humour out of what must have been a truly terrible time for them. BUSINESS AS USUAL chalked on what remained of bombed-out shops — that kind of thing. But the bombing! I know Coventry was devastated but that was the work of a single night. As for what the Maltese had to endure, I hardly know where to start. (And of course a year ago I couldn't have started at all.)

David paused in his reading in order to sip his tea. What did his father mean by that remark? Why couldn't he have told his wife about what was happening on Malta? Presumably because army censors wouldn't have allowed through any news that might, had it fallen into enemy hands, have brought aid and comfort to said enemy. Did that mean all the letters were read? Was his father writing in the knowledge that his private correspondence was subject to official scrutiny? Or had such scrutiny ceased by the time he was writing this letter. Or if not ceased then become more intermittent, less zealous. Yes, that would be it. His father was free, or at least thought he was free, to say more or less whatever he wanted.

He went back to the letter itself.

I'm told that in one month alone (December, 1941), the islanders were hit by no fewer than 170 air raids. That's over five a day. Some way of preparing for Christmas! Hitler wanted the island as a staging post to get supplies to Rommel. If he'd succeeded I dread to think what might have happened to us lot in North Africa. So the Luftwaffe poured bombs onto Malta. It seems a miracle that after so much tonnage the island hasn't simply slipped beneath the waves. Every time I take a trip anywhere here I see so much damage and destruction it comes as a huge surprise to notice that many buildings are still standing. You can imagine how many deaths there have been. Hardly a family hasn't been affected. Yet somehow they kept Hitler at bay. And have you heard what the Maltese air-force consisted of? I ask, because I've no idea how much people 'back home' really know about what went on here. Though the fact the island was awarded the George Cross must have made even the doziest sit up and take notice. Did the newspapers there report that when the actual medal arrived it did a tour of the island, went into virtually every town and village, before being put on show in Valetta? Since then, I notice that although some people shrug and pretend to play down the honour, they are in fact very proud of being recognised as the ones who, as I'm repeatedly told, "stopped Hitler in his tracks." And now they're equally keen to tell the story of the Maltese Air Force. There are photographs in the museum. A total of four superannuated Gladiators waiting to attack the Luftwaffe! One conked out almost immediately, leaving three, which the islanders dubbed Faith, Hope and Charity. Needless to say, they didn't last long. The Italian air force turned out to be useless — just like their army — but Goering's lot came over, bombed the airfields and wiped out the planes. The RAF with local help repaired the runways as best they could but it was a bit pointless, because our planes couldn't get through.

Nor could the ships. The worst period, according to those who had to live through it, was early 1942, when life here was absolute hell. Not any longer. We haven't had a single raid this year and unless matters take a sudden turn for the worse I doubt that we shall. Between them, the RAF and USAF seem to be in control of these southern skies and the navy more or less runs the Med. And both are truly beautiful. (The sky and the sea, I mean.) Until I arrived here, I had no idea how many shades of blue there can be.

Not that it's an unspoilt paradise. Quite apart from the bomb damage, there are natural hazards. Flies, for instance. Maybe not so many as in Egypt, but more than enough, squadrons of them droning all about us by day and half the night. And although convoys are now arriving, food supplies are still far from satisfactory, and quite a lot of the Maltese lead hand-to-mouth existences. Still, there's no comparison between the poverty here and what I saw in Egypt, especially Cairo, because the Maltese don't include professional outcasts and beggars among their population. Or of they do, I haven't noticed. In Egypt you can't avoid them. They're **everywhere.** To say that the hardship and suffering are dreadful is itself a dreadful understatement, but I can't really say more in a letter. Better to save it until I'm back with you all. Being in Cairo as a Brit. wasn't too bad, even for a squaddie (Alexandria wasn't quite as welcoming), but if you were a native of the place it paid to be connected to Farouk. He, by the way, is quite the most corrupt-looking man I've ever clapped eyes on. He doesn't give a damn for the sufferings of his people, all he wants to do is to play cards, be driven everywhere in posh cars, and bed as many women as possible. (Censor, if you're reading this, please note that this is what we **all** think.) And of course he butters the Brits. up. But ordinary Egyptians must hate us. We're in their country, creaming off the money and goods, while they scratch around for the precious little they can dig out with their finger nails. And most of the ex-pats I met in Cairo were especially loathsome. In their eyes, all "foreigners" — that is, the Egyptians themselves! — are wogs and dagoes, and anyone in the British army below the rank of colonel must be a frightful little oik. (Censor, if you're still reading, please note you too would count as an oik.)

So for all kinds of reasons, I was glad to have got away from Egypt. I never want to see it again. Whereas one day, after this bloody war is done with, I'd like to bring you here, show you and the kids around the island. I've made good friends with some of the islanders , including the man who cuts my hair, and his sister, who runs the town's bakery. And then there's Professor Zammit. Professor Zammit stands at the bottom end of the town. A scholar, a schoolteacher. A very dignified-looking man with a calm, far-sighted gaze. It's a surprise, a welcome one to an Englishman used to statues in honour of captains or colonels or knights-at-arms, to find this little town celebrating a man of learning!

But then Malta is full of surprises. The other day I walked up from our camp towards the coast, and headed for a huge mansion I'd been told about, the Inquisitor's Summer Palace. I had to scramble along an old donkey-track that ran between olive orchards with cypresses smoking up into the blue air, then, after what seemed an age, eventually came to an enormous baroque pile, though I couldn't get a good view of it because it was surrounded by high walls, and the only gate I could find was bolted and its wrought ironwork festooned in weeds. I was doing my best to peer through when an old woman came along, being led by a goat. Between her poor English and my worse Maltese, I pieced together bits of information, including the fact that in days of yore the place was famous less for the summoning of heretics than for its parties. Orgies, she meant. Then she crossed herself and said that servants were prevented from witnessing let alone joining in. Once they'd prepared the food and uncorked the wine they were sent back to their cave-dwellings. Their presence would have embarrassed the Inquisitor. Well, naturally. I suspect the caves she was referring to are the ones that warren the hillsides around here and more recently proved *useful as improvised bomb shelters for people working in the fields when the bombers showed up. (The big shelter down in Siggiewi, said to hold over 200 people, was regularly packed during the worst period, but now nobody goes there.) The palace by the way is not far from some extraordinary megalithic ruins I'd love you to see.*

Oh, there's so much else I want to tell you, but I'll have to stop now because I'm due in Valetta to bring back supplies for camp. I'll take this with me to post from there.

*My dearest love to you and to David and Sarah. I **ache** to hold you.*

David held the two, closely-written sheets in his fingers for some time before laying them face down beside the others. He was trying to hear his father's voice. What kind of voice was it? Gruff? Deep? Light? But it was gone for ever. He looked at the photograph of a young man in army uniform, now kept propped on the shelf above his desk as it had in boyhood been at his bedside. The lips were curved in a slight smile, the eyes gazing steadily into the camera lens. Studying the beret, the lightly curling hair, he thought, I'm twice as old as he ever was.

He looked again at the letter. I am alive. I want a future for us all. Both photograph and letter said that much. And here, now, was that long dead man's ageing son, sitting at his desk in the middle of a cold January night, aware that he owed it to his father, to his sister, and to his mother, to read his way through the hundreds, no, thousands of words, because somewhere in them must lie the explanation for that event which fifty years previously had so utterly altered all their lives.

He glanced at the next letter, then the one underneath and the one beneath that, noting their dates. They were in order. She had looked after them. Wasn't that, now he came to think of it, odd? After all, she had destroyed so much. He wound the ribbon about his fingers. True, she had hidden them at the back of her wardrobe. But they were there, curled in the dark, waiting discovery, and sure enough Sarah had come across them. Or had she meant the letters to take their chance. Discovery or destruction.

Let fate decide. For if Sarah, scrabbling about in the wardrobe, hadn't found them, they'd almost certainly have ended up on a rubbish tip or in an incinerator or paper shredder. But by good luck, if that's what it was, here they now were, lying open for inspection under the lemony light of his reading lamp.

He blinked, stretched, rubbed his eyes. Full inspection would have to wait. But before he re-tied the bundle he riffled quickly through, noticed how often the name of someone called Derek Southern cropped up. He stopped, went back to a letter near the top of the pile, then, reading rapidly, picked up the thread of a narrative and followed it through successive letters.

Southern was, it seemed, a young soldier whose romantic affair with a local girl called Anna his father knew about and whom he was advising, though the letters made plain that he saw himself as far more Father Lawrence than Pandarus. *"It's far from easy,"* one letter complained, *"because I can't be there each and every time they want to meet and yet her father and his brother Marcus expect it of me, or expect Anna and Derek to defer their meetings until I **can** be present. I'm pretty certain that I can trust Southern, but all in all I spend far more time at the bakehouse — their regular meeting-place — than I want to, and even so that isn't enough to please everybody. The trouble is, the Maltese fear that the hot blood reigns in the winter's pale. And family honour must not be insulted. That way lies certain death!"*

The note of grumbling disaffection, mostly good-natured but sometimes exasperated, ran through other letters, a kind of refrain to be taken up, dropped, re-introduced. *"Of course I'm seen as an old codger,"* one said, *"a grey-beard as far as most of the Company is concerned. Quite a few of the men are married, and often, I can tell, anxious about their wives, desperate not to be on the receiving end of a 'Dear John' letter. Some have children. But I'm not merely married and a father, I have a career to return to. For a lot of the men here, this is the first regular work they've had — if you can call this work. They are only just starting their lives, whereas I'm already well into mine, or so I can tell, that's what they think.*

David stopped, considered. His father had been born in March, 1910. That meant he was into his thirties when Southern and no doubt others turned to him for advice. He was also of course someone with a degree and a profession. A grammar-school teacher, he was different, but at the same time someone they trusted. He stood on the far side of a door which they had yet to try to push open, let alone walk through.

Birdsong, a full flurry of winter notes, made him look up. The first, grey light of dawn was beginning to smear his uncurtained study window. He could make out, just, the forked outlines of the garden's fruit trees and, beyond, the deepening of shade which signified the high brick wall over which the air darkened still further as it shaped the outline of a row of three-storey houses running parallel to their own. Soon the everyday world would be beginning its activities. Sure enough, as he gazed out at the greyness, sequent oblongs of yellow light appeared in the previously blank walls opposite, and over the rooftops came the first, distant sounds of car doors slamming, of engines starting up. Early commuters leaving for work. If he was to pretend to spend a day working on that bloody book Fitzroy Frobisher pretended they wanted to publish, he'd need to get his head down for a couple of hours. As for what happened to Southern and Anna, that, he thought, as he tidied the letters into shape, would have To be Continued, as the magazines used to say.

About to retie the bundle, his eye snagged on some words of a letter whose place in the order he was trying to determine from its date. *Tell me more about this Mr Krassner*, his father had written, *he sounds fun. I can imagine David's joy at finding someone to help him with his musical activities. But don't let the pair of them drum you out of house and home. (And apologies for so awful a joke.) I can't see that there's any harm in David inviting the man to the house, though if you're uneasy about it you must do whatever you think is right. But you'll probably be spared having to make an awkward decision. Given what you say about Beth Morton, I doubt Krassner will have much free time to tutor our son. By all means defend her, but at a shrewd guess she's already got her grappling irons into young Mr K.*

When had that been written? The date given at the top of the page was *Late June*. A bit vague, but then, as he had already begun to understand, many of his father's letters were put together over the course of several days, a paragraph or page at a time as he snatched at whatever free hours he had.

Once more David flicked through the pile. Yes, here for instance was one which amounted to a kind of journal: entries for *Tuesday, Thursday, Friday (pm), Saturday morning*. But *Late June*. It meant that his father was replying to a letter or letters that had at a guess been sent some two weeks earlier. In other words, he was putting pen to paper in response to hearing for the first time about Jay Krassner's entry into their lives.

∼ Chapter Three ∼

They had just finished dinner when the phone buzzed.

"David?"

"Sarah? How are you?"

"As it happens, well. Though it's not my health I want to discuss."

"I didn't actually think it might be," David said, smiling in answer to Maggie's raised eyebrow. "I was only being polite, honest." Sometimes, his sister's desire to cut straight to the chase seemed not so much brisk as brusque. Not, he had to admit, that he himself greatly liked the phone as a medium for communication. He wondered whether to say this, but before he could find a way of framing the words, Sarah was asking him whether he'd had time to read their father's letters.

"A good many of them," David said, feeling an obscure guilt in having to admit that he'd not yet finished the task, even though he'd brought the letters home only — what was it? — five, no six days ago.

"You've had the weekend at your disposal."

What was this, an inquisition? "To be honest, I'm not much enjoying the experience," he said. Then "no, that's wrong. I mean that I don't feel at ease reading them."

"Why ever not?"

Silently acknowledging the re-filled glass Maggie pushed towards him, David said, "because ... well, because they're very personal. It feels intrusive, prurient, like reading someone else's private love letters. In fact, they *are* love letters. And it's not as if they're written to a stranger, someone we don't know."

"*Exactly!*"

Her remark, uttered with such emphasis, as though she was proving a point in law, perplexed him and again he was struggling to find the words he needed when she cut in.

"When I said *exactly* I meant that from a glance at them, which you'll remember is all I had time for, they struck *me* as love letters."

"You sound surprised." David frowned across at Maggie, lifted his shoulders to indicate his puzzlement at the turn the conversation with his sister was taking. "But I don't find it surprising. Our father was hundreds of miles away, missing his wife and his children ... "

"Have you noticed the date of the last letter?"

"No, I can't say that I have."

"October 12, 1944."

There was a pause. David put down his glass. Maggie was now looking enquiringly at him.

"David?"

"Yes, I'm here," he said, mastering the tremor in his voice.

"Read it carefully," Sarah said, as in rebuke to a backward pupil. "It was the one letter I had time to look over. Of course, because it *was* the last letter I wanted to see whether I could find anything in it that would explain what happened. Not necessarily in what he says but in *how* he writes to her. I think — no I'm sure — that I'd have noticed if there'd been any difference between the earlier letters I flicked through and the way he writes that last one. But if there was, I couldn't see it, and the more I've thought about the matter the more I'm sure that when he wrote that letter nothing was amiss, not as far as he knew."

She paused, and when she next spoke her tone, far more than her words, suggested a certain loss of confidence, though perhaps it was more a diffident acknowledgement of uncertainty than any admission of failure. "I admit it was only when I got home that the significance of the date struck me. Do you see what I'm getting at? That letter is written by someone who doesn't know anything is wrong." She paused, waited. "Do you understand?" But there was no rebuke in the manner of asking. She was as much at a loss as he was.

He nodded. Then, belatedly aware of the fact she couldn't see this gesture of assent, he said slowly, "I think so. Yes. Yes, I do."

"So who told him?"

David took a deep breath. "You can't possibly be suggesting it was me."

"No, of course not." The briskness was back. "Don't be silly. She took jolly good care to vet all you wrote. 'Now, David, do send some cheer-up words to your father.'"

David winced at his sister's imitation, still cruelly accurate after all these years.

"She never said anything like that," he protested.

"It's what she meant. Don't let poor Daddy know what's really going on in his house. Not that you did know. Although I sometimes think there's none so blind ... No, sorry, forget I said that. But, David, who do you think *could* have told him?"

"Beth Morton?" he said, plucking the name from a past where it had lain dormant.

"Possible, but I doubt it."

"Godwin?"

Sarah laughed derisively. "Yes, if he'd had half a chance. He certainly disapproved of her 'goings on', as he no doubt called them and as I recently revealed to you. But I don't see how he could have come by our father's address. He'd have had to ask for it, and the only person he could ask was her.

David sipped his wine. "Not necessarily," he said. "After all, he was postmaster. She left letters and parcels for Malta in his safe keeping. He'd have had plenty of opportunity to note the address."

This time it was Sarah's turn to pause. When she spoke she did so slowly, almost reluctantly. "Well, perhaps. Yes, it's possible." For once, the fat boy at the back of the class had caught teacher's attention. "I admit I hadn't thought of that." Another pause. When she next spoke her voice was back to its most matter-of-fact. "I have a hunch that old Hetty Rayner will be able to tell us what we need to know. If anyone has the answer, it'll be her."

Another name from the past. "Why? I mean, why Hetty Rayner?"

"Because I'd bet with borrowed money that she knew everyone and everything in that village that was worth knowing. And she liked us, didn't she? Well, she liked our mother and she liked you."

"Hmmm." David considered. Then he said, "why do you say that she *will* have the answer? I thought we'd agreed that she's almost certainly be dead by now."

"No, that's what *you* said. But when I got back home I decided to do some sleuthing." The note of implicit triumph was unmistakeable.

"And?"

"She's alive," Sarah said. "The husband died some years ago, but she's still on planet earth and still living above the shop, though it's no longer her shop. Rayner's Bespoke Tailors has become Dirk's Adult Videos."

"I'm impressed. Amazed." And he was. "How do you know all this?"

"Easy," Sarah said, permitting herself a moment's laughter. "Census returns, Notifications of Change of Address, Street Directories. And, where needed, a little additional help from the Boys in Blue we meet in wine bars or health clubs. All very discreet and above board," she added, as though heading off any possible criticism. "There's no end to the roads we accountants can go down in pursuit of those who want to disappear without paying what they owe."

"I see."

"So," Sarah said, "I want you to go and talk to her."

David sighed. "I thought we might be coming to that."

"And now you're going to tell me that you can't possibly find time to pay her a visit."

Stung by the imputation of indolence or, worse, indifference, he said, "The fact is, Sarah, I'm trying to finish a book that's already behind schedule, and my publisher is breathing down my neck threatening to pull the plug if I don't get the typescript to him asap."

"Typescript! Gosh, I though you still spent much of each day sharpening your quill and replenishing the inkhorn. Anyway," her tone shifted to reasonableness, "this won't be difficult, will it? After all, you're in London and you know the old girl had a soft spot for you."

"But Sarah, that was fifty years ago."

"All the better. Old people enjoy reminiscing."

Then, as he drew in his breath, she said, "Oh, Christ, I'm sorry, that was bloody tactless. David, forgive me."

"Of course," he said. Then, sensing that she was waiting for him to say more, he went on. "You're right, though. We can't undo the past by trying to forget it. And to be honest, since our mother's death I've been thinking about it more or less non-stop."

"Well," Sarah said, her voice no longer that of the sister superior, but newly softened, "you may not believe this, but so have I."

Relieved by this sudden renewal of warmth between them, he laughed. "Why shouldn't I believe you?"

"Because you think me — oh, not a hard-hearted Hannah, perhaps, but as pretty well armour-plated. Britomart, is that the name? No time for personal feelings, present and future the only tenses we need to learn — that kind of thing. By the way, I am often armour-plated. Steel knickers, that's me." The defiance in her laugh rang not quite true.

"You're still my sister."

"So you *will* go to see her?"

Touché he thought. She's outsmarted me as usual. "I'll think about it," he said, but even as he took down the address Sarah spelt out and made him repeat to her, he knew that he'd do her bidding.

∼ CHAPTER FOUR ∼

On the short train journey up to Waterloo and the even shorter journey to his destination, David had time to finish *Anna of the Five Towns*. Anna married Mynors, discovering too late that she loved the hapless Willie Price, a bankrupt who owed her money and who disappeared from her life, apparently to make for opportunities of financial redemption in Australia though in fact he died before he could leave the Five Towns. Accident or suicide? Bennett did not say, remarking enigmatically that "the abandoned pit shaft does not deliver up its secret."

He killed himself, no doubt about it, David thought as he closed the novel and, a moment or so later, stepped out of the tube that had brought him to Brixton. Willie Price couldn't live with the agony of separation from Anna. To be on the other side of the world from her would have been more than he could bear. And at once he thought of the words of his father's last letter, a letter which, since at Sarah's prompting he had read it, was imprinted on his mind. It wasn't actually a letter, more a hastily scribbled note.

Yours arrived as I'm about to go on duty, so I'll write a full letter later. This is to reassure you that my love for you is constant. I know that being apart is hell for us both, but for me, and I think for you, 'the bonds of heaven' will never be 'slipp'd, dissolv'd and loos'd'. All my love, Stephen.

Walking down Coldharbour Lane, coat buttoned and collar raised against the bullying wind that hurled rain into his face, he replayed those words over and over, even muttering them aloud as he skirted cracked paving slabs and puddles, seeking an answer to the puzzle of why his father had written in that, for him, uncharacteristically passionate manner? Was he wanting to reassure his wife of his love, or did he want reassurance of hers for him? Yes, as Sarah claimed, it was a love letter, but the tone was ... Was *what*?

He was still brooding about this question as, following instructions, he turned right off the main road into a narrow, dead-end street. Here, there were fewer burnt-out cars and most of the paving-stones seemed as yet unbroken. The side of the road he walked along was lined with two-storey houses built of grey-yellow London brick, their bay windows, which you could almost reach over and touch from the pavement, either shuttered or with drawn curtains, in front of each a space of three feet at most before the pavement began. In some cases the flattened mud revealed long-abandoned attempts to maintain a strip of grass, although more often the gap, concreted over, was filled with bikes, prams stripped to now rusting frames, old refrigerators, washing machines, TVs. The detritus of urban living for those gripping the rim of the abyss. The terraced houses facing straight onto the pavement on the street's far side provided evidence that here the grip had largely failed. Several of the houses looked vacant, one or two had their doors kicked in, curtains billowed through windows that had lost their glass, and from the upstairs of one window a torn sleeping bag hung, twisting in the wind in such a way that it took David a second glance to assure himself it wasn't the dead body he'd at first, unnervingly, taken it to be. Decay, depression, abandonment. Hetty Rayner must surely find living here an unwelcome change from the green fields and lush hedgerows of her wartime village.

The end of the street was marked by two adjoined houses which had at an earlier date been turned into shops. One, with grille covering the ground-floor windows from top to bottom and glass door heavily reinforced with steel mesh, proclaimed itself WINSTONE WINES. Beside it, corrugated sheeting over windows and door prevented entry to DIRKS ADULT VIDEO'S.

David did as instructed and followed the narrow, foul-smelling alley beside the latter building until he came to a door set in its side wall. There was no bell push or knocker, so he banged with his fist. Flakes of red paint detached themselves from the wood as the door vibrated in its frame. He banged again, harder. This time he heard a dog yap and then a woman's voice calling from, he guessed, upstairs, "Coming, coming."

A few minutes later, the same voice said from behind the unopened door, "Who is it?"

"David Willoughby."

The safety chain slid back, there was a fumbling with key and lock, and then the door swung wide. "You have to be so careful these days," the old woman coming into view said.

Had she always been so fat? The aged face, its wide, fleshy nose and pendulous cheeks streaked with talcum powder, tilted towards him as, stepping inside, he bent to kiss her. Or short?

"My god, David, don't look so surprised. It's fifty years since we last met. You were a little boy then, and I'm entitled to be an old woman now. Here, Sylvie, this gentleman and me, we used to be friends." As she spoke, she bent stiffly to pick up the Pekingese that had been snuffling at David's feet, its eyes wet with rheum, and he noticed how much pink scalp showed through the white hair which Hetty Rayner had tried to arrange in neat curls across her broad head.

"Well, well," she said, patting his arm. "So here you are. In the flesh. Cold, too, I'll be bound. This dreadful weather. It gets straight to my bones, I can tell you."

As David stepped past her into the passage, she released the dog which thudded softly onto the passage's bare boards, shut and locked the door, then slipped the safety catch back on.

"I'm upstairs," she said and began to follow the dog as it hauled itself, panting, over each riser of the dimly-lit stairway, its mistress holding onto the banisters while she laboured upwards. Following slowly after, David had plenty of time to observe the plum-coloured dress stretched tight across her wide beam, her old-woman's legs encased in dark brown woollen stockings, the flat-back slippers that clack-clacked on the threadbare stair carpet.

"Coffee, maybe," she asked, turning to face him within the open doorway of the room that stood at the head of the stairs.

"Coffee would be fine," he said, speaking for the first time. The room they were in was larger than he'd expected. Without looking over-crowded, it was able to contain two easy chairs and a sofa grouped in a semi-circle, and at the further end from where they stood, a square dining table round which were grouped four hard-backed chairs stood in front of a swagged floor-length curtain. Beyond, in the back wall, a door presumably led to a further room or rooms.

"Take off your coat and make yourself comfortable," Hetty Rayner called as she disappeared through the inner wall's curtained doorway into what had to be the kitchen. "Sylvie, you come here. I try to keep her out of the best room when I've got company," she explained, shouting. "I know not everyone likes dogs." Had she guessed that he was among that number? Her head reappeared briefly round the kitchen door. "You want the toilet, David. It's out on the landing, second left. You'll find there's a clean towel."

"I'm alright thanks." He took off his damp coat and draped it over one of the dining chairs. Then, while she busied herself in the kitchen, he began an inspection of the room's many photographs. They hung on walls, were propped on the mantelpiece, lined up along the top of the bookcase, television set, they even crowded the surface of a small side-table that stood beside the sofa. Most were of faces he didn't recognise: wedding groups, formal family occasions, studio portraits, a few were of Hetty and a man he at once understood to be Michael Rayner. But this man was a good deal older than the one he remembered, had less hair and a more pronounced paunch. The cheerful smile remained, however. He looked for any evidence of photographs taken at the time he knew the Rayners, of the village, of the tea-dances, perhaps, but couldn't see any.

He turned back to one photograph he'd passed with an initial, perfunctory glance. A women's football team, framed within un-netted goalposts, the women at the front crouching, those in the back row standing with arms folded, purposeful.

"Lyons Ladies Eleven, 1938," Hetty Rayner said, from behind him. "Taken at Hackney Marshes. I'm second on the left, front row. Look." Silver tray in hand, she came to stand beside him, indicating with a jerk of her head the stocky, dark-haired young woman in quartered shirt, sleeves rolled up to show well-muscled biceps. The unrecognisable young woman stared back.

"I never knew there were women's football teams then," he said, turning to the present Hetty Rayner.

She smiled up at him, her wide, whiskery mouth accentuated by the uncertain application of lipstick. "Top of the season for three years running, we were," she said. "Best kickers in London."

"And Lyons?" He lowered himself into an easy chair while, having rested the tray on the table after taking care to put a mat beneath it, she poured coffee for them both. "So you weren't a seamstress then? Or were you an outsider, a ringer, smuggled in to the team because of your goal-scoring abilities?"

She laughed as she handed him his coffee. Good-quality china, too. "Never sewed a stitch until Michael showed me how. I was a pastry-cook, David. *Patissier.*" She spoke the French word with pride.

He breathed in the aroma of her excellent coffee. "But you're not French by origin, are you?"

She plumped down in a chair opposite him and on a stool she dragged between them set down a large, round plate with slices of thick fruit cake. "No" she said, looking at him with black eyes that now at last began to stir memories of fifty years ago, of the younger Hetty Rayner's intense gaze. "Vienna was where we came from."

David helped himself to a piece of cake. "Ah" he said, as the rich, warm, moist flavours filled his mouth. "I thought so. Yum, yum. I was hoping this cake might be like the one you used to make."

"I remembered how much you liked it."

"You're a wonder."

"For my age you're going to say."

He shook his head, laughing. "I wasn't, I truly wasn't."

"Well, I don't mind. At eighty-five I don't get many compliments. Thanks be to God I've still got my health, though sometimes I wonder whether I wouldn't be better off dead." She spoke matter-of-factly.

"I was sorry to hear about Mr. Rayner."

"Michael? He had a good life. He was alive right to the end, if you know what I mean. Still doing a bit of work, though we'd given up the shop by then. But he did some cutting and sewing for friends in the trade, read books, went for his walks, met friends. Then his heart —" she clapped her hands. "It stopped. Like that." She paused, stared reflectively at the dark blue carpet. "A shock to me, but for him — it was how he always wanted to die." Another pause. "We don't all have the choice, though." She still pronounced "have" as "haff".

"You know," David said, speaking into the awkward silence, "until this morning I never realised you were Jewish. I ... Well, I'd simply no idea. But then, looking at these photographs of weddings and what I suppose are bar mitzvahs ... "

"No need to apologise." Hetty Rayner's look contained a depth of sadness though something else stirred in it. "You were a small boy. Besides, we didn't go around advertising the fact."

"But people in the village must have been aware?"

A brief laugh. "Oh, they were, they were." And now the sadness gave way to a flash of bitter remembrance. "Michael told me he'd heard some of the workers in the hosiery factory discussing the war. He was pretty certain they wanted him to hear. They blamed the Jews for provoking Hitler. Yes, well bound to be our fault. I imagine their wives thought the same way."

He was stunned. "But nobody said that to your face?"

"No. That's not the English way, is it. So we didn't say anything, either. Let them think what they wanted about us. We'd got out of London because we didn't want to be bombed and, to be honest, at that time a lot of people took for granted a German invasion. There was a panic that once that happened, well then, London's Jews would be an easy target for the storm troopers. Lord Haw Haw used to read out lists on the wireless. I said, 'Michael, don't listen,' but he did. We all did. 'When we arrive we shall be looking for ...' Not us, of course, but prominent Jews, they were all on his list. No wonder there was a panic. So, like other Jewish families we knew at that time, we decided that anywhere but London was where we wanted to be, stuck a pin in the map and ended up in your village. And once there, we did our best to keep quiet."

"Not to disturb the even tenor of the village's ways."

"If you say so."

He drank his coffee. "But once the war was over you came back to London."

"Couldn't wait. I was never so pleased as when I saw the back of that place. Michael felt the same. We loathed it there." She grimaced, wriggled her shoulders in an expansive gesture of disgust. Then, noting his expression, she said, "I know that for you it must have been different. And you and your sister were so young, most of the nastiness would have passed you by. Well, until … " She waved away her own words, "An English village. A little bit of paradise. Roses round the door and cows up the lane. Isn't that what the English dream of?"

He laughed to oblige her. "Some do. Not me." But he felt shaken. By her words and by the bitterness with which she spoke them. He *had* been happy there. At all events, he'd been happy until the moment that brought life in the village to its abrupt, terrible end.

As though replying to his unspoken thought, Hetty Rayner said, "I don't know how your mum ever put up with it. She was a real pal, she knew what others thought and no doubt said behind my back, she could see the way they behaved when I was there — not all of them, I grant. The ones who helped with the dances were alright. But as for the rest! Never *said* anything mind, but you could see it in their little smiles, the way they had of not quite meeting your eye. But your mum always made it clear to them that she was my friend."

And now her words triggered a memory. Something stirred in his mind, the fluttering of wings, something struggling to free itself from the deep forgetfulness of the years. What was it?

Suddenly, he knew. Old sounds came back, her voice as it then was, an exchanged look. It had been when he was helping her clear up after one of the tea-dances and Hetty Rayner had said — but what had she said? Something about not expecting the village to care whether she ran the dances or not. In that case it must have been after the Americans had left for France No, the words wouldn't come. But what he *could* remember was the way she had spoke them, and the look on her face. The sense of hurt, or was it contempt? It came to him for the first time, with the force of a blow: *that* was why his mother had been so keen for him to help Hetty Rayner with the Saturday dances. She wanted it to be known whose side she was on. And *that* must have been why, on one never-to-be-forgotten occasion, she'd arranged for Sarah and him to stay a night at the Rayner's house, when it would have been just as easy — easier — for them to stay elsewhere.

He saw her now in a new light. Someone who'd set herself against the prejudices of a village life he still viewed through a haze of remembered happiness. By her actions, and perhaps words, she'd made herself its victim. The Rayners had after all escaped back to London. She had gone on living in the place. Could Hetty Rayner explain *that*, he wondered.

The old woman was talking again. "And you and Sarah came to London. Now that *was* a surprise, you telling me when you phoned the other day. Almost as big a surprise as hearing your voice." She gestured to his cup. "More coffee? And another slice of cake. Go on, it was made especially for you."

While she refilled his cup, he reached for the cake. "This is even better than I remember," he said, swallowing a sizeable piece. The Pekingese, which had been asleep on the sofa, woke, sniffed the air, then dropped onto the floor and waddled over to where David sat.

"Sylvie, come here," Hetty Rayner said. The dog obediently turned and shuffled back to its owner who, groaning with the effort of bending past her own bosom, scooped it up into her lap. She watched her visitor bite into the cake. "It's made with ingredients we couldn't get in the war," she said, her smile twisted, sardonic. "Though one thing I'll say for the village, it may have been lacking in human kindness but there was never any shortage of cream." She sipped her coffee, set the cup aside. "Now, I want to know how you were able to find me."

David cleared his mouth of cake. "It was Sarah," he said. "Apparently in her profession you learn ways and means of tracking down defaulting clients or clients of clients. So I imagine it wouldn't have been too difficult to discover your address. After all, you weren't trying to keep it hidden." She smiled to show she understood that he was joking. "Anyway, she did discover it and here I am."

"And it's lovely to see you here, after all these years. It brings back memories. I'd like to have seen Sarah, too."

Aware of the implied rebuke, he told her that Sarah lived in Manchester and that trips to London, while not infrequent, didn't happen so often as to allow her to join him for his visit to Brixton. But she sent her regards.

The old woman nodded. "And is she successful?"

"Very. She makes far more money than I ever have or will. University salaries don't compare with what top accountants earn. And unless I'm much mistaken, Sarah must be at the top or thereabouts. Mind you, job satisfaction in my field is, correction, used to be. ... " And he smiled wryly.

But she wasn't listening. "Eh," she said, sighing. "the last time I saw Sarah she was a little girl in pigtails. She used to trail a teddy bear around with her, I remember, and make it sit and watch her skipping. Mrs D, Mrs I, Mrs FF I ... " She clapped her hands to accentuate the rhyme and as she did so the Pekingese raised its doleful countenance to stare at the podgy, wrinkled, beringed fingers meeting in the air above its head, then grunted, licked its lips, yawned, and settled once more into a profound lethargy.

"She'll be married?"

"No". David set his cup down. He wondered whether to say anything more about his sister's personal life and could see no harm in adding, "for some years she had a live-in partner, but I gather they've gone their separate ways. Sarah seems happy enough on her own."

"And you?"

"Oh, married, as I mentioned the other evening. Two children, both adults, both themselves now married. Maggie and I are, would you believe, grandparents. It makes us seem very old."

But if he was expecting a disclaimer he was to be disappointed.

"No, I mean, do you like your work. You mentioned university.

Are you a lecturer?"

"Was. I've just retired. But I have a book to finish writing. After that, I don't know … ."

"So you never became a musician, a drummer, wasn't it?"

"No" he said, meeting her gaze, "No, that never happened."

"Pity. Your mother had such hopes for you. 'My little drummer boy,' she called you. Ah, she loved you two children."

She looked unblinkingly at him, shook her head and sighed.

Weighing the sombreness of her expression, he said, feeling his way, "You and your husband had no children."

Again, she shook her head. "No. I had two miscarriages in the early days, in London, that was, and the doctor warned us against trying again. Said my body was wrong, I don't know. So no, we had no children. And then we got out of London and came to live in rural England. Plenty of happy families there, of course." The satiric edge was once more in place, but was blunted by her next words. "We loved your mum and seeing you two about the village. I can remember … " and she began a series of reminiscences of the young Sarah and David with their mother or on their own, of Sarah's worries about her bear's health, of him in charge of music at the tea-dances, his concern always to choose the right records, his careful winding of the gramophone, the care he took to change needles. "Every ten sides, wasn't it? … "

At first he was startled and then moved by the old woman's words, her vivid recall of incidents he'd forgotten or which, now she brought him to share them with her, meant little enough to him, though for her they had a significance which, he realised, was intimately connected to her regard for his mother, whom she repeatedly referred to as that "lovely girl" or "dear thing," or simply but affectingly "your mum." For fifty years she'd held onto memories she now unwrapped in his presence so that they gleamed, untarnished. Whereas for him such memories, if he brought them up at all, were irreparably spoilt by how it all ended.

He said, "when Sarah and I went to live with our grandparents at Twickenham I didn't take the drums with me, you know. I'm not sure that such noise would have been encouraged."

He tried to keep his voice light, smiled in an intendedly

reassuring manner. "Sorry, I don't want to give you the wrong impression. They were a bit too old to be comfortable with the role of parents, but I'm not criticising them. They did their best to look after us and anyway," he shrugged, avoided her eyes, "once I'd left the village I rather lost interest in drums and drummers."

Hetty Rayner sat with her head lowered, studying her slippered feet. When she looked up again, her eyes were glowing with what had to be commiseration. She said, "that must have been a terrible time for all of you. I was very, *very* sorry. I still am." She paused, looked fixedly at him and said, with unusual fervour, "I hope you realise David, your mother was a good woman."

He looked back, uncertain how to reply. Then, "I'm not sure Sarah would entirely agree," he murmured.

"Sarah was a little girl at the time," she said urgently. "But later, when she was grown, surely then she could understand and forgive?"

"I don't know." But as he spoke he remembered the day of the funeral and of Sarah rebuking him for his own harsh words about their mother. "Yes," he said, "perhaps. Perhaps." He noticed how solemnly now she was studying his face and suddenly the question he'd come all this way across London to ask her seemed impossible to put.

He blew out his cheeks, said, "you must understand that once we'd left the village behind, we saw very little of her. Not in the remainder of our childhood, not in our teenage years, nor as adults. She wasn't welcome at Twickenham, of course, but as soon as Sarah and I were out in the wide world we made regular contact with her, that is we wrote, tried to get her to visit us, offered to visit her. But she always found some way of putting us off."

He paused, shook his head, plunged on. "Maggie and I invited her to our wedding but, as we feared, she found an excuse not to come. Then, when we had kids of our own, I was sure she'd want to see her grandchildren, but no. On the other hand, she remembered their birthdays. There were always cards and small presents — I don't suppose she had much money, though on the few occasions we saw her — on neutral ground — she wouldn't discuss the matter. This was when Sarah and I were adults, of course."

"Neutral ground?"

He smiled apologetically in answer to her quizzical look. "Oh, you know. From time to time she'd come to London and we'd meet at the Tate or some public place or other, maybe one of the big stations or a department store. And once or twice, when Sarah got her to Manchester, I'd join them there. But I think we both felt that the meetings were dutiful rather than … well, rather than," he hesitated, said again "rather than … " and stopped. He wanted to say "rather than warm, loving," but felt he couldn't use those particular words, and what other words would do. He went on, "And my guess is that each time we said goodbye all of us did so with a secret relief. She simply wouldn't let herself be close to us. It was as if — as if she didn't want to be forgiven."

He stopped. He felt wretchedly at a loss for words. Felt, too, that he was somehow called upon to defend himself and Sarah against an accusation that, although it hadn't been made, nevertheless hovered in the air of this over-heated room, an accusation of which, no matter how appearances might be stacked against them, they were innocent.

"And now she's dead," Hetty Rayner said softly, without taking her eyes off him.

He nodded. "Yes, I'm afraid so."

They sat in silence for a few minutes, eyes averted.

"David," Hetty Rayner said at last. "Tell me the truth. Why did you come here today?"

He felt himself blush. A small boy being brought to account. "Well," he said, trying to put together the words he needed. "The fact is, Sarah and I were wondering if you knew … if you could throw any light on what happened. I mean, it's difficult, I know, but … it occurred to us … As you yourself said, Sarah was so little at the time, and to be honest I wasn't much older, not old enough to … ."

"Not old enough to understand how dreadful it all was," she said, and then, more energetically, even heatedly, "and certainly not old enough to understand that nobody was to blame except perhaps the war itself. Terrible things happen in war, David, and not always on the battlefield."

Her words, and the manner in which she spoke them, made him feel as though he was in need of correction, that he'd misunderstood a matter on which it was vital she put him right.

But when she next spoke, her voice was altogether gentler. "I doubt there's anything I can tell you that you don't already know." She looked at him, looked away, looked back. "I imagine you know that as soon as you'd gone to your grandparents, your mother shut up the house and went away, she wouldn't tell me where. She wouldn't tell me anything, in fact, except that you'd gone to — where was it?"

"Woodbridge," David said, "that's where they were renting a place until the war ended."

"Woodbridge, yes, I remember now. But you could have knocked me down with a feather when you told me the other night that after the war they took you back to Twickenham with them. And that you and Sarah stayed there for the rest of your childhoods. I'd never have believed that."

"I don't think we could believe it, either," David said. "We expected her to appear any day, I think we told each other it was bound to happen; and that, when she came, we'd of course go off with her and stay together, the three of us. We even managed to persuade ourselves that on one particular day she'd show up, a Saturday it was to be, not long after we'd arrived at Woodbridge. It began as a wish, then it became a hope, then a belief, and from there it hardened into a certainty."

He laughed ruefully at the memory, wondering whether to go on. Then, seeing Hetty Rayner's look, the unmissable encouragement of her smile, added, "Sarah and I began to talk about it as though it was definite, egged each other on, made each other promise that it would happen, as if a promise was a guarantee. We even planned a party for the day, saved biscuits, made some flags to wave from the windows. The night before she was due we went to bed in a state of high old excitement. And the next morning when we went down to breakfast we'd both dressed in our best clothes. Of course, they — our grandparents — wanted to know why. So we told them. 'Our mother's coming today, she's coming to fetch us.' And I saw our grandmother's face.

Astonishment, then disbelief. 'Who ever told you any such thing?' And of course we didn't know. But as soon as we heard those words, let alone saw her face, our hopes flew away like … like scared birds."

He sighed, shook his head. "It wasn't their fault, of course it wasn't. But the sense of let-down, ah, that was difficult for both of us. We never mentioned it again but I think from then on we both began to resent her for not coming to collect us when we'd been so certain she would."

"And she didn't come later?"

"No," he said, "she never did. Once the war ended, they took us back with them to Twickenham. We never knew why and they didn't explain. She must have been in touch with them, and once or twice they'd say something like 'Your mother wants you to know that she's thinking of you and sends her best wishes' — never love — but that was as far as it went. And all that time there was no sign of her. They were kind, they did their best, but still they couldn't take her place, could they? Sarah cried herself to sleep night after night until I suppose she was out of tears." He stopped, said, "I'm telling this badly, I'm afraid. Sorry."

The old woman said nothing, merely motioned with her hand for him to go on.

"I remember that to start with we'd ask when our mother would be coming to take us home, but we never got a satisfactory response. Once though, our grandfather said, 'how long is a piece of string,' a remark neither of us understood, but which we sensed meant we shouldn't go on asking. And after a while, perhaps to stop us asking, they started to tell us 'this is your home now.' Though there was an occasion when Sarah, in a temper because she'd been told to eat some food she didn't like, shouted that she wanted to be with her mother, and our grandmother said, snappishly, 'well, you can't.' And I said, 'why, are you keeping her prisoner somewhere?' and there was a silence during which they looked at each other, and then my grandfather said, 'you shouldn't talk to your grandmother like that. But no, your mother isn't anyone's prisoner except her own,' a remark I understood even less than I understood his remark about the piece of string. Then nobody said anything for some minutes, until finally he told me, 'your mother isn't well.' And I thought he meant she was very ill."

Another pause. He looked across at Hetty Rayner, saw the unchanging gravity of her expression. "As in a way I suppose she was," he said, breaking off.

She nodded, this time vigorously. "Yes," she said. "She was. She came to see me after she'd put you on the train to Leicester where they were apparently going to collect you. Told me she couldn't face them, couldn't face anyone. She looked terrible, David, simply terrible. If I hadn't known how good a mother she was to you two, how deeply she loved you, I'd have been worried that she might do something to herself. She'd not have been the first. I even begged her not to try anything 'desperate'. And she promised me she wouldn't. So I believed her when she said she needed to get away on her own for a while. I phoned your grandparents once or twice — she'd given me their number — to ask after you. I knew you must still be with them because whenever I went past your house it looked shut up, curtains drawn, porch unswept. Once, I even went up the path and knocked on the door, but there was no answer. Then I had a card from her, from somewhere up north. It said nothing apart from the fact that she hoped to be back soon. But simply hearing that she was alive put my mind at rest."

"I don't remember my grandparents ever mentioning that you'd phoned."

"I'm not surprised. It was made clear to me that they thought I was pushing my nose in where it wasn't wanted, especially when I said I was a friend of your mother's. So I stopped phoning. And then, when it was time to say our not-so fond farewells to the village, I didn't know what to do. Your mum still wasn't back. So I popped a note through her door with our London address, hoping that once she'd returned she'd get in touch. You should have seen the mess the porch was in by then. I hated the place being in such a state. It felt completely *abandoned*. I went back home, fetched Michael, and together we swept the front path and porch, knocked down all the cobwebs, got the leaves and paper scraps into a sack, left it looking as clean as we could. That little house had been such a pleasure to visit. I loved dropping in there for a chat with your mum. It wasn't much of a place but she made it look, well, like a *real* home."

A memory of the freshly-painted bedrooms waiting for him and Sarah on their return from what proved to be their last holiday in Huntingdonshire came back to him, and then a far more vivid memory of the drab, comfortless house he and his smart sister had wondered disconsolately about after the recent funeral.

"She must have got back after you'd left for London," he said, when he could speak.

"I guess so. And then moved away, though you'll have to tell me where, because I don't know. I wrote to her a few times but by then she must have packed up and gone. I never had a line from her, and of course there was no phone in the house." She sighed deeply, shook her head. "I wanted to keep in touch, believe me. And if only I'd known of her death, I'd have done my best to go to the funeral. Where was it held?"

"In the village," he said.

She looked surprised. "I'd not have thought she'd have wanted to be returned there."

"She never left."

Hetty Rayner stared at him, mouth agape. "She *what?*"

"It's true. She stayed."

Disbelief gradually gave way to something nearer horror. Her eyes filmed over. Then, covering her face, she whispered, aghast, "But how *could* she."

He sat silent, unable to answer.

After a few minutes she lowered her hands and he saw that her eyes were wet with tears. "Poor, poor woman," she whispered. "To stay there, in that place, with nobody she could talk to, nobody to take her side." She shook her head, still in a state of shocked disbelief. A tear trembled on her cheek. Impatiently, she brushed it away. "What punishment." Another pause. Then, "and with nobody to take her side," she repeated, this time fiercely.

"I remember there was a woman, someone called Beth Morton. Wasn't she a friend?"

214

Hetty Rayner stared at him. "*What* do you remember of Beth Morton?"

Surprised by the anger in her voice, he shrugged, said, "nothing really. Only that she lived in a house down the road from us and that she was a friend. At least I thought she was."

"Beth Morton was no friend to your mother, I can tell you," Hetty Rayner said and her voice quivered with contempt. "A real cobra, that one, spitting poison wherever she could." Beth Morton had presumably been among those who whispered about Hetty Rayner behind her back. And what else might she have been responsible for? "Anyway," she went on, briskly now, "she disappeared with some fancy man even before we left the village. Came to a bad end somewhere, I shouldn't wonder."

Might she be hinting at more than she was prepared to reveal. "Do you think she somehow got in touch with my father?" he asked.

Hetty Rayner looked at him, a puzzled expression on her weary, lined face. She was, he suddenly realised, very old, and the emotional impact of what he'd told her had hit her hard.

"Why?" she said, "why should she?" Then her expression cleared. "Oh, I see what you're getting at. No, not her." She waved a hand dismissively and as she did so brushed against the Pekingese's head. The dog woke, looked mournfully about, then, seeing nothing to sustain wakefulness, subsided once more into sleep. "Beth Morton," she said, pursing her lips derisively, "I'd not thought of her for years, nor the rest of that precious bunch." Then, pulling her shoulders back, she said, "Doreen Hollis, she was all right, though. She used to help at the dances, remember? Yes, you do. Made sandwiches, washed up. Worked like a skivvy. No airs and graces about Doreen. No —" she hesitated. "No prejudices, either. We kept in touch for a while, postcards, but then one of us didn't reply to the other, can't remember whose fault it was. And that was that. My last contact with the village." She looked at him. "Until you phoned, right out of the blue. I don't imagine you or Sarah have any news about the place?" And when he shook his head, she asked "What about that friend of yours, Robin, wasn't he called?"

"No idea, I'm afraid. He and I lost contact once we'd left for Woodbridge." He told her then about the funeral, about the hour he and Sarah had spent in the pub, about what they'd been told concerning the organist and of Bert Mee's death. She nodded, but without interest. The names rang no bells. Of the house he said nothing, nor did she ask. He had the feeling that to tell her about its final dilapidation would cause her too much hurt.

When, soon afterwards, he stood up to leave she did not ask him to stay. But she laboured downstairs ahead of him, the Pekingese panting along behind them. Pulling open the front door, he promised to keep in touch, and she asked him to remember her to Sarah. "And tell her it's never too late to marry."

"I'll do that." He peered out into the rain.

"When we first came here this was a nice little street," she said, gazing under his arm at the drabness. Then, smiling uncertainly up at him, "I'm sorry I couldn't be more help to you."

He bent, kissed her wrinkled cheek. "You *have* helped," he said, meaning it. "And I will be in touch again, I promise."

* * *

Outside, he buttoned up his mac, began the walk back to Brixton station.

"Your mother was a good woman." Those words hadn't been uttered for form's sake, they came from the heart. Thinking of the fervour with which Hetty Rayner had spoken them gave a sudden lift to his spirits, provided some warmth to counter the chill of the rainy, windswept day.

Striding up Colharbour Lane and adjusting his stride to avoid as many of the cracked paving stones as possible, he began to whistle.

CHAPTER FIVE

He took the tube to Leicester Square, spent some time wandering about the bookshops of Charing Cross Road and Cecil Court, telling himself as he dodged in and out of various doors that he was on the look-out for works that might help him in the writing of his own book. Then, having found nothing that was within reach of his pocket, he made his way through a Trafalgar Square crowded with tourists huddling together as they posed, grinning, for cameras, determined to assert that they were enjoying themselves in the squally, cheerless weather. From there he walked across Hungerford Bridge, face stung by spray driven upwards on the buffeting wind, and arrived at Waterloo as the office crowds, released from their day's work, began to thicken in the late afternoon gloom.

But at home all was a glow. As he came through the front door, he heard music coming from the kitchen. Maggie was sitting at the scrubbed wood table, a glass of red wine in front of her, her face lit with smiles.

He stooped to kiss the top of her head. "What's that?"

"Schubert," she said. "Don't you recognise it?"

"What you're drinking? The String Quintet, of course."

"Correct, and I'm drinking a Cabernet Sauvignon." She showed him the bottle.

"To drown your sorrows?"

"On the contrary. I — you — we, have reason to celebrate."

He pulled out a chair, sat opposite her and, as she poured him a glass, looked speculatively at her. Had her agent reported good advance sales for the new show?

She gestured to him to take up his glass. "Susie's pregnant," she said.

"Oh, wonderful." And it was. They clinked glasses. "Tell me all about it."

He listened to Maggie's account of their daughter's phone call, which had come not long after he'd left the house. The doctor had confirmed Susie's confident assumption that she was two months' pregnant. "Which means a summer baby." Mother and daughter had spoken about where the birth would take place, Maggie relieved when Susie told her that she'd taken her doctor's advice to go into hospital for the delivery rather than have the baby at home. They'd also discussed how the flat would have to be re-arranged. Alex would move what he called his office out of the spare room. "He doesn't really need it, anyway. He's got plenty of space at school. That's one of the advantages of teaching art."

He refilled their glasses. "I ought to phone to congratulate her."

Maggie glanced at her watch. "Too late, I think. They're going to out to celebrate."

"Is that wise?"

She burst out laughing. "Oh, come on, David. There'll be plenty of times in the coming months when she won't feel like good wine and food. Let her enjoy herself while she can."

Through her words he heard the music come to its close.

"Well, if we're joining them in celebrating I'm not sure I'd have chosen that Schubert as appropriate to the present occasion," he said, smiling faintly.

I love it," Maggie said simply. "He may have been a dying man, but there's a lot of life in what he wrote." She paused, sipped her wine. Then, getting to her feet, she said, "I ought to attend to our casserole. Oh," turning back, "sorry. How was your visit to Mrs …Whatever she's called. I should have asked before but Susie's news has filled my mind."

"Mrs Rayner," he said, "and don't apologise. Your news is better than mine by far. Cheers." He rose, went across to her, put his arm round her and they kissed. Raising his glass, he said, "and here's to Hetty Rayner. She may be an old lady but there's still a lot of life in *her*. Surprises, too."

"Such as?"

"Such as the fact that she's Jewish."

"And you hadn't known?"

He shook his head. "It's more than that. We hadn't been meant to know. Our mother knew, but kept quiet about it. And in the light of what I learnt today, I can understand why. It seems that there was a good deal of anti-Semitism in the village I once thought of as paradise revisited." He raised an eyebrow as he spoke the last words, gave a wry shrug. "We might have spoken out of turn, as small children do."

"So how did it come out?"

"Photographs," he told her. "Photographs all round the room we were in. There was even one of her in a pre-war women's football team, can you believe. I'd never seen any of those before." And as she began to speak, he said, "We were in the Rayner's house on enough occasions, you know, and even if I'd forgotten some of the details I certainly wouldn't have forgotten the photograph of a women's football team. It's not the kind of thing a boy would forget."

"Point taken." Maggie opened the oven door and savoury smells filled the kitchen. "This is about ready," she said. Then, with her back to him, "perhaps they left London in a hurry and had no time to pack all their knick-knacks, photographs included.".

"It's possible." He reached into the table drawer for mats and cutlery. "Yes, it's possible," he said again, as he arranged their place settings. "But my hunch is that they chose to travel incognito. Either that or they took good care to hide the photographs as soon as they realised what they'd come to. 'My dear, *what* kind of a woman plays *football.*' 'My dear, need you ask.' And the fact that Michael Rayner was a tailor. It all adds up. I was thinking about her revelation on the way back. Those little signs you don't really understand when you're a kid. How I sometimes sensed that people kept her at arm's length. Not all, by any means. She told me about a woman called Doreen Hollis, a woman I can scarcely remember, who used to help out at the dances where I ran the music side of the business. The village's infant DJ! Ho, yus. Apparently Doreen was a real friend, and so was our mother. But there was another woman, Beth Morton, who I always thought of as a pucka wallah. Well, she had a fridge, the only one in the

219

village as far as I knew. If Hetty Rayner is to be believed, and I think she is, Mrs Morton was a very nasty bit of work."

"So much for the village idyll," Maggie said, bringing the casserole over to the the table. "There's a salad to go with this. OK?"

She served them both. "Terrific," he said, bending to sniff at his plate. "You're a wonderful cook. As well as being a first-rate sculptor."

Maggie bowed her silent head in mock acknowledgement of his words.

"But as for life in the village," he said, when he'd swallowed a forkful and taken a mouthful of wine. "No more the happy rural seat of various view, I'm afraid."

* * *

After they'd done the washing up and sat sipping coffee, Maggie said, "are you going to report back to Sarah?"

"Of course."

She looked at him. "But ... ."

"I'm worried about Sarah," he said.

"I can't think why. She's a successful business woman who earns twice what you do — did. And who from all I see and hear thoroughly enjoys her life. You've no reason to feel sorry for her."

The hint of tartness in her words made him wonder whether Maggie secretly resented Sarah's freedom to live much as she pleased.

"I didn't say I was sorry for her, I said I was worried about her." Then, curbing the tetchiness of his own words, he said, "I know she's good at her work and she's certainly not without material rewards. You should see the car she drives, paid for by a client, so she tells me. £20,000 I'd guess, probably more."

"Well then." Maggie smiled across at him. Don't let's quarrel, the smile said, especially not now, when we should be happy for our daughter.

He smiled back, became serious once again. "I know Sarah's life seems, well, seems wholly successful." He paused, wondered whether to go on, decided that he must. "But on the day of the funeral she said something that cut me to the bone. It was when she'd driven to me to the house for my first glimpse of it, before the funeral itself. I hadn't seen it for fifty years. God, it looked *awful.*" He shuddered at the recollection. "I can't remember what I said, but I must have given some indication of my feelings. And Sarah said, 'A house without love.' And it's true. That's *exactly* what it looked. A house without love."

He stared at the floor-tiles, then, looking up, he said, as though to himself, "and yet we *had* been happy there, the three of us. I wanted the house to have kept some sign of that. But it hadn't."

There was silence. Was he saying that unhappiness was stronger than happiness, would outlive it, erase it. Down their carved names the rain-drop ploughs.

"Perhaps," Maggie said slowly, "when you and Sarah left you took the happiness with you."

"Perhaps we did. I've been reading that novel of Arnold Bennett's, *Anna of the Five Towns,* the one Susie bought for me. Bennett gives poor Anna a pretty hard time of it. But at least he lets her remember the happiness she once experienced. Even when she's stuck in the dull, loveless routines of middle-age, she gets a glow out of her memories of the time she was young and happy."

"And you think Sarah doesn't."

He nodded. "She was only five."

"I had an old aunt who used to say 'happy as a sandboy,'" Maggie said, apparently inconsequentially. "I asked what a sandboy was, and she said that a sandboy was a boy who sells sand. Why should a boy who sells sand be happy? I suppose it's ironic, like Happy Arabia."

"'Happy Arabia' isn't ironic" David said. "Or rather it wasn't originally." As he spoke, he realised that Maggie knew perfectly well what she was doing, but he decided to go along with her diversionary tactics. No bad temper, no gloom. Not this evening. He stared over imaginary spectacles as he gripped the lapels of an imaginary gown. "Felix Arabia — Araby the Blest, though Milton's coinage is a mistranslation of the Latin, which means 'on the right hand.'"

"Cor," Maggie said, "you don't 'arf know a lot. Now, how about finishing the wine. And while you're doing it, tell me whether your Mrs Rayner turned out to be any help."

David poured what was left into his glass. "Not really," he said. "Or not in an obvious way. She couldn't throw any light on what happened. I'd not realised, you see, that the Rayners returned to London as soon as they possibly could. When they left the village Sarah and I were at Woodbridge. The old girl had no idea that after the war we'd been taken from there to Twickenham, she didn't even know that after they'd left our mother returned to the village and then stayed on. Hetty Rayner wrote to her several times, she says, as I've no doubt she did, but never got an answer, so assumed her letters hadn't been forwarded. She was stunned when I told her that our mother had been in the same house all those years. 'And without anyone to take her side,' she said." He paused there, drained his glass.

"So you drew a blank."

"More or less. She was keen, though, to let me know that she didn't blame my mother for what happened. I don't know how that can be true, but there's no doubt that she liked and admired her. 'Your mother was a good woman,' she told me. And she clearly meant what she said. That cheered me up, I can tell you. She had it in for some others, though, especially Morton."

"Tell me about her."

"Beth Morton? She was a friend of our mother's, at least I always assumed she was. Sarah and I saw quite a bit of her at one time or another. She lived further down the road, in a bigger house. I used to think it rather grand, 'swanky'. A fridge! Imagine! The only other one I'd seen was in an Abbott and Costello film, which made her seem like a film star. And that wasn't the only reason. She used quite a lot of make-up and looked — looked stylish, I suppose people would have said. Out of place in a village, now I come to think of it."

"And she was married?"

"Yes. Her husband — Dick, I think he was called — was quite a bit older than her. Too old to be called up. Anyway, I seem to remember he'd got a bad limp, he'd done some sort of permanent damage to a foot or a leg, I forget which. He owned a garage up in the village, which doubled as a kind of forge for the local farmers. Whenever I went past there'd be a tractor or two in for repairs. He wasn't without a bob or two. I imagine that caused some resentment."

"But that wouldn't be the reason your Mrs Rayner disliked his wife, surely?" And when he shook his head in agreement, she said, "So what was?"

"Dunno. She simply said that Beth Morton 'spat poison,' but she didn't give any details. Perhaps the Morton woman said unpleasant things about the Rayners behind their backs and her remarks got back to them. In a village as small as ours it wouldn't take long for rumours to circulate. 'Not that I'm one to gossip, but my dear, you should have *heard* what that woman said about you'".

He stopped. Then, suddenly, "of course," he said, slapping the table. "I've just remembered. She had a reputation for being a man chaser, except that that wasn't — what *was* the word my mother used?" He looked expectantly at Maggie as though she might have the answer.

"A scarlet woman?" she suggested, twisting her lips in an ironic smile. "Trollop? Baggage? She said such things to her son?"

"No, no. I never heard her say anything against Beth Morton. But I did once sneak a look at part of a letter she was writing to my father." Again he paused. "Dammit, I can't remember, but I think she was reporting back to him something he himself had called Beth Morton. No, I can't remember."

"Perhaps it will be in one of the letters?"

"Doubt it. All the letters are from him to her, not from her to him."

Another pause. Fist thumped into palm. "Got it! Yes, now I remember. Not what *my* mother said but what Robin reported *his* mother saying about Beth Morton. Yes. We were out one evening and Robin told me that he'd overheard his mother and grandmother chatting about who the old lady had seen in the village that day. Beth Morton's name was mentioned and his mother said, 'oh, that painted Jezebel.' Not that Robin had a clue what it meant. He asked me if I knew and I didn't but at the next choir practice I asked one of the choirmen and he said I wasn't to use such words, so of course Robin and I knew it had to mean something bad. And then" — he was talking faster now, grinning in triumph as the memories poured back in, "then Robin pointed out to me that Beth Morton used scarlet nail polish — she was the only woman we knew who did — and *that* had to be what was meant by her being painted."

"And Jezebel?"

"Ah, that we didn't understand. And it wasn't in the dictionary at home. But," and he raised his fist in a final victorious flourish, "when I first met Krassner he was with her. With Beth Morton."

"I see. And what was she doing with Mr Krassner."

"They were in a field near our house. I passed them when I was running home late one evening after choir practice."

"In a field, eh?" Maggie cocked an eyebrow. "Married woman and young American soldier out to inspect the local flora? Sounds dodgy. A Jezebel indeed."

Wife and husband looked quizzically at one another.

"You know," David said eventually, "appearances to the contrary, I don't think there *was* anything dodgy about it. Not on Krassner's side anyway, although Beth Morton may have had different ideas. But I can remember that my mother was determined to tell me I'd got it wrong, that it couldn't have been Beth Morton I saw with Krassner, whereas I knew it was."

Maggie stifled a yawn. "Sorry," she said, "it's been a long day."

"And I'm adding to it by digging up old tales." He gathered their plates together, stood to take them to the sink.

"No, no, you're not. Not tiring me, I mean. But I don't see how you're going to solve the puzzle of Rayner versus Morton. Not tonight. Anyway." And, pushing her chair back, she got to her feet.

"I suppose," he said, watching her as she stretched and prepared to leave, "I suppose it's possible that my mother thought it best not to set tongues wagging. She was trying to head me off from reporting to anyone else what I'd seen, knowing that if I did, it would be all round the village before you could say knife."

Maggie paused at the door. "That still wouldn't explain why

Mrs Rayner said that the Morton woman spat poison at others. Unless it was in retaliation."

"True. Or alternatively, as I say, that Beth Morton said unpleasant things about her, about Mrs Rayner."

"It's possible. But you're trying to avoid the obvious, aren't you?"

"Which is?"

"That it was your mother Beth Morton had it in for. Hell hath no fury ... ." She left the worn quotation unfinished. "Now," she said, turning away, "I simply must go to bed. You won't be long, will you? "

"No" he said, as the door shut behind her, "I'll be up as soon as I've told Sarah about today's meeting. She's probably waiting by the phone."

But Sarah wasn't. He phoned from his study and almost immediately her answer phone clicked on, inviting him to leave a message if urgent or, alternatively, to contact her office during business hours. Number and extension were given, though not, David noticed, any indication of the business hours themselves. "Hello, Sarah," he said slowly into the hated machine, "this is David, your brother, speaking at " — he glanced at his watch, ten-to-eleven, — "at a later hour than I'd intended. Sorry about that but Maggie and I have been celebrating. Susie's pregnant. Still, late as the hour now is, I thought you'd want to know that as promised I saw Mrs Rayner today. I was with her for a couple of hours. She's surprisingly fit and alert but she doesn't have much for us, I'm afraid. If you'd like the details, phone me tomorrow. She sends her best wishes and thinks you should be married. And she was pretty sharp about Beth Morton — remember her? Oh, and Sarah, she — Hetty Rayner —is Jewish. Did you know that? I didn't."

Replacing the receiver, he reached into his desk for the letters, though as soon as he began to untie the red ribbon he realised he was too tired to go through any of the as-yet unread ones lying beneath his hand. Besides, he was coming to feel that they contained no clues to guide his sister and himself to a proper explanation of what had happened all those years ago. The letters he'd so far read contained entertainingly vivid and sometimes comic accounts of Malta and those of its inhabitants his father had come to know, there were progress reports on the courtship by the young soldier Southern of the girl his father had taken to calling Island Anna, there were comments on the increasingly boring, even frustrating routines of army life without much active service, and each letter ended the same way. Protestations of enduring love for his family and of his longing to be home once more ... . No, he'd put the letters back in the drawer and join Maggie in bed. He glanced at the top letter as he prepared to re-tie the bundle ... *and as the British soldier has, bless him, shortened the Italian tedeschi for Germans to 'Teds', we make them sound almost cuddly. There's only one person I want to cuddle, though.*

When had that been written? 25th July, 1944. He thought about it. By then he and Sarah must have been at their grandparents in Huntingdonshire, leaving their mother alone in the village to paint their bedrooms. Would she have told her husband about that decision? And if so, what would he have said? He took up the letter again, began to look more closely at the neat lines of script. Yes, here it was, right at the beginning. Stephen Willoughby wrote that he was sorry she'd chosen to forfeit a holiday with her parents "being waited on hand and foot," but could understand why she'd prefer to use the opportunity of being on her own in order to paint and decorate the children's rooms. There followed an account of the tedium of daily life on the island, of the servicing of vehicles that would have been better left to gather dust, a report on swimming races organized for otherwise bored soldiers, and then, the final paragraph: *You must feel as I do, that with the Normandy invasion, which everyone here has been following with gathering excitement, the war is going to finish in the foreseeable future and that we four can plan to be a part of it. It isn't merely the Mediterranean blue which fills me with such hope. I can sense it all about me, can't you?* **We're going to be alright, ALL of us.**

With which good thought I'll end this, my dearest, sending you and the nippers my boundless, endless love.

* * *

How long he had been sitting at his desk, eyes shut, he didn't know. Shivering in the night cold, the central heating long switched off, he knew only that he'd been lost in a trance of speculation, of useless thoughts that encompassed the might-have-beens and what-ifs of so much of his, as of Sarah's, life. All that hope, that love, that belief in the future. Turning his sigh to a yawn, he tied the letters and returned them to the drawer. Then, shoes in hand, he tiptoed to the door and in the act of switching off his study light heard Hetty Rayner's words loud in his head, almost as if she was in the room, facing him.

"Terrible things happen in wartime, David, and not always on the battlefield."

∼ CHAPTER SIX ∼

Brother and sister agreed to meet in London. Sarah was due to see a client in the metropolis one day the following week — Tuesday was named — and she'd take time off for some lunch. But wouldn't the client expect "to factor in" lunch as part of the business? No, big brother, Sarah told him, she sometimes mixed business with pleasure but on this occasion she could and would plead that family matters took precedence. Over which, he asked — business or pleasure? Over accountancy duties, she said, naming a restaurant near Victoria and telling him how to find it. "It's Italian, good food, decent wines, not noisy." She laughed. "Nothing for you to grouse about."

After she'd rung off he sat for a few moments at his desk, staring at the letter on top of the unbound sheaf, before, lifting his gaze, he turned to look through his study window down at the darkening garden, where a few stray daffodils were being cuffed by the winds of early March. Then he heaved himself out of his chair, and taking the letter with him, went to join Maggie in the kitchen.

She was sitting at the table, checking a list of names on a narrow strip of paper that lay before her, an untouched mug of tea at her elbow.

"People I must remind Giles to invite to the opening," she said in answer to his speculative gaze. "Well?"

"We've arranged to have lunch together next Tuesday. Sarah has to be down in London on business. Or should I say we'll do lunch?"

"That's probably last year's talk. 'Do' as in make it, be pro-active, don't simply sit there. Anyway, you don't have the clothes for 'doing lunch.' No red braces, for a start." She laughed. "I'm happy to say. I wouldn't want to be married to a man who wears red braces. Where will you be lunching? The British Library cafeteria?"

It was his turn to laugh. "No, some Italian restaurant Sarah knows about. Probably costs a week's wages. She sounded very cheerful, by the way."

"Perhaps there's a new man in her life?"

"Isn't that rather a sexist remark?"

Maggie winked at him. "Not when made by a woman. Didn't they teach you anything at your university." She reached for her mug, sipped, screwed up her lips in a gesture which, after all their years together, still made him smile, said "yuk, it's cold." Then, indicating the sheets of writing paper he was holding in his hand, "You told her the contents of the letter?"

"Of course. I read it out to her." He pulled out a chair and sat facing his wife.

"And?"

"As I expected, she hadn't a clue. Couldn't recall anything. But you see she wasn't even six years old when it happened. She could barely remember who Beth Morton was, had only the vaguest memory of her house, and none at all of the fact that she and our mother had been friends."

"And yet you say Beth Morton was often in and out of your house?"

He shook his head. "I don't know about often. I think she preferred to be visited." He glanced down at the letter as though hoping to find there an answer that Sarah hadn't been able to give him. "Looking back," he said, "I imagine Beth Morton liked showing off what she'd got which the others lacked. She certainly provided a kind of open house for the local kids. Sarah does have a faint memory of being, as she says, 'parked' there on occasions when our mother had to be elsewhere. Morton provided a kind of baby-sitting service, I suppose."

"What, toys and toilet-training?"

He laughed. "No. I doubt that would have been her style. But I do recall that she got her charges to make ice-lollies. Take one egg cup, fill with water, drop in a dob of jam, insert tooth-pick, place in fridge, wait one hour and bingo. Quite good. I got a lolly once when I went to fetch Sarah." He made a mock-appreciative noise. Then, pushing the letter away, he said, "I don't think we're going to get far with this. Sarah can't recall Morton ever saying anything she thought was out of order. But at that age … ."

"And yet, as you say, the letter makes clear your mother must have had something pretty obnoxious to report."

"True." Reaching for the letter once more, he scanned it rapidly, found the place he was looking for and read out "*Of course you did the right thing, don't even begin to doubt it. But what an absolutely vile woman. I worry only that all over England there will be plenty of her kind, demanding a halter gratis, nothing else, for godsake.*" He put the letter down again. "I imagine she must either have thrown Beth Morton out of the house or told her she didn't want to see her again. And "the right thing" refers both to that and to our mother asking Hetty Rayner to look after Sarah and me for a night."

Again he picked up the letter. "Yes, here it is. *From all you tell me, the nippers will be fine with Mrs Rayner. Home from home. And it's only one night.*" He looked across to Maggie. "My guess is that she must have asked Beth Morton to give us a bed and that prompted Morton to make some remark about Hetty Rayner in which she showed her true colours."

"It certainly seems that way," Maggie said. "But how can you be so sure that's what caused the row?"

"Oh, those words about a halter gratis. It's what Gratiano says in *The Merchant of Venice*, at the end of the big trial scene." And when she stared at him, inviting further explanation, he said, "just after Shylock has had the tables turned on him and been humiliated by the Christians. Portia feels some sympathy for him, so she asks Antonio what mercy he might show Shylock. And Gratiano, one of those useless bits of aristocracy you always find hanging around, full of tenth-rate opinions and nasty prejudices, butts in and says, 'A halter gratis, nothing else for Godsake.' Gratis is his idea of a joke. Hang the Jew for free. But for the sake of keeping the Christian God — *our* God — free from taint, don't show Shylock any clemency. Mercy doesn't extend to Jews."

"I see." From studying his face she dropped her eyes

momentarily, then brought them up again, lips apart as though considering what to say. When she spoke the words came as a challenge. "That rather shows your mother in a different light, doesn't it?" And while he looked questioningly at her, she went on, "you're always ready to imply that she was at fault for all that happened, but on this occasion at least she obviously behaved really well."

He nodded. "Yes," he said slowly, "she did. Unfortunately, what she did gave Beth Morton a perfect opportunity to take revenge."

"She can't be blamed for that".

The sharpness with which she rapped out the words startled him. So, too, did the way she was looking at him, the sudden tightening of her lips. "For God's sake, David, stop sitting in judgement on her. That's self-pity. People fall in and out of love. These things happen. Besides, you don't, you *can't*, know all that occurred. If it comes to that, you still don't know that it was Beth Morton who told your father. This Hetty Rayner — *she* didn't think it likely, did she."

"But she didn't know about the row between our mother and Morton."

"She may well have done. 'A cobra, spitting poison.' You don't have to be in the Maigret class to work out why Mrs Rayner would have called her that."

He thought about it. "You could be right. But as to sitting in judgement." He paused, tried to choose his words carefully. "She more or less cut herself off from us, remember. Cards at Christmas and very occasional meetings in public places. Not much on which I can build a case for" — he was going to say "the defence" but something in her look made him change it to "sympathy."

But it made no difference. "*Case*," she jeered, "*case*. You should try listening to yourself more carefully. David, you're so bloody moralistic, so certain you're in the right. No wonder you're an academic."

"Not any longer," he said. "Though some of my best friends still are."

But she brushed the weak joke aside. Her eyes sparking anger now, she said, "Do you know what it is I most detest about your friends? I mean those in the university world? And, let's face it, you know precious few outside that world. It's their endless determination to put everyone else down. They're so used to talking to students who know less than they do that they assume *everyone* is a sodding student. It's always the other person who's wrong, who's ignorant, who's stupid, who's uncultivated … who can be sniggered at. And always, but always, it has to be someone else on the banana skin."

The outburst bewildered him less by its novelty — she had often enough voiced her irritation at what she called academic aphids — than by its timing. Why *now?* Perhaps, from the outside, it did seem as though he was blaming his mother for what lay beyond her control. Well, in his wife she had found a new champion. He wondered whether to say that he rather thought Sarah shared his point of view, and, after a moment or two, risked murmuring the thought aloud.

Maggie looked at him, the spark of anger already fading. Even so, "I doubt it," she said. "Women see these things differently." And with that he had to be content.

* * *

Sarah followed the waiter to a table at the rear of the restaurant, David tagging along at the rear.

"I hope you don't mind," she said to him as they sat and in a trice a stiff linen napkin was being shaken out and placed in his lap.

He looked enquiringly at her.

"That I reserved a table. The place gets so crowded at lunchtime." She glanced around her. "Good lord, there's Phil Partridge." David followed the direction of her smile and slight wave and took in the slim shoulders and crinkly hair of the man who smiled and waved back. Black-suited, as were most of the other men in the restaurant, Partridge sat opposite a woman who, herself now turning to stare in momentary languor at brother and sister, proved to be elegant in dark blue pin-stripe jacket and a discreet amount of what looked to be gold at throat and ear.

David turned back to hear Sarah tell him *sotto voce* that Phil was a one-time colleague who had come south a few years earlier. Then, giving her attention to the hovering waiter who was laying menu cards beside their places, she ordered mineral water for herself and for her dining companion … ?

"I'll have the same," David said.

"Sure you wouldn't prefer wine?"

David shook his head but was delighted when she ordered a half-bottle of Sancerre, "because you never know."

Without even glancing at the menu, Sarah pushed it aside. "They know what I have," she said. "You choose whatever you'd like. Lunch is on me. I must say Phil has good taste in bed partners."

She smiled conspiratorially at her brother.

"How do you know it's not business."

"Because I know Phil. Oh, not in *that* sense, he's not my type, and I don't suppose I'm his, wide though he casts his net. At all events, he's always been the perfect gentleman in his dealings with me." The words were uttered with a slight, satirical smile, though it faded as she said, "but he had to leave Manchester in something of a hurry. One of his clients took exception to the very close interest he was taking in said client's wife, an interest we heard was fully reciprocated."

"Well," David said gallantly, "his present companion is considerably less attractive than mine." He meant it. Sarah did look good, in fact, he thought, radiant might not be all that wide of the mark.

She acknowledged the compliment with a half-ironic inclination of her head and, as their drinks were poured — David accepted a glass of wine — raised her glass and gestured to him to do the same. "Life is good," she said, as they touched glasses. "I may even be in love."

"Sarah, I *am* pleased." He left it at that, smiling expectantly, but it seemed she wasn't about to tell him any more. Instead, she gave her full attention to the waiter, who nodded as she ordered. While she did so, David looked admiringly at his elegant sister. "Skin unfarded, lips hepatic". The words from a poem he had read years earlier came suddenly into his head but he as suddenly pushed them out. Sarah's skin was perfectly farded, her lips touched by the merest application of colour, her hair an immaculate cap of still rich chestnut, and as for her suit, which might or might not have been the one she'd worn on the day of their mother's funeral, it was perfectly set off by the pale blue silk blouse, its collar secured by a tiny gold clasp. In his old brown sports coat and dark grey cords he felt himself to be hopelessly out of place among the svelte occupants of the restaurant.

Once their food was placed in front of them, tagliatelli for Sarah, roast lamb and almonds for him, a green salad to share — "I've taken a calculated risk in ordering this for you," she said, waving her fork at it, "I should have asked if you've gone vegetarian like so many of my friends," at which he shook his head — they began, hesitantly at first, to talk.

"I've read all the letters now," David said, by way of making a start. He toyed with his wine glass then took an appreciative sip. Sarah had chosen well.

She stopped eating, raised an eyebrow but said nothing.

"And I'm puzzled." He swallowed some of his food, took another sip of wine, rolled it round his mouth. "The thing is," he said, clearing his throat, "the thing is, I can't find anything in *any* of them to explain what happened. As you pointed out, even the one he wrote on the day he died is completely without — is completely free of — well, it ends as they *all* do. With love. It's short but as he says that's because he has to go on duty. I'm reasonably certain it isn't because he can't think what to say or is covering his tracks. I simply don't think he's being duplicitous. 'All my love, Stephen.' He means it, surely."

Sarah ate another forkful then pushed her half-empty plate aside. "Yes," she said. "It was a love letter. Or anyway, a letter written out of love. Thanks, by the way, for making me a copy. I've read and re-read it since you sent it and I'm glad that you agree with me. You're the literary expert. Your kind can spot insincerity at ten paces, or so I'm led to believe." But her smile was intended to disarm. She drank some water, dabbed her lips with the napkin and looked into its folds as she said, "But that quotation he used, what was that about?"

He cut into a piece of meat, tried, clumsily, to balance slivers of almond on its sticky surface before putting it in his mouth, and, aware that she was watching him with a faint smile that included a measure of condescension, said in an effort to regain some ground, "a frustum."

"A *what?*"

He swallowed the meat, cleared his throat. "'Frustum'". And in answer to her quizzically raised eyebrow, added, "'The part of a solid, such as a cone or pyramid, contained between the base and a plane parallel to the base that intersects the solid.' Crabbe uses the word. The poet Crabbe. 'She minced the sanguine flesh in frustums fine.' That's how it's defined in the Oxford English Dictionary. I don't know why I remember it, but I do. Johnson is plainer. He says a frustum is 'a piece cut off from a regular figure.'"

She was staring at him in mock wonder. Then, "Good for Johnson, he sounds like a friend to the human race, whoever he may be," she said.

"Johnson, Samuel Johnson, Dictionary Johnson. Crabbe's father was a keen mathematician so I imagine his son got the word 'frustums' from him."

Sarah put her hands together in ironic applause. "Well, if the tutorial is over perhaps we can go back to my question. The quotation in that final letter. Where does it come from? If you know so much, you should know that." While she spoke she reached for the shoulder bag she'd hung over the back of her chair, fished out a notebook and began to flick through its pages. "Yes, here it is. 'The bonds of heaven will never be slipp'd, dissolv'd and loos'd.' I've asked several of my acquaintances but none of them knew it. Scarcely surprising, perhaps, given that they're not literary lads and lasses. But you, David … ."

He shook his head apologetically. "I'll have to disappoint you, sister. Frustums I can do. But not that quotation. Not a clue, I'm afraid." And, as she looked at him askance, he hurried on. "Though I can't see that it matters. He's telling her that he loves her and that their love will last."

"Not good enough."

"Well, then, rummage around in the copy of Shakespeare you

took. If it comes from one of the plays, or poems for that matter, it's always possible he marked it up. Or it may be one of Professor Zammit's *bon mots*."

In the act of pouring him more wine, Sarah paused, looked up at her brother. "Who?"

"Professor Zammit. A man, or rather the statue of a man in Ziggiewi, where our father was stationed. He mentions him in quite a few of his letters. He seems to have acted as some sort of silent oracle."

The waiter deftly removed their plates. Sarah smiled abstractly at him as he did so then, watching his retreating back, said, "But surely he'd have told her if he'd taken the words from something Zammit wrote? After all, she couldn't be expected to know."

"Perhaps he'd already told her in an earlier letter, one we don't have."

"Hmm. Could be." She thought about it, shook her head. "I want to believe we have all the letters that count, because I want to believe that she took care to look after them in the hope — hope against hope — that someone, us I suppose, would eventually find them, read them, and come to realise that … . Oh, that she needn't be condemned for ever."

"'Rest, rest, perturbéd spirit.'"

"Me or her?"

"Both, if you like," he said, smiling he hoped reassuringly, wanting to take the edge off her sharp question. How little I know her, he thought, as he looked across at Sarah's half-averted face, its air of brooding concern. She was far more exercised by the letters, what they revealed, what withheld, than he had expected, and he was newly aware of her as someone very different from the successful and, he realised now he had been too quick to assume, self-contained person he identified through her clothes, her brisk talk, her expensive car. Perturbed, yes. The word he had so lightly thrown off was, in fact, true of the woman who now lifted her eyes to meet his.

"I'm sure he's using the words to tell her something," she said. Then, after a moment's reflective silence, "and you tell me that you drew a blank with Hetty Rayner, too."

"Not quite," he said, feeling that he had let her down. "She doesn't think Beth Morton can be mixed up in it."

"Even though she dislikes her."

"Loathes her."

"Funny isn't it. I can't remember nearly as much as our time in the village as you can, for which I plead my age, but if I put my mind to it I seem to remember Beth Morton and our mother as good friends."

"Which they were until the day our mother threw her out."

"Which gave the Morton woman two motives for wanting revenge. Rejection by both our mother and by Mr. Krassner."

David shook his head. "I know we used to talk about that," he said, "but I'm pretty sure that she — Beth Morton — hadn't been involved with him, not romantically, as the papers say."

He paused as the waiter re-appeared. "Yes," he said then, in answer to Sarah's query, "I'd like a coffee." The waiter bowed slightly at her order, emptied the remains of the wine into David's glass and bore the bottle away, balanced upright in his open palm. David sat concentrating, trying to remember from fifty years ago the details of that first meeting with Krassner in bottom meadow. Hopeless of course. The intervening period had worn away the memory's edges and now he couldn't be sure what he actually remembered and what might be invention. .

"What are you thinking about?"

"That first meeting with Krassner. I was running back down the fields from choir practice when I came on them. Beth Morton had her back turned, she didn't want to be seen, and in fact when I told our mother about discovering them in bottom meadow, she refused to believe it *was* Beth Morton, though I knew it had to be her."

And then, suddenly it came to him. Of course, of course. Why had he never before seen it. Or, if he had, why had he never understood.

He *hadn't* discovered them. Krassner had discovered *him. Yes, that was it.* The American had simply walked out from wherever he had been and called out to David *after he had run past.* It was Krassner who, speaking to the boy's retreating back, had made

David turn round. But for that remark about his whistling, he'd have run on home with no knowledge of the soldier's existence, nor would he have had any inkling of Beth Morton's presence. Yes, *she* was embarrassed to be seen, but Krassner certainly wasn't.

To Sarah now, he said, almost exultantly, "There was nothing between Krassner and Beth Morton, I'm certain of it." And he told her why.

And yet Sarah wasn't convinced. "He might not have been embarrassed to be seen," she said, "because he was in a strange place, one that meant nothing to him. Why should he care what a small boy would think? He might even like the idea of showing off. See, I've already got myself a woman. But for the woman herself it was a very different matter."

"No," David said, "no, that wasn't it. Jay Krassner wasn't like that. He wasn't the kind of man who enjoys showing off, and he certainly wouldn't boast of 'getting a woman', as you put it. I'm absolutely certain of that. I admit that Beth Morton might have been attracted to Krassner but … . " And there he paused, watching in silence as the waiter placed between them a tray with a pot of coffee, milk jug and two cups.

A moment's silence and then, sipping the coffee Sarah had poured, David said, "Of course, that doesn't mean she might not have felt cheated, scorned, I don't know, when Krassner showed up at our house on a regular basis."

Another thought came to him. He put his cup down. "You don't think, do you, that our mother confided in her? My god, if so that *would* have been a mistake." He picked up his cup again, stared into it. "Oh, lord knows," he said, hunching his shoulders, as he looked at Sarah to get her opinion. "As Maggie said the other evening, we'll never know all that occurred. She thinks I'm too harsh on her, our mother, that is. You don't, do you?"

Sarah sat staring at him fiercely and when she did at length speak it wasn't at all the answer he had expected. "You know," she said, "I loved her. I really loved her." The passion in her voice confused and then startled him. Her fixed stare was ferocious. "Does that surprise you?"

Wondering how best to answer, he said, "you seemed very

unhappy at the end … I mean before we went to Woodbridge."

"Where I was of course deliriously happy. And as for Twickenham, paradise on earth."

"They did their best," he said simply.

Ignoring that remark, Sarah said, "you weren't in the house often enough to see how unhappy she was. You were off playing what that friend of yours, Robin. I'm not saying I blame you, but I was the one who saw her tears. Of course I was unhappy." And when he looked at her for confirmation of the remark she said, nodding, "I used to listen outside the door to the living room and so often she'd be in there sobbing that I think I began to feel it was all my fault. I remember once I went in and she was darning one of your socks, and she used it to wipe her eyes. I asked her if I could help but she said no, why didn't I go outside and play. Strands of wool had got into her eye-lashes and were on her cheek and I tried to help her pick them off but she pushed me away."

She stopped, stared into her coffee cup. "I think that was probably the unhappiest moment of my life," she said, her voice so low he barely caught the words. "I wanted to be with *her*." She shook her head. "I don't know who was the lonelier," she said, "her or me."

"I had no idea things were quite so bad." His sister's words had cut through his thoughts. "You never mentioned it when we were growing up. I mean when we were living at Twickenham."

"Ah, well," Sarah said, more briskly, draining her cup. "Burying the evidence, you see." And. pressing her lips together, she raised an index finger to them. "Mum's the word. Oh, what a dreadful pun. Not even pun. Mum *wasn't* the word, was it. Not allowed." She reached for her bag, took out her wallet, then gestured to the waiter for their bill.

"Do you remember once telling me that what was happening was all Krassner's fault and that he came to the house to see her, not me," David said. "It was that last holiday we spent at our other grandparents, her parents. I've thought about that since, but never liked to mention it. But you presumably knew what was going on between them. What did you mean by it being his fault?"

But Sarah shook her head. "I'm sorry," she said, "I can't

remember, I really can't." Then, as by way of justification, she added, "I know I saw more than you, I was in the house far more. But I was too young to understand. And I hadn't a clue what old Godwin was going on about that evening he came banging on our door. Anyway, I'm sure they never — you know — disappeared upstairs or anything like that when I was there. But I must have guessed that he was the cause of her not going on holiday with us."

"She was decorating our rooms."

"So she said." Then, with a shake of her head, she cancelled her words. "No, that's unfair. She decorated them alright, I remember that, though no doubt with his help."

A few minutes later, the bill settled, she unhooked her bag from her chair and prepared to stand. As she did so, she said with a wry smile, looking down at him, "I remember another thing. Perfume. I didn't know what it was, of course, but there were occasions when she smelt different — *enticing*, I think. That must have been when she was expecting him to appear."

Following his sister's actions, David got to his feet. Her words stirred a faint memory but it was gone again before he could catch it. Instead, fingers resting on the table as he looked down, he said, "I'm not especially proud of the way I thought or spoke of her over the years. Too much self pity. Maggie accused me of that the other evening, and she was right." He looked up and met his sister's gaze, found her watching him. "And now it turns out that you had to put up with far more than I ever did, both then and perhaps later. It helps explain why you so disliked our Willoughby grandparents. You did, didn't you?" He couldn't read her look.

"Let's just say that I was happy to get away from Twickenham," Sarah said. "Of course I knew what they were worried about. They wanted to ensure that I wouldn't turn into a scarlet woman like my mother. No fancy clothes, no boyfriends, and even at sixteen I had to be at home by nine thirty. You were spared all that. Son of their son, they saw you as. No fault there."

They moved towards the door, were bowed out by their waiter and stood for a few minutes on the windy pavement as David began to thank Sarah for his lunch, but she said, "You missed a good deal I had to endure at Twickenham, you know. All those grandparently lectures on the need for modesty, respectability, not dragging the family's name 'further' into the mud, above all not leading a man on ... " She drew a deep breath, said savagely, "they were doing their damnedest to poison my mind against her. Remember your sixteenth birthday?"

She looked quickly at him. "I don't want to be melodramatic about this, David, but I feel I've much more reason to hate them than to hate her. And I don't hate her, not at all."

They began to walk along the pavement, heads down against the cold wind, and he was at her elbow when she said, stopping and turning to him. "As we're in confessional mode, I'll tell you something else." He had difficulty hearing her speak above the steady thrum of the traffic, but almost immediately she resumed walking and they turned off into a quieter street. "About twenty years ago," she said, marching him along, "I went to the Heywood Gallery. Someone I was seeing at that time wanted me to go with him to an exhibition of work by an artist called Millet. You presumably know the work."

"Yes." David shouted as a motor bike thumped past, "French. I know. Peasants in a landscape."

She took his arm as she said, "that's right. I wasn't all that keen but once I started studying the pictures I was hooked. There was one in particular. A chalk drawing called 'Sewing Lesson.' Do you know it?" She looked sideways at him, and when he shook his head, she said, "it's a kitchen scene. Dresser, big table, bench. A mother and small girl, it must be her daughter, heads together. I imagine it was Millet's own wife and daughter and he'd come upon them like that and made an instant sketch of them, though perhaps he worked it up later. That's what the man I was with told me, anyway. But it stopped me in my tracks."

Suiting her action to her words, she came to an abrupt halt, her arm acting as a brake on his further progress. People strolled unconcernedly past the couple, a middle-aged pair having a lovers' quarrel, perhaps. "I found myself going back to look at it, again and again," she said. "In the end I simply stood there for I don't know how long." She watched as a van trundled slowly along towards where they stood. When it had gone by, she said, speaking slowly and deliberately, "I realised I was willing the two of them to raise their heads and look at me." A pause. "I knew who they were you see." She withdrew her hand from his arm and brushed it impatiently across her eyes.

Then, head still averted, she resumed walking.

A few minutes later, during which neither spoke, they came to traffic lights.

"The parting of the ways," she said, preparing to cross. "I must get back to my client. And you?" Her voice had lost the agitated emotion of a few moments before. She was back in control.

"I think I'll pay a visit to Malta," he said, the words and thought arriving in his head simultaneously.

About to step off the kerb, she stepped back, her eyes wide in sudden surprise. "Malta? Why? I mean, whatever for?"

"I want to see our father's grave." He spoke loudly above the low roar of restless traffic.

She looked at him, perhaps wondering whether this was his idea of a joke. "A bit late for that." She drew her coat around her throat, shivered in the wind.

"True. But I may be able to meet some of the people who knew him. You never know."

"They'll surely be dead by now," Sarah shouted, as they waited for the now red lights to change back to green.

"At least Professor Zammit will still be there."

The lights changed. "I'm going" she said, inclining her cheek for his kiss. "I'm glad you're not giving up the hunt. Keep in touch and let me know how you get on."

With what could have been a dismissive flip of her fingers she walked alertly away from him and was soon lost to sight among the crowd on the far pavement.

Standing there, aware of people jostling against him as they queued at the lights, David wondered in amazement at what he had just committed himself to. Malta? What on earth had put the thought into his head? And how come that without any forethought he had blurted the words out to his sister? He would have to phone her and say the wine, little as it was, had gone to his head.

Of course he wasn't going to hare off to Malta or anywhere else, come to that.

But then, he thought, why shouldn't I go? Answer, because the idea was madness. A moment of lunacy, sheer and simple. Blame it on the drink. And anyway, I have a book to finish. Buttoning his coat against another blast of wind, he hurried toward the nearest underground.

CHAPTER SEVEN

Leaving the tube at Euston, he walked the short distance to the British Library. Once there, he quickly crossed the apology for a piazza, determined not to glance at the sculpture whose massive dullness seemed calculated to warn all who entered of the oppressive weight of books, and was soon at his reserved seat, eager to renew the acquaintance of Anne Finch, for the airy cages of whose verse he had an especial liking.

The edition he had ordered was waiting for him. Full now of resolve, he produced a notebook from his sports coat and, opening Finch's Poems, soon found the poem he wanted. "To the Nightingale" was one of his favourites. "Free as thine shall be my song," she had written. Wishful thinking? And then, "Poets wild as thee were born," no doubt aware that as Countess of Winchelsea she had to mind her ps and qs. "Pleasing best when unconfined." More wishful thinking. But remarkable, too, for a woman who was dead before 1720, long before the "wandering bard" became a symbol for the true poet. As for identifying poet as nightingale. Ask most people who'd been first to do that and they'd answer Keats, though some would know of Milton's sonnet. But precious few would be aware of Anne Finch's poem, including virtually all the self-proclaimed experts on Keats's poetry. Perhaps Keats didn't know of the poem's existence. But Wordsworth, a note in his own writing told him, was "especially partial" to her. Back to the poem.

"Thus we poets that have speech." Philomel was denied speech. Anne Finch was taking good care not to identify her own experience with the poor girl who was first raped then had her tongue ripped out. The Countess was, after all, happily married and free to publish her poems. Besides, being childless, she had no experience of actual confinement. But then she wasn't literally writing about herself. The poet was in fact a "he".

And still th'unhappy poet's breast

Like thine, when best he sings, is placed against a thorn.

But by the end of the poem she was talking about poet tribe being envious of each other, most particularly when faced with those greater souls, poets of genius. Being a friend of Pope's, she'd have known about that. The thorn against *his* breast was what he himself called "this long disease," his dwarf, malformed frame. But it was also his "strong antipathy of good to bad," his contempt for scribblers, and their rage at him. Still, her nightingale went on singing, "Till thy business all lies waste."

Business. He suddenly recalled two lines that had lodged in his memory from student days. "Who for his business from his wife will run, Takes the best care to have her business done." *The Country Wife* was full of contempt for business people. Sir Jasper Fidget goes off to conduct business affairs, Horner comes to Lady Fidget to conduct a very different affair. And, free associating now, he thought of Lawrence telling Forster that he shouldn't have glorified those business people, the Wilcoxes. "Business is no good." This was the same Lawrence who had taken Keats to task for making the nightingale into a singer of plaintive anthems. "It was Caruso at his jauntiest." Might Lawrence have heard Caruso sing and if so, where? In London or Italy? He must try to find out.

But back, back to the poem.

Thus we poets that have speech
Unlike what thy forests teach,
If a fluent vein be shown
That's transcendent to our own,
Criticise, reform, or preach,
Or censure what we cannot reach.

"Oh, lord, I'm off on the preach again". Lawrence again, apologising to a correspondent for having spent several paragraphs in railing against art he didn't like. But it was the last line that made David stir uncomfortably. "Or censure what we cannot reach." We criticise what we can't aspire to, Anne Finch meant. But when you reach an understanding you're accepting a compromise. Poets mustn't compromise. But others? He thought back to Sarah's words. "I loved her. I really loved her." Unlike Sarah, and, he now knew, with far less reason, he himself had been ready to criticise his mother rather than reach an understanding of what had happened to her and its consequences for them all.

Was is that which had made him blurt out his mad announcement about going to Malta? Guilt breaking cover? Because he had, he was certain, absolutely no prior intention of speaking the words. They had come as much of a surprise to him as they had to Sarah. "I want to see our father's grave." What on earth had possessed him to say such a thing? Well, whatever it was, he knew he had no choice but to see it through.

He pushed away Anne Finch's poems, shoved his notebook back inside his jacket pocket, and left the library. It was time to reach an understanding of — even, perhaps *with* — the dead.

* * *

Less than an hour later, after quick changes on the Victoria and Bakerloo Lines and a scamper to leap aboard the train at Waterloo — one that left him out of breath, heart thumping and uncomfortably aware of the amount of roast lamb he'd recently packed away — he left Twickenham station and began to walk towards the river. For the first time since leaving university he was returning to the house where he and Sarah had grown to adulthood.

A burst of early spring sunshine lit the route he had trodden so many times in adolescence. Right turn followed by left turn followed by another right, curve left, and half-way along the road he was now walking down, a road of unexceptional double-fronted houses, many with bay windows and glassed-in porches and all of them screened behind privet hedges or low, decorative brick walls topped by black-painted metal chains, here, on the right, it was.

Stanmore Avenue.

For several minutes he stood at the kerbside, waiting for his pulse to slow. Only then could he bring himself to look along the cherry-tree lined vista to where, beyond those half-timbered semi-

detacheds, stood, he knew, the house where he had and Sarah had
lived out their adolescent years. Not stockbrokers' Tudor, perhaps,
but certainly answering to the house agents' description of Des.
Res.

My god, he thought, the road is exactly as I remember it. Forty
years and nothing's changed. The same air of net-curtained
respectability, of timorous propriety.

He looked again, this time more attentively. And now he saw
that there had been changes. More cars for one thing, new or
newish saloons lining either side of the road or drawn up on
what had once been patches of grass and were now concrete or
gravelled forecourts. Besides, most of the houses had gone over
to double-glazing or would it be noise insulation against the
planes using nearby Heathrow. As though to confirm this guess,
a jet lumbered hugely overhead, its cruciform body for a moment
blotting out the pale sun.

A breeze flicked his face as he began, hesitantly at first, then
more rapidly, to walk down Stanmore Avenue.

As he came close to number 37 he wondered whether to go
across and knock at the door of 40, on the off-chance that the
Haldanes still lived there; but then decided against it. Even if they
were alive and in residence, what could he say to them? The two
couples had scarcely been close. Had the Haldanes even attended
either of the Willoughby funerals? Probably, although he couldn't
remember them being among the small group of mourners who
came back to the house for tea and sandwiches following the
burials. And after so many years, he couldn't even be sure what
they'd looked like. The husband had sported a small moustache,
hadn't he? An image came of a slightly-built, grey-suited man with
brown trilby hurrying up the avenue at the same time each
morning, carrying a brief-case in one hand, brolly used as
walking-stick in the other, fawn mackintosh neatly folded, off to
catch one of the innumerable Southern Electric commuter trains
that would take him to the city where he worked as ... .

But no, memory threw up no information on that score. As
for the childless Mrs Haldane, he could remember only the hat
she wore to church each Sunday, a black straw boater, with a

green ribbon around it which, at the back, hung down in a tail, an odd, raffishly defiant note to set against a life otherwise unimpeachably ordinary. Grey is your theory, my friend, but green is the golden tree of life.

No such tree at number 37. No tree of any kind. Coming to a stand outside the house where he had spent ten years without ever feeling he truly lived there, he saw that the silver birch which had stood in the hedge between 37 and 39 was gone. So, too, the hedge. And where there had been separate plots of grass was now a shared gravel yard with space enough, he guessed, for at least four cars. Probably the two semi-detacheds had become flats. He glanced at the open porch and made out a brass-plate with what had to be bell-pushes and names beside the maroon-painted door through which he had passed so many times. The last was when he and Sarah had come back, during his final undergraduate year, to be the chief mourners at their grandfather's funeral as, scarcely six months earlier, and because of her husband's hospital confinement, they had played the same role at their grandmother's.

He thought idly of how, on the second occasion, the old couple's lawyer had taken their addresses in order that he could "communicate" the information of what they had each been left — not much, it turned out — adding that the proceeds from the sale of house and contents were to go to some religious charity but that they would be allowed to remove their own "chattels" first and to select and take away any single item belonging to their grandparents, provided its value did not amount to more than fifty pounds. David asked for, and was given, a sherry decanter which he still had, and that, after he had cleared his few books and a small desk, was that. Sarah, having begun accountancy studies while he was in his first year at university, was already living in a bed-sit she'd found for herself in Clapham. He visited her there once or twice and was impressed by her determined self-sufficiency. She refused to take anything from Stanmore Avenue. "I don't want to be reminded of the place" she told him. "I don't want to be reminded of *them*."

Recalling those bald, blunt words as he stared at the house's frontage, its white-painted bay windows, the black timbering above the porch that echoed similar decorative devices up and down the avenue, he felt a chill depression seize hold of him. The sadness of incomplete lives. He tried to summon up usable images of the couple who had once lived here, who, despite their own heartbreak, had cared for his sister and him as they grew up, who in their undemonstrative and fretful way behaved responsibly to and for their grandchildren, may even have loved them, and who were now gone, all signs of their lives erased as thoroughly as though they had never existed. But no memory stirred. No forms of old time walked here. It was too late to make amends.

He turned away, began to retrace his steps. A mistake to have come. At the head of the avenue, he hesitated, glanced at his watch. Not much past four o'clock. If he hurried, he could be at Waterloo before the great press of home-bound commuters. Then, on an impulse, he turned toward the river.

* * *

A few minutes later, he was on the towpath looking to his left at a pub which, now open all day, was still called THE QUEEN'S ARMS. This being the middle of the afternoon, the place was more or less empty. Standing at a bar very different from the dark, cramped one he had known, he ordered a pint of bitter and took it outside. Hunched in his coat, he sat on a wooden bench and watched the river pouring slowly towards Richmond. Arching over the water to his right was the bridge that led to Eel Pie Island.

As suddenly as his spirits had sagged, so, now, they lifted. He swallowed some beer, lowered his glass and then self-consciously raised it in a toast to the island. That, he told himself, is where I learnt to be happy, and then, aware of the words' portentousness, don't be so melodramatic. "But I was." Startled, he looked around but saw no-one. The pub forecourt was empty. What few drinkers there were preferred the warm interior to the chill of outdoors. Relaxing, he raised his glass again. "Here's to you," he said as memories of the island's tumble-down hotel took possession, memories now sepia-tinted and clamorous with those nights of his late adolescence when he'd re-discovered the music of his early boyhood.

Eel Pie Island. The sounds of jazz washed down the summer Thames, of the various bands who played there, Acker, Ken, Eric, Brown, others, whose music he came to hear, to drink beer and dance to; evenings when he would stand by the long windows mesmerised by the tarry water as it slid by, while all about him were the tangled smells of hops, sweat, perfume, tobacco and something stronger and sweeter, thickening the air and making it seem that Delta City itself had been transplanted to this spot. Or times when he'd push between newly-arrived couples as he climbed the steps beside the stage and fix his gaze on the drummer below him, studying his technique, wondering, if I'd gone on practising could I have become as good as that. It wasn't envy, this speculation, or if it was it was quickly lost to plain delight in the music, the release that music brought, the exultance, the joy. There'll be a hot time in the old town tonight.

He sipped some more beer, looked across to the boatyard and, beside it, apartment block that screened much of the island's near side. All new, surely. And then he remembered reading years earlier about a fire which started one night in the old boatyard and gutted many of the buildings around, shaking out those folk who, enjoying their alternative life-style before the phrase was invented, lived in shacks and lean-tos they themselves had constructed, sculptors, artists, oddballs, that devil-may-care bohemianism as vulnerable as the hotel when it went up in flames, although by then its glory days were past and, so the newspaper article informed him, it had become a venue for up-and-coming rock groups. This music crept by me on the waters, abandoning the place where for a while it had made its habitation.

Abandonment. Jay Krassner.

It was time to confront his memory of the American, to accept that he had to be included in any attempt to reach an understanding with the dead. *Was* Krassner dead? He might not even have survived the war, that blue-eyed, tall soldier-drummer with, as far as memory could lend its uncertain aid, a slow, easy way of speaking and slow, easy smile.

He might of course have returned home to — where? — yes, Gary, Indiana. He could have resumed his career as professional musician. But if so, there was no knowing. Every so often in his adolescent years David would glance through a school friend's copy of *The Melody Maker*, scanning its columns for the "personnel" listed in reviews of recordings by American bands, but he never came across Krassner's name. Which proved nothing. Perhaps Krassner opted for the life of professional drummer in one of those "rickety-tickety" outfits he affected to despise, accepting the regular pay and trying to forget his dream of being a second Dave Tough. Or perhaps — and this was as likely as any other supposition — once back in his native country, the American decided to hang up his sticks and settle for a nine-to-five life of married respectability. Most people did, including those who had in childhood dreamt of very different possibilities. The ant-trap claimed us all, well, the majority. He himself had been persuaded to leave behind the drum kit he'd insisted on taking to Woodbridge, though once there he hadn't been allowed to use it. Jazz, his grandparents explained, was not music decent people enjoyed.

In the years that followed, he and Sarah were told that there was a good deal you weren't supposed to enjoy. And what you couldn't enjoy you mustn't even mention. So he never again brought up the subject of jazz, not in their hearing. And he only once tried to approach it with his mother. On the rare occasions after the move to Twickenham when he and Sarah were permitted to see her — or, rather, she was permitted to see them — they'd sit in awkward silence broken by the kind of formal questions and answers which made it impossible for him to mention Krassner's name. Once, though, when they were in a café at Waterloo station, he got as far as telling her that his grandmother called jazz "an uncivilized racket." And though he didn't add that she'd also said that it was no wonder that such music came from *America*, giving the word a stress that made plain her contempt, his words were enough to send the colour pumping into his mother's face. She recovered herself sufficiently to ask Sarah a question about the school she was attending, one whose uniform of brown skirt and brown and white striped blouse Sarah loathed. "It makes me look like dog's poo," she said.

251

Oh, those meetings. At first so rare as to make her seem almost a stranger to them, which was no doubt the intention, they never amounted to more than half-a-dozen times in any one year. Brother and sister would travel by train to Waterloo, accompanied by their grandmother, who marched them to the appointed meeting place, the steps at the end of the concourse that led to the News Cinema. Their mother would be waiting for them, her face set in unsmiling rigour. The curtest of nods and exchanges between the two women as they settled on the hour when the children must be returned, and then the three would watch the older woman's unyielding, black-coated figure disappear among the crowd. Only then would their mother bend to kiss her daughter and son. And at the end of the day, punctual to the minute, they'd be passed back into their grandmother's control.

As to return journeys to Twickenham, they were managed with very little talk, sometimes none at all. They knew better than to discuss their visits to Madame Taussauds, the Tower of London, Regents Park Zoo, visits which, when they were at first mentioned, drew disapproving looks, the disapproval increasing in direct proportion to the degree of pleasure they voiced. So while they looked forward with an almost desperate eagerness to the meetings with their mother, they travelled back in a silence amounting in Sarah's case, David guessed now, to a sullen despair which their grandmother took to mean that they hadn't enjoyed the day.

And now, quite suddenly, he found himself remembering a ghastly occasion, one he'd long forgotten about. They were as usual early in returning to Waterloo. But on this occasion, instead of waiting in silence, his sister began to cry. Clinging to her mother, sobbing, she pleaded to go home with her. "I don't *want* to go with her. I want to be with *you*."

White faced, her mother had bent to her, then, as Sarah's crying became a howl of outrage, her whole body shaking, she looked over her daughter's head to David, her eyes begging for his help. What he could have done he had no idea, but anyway at that moment his grandmother arrived, pushing him to one side and confronting his mother and the now screaming girl.

What followed was a kind of torture, an agony of embarrassment and hurt, noticed by curious passers-by as they hurried to catch their trains. Even now, he found himself shifting uneasily on the bench as he heard his grandmother's words: "upsetting the child, as if you haven't already done enough damage to our family" — and his mother's words, the low, grief-filled, "you don't understand."

"I understand only too well, my lady."

Suddenly he was on his feet, clutching his glass so tightly that he had to relax his hold before he could set it down on the table in front of him. The words reverberated in his head as though, at that very moment, they'd been spoken aloud. He drew some deep breaths then, still trembling, sat down again, pain knifing his heart. The words were alive, cutting into him, a spasm so sudden, intense, that, slumping forward, head and shoulders bent, he had to rest his arms on the table, take further breaths to draw off the pain.

Eventually, the spasm subsided. How different from Sarah he was.

"I loved her. I really loved her." Sarah hadn't merely been denied that love, she had been denied the chance to show it. Because in later years her mother wouldn't, couldn't, believe in love. She kept her daughter at a distance as she did her son. She must have believed that her failure to act at the decisive moment had killed their love for her. And yet what, after all, could she have done? No doubt their grandparents would, if necessary, have had a court order taken out denying her access to her children. She was powerless against them.

Gradually, the pain eased. He could breathe more easily. His glass was empty but he was in no mood for more beer. Better get home. Once more he stood, buttoned his coat, gave a final glance across to the island, that place where he had found a happiness that Sarah had been denied, and was soon at the station.

* * *

And of course waiting for his train at Waterloo brought back further memories. Now his mind was open to the past they came swarming out of their hiding place. Mostly they came as voices, insistent, peremptory. The waiter in a Lyons Corner House who asked if the children were hers, "only you don't look old enough to have kids of your own," winking at her frown of displeasure. Her own voice when, unguarded for once, she had said to him as they came out onto the steps of the Natural History Museum, "You're getting to look quite like your father," followed by an appalled silence, then, turning from him, "I'm sorry," and the walk back along busy, traffic-clogged streets during which she said nothing else at all, not even when he tried to ask her whether she thought dinosaurs could ever have lived in England.

Sipping a coffee while he stood alone on the increasingly noisy, thronged concourse, he made himself remember how, in the summer after his first year at university, he and Sarah, having saved up the money, insisted on taking her out to lunch at a small restaurant near Leicester Square. There, perhaps, in the none-too-formal atmosphere of the spaghetti house Sarah had chosen, they could find their way back to being once again a family, talking as a family should talk. Could they perhaps cajole her into telling them what she knew about the deaths of her parents, killed, as they had heard from their other grandparents, in a car crash soon after the end of the war, though the information came to them some months after the accident itself. "We didn't want to upset you further," their grandmother had said when, the chance to be at the funeral long gone, she finally broke the news.

And beyond those deaths there was the heretofore unmentionable one, the death they'd never dared to touch on in her presence, even thought it invaded their lives on an almost daily basis, loomed over them all. No, that death had never been brought up. But over wine, the three of them together, mightn't the chance for talk, for *real* talk occur? Well, it was worth a try.

The meal was a disaster. She rebuffed every effort they made to get her to say something, anything, about herself. It was as though she wanted to cancel her life as completely as it was erased from the house at Twickenham. There, as the young Sarah pointed out to her brother, the photographs of Stephen Willoughby, of which there were a good many, showed him as a toddler, schoolboy, student, as a young man in cricket gear posed among his team, another, this one elaborately framed, laughing with a group of friends outside a pub. But of Stephen as bridegroom, as husband, father — nothing. His parents had expunged every trace of their son's life from the moment he married Jean Enderby. For them, their only child had died a single man. As a husband he did not exist. Nor did he seem to exist for their mother. If she would say hardly anything about herself, she would tell them nothing about him, their father.

They made an effort to dress for the occasion, to suggest a gaiety they hoped she would share. David had on a new, check sports coat and charcoal grey flannels, a dark blue shirt and red, woollen tie, Sarah wore a wafflepeekie blouse and green, pencil skirt which made her look older than her years but which, with her chestnut hair cut flat, and her vivid face, caused most men to stare after her. In a joint note, they had suggested that they wanted to make this lunch "a family treat for the three of us," hoping this would persuade her into better clothes than the drab skirts and coats she habitually wore. But they might as well have saved their ink. She sat facing them in the Italian restaurant in her shabby dark brown costume, her face, without make-up, pale except for the dark blue-black hollows under her eyes, her hair, though cut and washed, otherwise uncared-for. As to food, she accepted all suggestions with a silent nod, ate little, would drink no wine, and, though she roused herself to show some interest in her son's tales of student life and Sarah's of her experiences as trainee accountant, she seemed almost to wince at their efforts to please her.

* * *

"I understand only too well, my lady." But really he thought, as he turned into the road where his own house stood, how little we understand each other. I didn't really understand what my own sister went through at Twickenham, and probably the old couple who brought us up deserved more understanding than Sarah and I ever considered necessary. They lost their only son and they didn't get much by way of love from their grandchildren. As for our mother … .

Pushing open the front door, he heard Maggie calling to him. "Here," he answered, profoundly glad to hear her voice. "I'm home."

~ CHAPTER EIGHT ~

The hotel arranged for him to be collected from Lucca airport. "All part of the service, sir," the hotel manager said when David phoned to confirm his time of arrival. The man's precise, clipped delivery made him sound English, but as the car steered through Valetta's midnight streets and David looked out on a succession of six-storey buildings, their shuttered windows and wrought-iron balconies, it was Moorish Spain he was reminded of, although these streets were deserted and eerily quiet, and when he finally hefted his case through the hotel's swing doors, the manager who, despite the time stood impeccably groomed behind the reception desk, was olive skinned.

"Ah, welcome, welcome Mr Willoughby. A pleasant flight, I hope." His smile seemed perfectly to echo a civility known to David through old black-and-white films, as though modelled on Richard Wattis or Cecil Parker.

Breakfast, he was told, would be from 7.30 until 9 a.m. "I think I'll sleep in," he said.

But in the event, he woke early. The previous evening Maggie had driven him to the airport through wild squalls of April rain, but here a keen blade of sunlight sliced through the shutters he'd closed before falling exhausted into bed. He crossed the carpeted floor, prised the shutters open and staggered back as sunlight slammed into his face. Then, blinking, he part-opened his window and at once street noises battered his ears. Craning for a better view, he watched as far below him smartly-dressed men and women, many of them carrying what looked to be brand-new leather briefcases, strode purposefully along the pavements. Early to bed and early to rise. David tried to imagine the city as his father had described it in his letters, its bomb-damaged streets like "frozen torrents of marble," metal girders bent and twisted as easily as if they'd been made of plasticine, house walls sliced away. "*You can't imagine how vulnerable, almost indecent, the exposure of a house's interior seems,*" he had written, "*I feel like a voyeur peering in on someone's shameful secrets*"; other houses reduced to blackened stumps, and everywhere, despite the danger, children scrambling among the ruins, families re-instating themselves in what remained of their homes, searching through the rubble for anything that could be saved, that could assert some defiance of the terrible devastation of their island homes.

But on this spring morning, the massive well-groomed buildings, their stone exteriors honey-gold in the vital sun, were innocent of any scars of war. Like the Maltese moving rapidly to and fro in front of them, they gave off an air of untroubled prosperity, of solid, permanent ease. War was not merely a lost memory, it had occurred on a different planet.

Glad of the sun-glasses Maggie had made him pack, he breakfasted on the roof terrace. There, as he sipped his coffee, he riffled through some of the letters he'd brought with him, lingering over one in particular. *No matter how awful the life here,* his father had written, *the singing hardly ever stops. I arrived here after the worst of it, but men who were on the island during that time tell me that the Maltese sang as much then as they do now. Perhaps it's the Catholic heritage, although I'm told they sing far more folk songs than they do hymns, but whatever lies behind the habit* [the word was scored through and over it was written *compulsion*] *it tugs at the heartstrings to hear them. For all the misery and abominable suffering they've had to endure, the Maltese* **can't be silenced.** *Old hands tells me there was a period when Jerry flew as many as five sorties a day over Valetta alone and that altogether the city had to put up with more than a thousand raids. Imagine that! I don't know how many raids London has been hit by but my guess is that it will have been far fewer. And after all, people can get out of London. The Rayners did and I wish my parents would. But here there's nowhere to go. A quarter of a million people were simply stuck on this tight little island with nothing but air-raid shelters to protect them or, where they could find them, caves, and nothing to look forward to but death falling from the skies. And yet*

*they went on singing. As Dave Morris remarked, not even the Victory
Kitchens could stop that, though they sang a whole lot more
cheerfully once the kitchens were themselves stopped.*

Having spent the previous fortnight reading up on Malta's
war, he knew about those hated Victory kitchens. He glanced
around him, took in the well-dressed people breakfasting here in
the clear air above Valetta's noisy streets. Odd to think he might
know more than any of them about the kitchens, set up at the
time of the worst food shortages, when convoys could hardly ever
get through the ring of U boats and mines slung around Valetta's
harbour. Not difficult to understand why the islanders grew
resentful of the boring, repetitive menus they provided, why,
according to one account, there had been a near-riot when goat
stew was served for five continuous days.

Folding the letters into his jacket pocket, he drank the last of
his weak, tasteless coffee, and strolled across to the terrace edge.
From the parapet he looked down into the waters of the Grand
Harbour where, fifty years ago, Italian Cants and then the
Luftwaffe's assorted bombers had blown up and sunk the harbour's
crowded contents: cargo boats, grain ships, troop carriers,
harbour vessels, dredgers, wherries, pleasure craft, all set ablaze
in a seemingly unending orgy of destruction. Now, under a
flawless blue sky, the few container ships tied to wharves and the
French naval cruiser riding at anchor as ratings in white ducks
swabbed down its steel decks or watched a small motor-boat ride
out with a plume of spray cockily tailing it, had no connection to
violence.

It was the same at street level. Walking post-breakfast through
Triq ir Reppublika, noting the elaborately-carved balconies of the
tall buildings, the many second-storey alcoves in which stood the
plaster figures of saints, the air of calm prosperity the place
exuded, he realised how his father's letters and the books he had
recently read unfitted him for this city of well-stocked shops,
their window displays of glistening, whorled pastries, ropes of
garlic sausages flecked white and red like the bell pulls he had
known as a child, the geometrically exact pyramids of oranges,
apples, melons, the elegantly-dressed window-models whose

slender grace bore little resemblance to the stocky men and women among whom he dodged as he made his way towards the Cathedral of St. John. Maggie had ordered him to report back on the famed Baroque interior.

But entry to the cathedral was cordoned off by police.

"What's going on?" he asked a bystander, one of a group of mostly aged men who stood peering over and under the policemen's shoulders.

"Funeral," the man answered in passable English. "An old actor." A name was offered, though it meant nothing to David.

"I saw him at the Coliseum here, in 1943, imagine. You are English? Well, your Mr George Formby, he was here, too. He played the mandolin."

"I expect it was the ukelele."

The man shrugged. "OK. The ukelele. But he was here. I think he is dead now?"

"Yes," David said. "He died years ago."

The old man sighed. "Soon we all die. It is God's will," he said and crossed himself.

David turned away. He could come back later.

Almost at once he found himself plunging down a stepped pavement along a narrowing street where the shops, at first grandly double-fronted plate glass, increasingly seemed like the entry to caves. Here were cafés, greengrocers, vintners, jobbing tailors, electricians, among whom, for all he knew, was the draper's shop outside which his father had seen a sign which read

Blitzed three times

Back I came

Three times more?

I'll do the same

As he continued his jolting, uncomfortable descent of the long, unevenly cobbled street, he saw, as he had hoped, that he was coming down to a high wall of massive limestone slabs. St. Elmo's Fort.

Arrived at its base he turned left and, having paid his entrance fee, was allowed into the National War Museum.

Two hours later he sat on a stool at a nearby bar, staring at the glass of lager he had ordered but which he couldn't as yet bring himself to touch. Scarcely conscious of his whereabouts, he huddled, frowning, abstracted, until he became vaguely aware of a solicitously-voiced enquiry. Was sir well or would he prefer to step outside for some fresh air.

He took a while to realise the words were directed to him. Then, lifting his eyes, he met the barman's stare. "I'm fine," he said, "fine," and tried to smile.

Smiling back, though none too certainly, the man went to deal with orders that were being shouted from further down the bar.

The words calmed him. Hands no longer shaking, David again brought the glass up to his open mouth and this time managed to swallow some lager before returning his drink to the counter.

Had that been his father? There was no way the museum, which lacked a catalogue as it lacked postcards, could help. And yet it was as though the photograph, which he might easily have passed by, stuck as it was in an obscure corner of a room he had almost decided not to visit, summoned him to it, reeled him in, demanded his attention. An indistinct, faded, amateurish snapshot, and yet ... .

He'd come on it, or it had called to him, at the moment when he had, as he thought, finished with the museum. He'd spent time poring over photographs, maps, newspaper-cuttings, memorabilia, all relating to those desperate months when every attempt to get convoys through to the beleaguered island ended in failure, until failure itself ended with what seemed like a Boy's Own story of triumph over impossible odds as the tanker OHIO, decks awash, steering gear smashed beyond all hope of repair, at one moment actually ablaze, nevertheless managed to limp into Grand Harbour, bringing with it, as someone watching from on shore was reported to have said, "flour to us and nuts to the Germans." On its own, the story was enough to justify the king's award to "Fortress Malta" of the George Cross, the tight-lipped citation for which was shown alongside Roosevelt's far more eloquent tribute.

As he turned away, it struck him that, considering how full the museum was, it was unusually quiet. He watched a man of elderly middle-age, in open-neck check shirt, shorts stretched tight over his pot belly, himself turn away from the display case in which he'd been following the account of how HMS BRECONSHIRE, veteran of six convoy runs, was lost on the seventh, saw the man dig the heel of his hand into one eye, then the other. Meeting David's gaze, he shrugged as though in mute apology for his tears. No need, David wanted to say, I understand, before beginning to study the contents of display cases which housed life-size dummies of men in service kit.

To the left of one of these cases was a motorbike and sidecar, and propped against it a floor caption which read **"Norton Big Four 633 cc. Motorcycle and side-car in 'Rubble-wall Camouflage."** The camouflage was so absurd that David wanted to laugh aloud. Hatched across the off-white in which the machine was painted were thick green lines which made the bike look from above like some compressed sea animal that had crawled onto land, wonder to all whom it did espy. Though perhaps from the air espial wasn't easy.

A photograph was pinned to the wall above the bike. Nothing remarkable, a snapshot of a group of young men and women astride motorcycles identical to the one he'd been inspecting. Dressed in makeshift uniform, battledress, cap, boots, all looking as though they'd been hastily donned for the photograph, they posed, laughing, some brandishing their fists, others giving victory salutes. The caption explained that they were Yugoslav partisans **"in training."** Behind them a few British soldiers, probably their trainers, stood at ease, their faces partly blurred by shadow, partly by distance. He moved away.

And then turned back. He looked again at the British soldier who stood tallest among the group at the rear. Skin prickled. His palms began to sweat. Fair, curly hair cut short, lean of face, unsmiling but not unfriendly, Stephen Willoughby stared confidently out of 1944 to where, fifty years later, his son stared back.

* * *

"And you're sure it was him? The date fits, I suppose, but does anything else?"

"Like what?"

"Well, does he mention the partisans in any of his letters?"

"Maggie, of course not. How could he? Any information like that and the censors would have spotted it and he'd have been strung up." Stretched out on his hotel bed, receiver pressed to his ear, David stared up at the ceiling, trying to remember the face which, blurred though it had been, signalled to him across the years. "But it *was* him, I'm sure of it."

"And how did he look?"

"He looked like my father." He knew that wasn't what she meant, but he also knew he couldn't play amateur psychologist over a blurred snapshot taken half a century ago. "I don't know exactly when the photograph was taken but I can probably pin it down. Someone somewhere will have a record of when those partisans were on the island and, more important, when they left for Yugoslavia."

"Will you take a copy."

"I've thought about that. I may, if I'm allowed to. Trouble is, the three people who could have identified him are all dead. "

"What about Hetty Rayner?"

"No, the Rayners arrived after my father had gone." And before she could ask, he said, "and Sarah was so young when he went that she doesn't have any memory of him."

"So, what next?"

"Well, if you're sure you don't mind my skipping the cathedral visit, I'll get on the road first thing tomorrow, drive to Siggiewi, see whatever's to be seen. I can at least pay my respects to Professor Zammit"

"Who? Oh, I remember. That statue you say your father mentioned in his letters."

"*Often* mentioned. The wise man of the island. Prospero without the nastiness." And when he heard Maggie's sceptical laugh, he said, "Obviously I don't know what my father saw in him, but now that I'm here I want to meet the old man." A pause while he shifted the receiver to his left hand. "And you never know, there may still be a few old people left from 1944. Besides, I do want to see the town where he was stationed and where he died. Hello? Maggie? Are you still there?"

"Yes," she answered, "I'm still here. But David, take care. I'm worried this may upset you more than you anticipate."

"It can't upset me more than coming on that photograph did. To see a man you've consigned to death looking at you from eyes half the age of yours … ."

"I can guess."

He was grateful for the concern in her voice, but, laughing lightly, all he said was, "I rather felt I ought to have been a small boy, not an ageing gent with a stoop."

Humouring him, she said, "Silly, you don't stoop."

"I didn't when you last saw me. A lot has happened since then. How's life on the farm, by the way?"'

"Both children phoned. Paul to ask how you were — he's fascinated that you're on Malta in pursuit, as he puts it, of the grandfather he never knew, Susie to say that all's going well and that she's turned down the offer of being told the baby's sex. And of course both send their love. As I do. I'll see you tomorrow night and you can tell me then about your visit to wherever it's called. Now, please *do* take care."

After he'd replaced the receiver he lay in the dark, weighing her words, their mixture of regard and tender admonition. She was, she had made plain, concerned about what he'd told her of his visit to Twickenham and its aftermath. "I worry for you, David," she'd said. "I don't think you're good at dealing with emotions, my love." And now here was a further cause for anxiety. But then, crowding out his thoughts about Maggie, unbidden, unignorable, came again the image of the man he had met earlier that day, the face which, for all the blurring of time and the camera's imperfections, was surely the same as that in the photograph he kept above his desk. I'm getting closer to him, he thought, and with the stir of excitement came a feeling of apprehension, of fear.

* * *

Driving out of Valetta early next morning, David noticed the number of English names over shop doorways, cafés, bars. Adverts for English Ales, for full English Breakfasts, for Harris Tweed. People who'd walked straight out of their lives in England and then, when they'd arrived here, walked straight back into them. The Roman poet was right. You could change your skies but never your soul. And yet, if his father's letters were to be believed, that young soldier Southern was prepared to change his soul, his conversion to Catholicism proof that he intended to become a true Maltese husband to his island girlfriend. But did he? Did the marriage take place? For of course the letters stopped while the romance was still going on. Was there a happy ending for that couple at least? If so, Southern might even be on Malta still. And if *that* was the case, and if David could somehow find him and get him to talk, then who knew what ... .

He switched his attention to studying the dry, limestone walls separating fields he passed, walls that had plainly been the inspiration for the camouflage he had yesterday thought so absurd but which he now humblingly realised made ingenious good sense. Then came walls at once higher and blanker, behind which he caught flashes of corrugated-iron roofs, buildings that might once have been barracks, army stores, even aircraft hangars. He was travelling back in time, back to the Malta his father had known, when men and women were beginning to emerge from years of terror and, for some, despair, once more hoping for a new start. Through the car's open windows scents of new-mown hay drifted, mingling with earthier smells of spring. He began to whistle.

The lane he was now in, which had obviously been cut for the convenience of local farmers, ended, as it had begun, at a T junction. He turned right and in a few minutes the flanking hedges gave way to houses, a few at first, then more of them, lining either side of a road which widened as it approached a town. He came to the edge of a small square, stopped the car and got out. He knew where he was.

Grass and trim flower beds surrounded by gravel, and in the centre was the statue of a man erect on his plinth, gazing imperturbably along the road in the direction from which David had come. David walked towards him. The man stared over his visitor's head, his expression one of calm assurance. Right hand resting lightly on his hip, the left, open-palmed, pressed down on a pile of stone-cut books, themselves atop a marble block on which was carved the serpent of wisdom. At its base two more books lay adjacent to the man's left foot, as though he had set them carefully down in the full awareness that at any moment he might need to refer back to them.

"Good morning, Sir," David said aloud.

Professor Nikola Zammit, Philosopher, Architect, Poet, 1815-1899, looked steadily ahead. His untroubled gaze, the moustache that followed the curve of his generous upper lip, his frock coat, neatly-buttoned, the trim-lapelled waistcoat and correct sit of his bow tie, suggested a man in whom knowledge and, yes, sagacity were combined.

David glanced around, saw he had the square to himself. Looking up to Professor Zammit, he said, again aloud, "I think you knew my father. Or perhaps I should say he knew you. You had certain things in common." The professor's gaze didn't suggest that he would reject this claim. "I'm very pleased to have met you at last," David said. "He thought you were a good man, and I would like to think that my father was also a good man. But he died before I could know him and that is why I'm here. Yesterday I believe I came face to face with him. Today, I want to see the town where he died."

He paused, again looked around, then back up at the professor. The professor's image had blurred, seemed to waver. David pressed fingers to his eye-lids, stood in silence. When he looked again, Professor Zammit had returned to contemplative stillness. "Now," David said, "I must go, because I don't want to waste what little time I have. Goodbye."

He walked back to his car and, as he reached it, turned for one last look. Professor Zammit was still gazing intently along the road that led to Valetta and the world beyond.

* * *

A labyrinth of narrow, winding streets led him to the town centre. Parking near to the top end of the main square, he walked out to confront the massive church of St Nikola, then, drawing one of his father's letters from his shirt-pocket, turned to look down at the square's far end, where he could see the two smaller churches his father had sketched, to the side of one of them the pencilled figure of the saint who gave the church and indeed Professor Zammit his name, "*clutching in his hand a most improbable basket of loaves*" his father had written, "*which to be honest look more like primitive hand grenades,*" and a cross marking the place, half-way down the square, where Maria's bakery stood.

But he wanted to approach the square as his father would have approached it when he came down from his barracks at the town's far side. The sketch showed how this was done. There was the arrow pointing to the street along which Stephen Willoughby came, an attempt at a barber's pole which had to signify where Marcus's house stood, near to a cross identified as "*Church of the Beheading of John the Baptist,*" and, at the very edge of the square, some stick figures against which his father had written, "*air-raid shelter, not needed now except by locals wanting to evade the prying eyes of Dogberry and Verges.*"

Turning away from the square, David re-entered the labyrinth of narrow streets, working his way down-hill until he judged he must be on a level with the bottom of the square. A few more turns brought him out to what, as he'd hoped, was the Church of the Beheading.

But where in that case was Marcus's shop? He studied the glass doors of a bank on the other side of the street. Had that once been a barber's? Should he ask the policeman who lounged wearily outside the bank's doors, scarcely bothering to scrutinize the few customers passing in and out? No. Instead, he walked the few yards to the bottom end of the square, then, screwing up his eyes, stared up its expanse to St Nikola's which from this vantage point he could see was a grandly baroque church, made more massive by its dominant position.

He reached for his sunglasses and, as he did so, realised he'd left them in the car. Damn. How remote the rainy England he'd left seemed from this world of heat, dust, dazzle. And how remote it must have seemed to all those thousands of servicemen who fifty years previously had been dumped here. All he had to do when he finished was drive to the airport, board a jet, and he'd be home in a few hours. For them, England was a lifetime away.

He looked about him, trying to imagine those young men in war-battered Malta, amid the alien — not corn, but alien culture, a culture of which hardly any of them would have prior knowledge. Was this what was meant by exotic? Exile, exodus, exogamy, expropriation, exscind … Yes, to destroy. So much of Malta destroyed by the war. So many lives, too. And among them, a tiny episode in the general cataclysm, his father's death, the damage done to his family … .

But now the eager sense of anticipation which had been with him on the drive from Valetta and which had been sustained, strengthened even, during his meeting with Professor Zammit, was ebbing fast. I am hoping to understand. Some hope! The dark certainty of Cowper's words came back to him." And in the dust, sifted and searched in vain, The undiscoverable secret sleeps."

But did it? Could he wake the secret? What was the point of making this visit if he didn't at least try. Shielding his eyes against the sun's glitter, he looked up the square to the point where he judged Maria's bakery would have been, fixing his gaze on a man who appeared from out of a doorway, bag of groceries in one hand and, in the other, an ice cream which he held out to the girl who came skipping up the steps to where he stood. She took the filled cone and ran across the square to a parked car. The man followed her, lobbed the groceries into the back of the vehicle, said something to the little girl, then stepped onto the far pavement and disappeared through a door above which a painted board announced BAR — ALL WELCOME.

Walking slowly up the uneven, flagged pavement, David came to the spot from which the man had emerged. It was, he saw as he approached, a single-fronted shop. He pushed through the plastic strips that curtained its doorway and found himself in a small, general store. Behind the crowded counter a woman stood. Grey-haired, dressed in black, she looked at him enquiringly.

"I wonder whether you can help me?" he said, quickly. Then, as she shook her head, he went on, more slowly, this time: "I'm looking for someone who used to own a bakery, I think on these premises. She was called Maria."

The woman did not return his smile. Nor did she speak. She merely stared blankly at him.

"I'm afraid it was a long time ago. In the war. I imagine she will be dead by now, but perhaps you or someone local remembers her."

No answer. No change of expression.

He tried again, by now aware of the futility of his quest. "I have come from England. My father was in the British army here. He was stationed at Ziggiewi. In his letters he mentioned Maria's Bakery."

Still nothing.

One more time, he thought, then I'll give up. "Maria had a brother called Marcus who was a hairdresser. His shop was just beyond the square," and he pointed to the way he had come, although she did not take her eyes off his face. "I am hoping to find out if anyone here remembers them."

She came out from behind the counter, then, beckoned him to follow her to the doorway. "No speak English," she said in a wispy voice. She tapped a finger against her lips. "There," she pointed across the square.

"I see." He nodded, hoping he had understood. "Many thanks." But already she had disappeared through the curtain.

In the bar three men sat round a table, smoking. They stopped their talk as he appeared through the curtained doorway blinking in the sudden gloom, looked first at him, then at each other. He went across to the wooden bar, against which leaned the man of groceries, shoulder to shoulder with the bartender as they studied a newspaper spread open before them. The bartender looked up, his nod part enquiry, part welcome.

"A beer, please."

"What kind of beer?" The accent was gutteral, the words laboured, but at least the man understood English.

"Anything, so long as it's cold."

The man stooped behind his counter, brought up a can of lager beaded with moisture, and pushed it across. He gestured to David to take one of the inverted glasses on the bar beside him and was about to return to the newspaper when David asked him, "how much?"

The man thought about it, as though he had never before been asked such a question. "A lira," he said at last.

David paid him and went to join the men at their table. "Thirsty weather," he said as he unzipped his can and began to pour the foaming liquid into what, even in the bar's dim light, he could see was a smeared glass.

One of the men, the oldest by the look of it, said in a low, halting voice that lengthened the syllables, "Eng-er-lish?"

"Yes. English."

The man considered this. Then "Me. I am Nick," he said, slowly extending his hand for David to shake. He had a deeply-lined face, a grey, almost white fringe of hair round his shallow domed head, and like the others was wearing an old black jacket over a collarless white shirt.

"My name is David. David Willoughby."

The three of them watched him drink but did not respond when he raised his glass in intended good cheer. Then one of them muttered something to Nick, who nodded and said to David, "Peter ask me to ask, why you are here."

No hostility was implied, David guessed. It was rather that the little town saw so few strangers that any outsider was bound to arouse curiosity. But it gave him the opening he needed. "I'm on a sentimental journey," he said. And noting the puzzlement in the other's eyes said, "My father was in the army here during the second-world war."

"Your father, he was *here*?"

"In this very town."

Nick spoke to the other two men who looked at David with new interest.

"His camp was about a mile away, I think, but he used to come down to Ziggiewi as often as he could. He often mentioned two local people. Marcus, who cut his hair, and Marcus's sister, Maria. Maria ran the bakery which was on the other side of the square, perhaps where the shop now is. She baked bread the soldiers liked, which my father spelt f-t-i-r-a, though I don't suppose I'm pronouncing it correctly, and she took in their washing, too."

He paused while Nick passed on this information.

He had their attention now, no doubt about it. The man who had not yet spoken tugged at Nick's sleeve and began to speak in a rapid monotone, from time to time jerking his head in David's direction.

When he finished, Nick said to David, "Manoel understand some English words but he don't like to speak it. He has lived here all his life, but me, I am new. I live here only thirty years." He exchanged smiles with David, then added, "I was from another town, Zebbug. I think I do not know about Marcus or Maria, but Manoel he say he know them and they are dead."

The excitement, that had begun to build as Nick spoke, fell at his last words. David sighed, then shrugged. "A pity," he said at last, and drank some more lager, wanting to hide his disappointment. "I would like to have met them. Judging from my father's letters they were very nice people."

"Your father wrote to you about these people?"

"To my mother, mostly. I was a small boy at the time."

"And then afterwards, when he is back to England, perhaps he tell you about such things. He tell about us, about this place?"

The moment had come at last. "He didn't return to England," David said, speaking slowly. "He died before the war ended. He died here."

"Ah". Nick shook his head, in grave sympathy. "I am sorry. Very sorry." He spoke in Maltese to the others, who looked equally grave. Peter reached over and patted David's arm. "He is very sorry," Nick said, "Manoel, too, of course." He was going to say more but Manoel began speaking rapidly to him, Nick tilting his head to listen to the other man's words. When he finished, Manoel nodded towards David, clearly intending Nick should explain. "He would like to know when your father died."

"October, 1944," David said, not having to think about it.

"And he was ill?"

While he was trying to think how best to reply to the question, Manoel, who was watching David's lips, now took hold of Nick by the shoulder, drew him close, and began whispering in his ear. As he spoke, the expression on Nick's face changed from the calm resignation of a moment earlier to one of puzzlement, then concern, then agitation. Peter, too, looked upset, and the bartender, whose companion had left, was also paying attention, too far off to hear anything Manoel said, but watching every move that he and Nick made.

For now Nick was whispering back, shaking his head, sighing, as Manoel gesticulated with his free hand, chopped at air, then brought his palm down flat on the table.

"What's going on?" David asked.

"You say you are called Willoughby." Nick had difficulties with the lls.

"Yes, that's right. Why?"

There was an awkward silence during which the three locals exchanged glances. Then, his eyes sliding away from David's face, Nick said, "Manoel remember a soldier with that name had accidental death. He don't know, but he heard about it."

David was shocked. He had always assumed that the army would have hushed the death up. But then, he thought, news travels fast especially in a small place like Ziggiewi. And of course some people, Marcus and Maria chief among them, would have wanted to know what had happened to the soldier whom they treated as a friend, would have pestered other soldiers to tell them why he no longer came to town for his haircut or to visit the bakery.

Nick said, "Manoel, he was here, in the square, when the army take the man away."

"*What.*" Then, trying to recover himself, he shook his head. "But that's impossible." His look of stunned amazement must have communicated itself to the others, for Nick said, more gently, as though to exculpate his companion, "Manoel, he was young boy. He don't see all what happen."

But David wasn't thinking about that. He said, "You're telling me that the death happened *here* — in the town?"

Nick turned to Manoel and in answer to what must have been his question the other nodded, lips pressed firmly together.

"Yes," Nick said to David. "Manoel is sure. He don't make it up."

He was appalled. All these years they'd believed what they'd been told, that the body had been found in camp, that Stephen Willoughby was discovered in his own quarters. Now it appeared that his death had occurred in Ziggiewi itself. But why? Or rather, why had they been lied to? The army took the man away, Manoel had said. Then the army knew more about the circumstances of Stephen Willoughby's death than they were prepared to tell his family. And again the question formed, but why?

Once more Nick turned to speak to Manoel before repeating to David, "He say, yes. For sure, he die here, in town."

Too aghast to do more than nod, David slumped back in his chair, looking from one to the other of the three men. He had come here hoping to discover something, *anything,* which, insubstantial as it might be, could give him some inkling about the man whose life, especially his time on Malta, remained so mysterious to his son. And now even the little he thought he knew turned out not to be the case. Instead of becoming more knowable, Stephen Willoughby was becoming less, the already insecure fabric of his image disintegrating into a dust of rumour and speculation, of old men's friable memories.

The old men looked back at him, their leathery, wrinkled faces settling into impassivity. He must get away from here. Pulling himself to his feet, he held on to the table until he felt safe to move, then, still unable to speak, he lifted a hand in farewell and walked numbly out into the sun.

* * *

A little while later, he was following the coast road that would eventually bring him, so his map indicated, to the megalithic temple of Haga Qim. As the car rumbled up a steep incline, he made out not far ahead a small, handsome baroque church which a roadside board identified as the Tour Providenza. A pause here might calm him, ease the yammering in his ears, unclench the pain still gripping his heart. He parked beside the church, then walked towards and round the building, concentrating his attention first on the elegant portico, then craning his neck to study the neo-classical figures ranged round the hexagonal roof. Feeling more in control, he was about to return to his car when he noticed a high wall behind the church, beyond which was a row of curved, corrugated iron roofs.

The thudding in his ears started up again. Of course, he thought, of course. He walked across to a wide, steel-mesh gate set in the wall, and, peering through, knew without a doubt that he was standing at the entrance to the camp where his father had once been billeted. Through the mesh he could see, stretching in both directions, long, single-storey hutments, formerly barracks, now the enforced homes, so those mingled smells and low, crooling sounds told him, of battery hens. In the middle distance was a weed-infested area the size of a football pitch, which once would have been the parade ground, although the only thing now stirring was a lean-looking guard dog, the size of an alsation. The dog wandered morosely between a few, mud-caked and rusty farm vehicles parked on the parade ground's cracked, concrete surface. To the right, just inside the gate, stood a box-like structure scarcely bigger than a telephone-booth, also made of concrete. The sentry box.

As he took all this in, the dog, aware of a stranger's presence, came bounding across, barking as it hurled itself at the wire, its yellow eyes glinting in an ecstasy of rage. The noise attracted a youth who emerged from the nearest hutment, lumbered over to the gate, shouting at the dog as he came and, as the dog cringed at his approach, looked at David in sullen enquiry.

David tried to explain that he was trying to trace the whereabouts of a British army encampment.

"Not army now," the youth said. "Farm. You go. OK." He jerked his head contemptuously at David. So David did.

* * *

A few hours later, after a desultory inspection of the megalithic tombs which he photographed for Maggie's sake rather than his own, and a visit by way of an overgrown, grassy path above the sea to the memorial to HIS EXCELLENCY SIR WALTER NORRIS CONGREVE, whose inscription his father had written out in one of the letters now tucked inside his breast pocket, David sat in the airport waiting for his flight home.

Had it been worthwhile, this trip to somewhere he had never, before that lunch with Sarah, intended, still less wanted, to visit? He didn't know. On the plus side, he had perhaps come face to face with his father. That was something, might even be much. But to set against it, what the old men at Ziggiewi had told him left him more confused, no, more baffled, than ever. The photograph had perhaps brought his father closer. But Manoel's words had without doubt pushed him further off. What do I really know, he wondered, and thought dejectedly, not much, not much at all. However he weighed it, his two days on Malta had resolved nothing. On the whole, he'd have done better to stay at home. And this was the feeling he dragged on board with him and which weighed him down on his return flight.

He finally woke, blinking. A glance at the bedside clock told him the time was already gone 10 am. Hauling himself from bed, he showered, pulled on an old shirt and pair of trousers and wandered down to the empty kitchen. A note from Maggie was propped beside his breakfast plate. "Gone Shopping" it said, and as though to verify its accuracy she now stepped through the back door with a full carrier-bag which she plonked on the table before stooping to give him a perfunctory peck on the cheek. "Hello," she said, "what time did you get in then?"

"Dunno exactly," he said, reaching an arm to encircle her waist "The wee small hours of the morning. I didn't wake you, then?"

"No."

He nodded, satisfied. He'd asked the taxi to stop some houses down from theirs and had been as silent as possible in unlocking the front door, then creeping up the stairs, shoes in hand. "I should have been a cat burglar," he said, "I could have been a contender."

Releasing herself from his clasp, Maggie shrugged off her coat and began to unpack the carrier bag, looking enquiringly at him as she showed him its contents: coffee, milk, bread, apples, eggs.

"Coffee and toast will be fine," he said.

"And while I'm slaving over a hot stove you can tell me about Malta."

"Ah, Malta," he said, then sat silent until Maggie pushed across to him a bowl of black coffee. Bending his head to inhale the deep fragrance, he sighed appreciatively, and spoke. "I'll tell you this for free, as my friend Robin used to say, your coffee is a damned sight better than anything the Maltese served up." He sipped, savouring the dark, slightly bitter taste, buttered a piece of toast, reached once more for his coffee, and, scrutinising the cup he was lifting, asked, "Didn't we buy a set of these in France?"

"We did, many years ago, when we were young and foolish."

"No use to talk to us."

"Well, now you can talk to me about your trip. I want to hear about that place you were at yesterday — Siggiewi?" She pronounced the word experimentally, testing, weighing out its four splintery syllables.

Chewing his toast, he looked out of the window as ragged sweeps of grey-white clouds shut out the sun, wondered how to explain to her yesterday's shifting moods, moods over which he had brooded on the plane back to England, increasingly certain that he could hardly explain them to himself.

At last he said, "To be honest, Mags, Siggiewi was … well, it was upsetting. Not at all what I'd expected. I don't mean in appearance. The place must have changed since my father' time — in fifty years you'd expect that. All the same, some of the features he describes in his letters were still there. The statue of Professor Zammit, for example."

He paused, looked at her. And when she nodded, smiling encouragement as she sat down opposite him, he went on, "Zammit was the first thing I came to when I drove into the town. I spent some time studying him, introduced myself, you might even say. I'd thought all those references to the old man were a bit fanciful, putting him on an even higher pedestal than the one he occupies, but now I think I can see why my father admired him. Zammit's a man of wisdom." He stopped, shook his head. "No, that isn't quite right. I mean he *does* look wise, but there's more to it than that. And although he's standing beside a whacking great pile of books, it isn't book-learning the good professor exudes. Forbearance, perhaps, magnanimity." He paused, searching for the right words. "You feel that he knows the worst the world can offer and yet isn't afraid. 'If way to the better there be,'" he paused in his quotation, then added, "'It exacts a full look at the worst.' Hardy could have written those lines with Zammit in mind."

"So at least the Professor wasn't a let down" Maggie said, reaching to pour him more coffee.

277

"Absolutely not. Zammit's fine." He finished his toast, then told her about working his way round to the far side of the little town so that he could approach it from the direction his father would have taken of an evening when he came down from barracks.

"And did you find the route."

"I think so, yes. I got onto a road that led slap bang into the town square with a rather silly statue of the patron saint handing out loaves of bread. Not a patch on Zammit, that's for sure. I think I must have passed Marcus's shop where my father went to get his hair cut, though I can't be certain. But I'm pretty sure I *did* find Maria's bakery — she was Marcus's sister, and, so the letters suggest, a motherly sort. Took in the soldiers' washing, did their darning, even sorted out their love affairs. Not that it's any longer a bakery. If I'm right it's now a now a small store, half way up the square towards the church. I tried asking the woman in there about Maria but she didn't speak any English. She sent me across to a bar."

He drank the remains of his coffee, held out his cup for a refill. Then he said, "I managed to get into conversation with some of the local men in there."

"And?" Maggie asked, watching his movements.

David looked up at her before answering. "Well, this is pretty weird. There was an old chap in the bar, Manoel he gave his name as, old enough to have been a teenager in the mid-forties, who claims to remember my father. Not only that." David met Maggie's gaze. "He claims to have been there when my father shot himself."

"Oh, David." Maggie reached for his hand. "My poor love." They sat silent, looking into each other's eyes.

Then, slowly, her look of concern began to change to one of puzzled enquiry. "Did this man Manoel tell you what he was doing there? I'd have thought the barracks would be off limits to the locals. Besides," and now her expression was one bewilderment, "I'm sure you always told me that your father's body was first discovered by one of the other soldiers a little while after his death?"

He said quickly, "According to Manoel, my father *didn't* kill himself at camp. The shooting *didn't* take place where we thought

278

he … where we were told it happened." Then, more slowly, he added, "If Manoel is telling the truth, he shot himself in the town square, in full view of anyone there at the time."

She was amazed. "And you believe him?"

"Yes," David said, "I do." She put a hand to her mouth, aghast at the implication of what he was saying. "Oh, I know there are always people who claim to have witnessed events at which they can't possibly have been present. Fantasists, people who manage to persuade themselves they know more than they do. Anything for publicity: A moment on camera, the chance to speak into a microphone, to see their name in a newspaper. But Manoel didn't strike me as one of those. Anyway, what was he going to gain by it? I wasn't any kind of a reporter." He frowned, then went on. "Not only that. When he told me about being there, he didn't know I'd be shocked by the discovery. He must have thought he was telling me what I already knew. No," he said, staring into his cup, "I'm a hundred per cent sure that Manoel was telling the truth."

"How terrible for you," Maggie said.

He looked at her then. "Not pleasant, that's for sure."

"And it's so … well, without being insensitive, I have to say it seems so melodramatic."

He nodded, wanting to dispel the look that had come into her eyes, its flickering awareness of having overstepped the mark. "You're right." He shook his head, went on, "I think I'd always clung to the hope, well, chance, that his death would turn out to have been an accident, and, if not, then at least his suicide, because it was in private, would have had some sort of dignity to it. But now … ."

After a few moments' silence Maggie said slowly, "It makes you think, doesn't it, that there's sense in the coroner's words about people committing suicide while — how does it go? — the balance of mind is disturbed." And when he said nothing, she added, covering David's hand with her own, "that at the most terrible of moments perhaps even the sanest among us can't be held responsible for our actions."

He looked away, then drew his eyes back to meet hers. "I don't think any the worse of him, you know," he said.

"Of course not." She gave his hand a squeeze.

He smiled, grateful. Then, once more frowning, he said, "they didn't seem especially sympathetic, even."

Still holding his hand, Maggie said, "Malta's a Catholic country, and despair is a cardinal sin."

"And suicide is an act of despair and 'no end is limited to damned souls.'"

"You don't believe that, do you?" she asked, troubled.

"No," he said, emphatically. "But I think my father's parents did. 'Cut is the branch that might have grown full straight.' My grandfather was always quoting that, though I doubt if he knew where it came from. He wasn't a Catholic, neither of them was, but they were both what they thought of as religious. They certainly hated my mother for forcing my father into taking his own life. That's how they saw his death. Caused by her betrayal of the marriage."

"Hatred doesn't go with Christianity. Forgiveness does."

"They wouldn't have seen it as hatred."

"But it was."

"Oh, yes," he said, "it was hatred, alright. That was what Sarah realised and I was too — too, well, *accommodating* to accept." He eased his hand out from under hers and stood up, shaking his head as he did so, as though trying to clear his vision. "But I doubt they hated her as much as she hated herself."

"And now you suspect that your grandparents knew more about your father's death than they told you and Sarah?" This time it was a question.

He sat down again. "I thought about that, after Manoel's revelation, but no, I don't think they did." His smile was a mere twist of the lips. "I've no reason to believe that they spared us anything. Of course, for a long time after we'd gone to live with them they told Sarah and me precious little. Our father had died on Malta and our mother couldn't cope. That was about the extent of it. That seemed strange, because after all she'd been coping ever since he'd gone off to war. But when you're young you believe what adults tell you, no matter how mysterious. You trust them to know, and in the period leading up to our being whisked off, first to Woodbridge then Twickenham, she'd certainly become wretchedly unhappy. I came to realise that later, though at the time Sarah and I were simply bewildered, couldn't understand her moods, couldn't understand what had happened to the mother we'd known." The words began to spill out of him now. "We'd try to please her, do things for her, hope to make her laugh, and sometimes it would work, the sun came out and she'd be her old self again; but at other times she'd snap at us or simply push us away, shut the door to the living room in our faces, tell us to go and play. Be out of her sight, she meant. And then we — Sarah more often than me — would hear her crying and think it was something *we'd* done, that *we* were responsible for her unhappiness." With an index finger he traced crumbs around his plate. "Once or twice Sarah blamed the American soldier, I mean she told me that it was all *his* fault, which in a way was true, although of course neither of us had a clue as to what had actually gone on." He held up his finger, licked it, said, "And to be honest we still don't know, not for sure. But there must have been some sort of an affair, though they couldn't have been together for very long."

"Long enough for her to want to leave her marriage?"

"Who knows? Anyway, Krassner was gone by the time Sarah and I got back from that holiday. I doubt she ever heard from him again."

"Poor kids."

"Poor her, I now think. Anyway, I don't any longer blame her, though I used to think she was at fault. The priggishness of the young."

Maggie looked at him, but said nothing. As though in self-exculpation, he said, "you have to remember that when we left for our holiday that summer, she was, as she might herself have said, as happy as Larry. When we came back she was completely different. I remember that once, when she'd been especially short with us, Sarah crept into my bedroom and whispered that in our absence our real mother had been captured and taken away and that the woman downstairs was a witch in disguise." He looked at Maggie, laughed briefly. "In a sense, Sarah was right." He shrugged, slapped his hand down on the table. "And then, suddenly, we were carted off to Woodbridge, 'for our own good.' Father dead, mother incapable. End of family. And in the following years, on the few occasions we were allowed to see her, she was always so constrained, so held in, that our meetings were miserable for us all. She'd become a stranger."

"So when did you find out more. I mean, when did your grandparents give you a full account of what had happened?"

"I've told you, surely?"

"Let's pretend I've forgotten."

And when he looked at her, puzzled, Maggie said, "David, my love, you've never said *very* much about your earlier years. In fact, during this last half hour I've heard a good deal more about the young David Willoughby than I've ever before been told. Not merely about what happened to you and Sarah but about how you, David, felt."

"Ah," he said, "you're going to tell me again that I'm not very good at communicating my feelings."

But the steady seriousness of Maggie's gaze rebuked the attempted lightness of his tone. "Why make a joke of it?"

"Sorry." He was silent for a few moments, chastened by his wife's rebuke.

"Perhaps," he said, matching her tone when he spoke again, "this visit to Malta has kicked open doors, shown me not merely some things I didn't know about but others I'd chosen to forget or to bury."

"Such as?"

"Well, for one thing I discovered that my father died in a way — correction, in a *place* — I'd not expected, though the place also implies a manner of death that shocks me. For another, I looked in at the camp where he must have been stationed. It's a farm now, with a young thug in charge. That was another jolt."

"But you surely didn't expect the place to be the same? Not after fifty years."

"No, of course not. But — I don't know — but perhaps I wanted ghosts to start to life, and the truth is that between them, farm and thug had simply *cancelled* the past, rubbed it out. Gone, all gone." He waved his hands in a gesture of frustration.

"And what of the things you'd chosen to forget? I'd like to hear about them."

"Such as exactly how my father's parents — our 'guardians' as they called themselves — told Sarah and me the facts about our father's death. Or anyway, the facts as they knew them?"

"Such as that, yes." She got up, went to make more coffee, then, turning back to him, said, "Don't you think you owe it to me to tell me about that? Don't you think you owe it to our children."

"Owe?" he said, startled. "How?"

Maggie shook her head in exasperation. "David, David. Make the connection, can't you. You go chasing off to Malta to find out all you can about your father, and yet whenever your own children asked you about *your* early years you fobbed them off with remarks like 'oh, they're of no consequence,' or 'some other time.' They got more out of me than they ever heard from you, and I could tell that they were dissatisfied with the little snippets I fed them. I don't blame them, either. They probably thought I was keeping back information I could have passed on, whereas of course I told them as much as I knew. Which was as much, or as little, as you chose to tell me. And that, to be honest, was precious little. You've never *really* told me about those years. Not when we students together, not in our days as lovers, not since our marriage. I've never liked to push you, but hasn't it *ever* occurred to you that your children see you as a mystery man? You wouldn't even take them to look at the house in Twickenham where you lived for all those years — from, what was it, a ten-year old to graduate? Ten years, David. A whole decade."

He shuddered faintly. "Bad karma," he said. "I must have wanted that part of my life to be finished with, done and dusted. And after my grandparents deaths there was no reason to return."

Maggie brought the re-filled coffee pot back to their table and, as she poured for them both, said, "But can't you understand that it's natural for children to want to know about their parents' early lives, and for that matter, to know about their grandparents, even their great grandparents."

"All of whom were dead — I mean the grandparents were — by the time Paul and Susie were born." And, as she opened her mouth to speak, he said, "anyway, I did tell them about my parents, *and* I told them about how Sarah and I went to live with our grandparents, I mean my father's parents."

"That still leaves a great deal you *didn't* tell them," Maggie said. "I'm not sure you ever realised how often I was pestered for information about your early life. And what could *I* tell them?"

"You didn't need to. Wasn't it enough for them to know that my mother was ill and couldn't be visited? And they knew my father was killed in the war. What else was there to say?"

Maggie looked at him, shook her head. "Alright," she said, "I know it must be painful. But won't you tell me, now, as we're sitting here, tell *me* at least. I really do want to know how your grandparents broke the news about your father's death. You never have told me, you know." She was pleading but perhaps less for herself than for him.

He took a deep breath. "Alright. But, Mags, it was over forty years ago, and I'm not going to be able to remember everything." He drank some coffee, slowly, as though using the opportunity to clear his thoughts. "OK. Well, they'd been promising that on my sixteenth birthday I'd be told something special, though what that would be they didn't say, and I didn't ever think I could ask. There wasn't much affection between us, you see. No closeness. I don't want to give you the impression they were unkind because they weren't. We were always well fed and clothed, they took us on holiday — Bognor, Worthing; there were days on the river, visits to the cinema, theatre, museums, we went to the Festival of Britain. In fact, it was at the end of a day seeing some of the Festival sights that we all went to a restaurant to celebrate my birthday."

"And?" Maggie broke the silence.

"And I can't remember what we ate. Rubbish, I expect. After all, food was still rationed. But I can remember being startled by the fact that the waiter who showed us to our table was wearing a black bow tie. I thought only band leaders wore those. But as for the food ... ."

"Cut to the chase" Maggie said.

"Alright. Well, this is the part I *do* remember. Plates cleared away, grandmother sitting hands folded on the table in front of her, staring at our grandfather, both of us nervously aware that something momentous is about to be said. Sarah, by the way, had on a white, woolly cardigan and a plaid skirt and I was in the grey suit that had just been bought for what they called 'Sunday best.' We'd been told to 'dress properly' for the occasion and so we put on the same clothes we wore whenever we visited friends of my grandparents. I can't remember what they were wearing, except that my grandmother must have been in the same hat as always, a dark red beret, surprisingly *chic*. Anyway, there we are and my grandfather says, not looking at me but across at his wife, 'Now, David, your grandmother and I think you are old enough to hear the truth about what happened to your poor father on that terrible day in October, 1944. And, David, we are expecting you to help your sister cope with what you are both about to hear.' And only then did he turn to look at me."

Maggie was staring at him now. "Yes," he said, "if I couldn't be told until I was sixteen, what about Sarah, who was that much younger? Perhaps they thought she needed to know the truth about her mother at an early age — a deadly warning to prevent her from setting out on the primrose path. You know," he paused, considering his words, "I've never been able to decide whether they actually took pleasure in telling us."

"I doubt it."

He shrugged. "Maybe. Maybe not. Their grief was genuine enough, I've no doubt about that, but over the years it had turned poisonous. I've always felt that a part of them relished the chance to let us know how and why they loathed their daughter-in-law. No doubt they hoped we'd loathe her, too."

"But it didn't turn out that way."

"No. We'd struggled with our feelings about her, I couldn't somehow believe what they said about their son any more than Sarah could believe what they said about our mother. From that moment on, though, Sarah loathed *them*. I don't actually know how much she took in of what was being said but afterwards she made it plain, to me at least, that she detested her grandparents. Whatever her mother had or had not done, she wasn't prepared to — well, a behavioural psychologist would no doubt say that she wasn't prepared to have her feelings manipulated."

"So what did exactly did your grandfather tell you?"

"Oh, that our mother was an adulteress — his word, which I don't think I fully understood but which I knew was as bad as it could get. That she had besmirched her married name, had betrayed her husband with an American, and, worst, had driven their son to suicide. I doubt I took it all in, but I was stunned by the vehemence of the old man's words, we both were. I remember looking across at Sarah and as he went on so she turned first red then very pale, gripped her bottom lip between her teeth. So as not to shout out, I suppose. When he finished, he said he was sorry if anything he had revealed might have spoiled my birthday celebrations, but it was better not to nurse illusions. I suppose he meant that from now on I could be expected to have no lingering sympathy for the woman who had as good as killed their son. It was some birthday, that."

He stopped, looked down at the floor, then back to his wife. "So now you know," he said.

Maggie bowed her head then raised it to meet his gaze. "Thank you," she said.

Her voice was still grave when she next spoke. "I can understand why you wanted to forget so dreadful an occasion," she said, "though I'm glad you've at last been able to tell me about it. But David, one thing I don't understand. How did your grandparents know about this American — Krassner?"

"Because she told them."

"*What?*"

"She must have done. When the official letter telling her of his death came she must have guessed that someone in the village had managed to tip him the wink about what was going on, though goodness knows how. That's a question Sarah and I are trying to find an answer to. But she had her enemies in the village, Hetty Rayner confirmed that. According to my grandparents, after their son's death our mother went to Woodbridge, and, so my grand-father told me, 'made a full confession.' That was part of the story I heard at my birthday meal, and that was why they couldn't 'dream of allowing innocent children to stay with the woman who had forfeited the right to be their mother.'" A pause. "I think I've recalled his words aright," he said, permitting himself the ghost of a smile. "Anyway, from then on, we lived with them and she was only allowed to see us at rare intervals, which they had to approve."

"Happy families," Maggie said, her voice full of distressed wonderment.

"Well, we survived. And, as I say, we couldn't complain of being badly treated. I can't say I ever felt much love for them and after that occasion I felt none at all. And Sarah ... ." He shook his head, sighed. "She was determined to get away just as soon as she could. I can't say I blame her, although on later occasions I tried to get her to see matters from their point of view. After all, they really did feel that they'd lost their only son in pretty ghastly circumstances. I imagine they were reconciled to the possibility of him being killed, but nothing could have prepared them for the manner of his dying."

"No," Maggie said, "I can see that." And she shuddered. "It doesn't bear thinking about. But I can also see why Sarah must have so disliked them. God, what a mess."

She made to stand, then sat down again. "Can I ask you one last question?" And when he looked enquiringly at her, she said, "that remark about not believing what they said about your father. What exactly did you mean?"

David rubbed his chin, considering. "Good question. Hope against hope, perhaps? That he hadn't meant to kill himself, that it had been an accident. I think that in some remote part of my brain I even wondered whether it mightn't have been a case of mistaken identity, that the real Stephen Willoughby was somewhere out there, still looking as he did in that photograph I had of him in his army get-up, and that at some time in the future he would come striding home to reclaim his family. The wandering Odysseus finally returning to his son and the faithful

Penelope." He stopped. "Well, with some necessary adjustments." A sigh. "Mere dreams, mere dreams, I know." Another pause. "And yet seeing that face in the museum yesterday I found myself thinking all over again, No, *this* man couldn't have pointed a gun at himself and pulled the trigger."

"But you don't *know* the man was your father," Maggie said softly.

He said, resolute, "I'm sure it was."

When he spoke again, his voice was darker, troubled. "That was why what I heard from Manoel was so dreadful. After *that*, I couldn't go on believing that my father's death was accidental."

"And all these years you hugged this … this theory — this hope — to yourself." There was the faintest hint of reproof in her voice.

"Sorry," he said. "This is hard to explain, but I always felt that if I brought it up with you you'd simply shred it, clip the angel's wings. And I didn't want to risk that. Especially as there were no rational grounds for what you call my theory. Anyway, my grandparents were completely satisfied with the official story. After the war was over, they got in touch with the man who found him, a Corporal Morris, or he came to see them. I'm not sure of the details, but Morris was a friend of my father's, one he mentions in several of his letters. He apparently found my father's body with his service revolver lying beside him. I know, because that was part of what Sarah and I were told at my birthday celebration. My grandfather even brought with him the letter from Malta reporting my father's death and saying that 'Nobody else was involved.' That's code for suicide."

"But still you couldn't bring yourself to believe it."

"Until yesterday. But Manoel's story about my father shooting himself in the square knocks for six my fantasy about an accident." He grimaced. "To kill himself in public. Almost as though he wanted an audience. Poor, poor man."

He got up, went over to the sink and poured himself a glass of water.

"What shall you do now?" Maggie asked.

"Phone Sarah. She needs to know."

As he made for the door, Maggie said, "You've not told me whether you found your father's grave."

He paused, hand on the door-knob, back to her. "Yes," he said, "I found it alright. No problem. It's in the British cemetery, on the outskirts of Valetta." He turned back to her. "There's a complete plan for the cemetery, names listed, plots numbered. All in order, all very tidy."

"And?"

He breathed in, deeply. "Nothing much to report. A plain, white slab. His name, his rank, his dates. That's all. Nothing else. The anonymity of death. 'Quiet consummation have, And renowned be thy grave.' Some hopes." And he left the room.

* * *

Half an hour later he sat at his desk, repeating to his sister most of what he'd told Maggie.

"Phew," Sarah said, when he finished telling her about the meeting with Manoel, "that must have come as a shock."

"It did," he said, moving the earpiece to his right hand so he could make a note on the pad in front of him. "But Sarah, it's suddenly occurred to me that there's something odd about it."

"Odd? How do you mean, odd?"

"Damn, I should have thought of this before. But look, if this fellow Manoel is right and our father killed himself down in the town square, then his body couldn't have been found by Dave Morris, could it? In fact, Manoel said that some soldiers — plural, not singular — came to take the body away. But *we* were told that our father's body was found up at camp by Corporal Morris. Our grandparents told us that, remember, and they got it from Morris when they met after he'd come back to England."

"Hold on," Sarah said, "don't gabble. Are you sure you heard Manoel correctly?"

"The trouble is I didn't hear Manoel at all." David paused, drew breath. "He couldn't speak any English, so someone called Nick had to translate for him."

He thought back to the previous afternoon's halting conversation. Then he said, "I may not remember every word, and of course I don't know that Nick translated accurately, though his English was pretty good. But, Sarah, I'm sure Manoel was telling the truth."

"Hmm."

"You don't believe me."

"Oh, I believe *you*. But fifty years is a long time, brother. Time enough for this Manoel to embroider a tale or to forget certain details. You've no idea how, in my line of business, I come across people who won't believe us even when we produce the evidence to show they were in receipt of monies of which they claim to have no knowledge. I sometimes think us humble accountants are called on to serve every Alzheimer's sufferer there is."

"That's different."

"Yes, alright, but my basic point remains. But put it differently. Suppose Manoel is right, why should this Morris want to tell porkies about our father's death? What's in it for *him?*"

"That's what I hope you'll be able to find out." He squinted at the note he had written himself. **Morris????** "Is there any chance you might be able to find out where Morris lives?"

"Why on earth should I do that?"

"Because if it's at all possible, I'd like to speak to him."

"You don't want much, do you. Morris. There can't be more than the odd million living under that name in London alone, though anyway the chances are that the poor man's long dead."

"You found Hetty Rayner. And," he added, "she's still alive."

"Women live longer than men. Something to do with life styles and being under less stress."

"I did you a favour in going to see her, remember," he said, pleading. "It was that visit, you know, that first set me thinking about paying a visit to Malta."

"Was it? Why?" She sounded genuinely surprised.

"Something she said, about terrible things happening in war and not only on the battlefield. Terrible things happened to our mother, I know you feel that."

"Yes," Sarah said slowly, emphatically, "I certainly do."

"So you can understand why I want to find out all I can about my father, and if Morris *is* still alive … "

"You said 'my father.'"

"Sorry, *our* father."

"No, don't apologise. If I'm honest, he means little to me. I never knew him, that is, I have no memory of him, whereas *our* mother … . " She left the sentence hanging in the air. After a brief silence, she said, "Alright, I'll see if there's any way I can track down this Morris. Start with the Regimental records."

"And Sarah, there's another man, someone called Derek Southern, my — *our* — father mentions in his letters. Someone who was involved with one of the local girls. I was wondering … "

"Now you're pushing your luck."

"I know," he said, hoping his voice sounded suitably contrite, "but the three of them were in the same place at the same time and you're a whizz at this kind of detective work."

"Flattery will get you only so far," Sarah said, and rang off.

* * *

She phoned again late the following afternoon. David, who was at his desk wondering gloomily whether he had anything that was worth saying on Mary Leapor's poetry, let the phone ring until he heard his own recorded voice inviting the caller to leave a message, followed by Sarah's curt "David, will you please get in touch as soon … . "

"Sarah, sorry. I'm trying to make up for lost time on this damned book."

"And what damned book would that be?" The enquiry was not especially friendly.

"Oh, it's my last say on eighteenth century poetry. My publishers are chafing because it's long overdue."

"Publishers. How grand."

Fitzroy Frobisher? Grand?

"Anyway," Sarah the brusque businesswoman said, "you can forget about your Mr. Morris. He emigrated to Australia in the early 1950s, after his mother's death, and according to our Sydney office he died two years ago. His wife predeceased him. So, end of trail. End of story."

"Damn." Then, tamping down his disappointment, he thanked her and complimented her on her ability to find out so much so quickly.

"As remarked before, we accountants have our methods." She was softening.

He could hear a rustling of papers. "Nor is all lost, you will be pleased to know. I've located a Mr Derek Southern who has, I think, to be our man. At all events, this Southern's details match the army records of a Southern who was stationed at Siggiewi in 1944. Place and date of birth, middle name — Frederick by the way — education, such as it was. Left school at the tender age of fourteen. In the most recent information we have on him, his occupation is given as engineer. That of course tells us nothing. He could be a car mechanic. He may design oil rigs." She laughed. "Though in view of his address I think we can rule out the latter."

"Where does he live then?"

"Putney."

"*Putney*?"

"There's no need to yell at me. What's so odd about Putney? As far as I know, it's a perfectly respectable place, at least so I've always been told." She was starting to enjoy herself.

"Nothing's odd about Putney," David said. "It's simply that Putney isn't far from where I live. I thought you were about to tell me he's in some remote corner of the kingdom. Now I know he lives at Putney I can easily arrange to see him."

"If he wants to see *you*." And then, without giving him an opportunity to reply to that remark, Sarah read out an address and telephone number — "which I really shouldn't let you have so if you *do* phone don't you dare tell him where you got it from" — and waited as he wrote the details down. "Good," she said, when he repeated them back to her, "now you can don your deerstalker and go a-sleuthing."

"I'll have first to make contact," David said, "drop him a line. Sarah, I'm truly grateful for all this." He was about to put the phone down, then, checking himself, asked "is everything ok with you?"

"Why shouldn't it be?"

But the question, far from being issued as a challenge, seemed to invite further enquiry. "You seemed a bit, well, a bit brisk."

She laughed. "Us businesswomen, you know. But as it happens, I'm trying to clear my desk before we fly off for a couple of weeks of sun."

"We?" He risked the next question but kept his voice light. "Which means, I take it, that all's going well. Romance is in the air."

"Oh, ar," Sarah said, "orl cudden' be better."

"I'm so glad" he said, feeling a sudden rush of regard for his sister. "Where are you heading for?"

"St. Lucia," Sarah said, "I think I *might* have preferred Barbados, but Jeremy insisted that St. Lucia was more private, more 'us'."

As though to prevent him from probing further, she said "And now I must get back to work. Happy hunting." Then, more gently, she added, "and let me know how you get on with this Derek Southern."

"Of course I will," he said, hoping his voice conveyed the depth of his regard. "And Sarah, many, many thanks."

He put the phone down, sat looking at the address he'd been given. Clever Sarah. May she be happy, he thought.

He glanced at this watch. Too late for the day's last postal collection. Never mind. For now he'd force himself to put in some more work on Leapor and then tomorrow morning, first thing, he'd write to the man Southern.

∾ CHAPTER TEN ∾

But Southern didn't want to see him.

David made several attempts to draft a letter, tore each up in increased irritation at not being able to strike the right note, and at last decided that the briefest communication would best serve.

Dear Mr Southern,

My name is David Willoughby. After the recent death of my mother I came into possession of letters my father wrote to her from Malta, where he served in the army during the second-world war. As there are friendly references to you in several of these letters I am writing to ask whether you would be willing to share with me any reminiscences you may have of my father, whose early death means that neither my sister or myself knew him very well.

Should he explain why he believed the person his father mentioned to be this Derek Southern and how he had come by his address? No, that could come later. He underlined his own address and telephone number and sealed the envelope.

A week went by, during which he put in long hours working with increased absorption on poets who, slightly to his surprise, he found he was becoming increasingly to respect and even admire, and then, having heard nothing from Southern, wrote again. Another week and still nothing. A card came from Sarah, showing a cobalt-blue sea edged by white sands and backed by lush vegetation, on its reverse two brief queries: "*Would you like one of these for your garden? What news of Mr Southern?*" Underneath Sarah's signature Jeremy had written his own name, with the message, "*Look forward to meeting you.*"

"What would you say that means?" he asked Maggie, pushing

the card across the breakfast table to where she sat, nibbling toast.

Without picking it up, she glanced at the words. "Love is in the air," she said. "Sarah and Jeremy must be intending to go public with news of their forthcoming marriage." And then, registering his look, she said, "well, you asked."

David laughed. "You could be right. I hope you are."

"This Jeremy. Is he love's middle-aged dream?"

"A successful accountant, or so I gather. He and Sarah used to be an item but then something went wrong, I don't know what, Sarah never talked about it. He disappeared to America some years ago, but now he's back and normal service has apparently been resumed."

"I remember you mentioning the name. But you never met him, did you?"

"No," David said, drinking his coffee and preparing to leave the table, "Sarah's always kept her various loves pretty much to herself."

"Ah, well, understandable, I suppose."

Only when he was seated at his desk, set ready to begin his morning's work, did it occur to him that the quizzical look with which Maggie had accompanied her words had been her way of suggesting that Sarah's silence might well have been a lesson derived, no matter how obscurely, from her childhood. Was Maggie right? Possibly. He guessed that Sarah felt more deeply than he did the dreadful sadness of their mother's later years, the injustice of her self-inflicted punishment. Suppose, after all, she had said nothing about Krassner to her parents-in-law? They'd have had their suspicions but they couldn't have proved anything. They almost certainly couldn't have taken her children away from her. But she conspired in that decision. No, conspired was wrong. At some deep core of herself, she felt she no longer had the right to them, had betrayed them, her husband, their lives together. And, without ever saying as much, he knew he had always accepted that, had gone along with the belief that she had indeed betrayed them all. Whereas Sarah hadn't. Sarah had never ceased to love her mother.

Enough. He began to sift through his notes on Langhorne's

poems. But it was no good. Almost at once his thoughts turned again to mother and daughter. What had they talked about on those rare occasions when they met in Manchester? What silences lay between them? What gaps that no words could bridge? Imagining them facing each other, unable to cross that gap, he was gripped by sadness. Langhorne would have to wait. Frobisher would have to twiddle his thumbs for a few more days. He reached across his desk and picked up the phone.

Nobody answered nor did an answerphone cut in. Either Southern isn't there, he thought, or he's sold up and left, or for all I know he may be dead. Sarah's information could well be out of date, I should have asked her …

"Yes?" It was an old man's voice, curt, suspicious.

"Is that Jackson's garage?"

"You got the wrong number, mate." The line went dead.

Trembling, David replaced the receiver, rubbed his damp palm on his shirt. Sod it. His attempt at a Cockney accent had been pitiful. Even now Southern was probably punching in 1471 or preparing to dial back, wanting to know who had been on the other end of the line. He sat for several minutes staring at the phone, willing it not to ring. It stayed silent. Back to Langhorne.

* * *

At the end of the morning he went out to the empty kitchen — Maggie had gone to her studio — and helped himself to biscuits and cheese, which he ate while pacing round the table. Food stowed, he drank a glass of water, put on his jacket, checked that he had Southern's address, pulled the front door shut behind him, and a few minutes later was at the station.

At Putney he glanced at the directions he'd taken down from his *London A-Z*, walked up the High Street, took a left turn as indicated, then the second right, and now, heart thumping against his ribs, found himself at the head of the street where, according to Sarah, Southern lived. No. 23 was on the left-hand side, one of a pair of small semi-detacheds which bold lettering across the joint porch identified as *LABURNUM VILLAS*. Bay windows, their once-cream paint now flaked and scabbed, stood just back from the street, dark green curtains pulled tight across, denying the passer-by a view of the front room. David pushed past the sagging front gate and stood on the cracked orange-and-black porch tiles. In the absence of a door bell, he gripped the heavy, wrought-iron door knocker, brought it crashing down once, twice, three times, before trying to peer through the door's frosted glass panels. No shadow moved within. Once more he brought the knocker down, this time more heavily than he had intended. The door shook in its frame. That would waken the dead, he thought.

Nothing. He began to turn away and as he did so the door creaked open and a man's head and shoulder came into view.

"What you want? You're not one of them bible thumpers, are you?"

Grey hair, a deeply-lined face, scrawny neck with grey chest hairs sprouting above a grey, open-neck shirt and dark blue pullover.

"Mr Southern? Mr Derek Southern?"

The other looked at him but said nothing.

David tried again. "My name is David Willoughby. The son of Stephen Willoughby. I think you and he were in the army, on Malta, during the last war."

It was as though platelets had shifted deep within the man's eyes. He cleared his throat and, almost imperceptibly, inclined his head. But still he did not speak.

"May I come in?"

The man's silence, his implacable stare, was making David nervous. Smile, be friendly, show him he has nothing to fear.

It worked. After seeming to consider the question for a long time, the man finally said, "suppose you'd better." Pause. "Now you're here." The voice was little more than a gruff whisper.

David stepped back up onto the porch, then edged into the narrow hallway as the other man stood aside to let him enter. Southern used his shoulder to ram the door shut, gestured with a nod of his head to the far end of the lino-covered passage. "We'll be alright in there." The man of few words had beer on his breath.

The kitchen was sparsely furnished. Pale green walls, cupboards white, recently painted, dark-red floor tiles. Below the picture window through which David could see a small, fenced garden, trim vegetable beds on three sides of a tiny, square lawn, was a sink unit, on the metal draining-board of which stood an inverted cup and, tilted against it, a round, white plate. Spick-and-span orderliness.

Southern motioned David to one of the two straight-back chairs drawn up to the formica-topped kitchen table. On it was a folded newspaper and a cheap notepad in which, given the uncapped biro beside it, Southern had presumably been writing when David came banging at his door.

"Shopping list," Southern said, following David's eyes. "Not that a man on his own has many needs." He made no offer of tea.

"I ought to explain why I'm here," David said and saw the flicker in Southern's eyes. Something's worrying him, he thought. Something I don't understand.

He leant back in his chair, the better to see Southern's face, for the other man still stood, hands gripping the back of his chair, looking warily at his visitor. "The fact is, my mother recently died and when my sister and I were going through her — her effects, we came across a bundle of letters my father had sent her from Malta. I took them away to read and found that your name cropped up in several of them. Always friendly references, he obviously liked you, and so we decided to try to trace you, see whether you could throw any light on … well, on what happened to him. I did actually write to you explaining something of this, wrote twice in fact, but I assume the letters didn't reach you."

Southern pulled out his chair and sat down. "No, I got 'em alright," he said, looking hard to David. "But there wasn't a dickie bird about how you found my address. I didn't like that. Made me feel you were … *after* me."

"No, not at all. No, I'm very sorry if we gave that impression." After a moment, he added, "my sister's work brings her into contact with the sort of people who, well, who are able to help her in various ways … ." He stopped, aware of how inadequate, evasive, the words sounded.

Fortunately, Southern had lost interest in the attempted explanation, as though David's mere presence in his kitchen was explanation enough. "When did she — your mother — die?"

"Three months ago. February."

"A month after my wife, then. I've had plenty of things on my mind, savvy? I didn't feel up to answering letters that dropped out of the blue." The words, uttered matter of fact, were edged with pain.

"I'm very sorry and of course I understand." David stood up. "Would it be better if I came back another time."

Southern looked at him, his face expressionless, then motioned to him to sit down. "No, no. Like I said, now you're here." He jerked his head about. "Been doing some decorating," he said. "Keeping busy. No point in letting things go to the dogs. And she'd not have wanted me to mope. I hang onto a routine. Work in the morning, down the boozer for a pint and sandwich at lunch, bit of a kip in the afternoon — I had my head down when you come banging." It was as though he felt the need to justify himself.

"I didn't mean to disturb you."

"Nah, forget it. I was due up anyway. Like I said, I've got the shopping to do." He pointed to the notepad. "Need to make a list, my head's like a sieve these days." A pause. "If you're wondering why I don't shop on the way back from the boozer the answer is because any excuse to get me out of the house is gratefully received. Two trips a day is more than twice as good as one, believe me. Fancy a cuppa?"

Talk had loosened him up, warmed the atmosphere.

"I'd love one."

Southern stood up, gulped for breath, as though the sudden action had taxed him unreasonably. "Steady the Buffs," he said. David followed his movements as he filled the electric kettle, switched it on, then, with almost a flourish, opened a cupboard door and fetched out a cup and saucer. While the water boiled, he brought a biscuit barrel over to the table, undid the metal hasp and, lifting the hinged wooden lid, made a show of peering inside. "Hasn't been opened since she went," he said gruffly.

"You don't see many of those nowadays," David said, hoping he sounded suitably appreciative.

"Bought at Brighton," Southern said. "Not long after we were married, that was. Our first holiday. I'd like to say help yourself but there doesn't seem much there." He closed and re-fastened the barrel. "I've got some cake." He took the barrel away and brought a round tin to the table. "Seems alright," he said, having prised open the lid and sniffed the contents. "Dundee. Now then, plates and a knife."

David sat and watched. Hospitality and nervous apprehension mingled in Southern's busying himself, his sudden wariness about meeting his guest's eye as he brought across a tray complete with tea pot, jug, sugar bowl, cups and plates. "Milk, sugar?" He poured for them both, cut thick wedges of cake and then, having pushed David's loaded plate across to him, finally sat.

The two sipped their tea and David broke off a piece of the cake which, as he popped it into his mouth, he discovered was surprisingly moist.

"Your father," Southern finally said. "His death was a bad business. I'm wondering what you know about it?"

David decided to keep his answer to the minimum. "Well, we know the worst," he said. "The army told us. That is, they told our mother. He shot himself."

Southern, frowning into the cup he held between clenched hands, nodded, bald spot on his crown brown against the surrounding clipped white hair.

"There was, though, some doubt as to whether it was an accident or whether he meant to kill himself. It was all left a bit vague."

"Meaning?" Southern looked at him from under his eyebrows.

"Oh, I think there was a statement to the effect that nobody else was involved. But we all assumed he'd committed suicide."

He was going to leave it there, but then, quite suddenly decided to trust Southern. "The truth is," he said, "that our mother had been having an affair — a very brief one — with an American soldier, and Sarah — that's my sister — and I are certain that someone in the village must have written to tell our father about

300

it, although we don't know who it was, and by the time he got the news the affair was long over. The American had gone. Posted to Normandy in all likelihood. But our mother had her enemies."

He looked across to see that Southern was staring at him in disbelief. "Yes, difficult to believe, I know. The English village: an idyll of tranquil contentment where never is heard an unpleasant word." He wondered whether to tell Southern about Hetty Rayner's experience of that idyll but decided against. He said instead, "At the back of my mind I think I always hoped to find evidence that my father shot himself by accident, but now I know it was deliberate. He committed suicide. No doubt about it."

Southern was still staring at him as though he couldn't credit David's words.

"I know there was no death note," David said, wondering for the first time whether such a note might have existed and, if so, that was why Southern looked so dumbounded by what he was now hearing. Perhaps it had been destroyed so that Stephen Willoughby's family could be spared the worst. But no, that didn't make sense of Southern's reaction. He couldn't have had prior knowledge of this tale of war-time infidelity and its consequences. Or could he? Was he shocked, not because he was hearing this for the first time, but because he had been privy to the destruction of the note and so couldn't work out how David nevertheless knew what had led to his father's suicide?

He had to feel his way. "I'm beginning to wonder," he said, "if after all there *might* have been such a note. Although if so I don't think our mother could have been given it when she received his other effects." And then he thought, but I don't *know* that, remembering as he did so that, at her instructions, his father's possessions had been returned to his parents. Had they found the note she perhaps had missed, and was that why their loathing of her was so implacable? In which case, he was wrong to assume that his mother had confessed her affair to them, or rather she only admitted it when they confronted her with the evidence the note supplied. But then that couldn't account for the guilt she'd obviously felt and, as it were, declared as soon as news came of her husband's death. She didn't need his parents to point the finger. From all he'd been told, it was plain that from the very moment she heard of Stephen Willoughby's death she was ready to accuse herself. Why otherwise should she have gone to see her parents-in-law to tell them about her affair with an American soldier and why else would she accept that they should take her children from her?

He drained his cup. Wordlessly, Southern drew it to him, poured more tea, then pushed the rattling cup and saucer back to David. The meniscus shivered before tea slopped over and ran in thin streaks down the cup's blue floral side. "Anyway," David said slowly, "note or no note, our mother knew alright. They were a very close, loving couple." He winced inwardly as he heard his own words, their trite, threadbare emptiness. How could he possibly convey anything of the love, the hopes, the certainty, that had run through his father's letters, letters that must have been an antiphon to those that came to him from her. Elbows on the table to steady himself, he watched his hands grasp the full cup and lift it, though he made no attempt to drink. Then he returned the cup to its saucer.

"You see," he said at last, "she knew she was responsible for my father's death."

"*Jeeesus.*" The long, drawn-out word seemed an utterance of final incredulity. Head in hands, Southern stared at the floor.

"You could say that his death finished her life," David said. Now he had started he might as well tell Southern the rest. "She went into a sort of depression, one that lasted until she died. Shut herself away, could hardly bring herself to see us. My sister and I were sent to live with my — our — father's parents." This time he found he could lift the cup to his lips. "She took all the blame on herself."

The words brought him to a momentary halt as the memory of others came to him. Had his mother been stricken by the injustice of the skies for punishment? She didn't seem to think so. Unmerciful, perhaps, but not unjust. "Anyway," he said, looking at Southern's averted face, its curiously abstracted air, "after our mother's death I suddenly felt I wanted to discover more about the father I could scarcely remember. My sister doesn't remember him at all because she was a tiny girl when he went away. But we've been helping each other. I want to find out whatever I can about his time on Malta, Sarah — my sister — wants to find out who poured poison in his ear. Although she hasn't said as much, I think she feels that knowing this will go some way towards lifting the weight of blame off her mother."

He was feeling his way again. "I'd say that from Sarah's point of view, she lost the mother she loved long before time or justice required."

Then, as Southern still said nothing, sat avoiding his eyes, he went on, "and that's why I'm here. It's also why I recently went to Malta."

"You *what?*" Southern sat up, looked hard at David.

Startled by his vehemence, David said, "perhaps I didn't mention that in my letters," and as Southern shook his head vigorously, he added, almost apologetically, "it was a spur of the moment fancy. I wanted to see where my father had been billeted. And I suppose I hoped that I might bump into one or more locals who'd be willing to share memories of the war years, who might even have remembered him. He mentions quite a few in his letters. So I went, spent a day in Valetta then went onto Siggiewi."

Southern's eyes were fixed on his, now, his look had become wary, or was that expression one of alarm.

"The war museum is full of information about the war. I don't think until I spent a morning there that I'd realised just how much the Maltese had to put up with. By the way," as Southern nodded in terse agreement, "would you happen to know whether my father was at all involved in training Yugoslav partisans?"

"We all were," Southern said, "why d'you ask?"

David told him.

Southern thought about it. "Could have been," he said. "You got a copy of the photograph by any chance?" And when David regretfully shook his head, Southern said, "no, well, who knows. I might have been in it myself."

David wondered whether to point out that in all truth there was only one face in which he was interested, so he was hardly likely to have retained other images, and even supposing he'd done so there was the little matter of a fifty year gap between the aged, stoop-shouldered man who sat facing him and the youthful figures who stared out of the 1944 snapshot. But no. He did, though, tell Southern that when he drove over to Siggiewi he was able to locate the statue of Professor Zammit, whose name featured in his father's letters.

"Funny old geezer on a plinth, with books piled up all around him. Yes, I remember. It figures. Your dad always had his nose in some book or other."

"And after that," David said, "I went on into the town itself, intending to make enquiries about a brother and sister my father wrote about. Marcus and Maria. Do you remember them?"

"'Course I do." Southern straightened his shoulders, looked hard at David. "You're not going to tell me they're still alive. They'd be in their nineties, probably more."

"No, they're dead, and the barbershop's gone. At least I couldn't locate it; and as for the bakery, I think it's now a general store. But an old man in the bar opposite, Manoel, told me something that shook me up."

Eyes fixed on his, teeth gripping his lower lip, body visibly tensing, Southern gave him his full attention.

"I'd always assumed, you see — perhaps it had been implied to my mother — that our father's death had been in private, that he'd been on his own when he, well, pulled the trigger. But according to Manoel, who claims to have been there when it happened, he shot himself in the town square. After dark, it's true, when most people would perhaps have been indoors, but still … ."

He left the sentence hanging in the air. Southern was looking at him, unblinking, silent, his expression hard to read.

"Poor, poor man." David shuddered at the thought. "He must have been out of his mind. Anyway," sighing, "assuming Manoel's telling the truth, it puts paid to any lingering hope I had that the death might have been an accident."

Southern unlocked his gaze, sat staring into space for a moment. Then, as though making up his mind, "You're right," he said at last, "it wasn't an accident."

"As I have now to admit. But I wondered whether you could tell me anything that might help me to understand … ."

"It wasn't an accident," Southern said again, more emphatically this time. Then his gaze once more met David's. "He didn't kill himself."

Had he heard right? The words made no sense. He stared at Southern. "I don't follow … ."

"He was shot."

The words echoed crazily in his head. This was madness.

"You mean … well, what *do* you mean.?"

"I mean what I say. Your dad was shot. Murdered, good as."

Stunned into silence, unable to grasp the sense of Southern's words, David shut his eyes. He took two, three, deep breaths, felt he was tumbling into a weightless cavern, gripped the chair seat hard to regain stability, opened his eyes, looked around, then at Southern, amazed to see the man was still sitting opposite, that the room was the same room, the cup at his elbow still held the remains of tea, that cake crumbs freckled the plate beside it.

The world was the same, the world had entirely changed.

After a minute — or was it a lifetime — he asked, "Can you please explain?" He thought his voice would emerge as an outraged roar. In fact, it was a whisper.

Southern sighed an old man's sigh. "May as well," he said, "now we've got this far." He stood up. "Fancy a drop of scotch?"

"NO".

The shout made Southern blink. "No beating about the bush. Simply tell me. Tell. Me. What. *Happened*."

But Southern went over to a cuboard next to the sink and reached out a half-empty bottle of whisky together with two tumblers. He splashed scotch into both, shuffled over to fill a jug with water, and only when he had poured some into his own did he re-seat himself. Pushing the other tumbler in front of David, he said, "in case you change your mind."

He raised his glass as though about to propose a health, thought better of it and drank quickly, grimacing as he set the glass down with both hands, stared reflectively into it.

"I suppose it was bound to come out sooner or later," he

eventually said, "although at the time we thought we'd get away with it." He looked at David, turned his head aside. "And for fifty bloody years we did. No, don't get me wrong. It wasn't one of us that shot your dad — we liked him a lot. I mean you *did* sometimes hear about an officer commanding, even some NCO, getting a bullet in the back which nobody could prove didn't come from enemy fire. But no chance of that with your dad, believe me. He was a good bloke, one of the best. That's the irony of it. If he hadn't been he'd have stayed away from trouble."

"Trouble? What trouble."

"The trouble I got him into. Well, me and Anna."

"Your Maltese girlfriend? He mentions her in his letters."

David reached for the jug, poured water over the glass in front of him until it almost reached the top, then took a mouthful of diluted whisky.

"Well, go on," he said, setting the glass down, "tell me about the 'trouble' you got my father into."

"We were sweethearts," Southern said, using the old word with no trace of irony. "But, see, she was a Catholic, and being Maltese she was under her father's thumb. And a bloody great thumb he had, I'm telling you. A right bastard, George, Marcus's brother was. But perhaps your dad mentioned that in his letters?" He waited for David's nod, then went on. "No prizes for guessing his reaction to me. 'Don't you go with no Tommy, they're only after one thing, you've got to be pure on your wedding day or I can't sell you.' Well, no, he didn't say that but it was like he worried she'd be damaged goods if I so much as laid a finger on her. Besides, he didn't like us Brits. Malta for the Maltese, that kind of thing. Wanted us out. Can't say I entirely blame him although he riled me when he banged on about how Hitler only tried to flatten Malta because it was a British base. I mean, if the Brits hadn't been there, the Krauts would have been swarming all over it, wouldn't they, back up for Rommel's lot. But I didn't argue with about it. When he began one of his rants I kept my trap shut. It was Anna I was there for and I didn't want anything to go wrong between us."

He paused, drank some whisky. When he spoke again, his

voice was softer, reminiscence warmed by emotion. "I was so in love with her I'd have agreed to anything her old man ordered. At first, that is. You know, seven year ordeals, twelve labours, that sort of thing. They wanted me to become a Catholic, which was alright by me. The army had me down as Anglican, but I didn't believe in anything much, so I reckoned I might as well be a Catholic as a heathen. I started to take instruction from the local priest. Didn't understand much of what he was going on about but Anna interpreted."

Another mouthful of scotch. Then, more briskly, "Anyway, your dad agreed to be a sort of chaperon. I think Maria put him up to it but he took his duties seriously. Gave me a right bollocking once when she and me were spotted on our own way out of Siggiwiggi down the coast, near a place called the Blue Grotto." He smiled, shook his head. "After that, we were careful to keep within limits. Didn't want to risk upsetting the apple-cart."

David ran the tip of an index finger round his glass. "One of his letters mentioned that he was worried for you both."

"With good reason. Her old man seemed to soften a bit when I started going to church, but I don't know whether he ever *really* trusted me. Like I say, it was Malta for the Maltese as far as he was concerned. Kick the bloody foreigners out. They were what caused us all our grief."

"He had a point."

"Granted, although by 1944 the heat was off. Food, booze and smokes were getting through and as far as the Brits were concerned we were bored. Malta for the Maltese. Alright then, George, have it your way. Most of us wanted shot of the place. I did, or would have, but for Anna. "

"So what was the plan."

"That we'd get married and I'd take her to England. I mean, the details were vague but that was the plan. Leave George to his dream of the socialist republic of Malta."

"Judging from his letters, my father was a socialist."

"He was. We all were, well, sort of. All for change once the bloody war was over. No going back to the bloody Tories telling us that being out of work was God's plan for the universe. Come a long way, haven't we. Lamont, Major ... ." The laugh was more of a snort. He poured more scotch for himself, held the bottle up enquiringly, and when David shook his head, said, "I'd better get to the point. You have to understand that Anna and me were sweethearts, not lovers in the modern sense. Snogging, yes, some of that, but no sneaking off into the bushes, no 'going all the way' as it used to be called, although most of the blokes I was with used more direct words. For that, they hopped over to Valetta, to the water-side brothels. Us two went for walks. And when we didn't," he paused, sipped his whisky, "when we didn't, there was the shelter."

"Shelter?"

"At the edge of the town square. An underground cave, I guess. Anna said it had once been used for holding smuggled goods, though it could just as well have been a dungeon. Anyway, it had been enlarged at the beginning of the war and you could fit more'n a hundred people in there. Any time the siren went up — Jerry's coming — the locals dropped what they were doing and legged it for the shelter. Not that Ziggiwiggi got hit that often but the shelter kept everyone safe. Well, that was the idea."

"But by 1944 the raids had come to an end."

"Got it in one," Southern said. "So the shelter became a place where courting couples could go, keep away from prying eyes."

"And you and Anna went to the shelter."

"Not just us," Southern said. "Half the bloody time it was more crowded than Epsom on Derby Day. But it was all proper enough. A bit like going to the flicks really, only with no film to see."

David drank from his glass and saw Southern register his grimace.

"Not used to whisky?"

"Not at this hour of the day."

"Give it time," Southern said. "You can get used to anything. Loneliness for starters." He toyed with his tumbler. "Where was I? Oh, yeh. The shelter. Like I say, nothing bad ever went on down there and maybe that was why people stopped coming. You know, you couldn't get down to business with others present. See, it wasn't fully dark, you'd be surprised. Someone had run a cable down there and rigged up a light. Shut the door and from outside you couldn't see a thing. But inside it was a different story. Not exactly the Eddistone lighthouse but Anna told me that when a raid was on people down there could see well enough to play cards. One or two even read. The light came on automatically whenever the door was opened. And the bulb was in a meshed recess so you couldn't get at it. A good system."

He drained his glass, considered a refill but delayed. "Not good enough for some, though. One evening when I went to collect her, Anna told me that Mr George had ordered her to stay away from the shelter. It was a sink, a sewer, fit only for those who had no reputation to lose. Made me furious to hear that. It wasn't as though we were doing anything wrong. I told her it was time she stood up to him, he was a bloody tyrant, she was old enough to make up her own mind. Poor girl, she was in tears. I dunno whether she loved her father but she was dead scared of him. I pointed out that she was supposed to love me, too, and that we were going to be married. Didn't I count?"

He sighed, lifted the bottle, looked at it without removing the cap and set it down again. "To be honest, I didn't even want to go to the shelter that night, I'd have been quite happy walking up to the bakery and sitting with her and Maria and whoever else was around. But his ordering her about made me mad. It was a battle of the wills." He paused, looked at David, shook his head in a kind of weary despair. "Just how stupid can you get," he said. "Anyway, in the end she agreed to come with me." Another pause.

"And?" David prompted.

Southern's eyes were clouded. "And someone must have told her father. Because we'd hardly got down there — believe it or not, we had the place to ourselves — when your dad came running in telling us to scram, the mad sod's on the warpath, got a gun with him. Dunno how he knew, but someone must have seen us. Perhaps that bloke, what d'you call him — Manoel."

He scratched his chin, stared about him as though the kitchen had become a prison cell from which he wanted to escape. "So Anna says she'll go off and find him, try to reason with him, and she leaves and almost at once we hear screaming and yelling. He must have been at the top of the shelter steps." He rubbed his eyes. "Oh, christ, don't think I haven't gone over what happened next a thousand times."

"What *did* happen next?" David said, his voice no more a whisper. Because he knew.

"Your dad says he'll go up and try to calm the bastard down, so he goes and then — bang. The fucker shot him."

Head bowed, staring at his shoes, David tried to take it in.

"But why shoot my father," he said at last, looking up at and into Southern's grieving eyes. "Did this man George think he'd failed in his duty. For god's sake," he was suddenly, violently angry, "he wasn't being *paid* to do it. I know from what he says in his letters how often he wished he could be free of looking out for the pair of you. My father was shot for *nothing*."

He was shaking with sudden rage.

"It was a mistake. Her dad thought it was me who'd stop the bullet," Southern said dully. "He took it for granted I'd be next through the door. He didn't know your dad was down there."

The silence lasted a long time.

David's thoughts drifted among questions he wanted to ask, questions to which he realised there could be no answer. The tangle of confusions that had ended his father's life couldn't be straightened out, not now, not from this distance. But Southern was obviously telling the truth. Had Manoel been the person who told George about his daughter's act of defiance? Perhaps. Perhaps not. None of that mattered. What did was that his father had been murdered and because of that another life had been needlessly ruined.

He became aware of sounds filtering through to where he and Southern sat. From next door a child's yell, "My turn, my turn." A woman was calling out that tea was ready, there was the muffled throb of an aeroplane heading into or out of Heathrow. Noises that between them shaped an average dailiness, coming from a world where someone was just walking dully along.

"There's something I still don't understand," he said at last, his voice breaking the thick integument of silence that surrounded them. "Something that doesn't seem right."

"I've told you all there is to know." Southern's voice was depleted, drained of energy.

"Almost. But there has to be something else." He raised his head to meet Southern's answering gaze. Go on, the gaze said, let's get this over with. "If my father was killed in the manner you've described, why were we led to believe he'd killed himself?"

The ghost of a smile from Southern, a sad, weary smile. But he said nothing.

"If that man — if Anna's father killed him, why on earth wasn't he put on a charge of murder? And why weren't we told what had happened?" Bile swarmed to his throat. His mother's wasted life, his own and, far more, his sister's miserable years at Twickenham, even the bitter sterility of his grandparents' later years, all predicated on a lie.

Southern shook his head, sighed. "There were no witnesses," he said.

"Of *course* there were. You and Anna."

"We weren't there."

"What do you mean … "

And then, at last, he saw.

He lent back in his chair, took a deep breath to control the trembling of his limbs. "What you're telling me is that to save your own skin you let it be thought my father had killed himself."

"It's more complicated than that," Southern said, shifting his gaze, then looking back to David. "But don't think I'm proud of what happened."

"You mean, what didn't happen."

"I don't follow." Southern frowned, looked genuinely puzzled.

"I think you do. If you'd admitted to being there, my father's murderer could have been brought to justice."

The laugh which accompanied Southern's shake of his head was short, dismissive. "Not a chance. There were no witnesses. I didn't see what happened, Anna was already on her way home, orders of her father, and nobody in the town would have spoken out against George."

"Wasn't anyone else in the shelter?"

A shake of the head. "I told you, not that night, no. Not that it would have made any difference."

"What about Manoel? He was in the square."

"So he tells you fifty years after it all happened. Well, maybe he did see something, maybe he was the one who made George come running. But if so he'd not say anything, would he? And nor would anybody else, not any of the townsmen, and who else was there? Where was the evidence?"

"The gun." David almost shouted the words, struck suddenly by the gap in Southern's account. "My father wasn't shot by his own revolver but by that man's gun. You're not trying to tell me nobody noticed *that*." A further thought. "And why was Corporal Morris said to have identified my father's body — back at camp? It doesn't add up."

"It was a fuck up, I'll admit that," Southern said, "a complete fuck up. But it adds up alright, just so long as you don't look too closely at the sums." Another thin smile, more of a grimace, as he emptied the last of the whisky into his glass, splashed in some water, sipped, then said slowly, as though trying to ensure every detail was in place, "See, this is what happened. I hung about in the shelter for a few minutes, then decided to risk it, going up. When I got out I almost fell over your dad's body, he was lying right in front of the entrance. I felt his pulse, course I did, but there was nothing. He was dead. No sign of George, nor of Anna. So I legged it back to camp, quick as I could."

Suddenly, his face twisted in a rictus of pain, his hand went to his heart, he bent over, gasping. Then he straightened again.

"Angina. Gets me sometimes," he said. He brushed at his eyes with the back of a liver-spotted hand. "Phew. I've never talked about this before. Never had to."

"Do you need some water? Fresh air?"

Southern acknowledged the concern in David's voice with a grateful smile. "No, I've got pills." He straightened his shoulders, took some deep breaths. "Let's finish the story. What happened was, the Redcaps found your dad's body, brought it back to camp and the rest followed."

"Meaning?"

"Well, I don't know all the ins and outs but what we heard was that those in the know, meaning the blimps, assumed he'd been helping himself to the local talent and for his pains had been shot by a jealous lover or husband. Now, that wouldn't have put a stop to enquiries being made except for the fact that we were under orders not to stir up bad feeling among the locals. It wasn't just that they'd been battered by Jerry and so deserved our gratitude. We were given regular warnings that there was an Independence movement to get us out of Malta for ever and that this had to be resisted. Malta was British. Malta had to stay British. The last thing the army needed was any accusation that there'd been a revenge killing because some soldier or other had tried to dishonour one of the local girls. Malta had to be kept sweet. Savvy?" He looked at David for reassurance, then went on. "So someone concocted a story that your father shot himself at camp where Dave Morris found him."

David was aghast. "But that's ridiculous. You know it wasn't like that. Didn't you say something?"

Southern's eyes slid away. "I tried to. I told you, everyone who knew him liked your dad, nobody believed he'd shot himself, and of course there were rumours about what had happened in Siggi because the town was put off limits for a month. You'd hear blokes say that there must have been a dust up with the locals and probably he'd been shot by one of them. But, see, it was wartime, deaths happened. Besides, soon afterwards a lot of us were transferred to Italy, and Malta was forgotten about. New scenes, new stories, new fuck ups. And then, as I say, the top brass was dead keen that we didn't do anything to antagonise the Maltese. Start an enquiry and all kinds of dirty washing might be exposed."

"Yours, you mean".

Southern registered the bitterness in David's voice but was defiant. "There was nothing wrong in what me and Anna was doing," he said. Then, "but I've never got over feeling guilty about your father, that I will admit. And when your letters came … . Well, they shook me up. I didn't know what to do. And then, when you phoned I knew you weren't going to give up."

"I wondered about that."

"Jackson's garage." Southern allowed himself a faint smile. "Sounded dodgy. At first I thought it could be a burglar, checking to see if the coast as clear. So I dialled 1471 and up came your number. After that, I knew it was only a matter of time before you'd come knocking."

David glanced at Southern's half-averted face. Grey, deep-lined, the lips down turned, jaw-line sagging with weariness. He looked at his own still half-full glass of whisky but decided against drinking any more. As he made to stand up, Southern, as though he had forgotten his visitor's presence, jerked out of reverie, his eyes re-focussing on the man opposite, on the present.

"I need to get away to think about all you've told me," David said, resting his knuckles lightly on he table. "As I'm sure you can understand, what I've heard has … " but he didn't bother to finish the sentence.

Southern stood also. In silence he led the way along the narrow hall to the front door, wrenched it open.

"I'm sorry about your wife's death," David said, stepping past him. Then, in the shabby porch, he turned to face Southern. "What ever happened to her father, by the way?"

Southern looked at him, perplexed. "Her father? He died years ago."

"At home, no doubt. Safe in his bed and surrounded by loving family, I shouldn't wonder." A gust of renewed bitterness shook him. "There's not much justice is there."

Southern's look of bewilderment changed to one of understanding, then relief. He shook his head. "You're thinking of that old bastard, George. Anna's dad. My father-in-law was a decent old bloke, lived and died a Londoner."

It was David's turn to look bewildered.

"See, after that night I never saw Anna again. It wasn't possible. Like I told you, the town was put off-limits for a month and then when I tried to get back in touch her family wouldn't let me near her. Not after what had happened. No, that was the end for Anna and me. I was in Italy before the year was out. End of story."

He looked away as though seeing through a fifty years' haze the girl he had lost. "I really loved her though." The words came as little more than a whisper, spoken to himself, less reassurance than affirmation of the truth. His Adam's apple gave a sudden leap, a spasm of pain passed over his face, was gone. "I told you it was a fuck up," he said.

Then he stood there silent, twisting the grey hairs that sprouted from his shirt, his gaze unwavering, as though willing himself to remain dry-eyed.

Slowly, hesitantly, David extended his hand.

Slowly, hesitantly, Southern took it. "And I'll tell you another thing," he said, his handclasp tightening. "Your voice. You wouldn't know this, but your voice is just like your dad's."

Then, releasing David's hand, but without taking his eyes off him, he stepped back into the hallway and closed the door.

He unlocked the front door, as he did so calling out a greeting. No answer. In the kitchen he found an opened bottle of red wine on the dresser and carried it over to the table where he poured himself a glass, then sat in the gathering gloom of the late spring afternoon, not tasting the wine but seeing as he stared into its magenta depths Southern's face, the deep lines of sadness etched round the man's eyes, his hollowed cheeks, the grooves that shadowed his mouth, and hearing his words. "I told you it was a fuck up." Which, in its blunt, direct way, repeated what Hetty Rayner had earlier said. Terrible things happen in war, David, and not only on the battlefield.

You can say that again.

Startled, he looked round him, got up, glad of the reassuring sound of chair legs scraping on the slate tiles, went to shut the connecting door to the square hallway, then snapped on the lights. The kitchen became its usual, unmysterious, foursquare self, the large window now turned to a glossy black square set into white walls, the fitted wooden cupboards trim, orderly, reassuring. Returning to his seat, he sipped some of the wine.

"Your voice is just like your dad's." Had Southern said that to appease him, to offer clumsy assuagement for all that David had learnt in the previous two hours? No, he meant it, though he could hardly be expected to remember accurately a voice he'd last heard fifty years ago.

So what would my father have done now?

Again, he looked round. I'm talking to myself, he thought.

And at that moment he heard the key in the front-door latch and a few moments later Maggie came to join him, bringing with her a large carrier-bag. "New dress for the private view," she said, in answer to his speculative look, "must look my best if I'm to sell anything."

"You always look your best."

"Thank you, young man." She rested a hand on his shoulder and stooped to give him a quick kiss on the cheek. "Celebrating something?" she asked, motioning towards the bottle, "or are you drowning your sorrows?"

"Good question."

She sat down facing him, and as she looked into his face her smile disappeared. "David? What's the matter? You look as though something ghastly has happened." A hand went up to her mouth. "It's not Susie is it?" She stared at him, anxiety flaring into outright alarm. "Don't tell me that … ."

"No, no," he said, "nothing to do with Susie."

"Thank god for that." She breathed out. He knew what she meant. And as though to confirm this, she said, "She's so *set* on having this baby."

An odd way of putting it, he thought, as he did so reflecting that naturally enough Maggie was equally set on her daughter's well-being.

"Well, you can rest easy on that score."

"So what is it?"

"I went to see Southern," he said, "you know, the man whose address Sarah found for me."

"You heard from him, then. I thought you'd rather given up hope of a reply to your letters."

"I had. But late this morning I decided to hunt him down. I took a chance and went to his house."

Maggie stood up. "I'm going to make myself a cup of tea," she said. "I have the feeling that what you're going to tell me isn't good news."

David told her.

* * *

Later, much later, husband and wife sat silently at the table on which stood the now empty bottle of wine, looking first at each other, then away, then almost shyly back.

Eventually, Maggie spoke. "I don't know," she said, "that I can find words that will even begin to … to say what I feel. And as to what *you* must feel … ."

"And what Southern feels," David said. "His life was turned upside down. Losing the woman he loved, having to go for all these years knowing he was at least partly responsible for the death of an innocent man." He shook his head, his lips pursed in rueful wonder. "I'd like to think his finally being able to speak about it came as some sort of relief, but I'm not sure it did. When we said goodbye his face …" He paused, sighed. "Mags, Southern's face was the saddest face I've ever seen." Again he paused. "We're always being told, aren't we, about the need for 'closure'. Some bloody counsellor or other advising us to get the bad news out of our systems and move on. Psychobabble, if you ask me. An invitation to forget, to feel good about yourself. But some things can't be forgotten."

He stopped. Then, as she was about to speak, he blurted out, with a vehemence that he himself was unprepared for, "Nor should they be."

Maggie took this in. "And Sarah," she asked. "What will she say?"

"I'm not sure what she'll say but I'm pretty sure she'll think more strongly than ever that her mother's life shouldn't have been thrown away in recrimination, that the poor woman did penance for a crime that never was."

"Murder's a crime," Maggie said gently.

"And so is, or rather was, suicide. But our father didn't kill himself. He didn't *know* about that fly-by-night affair. Sorry," he said, seeing her flinch from the savagery that had surged into his voice.

They fell back into silence.

"So what now?"

The question brought him back to the present. He shrugged. "Goodness knows. Tell Sarah all that Southern told me as soon as she's back from her holiday, and in the meantime try to finish my book."

Maggie stood up, reached over and touched his cheek. "And before that even," she said, "I propose supper."

He looked up, grasped her hand and drew her towards him. "Seconded," he said gratefully, kissing his still lovely wife.

* * *

A week later, the private view had come and gone, the exhibition had been pronounced a success and, so Maggie reported, Giles Lashman was purring over sales even more than she was delighted — relieved was her actual word — that the reviews had proved generous. "Tactility and taste coming together in rare accord," so the *Times* reviewer claimed, which, as Giles said, might mean bugger all but at least guaranteed the interest of buyers, including some from foreign parts. A New York gallery was enquiring about the possibility of a future show there.

"Though Giles warns me not to get my hopes up," Maggie said, plainly thrilled by the news she reported to David as they sat over their evening meal. "I gather these enquiries blow in more frequently than a call girl drops her knickers."

Laughing, he asked her where on earth she got that expression from.

"Giles, who else. Though I suspect his best lines come from his boyfriend. Charlie. 'Roughhouse Charlie' as he's called."

David knew at once whom she meant. The man had looked out of place at the private view, not because he was in leathers, there were plenty of those, men as well as women, sporting nose studs, chains, earrings, as well as city types in dark suits, even one or two in tweeds. What set this man apart was his pronounced indifference to everyone in the gallery. David watched him watching them, the art crowd, drinking, exchanging air kisses, words and smiles, eyes swivelling in search of recognisable faces. From time to time someone might be drawn to glance at the slim figure in black leather jacket, black leather trousers and black T shirt who leant, immoveable, against a pillar, an air of unabashed, undeflectable contempt marking his thin smile, but they soon looked away again. Knowing few among all those crowded into the gallery, David had at one point wandered over to stand beside the man whose appearance of self-containment might, he thought, be a show to mask his unfamiliarity with the invited guests, but as he opened his mouth to make some tritely innocent remark, the other turned momentarily towards him, his pale blue eyes so nakedly hostile that David was halted from uttering a word.

So, "Roughhouse Charlie," he said to her. "Yes, I remember. Not much of a conversationalist, is he? Not Goodtime Charlie, that's for sure."

"Although a roughhouse is some people's idea of a good time," Maggie said.

"Not mine."

"Nor mine. I prefer something or someone I can be at ease with."

And at that moment the telephone rang.

It was Sarah. "We're at Heathrow," she said, "our flight was delayed by an hour and it's now too late to get back to Manchester this evening. I know it's short notice, for which I apologise, but I wonder, brother mine, whether you could offer us a bed for the night."

David looked at the wall clock. 7. 30 pm. "Of course we can," he said. "Do you know how to get here?"

"We can splash out on a taxi." The exuberance was unmissable.

"Is the spare bedroom useable," he asked, as he put the phone down, explaining about his sister's request.

Maggie nodded. "Though it's hardly too late to get back to Manchester this evening, surely."

"I think she wants to see us," he said. "She sounds excited about something or other. She has news to share."

As indeed she had. Less than an hour later, the four of them sat round the table on which Maggie had put out bread and cheese while David uncorked the bottle of wine Jeremy presented when they arrived, tanned, smiling, laden with baggage. "Clos Trimoulet," he announced, reading the label. "Saint-Emilion. Grand Cru. Not your ordinary vin. So what are we celebrating?"

"This." Sarah held out her left hand and they saw the pale gold band on her ring finger.

"Sarah!" Maggie shouted in surprised delight. "How wonderful." Standing, she leant over and kissed her. "You, too, Jeremy."

320

While Jeremy stood to accept Maggie's embrace, David took the chance to inspect his new brother-in-law. Tall, solidly-built, curly black hair flecked with grey, square-faced with generous lips, jaw line beginning to sag but otherwise in good shape for a fifty-something, the dark-grey sports jacket over open-neck blue wool shirt expensive without being ostentatious. Jeremy Ross more than passed muster. And his handshake, David was pleased to discover, came free of he-man pressure.

Glasses were raised, toasts proposed, healths drunk. "We didn't want to tell anyone," Sarah said, "not till the deed was done. A bit late in the day for me to walk up the aisle as a blushing bride and beside, this time Jeremy was determined to avoid fuss."

David and Maggie exchanged smiles. This time? Jeremy had presumably been married before. Well, plenty of second marriages lasted.

"So," Sarah said, cutting a piece of stilton and passing it on the point of the knife to her husband, "we combined holiday, wedding and honeymoon. You're the first to know." She was glowing with laughter and, as she fed Jeremy the cheese then took his hand and pressed it against her cheek David thought how beautiful his sister now looked.

Talk was inconsequential, floating on the deep current of pleasure that flowed between them all.

Then Sarah asked, "that man, Southern. Did you manage to make contact with him, David?"

He looked across at Maggie but her face was averted. "Yes," he said, slowly, "yes, I did."

"And?"

"Well." He took a deep breach, swallowed his wine and said, "This is hardly what you'll want go hear at a time when you should be celebrating, but … " And for the second time he found himself rehearsing the story of his afternoon with Derek Southern.

"So you see," he said, as he finished, "all that suffering of our mother's needn't have happened." He looked across to where Sarah sat watching him, her eyes dark, fixed on his. "I'm sorry to have to tell you all this," he said. "Very sorry."

But to his amazement, Sarah said "I knew it. I *knew* it." There was a note of near exultance in her voice. "David, it fits with what I've worked out, makes perfect sense."

She turned to Jeremy, demanding his agreement. "Doesn't it?"

Smiling, he said, not to her but to her hosts, "I've been having a Brush Up Your Shakespeare course these last two weeks."

"And it's done you no end of good," Sarah said, satirically, "broadened your mind. Given you quite a new view of the law."

"True," Jeremy said. "I've decided that on the whole I'd rather be Lucio than Angelo."

"But it wasn't *Measure for Measure* that gave me what I was looking for," Sarah said. "No need to look so puzzled, David. " She leant over, stroked his hand, her smile reassuring, almost loving. The new Sarah. "You remember that quotation our father used in that last letter he wrote. I made a copy of it, because I was sure it meant something we didn't understand. Get it, will you."

Without a word, David rose and went to his study. A few moments later he was back, untying the bundle of letters, the final note laid in front of him, the rest to one side.

"Read it."

He read. "*Yours arrived as I'm about to go on duty so I'll write a full letter later. This is to reassure you that my love for you is constant. I know that being apart is hell for us both, but for me, and I think for you, 'the bonds of heaven' will never be 'slipp'd, dissolv'd and loos'd.' All my love, Stephen.* That's it." He looked up, saw the three of them watching him.

"And you remember I asked you where that quotation came from?"

"And I didn't know." He shrugged apologetically. "Still don't, I have to admit."

"Well, I *do* know."

"Though it took the best part of our honeymoon for her to find out," Jeremy said. "Nearly led to instant divorce, I can tell you." But his smile, the way he leant his head on his wife's shoulder, told a different story.

Sarah said, "you remember our father's copy of Shakespeare which I rescued from the house. I decided to take it with us to St.

Lucia. You get the Bible and Shakespeare on your desert island. Gideon for the hotel room and Shakespeare for the beach."

"And what was your luxury?" Maggie asked.

"Jeremy," Sarah said, reaching for her new husband's arm and giving it a squeeze. "He's my luxury."

Jeremy had the grace to bow his head in mock-bashful acceptance of his status.

Banishing from his mind as unworthy the old meaning of the word luxury, David fixed his attention on what Sarah was now saying. Every day, she told them, she spent some hours working her way through the plays, hunting for the words she was certain must come from there.

"Not necessarily," David said, "his letters are full of quotations from poets. I think he must have had yards of poetry by heart."

"Possibly, but I had a hunch about this. Though I admit I began to think I must be wrong. He'd made so many marginal comments in his copy of the plays I thought they'd be bound to lead me to what I wanted. But no. In fact, it was only two days before we were due to fly home that I found it." her eyes gleamed, exultant. "But I did find it. I did, I did!"

Caught up in her excitement, David and Maggie asked together, Where?"

"*Troilus and Cressida,* that's where." She sat back, looked expectantly at her brother.

"The play about infidelity?" he said, bewildered. "The false Cressid? You mean, our father was accusing his wife of being like Cressida?"

"Not at all." Sarah slapped her hand on the table. She reached into her bag, drew out the old, battered, dark-green copy of Shakespeare's plays he recalled from his boyhood. "Listen." She turned to the place she'd marked with a strip of paper. "It's in Act 5. Troilus has been shown Cressida flirting with Diomed after she's been handed over to the Greeks, and after she's promised to be eternally faithful to Troilus. And Troilus says ... ." She ran her eyes up and down the page, found what she was looking for, took a breath, and read in a voice wavering with emotion but intent, measured, even emphatic

"Cressid is mine, tied with the bonds of heaven.
Instance, O instance, strong as heaven itself:
The bonds of heaven are slipp'd, dissolv'd and loos'd,
And with another knot, five-finger tied,
The fractions of her faith, orts of her love,
The fragments, scraps, the bits and greasy relics
Of her o'er-eaten faith are given to Diomed.
Do you see?"

David, taken aback by Troilus's words, their almost unhinged disgust, sat silent.

But Maggie said, "Yes, I understand. The note David's father sent was meant to be one of reassurance, is that it? He wasn't accusing his wife of behaving like Cressida. Or, at all events," her voice quickened as she saw Sarah nodding, "he was telling her that it wasn't going to change anything between them."

"*Exactly.* He's telling her that whatever she's done, his love — *their* love — is still strong. *Now* do you see. The note is an answer to a letter she sent him. It *has* to be."

David looking round the table, saw the others watching him. "Yes," he said at last, "I see." He put fingers to his forehead, massaged it, as though trying to rid himself of a sudden headache. "God, what a mess."

"A terrible, terrible mess," Sarah said. "Our poor mother."

David nodded. "She must have decided to risk telling him about her fling with the American, knowing or at least hoping he'd understand".

"Which he did, as the quotation makes clear. To her, if not to us. They must have read the play together, don't you think? Because he obviously expected her to understand the reference."

"And the next thing she hears is that he's killed himself."

"And thinks therefore that no matter what his note said he found he couldn't cope with her admission of infidelity. And so she's responsible for his death."

"Rather than some madman with a gun out to defend his daughter's honour."

Brother and sister sat looking at each other and in Sarah's eyes David could see the gleam of subdued triumph. She had set out to vindicate her mother and in many ways had been proved right.

But there was something else that needed to be cleared up. "Sarah', he said, "when you went through our mother's address book, do you remember coming across the name Eve Roberts?"

Sarah looked puzzled. "Eve Roberts? I don't think so. I can check when we get back. I've kept the book. But no. Eve Roberts. I'm pretty sure I don't recall that name. Why? Who is she?"

"The woman our mother said she'd been looking after the night we came back from our holidays in 1944. The night we stayed with Mrs Rayner."

"Good god," Sarah said, "Yes, I do remember. That is, I've got a vague recollection of our grandparents telling us about a woman in trouble. But I don't remember a name." Then, more slowly, she asked, "why do you want to know? Does it matter?"

"It does if she doesn't exist."

Sarah looked at him. "Oh," she said, "I see."

"A last night with her lover," Maggie said. "Is that what you're thinking?"

"Or worse."

He kept his eyes on Sarah, watching for any sign she understood his meaning. She did. But she shook her heard.

"I'll admit there have been times I've wondered about that," she said, "but I simply can't believe she'd have risked it. Not a back street abortion. Anyway, given the few weeks she and Krassner had together, there'd hardly have been enough time for her to know whether she was pregnant."

"Perhaps." But he wasn't altogether convinced. There are some things we'll never know, he thought, the door of the past has slammed shut and we can't open it again.

"At all events," Sarah said, "she risked enough telling our father about Krassner."

"And as you said, in the light of what then happened must have thought she was responsible for his death."

Trying to wipe the record clean, he almost added, as some memory stirred, the image of a broken gramophone record, his mother's voice ordering him to throw it out. But as quickly as it had come, the memory disappeared, and he said nothing.

It was Jeremy who broke the silence. "I gather that the critics don't think all that highly of *Troilus and Cressida*," he said. "Why not?"

David dragged his thoughts away from his parents' tragedy. "Too dark," he said, trying to give his attention to Jeremy and at the same time scrambling together all he could recall about the play. "When I was an undergraduate the orthodox view was that it was a problem play. One without real heroes, cynical, nihilistic even. There used to be a theory that Shakespeare wrote it when he was suffering from the clap, which would explain why he took a dim view of sex."

"What balls." As though surprised by his own vehemence, Jeremy blushed under his deep tan, added, "I'm no expert, but *Troilus and Cressida* seems to me pretty accurate about the mess of war. Great suffering, little glory."

"And no heroes," David said, "that's what the critics found difficult to stomach. No 'moral centre'. Ulysses a liar, Agamemnon a thug, Hector vain, Achilles a cheap killer ... I mean, not much of a model for public schoolboys to follow. And then Thersites' claim that 'All the argument's a whore and a cuckold.' I do remember that from my reading."

"That's not *all* the argument," Jeremy said. "I know there aren't any real heroes in the play and certainly no heroic deaths. But then there aren't many heroic deaths in actual warfare, are there? Not much morality, either. Soldiers, sailors, airmen, they're killed in their thousands: blown up, sunk, shot down. Where's the glory in that? And as for the millions of civilians who are wiped out ... ." He left the remark unfinished. "Perhaps the world needs to catch up with Shakespeare," he said.

David thought about it. "Yes," he said slowly, "you're right. I should have taken more notice of the play than I did. Well, there's still time. All the time that Shakespeare is for."

"'When waterdrops have worn the stones of Troy'," Jeremy said, draining his glass as he got to his feet.

Taking her cue from him, Sarah yawned. "It's been a long, long day. Would you mind if we took ourselves to bed?" And, suiting action to words, she too stood, smiling her thanks and signalled goodnight to her hosts.

* * *

They left early next morning after a hurried breakfast. As they climbed into the taxi summoned to take them up to Euston, Sarah said, "you must come up and see us once we're settled in our new home."

"I'd love that," Maggie said, kissing her, and David, shaking hands with Jeremy, wished the pair good luck.

"What do you want me to do with the letters," he asked, as Sarah made to close the cab door.

"Keep them," she said. "If you can bear to."

He nodded. "I can," he said.

"Do you think it will last?" Maggie said, as they stood, shading their eyes against the sudden shaft of spring sun that ignited the windows of a parked van round which the taxi veered before disappearing into the distance.

"Why not," he said. "Late flowering love has its own perfume, sweet durability."

"That's probably a quotation," Maggie said, "but I'm not going to ask where it's from. Come on." She tugged at his sleeve. "There's still some coffee left."

Arm in arm they went back indoors.

He sits at his desk looking out at a green June evening lit by a declining sun that even at this late hour still fingers the aged apple tree he means to prune but somehow never does. Before him is the untied bundle of letters, lying across them a ribbon now frayed and thinned to a wispiness that might almost be the colour of dried blood. Beside them is the edition of *Troilus and Cressida* he has just finished reading. Jeremy was right. It's all there, what war does: the lies and distortions, the misguided actions, the well-intentioned but botched decisions, the plans gone awry, from best to basest. What do we really know of the past, what *can* we know? We are all victims of envious and calumniating time. Not this minute, perhaps, but at some future moment we can't predict. Opening the play again, he leafs through until he finds the speech where Cressida declares her undying love for Troilus, and vows that, should she prove false

> When time is old and hath forgot itself,
> When waterdrops have worn the stones of Troy,
> And blind Oblivion swallowed cities up,
> And mighty states characterless are grated
> To dusty nothing, yet let memory,
> From false to false, among false maids in love …
> Yea, let them say, to stick the heart of falsehood,
> 'As false as Cressid.'

"When waterdrops have worn the stones of Troy". Words Jeremy, that man of surprises, had spoken on the evening when the four of them finally unravelled something approximating to the truth about what had happened all those years ago.

Closing the play once more, he takes up and begins to wind the ribbon about his fingers. What do we owe the dead? Truth redeemed from time's rumours? Hopeless, of course. Full redemption isn't possible. Sooner or later, it all comes to dusty nothing. But at least Sarah had shown him that there's nothing wrong in the urge to discover the truth. It's a matter of responsibility. In this all-important sense, he thinks, *Troilus and Cressida* isn't a cynical play. The truth is always trickier, more complex, than the assumptions on which people build their stories, the materials out of which they make heroes and villains.

So. What to do about the letters. Keep them, as he'd promised Sarah he would do. But to what end? On their own they make little sense, don't explain the story he alone can tell. It's a matter of responsibility.

He sighs, reaches across his desk for a pencil and notebook, and yet again begins to read the topmost letter, transcribing the words as he does so.

Darling,

I can't tell you how wonderful it was to get your last ...